C000150920

The Mystery of the Golf Club Murder

The First in the Tom Colt Mystery Series:
The Life, Loves and Times of
a Golfer Who Solves Crimes

Brian Hill

Off the Grid Productions

© 2022 Copyright by Brian Hill

All rights reserved. No part of this book may be reproduced, stored in a retrieval system or transmitted in any form or by any means without the written permission of the publishers, except by a reviewer who may quote brief passages in a review to be printed in a newspaper, magazine, journal, or electronically.

ISBN# 978-0-9740754-4-0

Cover design by germancreative

Note from the Publisher: This is a work of fiction. The character Tom Colt, his golf career and detective exploits, are inventions of the author's imagination. In certain scenes, the golf tournaments depicted are based on actual events. Certain scenes also depict well-known business establishments that existed at the time this work of fiction takes place. Apart from those scenes, any resemblance to persons, living or dead, locations, events or business establishments, is purely coincidental. The persons and business establishments depicted have no relation to any person or business establishment with the same name or names.

Off the Grid Productions

PO Box 1210
Tonto Basin, AZ   85553
writers@offthegrid-productions.com

Javelina House
PUBLISHING

Acknowledgements:

This book is dedicated to all the wonderful friends who are no longer with us, both two-legged and four-legged. I look forward to when we will be together again.

Preferably, though, not anytime soon.

I wrote parts of this book at public libraries while traveling across Arizona. A special thanks to all of them, starting with the wonderful Tonto Basin Public Library and the resources they provided for me to research life in Arizona in the 1950s and '60s.

Also, the Greer Memorial Library, Alpine Public Library, Round Valley (Eager, AZ) Public Library, Cottonwood Public Library, Payson Public Library, Prescott Public Library, Scottsdale Public Library and Fountain Hills Public Library. Libraries have always been among my favorite places. Along with golf courses.

Brian Hill

Somewhere in Arizona, March, 2022

"Courage is being scared to death, but saddling up anyway" -- John Wayne

Chapter One   1962 - Phoenix, Arizona
Trouble in Paradise Valley

Seasoned law enforcement officers, or LEOs as they sometimes call themselves, like my good friend Det. Mathers with the Phoenix PD, say you can sense the presence of trouble--and danger--in a place when you first arrive there. But I'm Tom Colt, a young professional golfer, not a seasoned LEO. So as I walked up the native stone steps to this sprawling ranch-style house on the rapidly growing and increasingly fashionable east side of Phoenix, the town of Paradise Valley, incorporated just a year earlier, all I sensed was an eerie quiet. It seemed no one was there.

The house was owned by Arizona State Sen. Richard Luck, a fast-rising politician seeking national office who shared the home with his wife Lisa Prentiss Luck. I knew them slightly only because I was Lisa's golf instructor; they were fixtures in the local party scene of the wealthy set. By virtue of my golfing notoriety, I was invited to some of these parties even though I was far from wealthy at the time.

It was 6PM on an unusually warm day in April. I was wearing my work clothes--don't laugh, golf is work--light blue IZOD golf slacks and a white Munsingwear polo shirt, as I had rushed over to the Luck residence after receiving a cryptic and jarring message sent by Lisa that had gone to my answering service. At the time the message came in, I was giving golf lessons at the upscale (and incredibly snobby) Valley Vista Country Club, located in an almost deserted stretch of desert in North Scottsdale, east of the city of Phoenix. The members of Valley Vista referred to it as The Club, as though there was no other.

I said I was a competitor on the professional golf tour. Indeed I was and very proud of it, but in '62 the prize money on tour was only a teeny, tiny fraction of what it is today. Many of us, who weren't as successful as Ben Hogan or Sam Snead or Arnold Palmer, or rising stars like Gene Littler and Ken Venturi, had to work another job between tournaments and in the offseason.

So I endured endless afternoons of helping hopeless rich hackers improve their golf games. The upside was, many of these hackers told me their secrets as I worked with them on the practice range at The Club. Juicy gossip, it was for sure. It kept me entertained--and often shocked.

Lisa's message that summoned me said, "Tom, please come over to my home as soon as you get this. I am so afraid."

Why did she call me? We were not exactly close friends. She enjoyed taking golf lessons from me. And she knew I occasionally assisted wealthy people at The Club who found themselves in a spot of trouble. That was me, Tom Colt, professional golfer and amateur private detective. Or maybe part-time Knight was how I really thought of myself. On the day that turned out to be the last golf lesson I gave Lisa, she expressed to me that trouble may soon be finding her, and she might need my detective services sometime.

I got to the front door, saw it was ajar. I swung it open slowly, like a wary protagonist in a vampire movie entering the castle. I walked into the entry way and saw the house was vast, with a soaring ceiling in a living room that led to long corridors of bedrooms on the left, and a large kitchen/dining area on the right.

"Hello, anyone home?" I said rather weakly. Something just didn't feel right...

With the proviso that I lived in a small crappy apartment with hardly any furniture, decorated in what could be called mid-century golf bum style, as I walked through the living room it seemed to me the décor of the Luck house screamed WE'RE REALLY, REALLY RICH! It was a bragging kind of house, with dark heavy furniture that may have been expensive antiques, or just expensive reproductions posing as antiques. The beige carpet in the living room was deep enough for an unfortunate raccoon to get lost in, should he have accidentally wandered into the house. A bragging house, but also a cold one, it seemed to me.

I continued my lonely tour, reaching the kitchen area. This was a garish yellow room with garish yellow appliances. But something caught my eye through the sliding glass doors that led outside. Past a large expanse of perfectly manicured grass, good enough for me to practice pitch shots on, at the open pool area (no pool fencing laws in those days) was a figure reclining on a lounge chair.

The path across the lawn to the pool was at least 100 steps. When I was halfway there, I recognized the reclining figure as Lisa Prentiss Luck, evidently sunbathing, gathering in the last rays on this unusually warm afternoon. She was a lissome blonde with stunning large violet eyes and a soft breathy voice, as though Marilyn Monroe had been her vocal coach.

I was quite surprised to see Lisa was sunbathing in the nude.

I let out a sigh. Was this just a clumsy attempt at seduction? Her husband is off at yet another campaign fundraising event, and lonesome Lisa decides to have a dalliance with a man she barely knows? I can tell you from my years in tournament golf, lots of women find golf pros attractive, which I am only partially ashamed to admit I took advantage of every chance I got.

Lisa was a popular subject for the gossipy men in the Valley Vista Club locker room. One old guy told me she regarded the bonds of marriage as a low fence that was no problem for her to hop over like a rabbit, whenever she pleased.

But this seemed a bit much, even if the gossip were true. There must be another explanation.

I approached her from her left. Her right leg was raised, bent at the knee, as though to focus attention on how shapely it was.

I followed the curved path until I got to within a few feet of her. I thought it odd she didn't stir. She must have heard the clicking of my maroon loafers on the stone steps. I expelled an irritated breath. What was going on here?

When I came around to her right, this time the noise coming from me was a gasp that caught in my throat. On her right temple was a nasty and bloody gash, looked to be the work of that proverbial blunt instrument. I took her pulse but knew the horrible truth before I touched her delicate diamond-braceleted wrist.

I had gotten there too late. Lisa was dead.

Not having any prior experience with violent death, I immediately got extremely dizzy. I sat on a nearby chair for a few moments. My first thoughts were, what a shame, what a waste. She was maybe 30, with her whole life ahead. But my next thought was, I'm not really surprised. Everyone knew the Luck family, their many supporters and detractors, were a simmering pot of tensions, discontent, and restless passions.

The pot had boiled over today, and Tom Colt was smack in the middle of the hot mess.

I took a few deep breaths to restore order in my nervous system and trotted back to the house where I found a garish yellow rotary dial phone in the garish yellow kitchen. I dialed a number I already knew by heart, the Phoenix Police Department, and asked for my buddy Det. Mathers. I told the operator I had found a body at the Luck residence and it was a possible homicide.

I was told he wasn't there and was connected to another detective on the force, J. B. Leeves. I could tell by his gruff voice and the slight wheeze in his breathing that JB was an old-style Arizona cop, complete with ever-expanding belly that lapped over this gun belt. He ordered me to not touch anything, and not to leave.

Waiting for the police to arrive, I toured around, I guessed you called it, the Crime Scene. A red shortie terrycloth robe was on the path that led from the pool area to the master bedroom. I knew enough to not pick it up and examine it, but from the odd position it was in, and the tear on the right sleeve, the robe appeared to have been torn off someone rather than merely dropped and discarded.

Had Lisa been in the shower and heard an intruder? Had the killer ripped the robe from her in a fit of anger?

I looked back at the body. How can you be bashed in the head and then sit down in an elegant pose on a lounge chair, complete with a sexy leg posed perfectly to attract attention?

The answer is, you can't. Someone killed her elsewhere, tore her robe off, and then moved her to the lounge chair--and posed her perfectly. But why? What sense does that make?

Then, I thought, *STOP IT TOM!* The police won't give a rat's ass about your observations or half-assed conclusions therefrom. I had loved solving puzzles since I was a child. I devoured the *Hardy Boys* mystery books and as I grew up, Agatha Christie's adult mystery stories. Maybe a part of me was always a detective. I just happened to be extremely good at the extremely difficult game of golf.

The sound of car doors opening and shutting pulled me from my thoughts.

When Det. Leeves and a young, excited over-eager patrol officer named Rudy arrived at the Luck residence, I found my impressions from the phone call were completely correct. I should add that ol' JB was what we called then a chrome dome, completely bald. He had a habit of rubbing the perfectly smooth surface of his head, which he did after he opened a small spiral notebook and said: "You are Tom Colt, who called this in?"

"Yes, sir, I called immediately after I got here at 6PM," I said, in a submissive way designed to give the detective the satisfaction of being in charge.

Leeves gazed over at Lisa's body. This veteran detective had no emotional reaction to either her nudity or her death. He did a 360 around the lounge chair. Repeated my reading of the pulse, then stepped back.

"Looker," he finally said.

"In life," I added without knowing why I said it.

"Ummm," he said.

Leeves gazed across the pool area. "Rudy, look around the property for a weapon. Could be a baseball bat, some kind of lawn tool. The fracture area looks too broad for a hammer or something like that."

Rudy nodded and went off bloodhound-like. Rudy, I learned later, had a long last name tangled with too many consonants for most people to attempt pronunciation. So everyone called him Officer Rudy.

"Mr. Colt, you said you got a message to come here tonight."

I fished the phone message out of my pocket and gave it to him. He read it. Then fixed his attention on me with that hard, cold cop stare designed to elicit immediate confession.

"You touch anything after you got here?"

"Her wrist. I didn't need to even touch the door handle. Door was ajar."

"She left the door open for you."

"I...can't...I don't know that." Leeves was good. I was already feeling guilty.

"You and the deceased were friends?"

I tried to laugh at that notion, but it didn't come off with any confidence. "No. I hardly knew her."

"Have you ever been intimate with the deceased?" He looked at his notebook and then back at me as though that little notebook contained the names of every woman I ever slept with.

"No."

"So rich beautiful lady was in a jam of some kind and picked you out of all the people in the Phoenix, Arizona metropolitan telephone directory to help her. It doesn't add up. And remember before you answer my next question, it takes a while with the phone company records, but I can find out if she actually called you earlier today."

I didn't like his tone. But I didn't say so. Leeves was the bullying type of cop who thought it part of his job to be as rude as possible to anyone he meets. Since I had no involvement in Lisa's death, I should remain cool, I told myself. But you can't really do that in those circumstances. Believe me.

"That would be great, Det. Leeves, if you can confirm it." I smiled brightly. He didn't return the smile. "You know it might save some time if you just call Det. Mathers. He can vouch for me."

"How do you know Mathers? Were you conveniently on the scene of another recent homicide?"

"I'm his golf instructor."

"Mathers plays golf???" he said rather in the fashion of: Mathers picks his nose?

"Yessir. He's quite keen on the game."

Leeves made a lemon-sour expression.

At this point Officer Rudy came scurrying across the lawn carrying what I immediately knew was a golf club, a number one wood, called the Driver.

"Look at this, JB!" he exclaimed with exuberant pride. "That looks like blood on it."

Rudy extended a rubber-gloved hand and Leeves examined the face, the hitting surface of the club.

Leeves looked over at me with a kind of smirk. "Golf club, isn't it. Come over here and tell us about it, Mr. Pro Golfer who gives lessons at the country club.

I walked over and took a look. I tried very hard to not betray any surprise. I had no idea if I succeeded. It was a new First Flight brand persimmon driver. It still had the price tag on it, when it had been on the driving range at the Valley Vista Country Club earlier that day, for all of us to test out. There were probably 20 partial sets of fingerprints on the comfortable leather grip of the club. Golfers love to try out new clubs, in the vain notion that if they could only find the perfect tools, they would immediately become good players.

Everyone on the driving range today gave that beautiful club a try. I should let you know that in 1962, at age 27, I was already considered one of the best drivers of the ball on the pro golf tour. Everyone knew how much I loved hitting the number one wood long--very long--and straight--sometimes. Well, rarely straight actually.

This afternoon one of my students, dreaming of hitting a golf ball like I do (to dream the impossible dream!) asked to try this very same First Flight driver. He hit a few shots, with no noticeable improvement from his usual weak hundred-fifty-yard duck-hook. Then he said to me, "Tom, this club is swell! You try it."

So I did. My effort was of course much better. I drilled the ball 265 yards down the heart of the driving range, with that smart, sharp, inevitable sound a professional's drive makes. My student looked over at me with admiration. Awe perhaps. The club was Excalibur in my hands, no more impressive than a garden rake in his. I loved moments like that.

But then I realized that my fingerprints were the most recent—besides those of the killer--and freshest on the brown leather grip of that particular driver, which may very well be the weapon that took Lisa's life.

It dawned on me that I may be screwed. And then I chuckled at the irony. Because out of the 20 or so gentlemen who tried that golf club today, I was the only one I knew for certain had never screwed Lisa Prentiss Luck.

"Something funny," Leeves asked.

And I hadn't told the Detective the whole truth, as they say. Lisa had enjoyed the time I spent with her teaching her golf. And I enjoyed my time with her.

I must have let many seconds pass before I answered. Eventually, I knew what I had to do.

"I believe, Detective, that you may find my fingerprints, along with those of several members of Valley Vista Country Club, on the grip of that golf club the officer is holding."

"Really?" JB Leeves finally smiled, revealing a set of yellow, tobacco-stained teeth.

Chapter Two   2004 - Scottsdale, Arizona
Tom Requires Serious Convincing by Brooks Benton
Unexpected Visitors Come to Brooks' Rescue

Twilight darkened the verdant, painstakingly manicured acres of Valley Vista Country Club after a perfect March day—the kind Phoenix, Arizona is known for in the springtime, the kind that draws the throngs of tourists down from the frozen north. Temperatures had hovered near 80 degrees as the members of the club faced this extremely challenging golf course with varying degrees of success. Many of the golfers looked weary, even whipped by the time they made the steep ascent up the 18th fairway.

This course was designed in the early '50s to be a test of skill, not merely a recreational course for tourists or rich old men. The movers and shakers of the era congregated there; it was not unusual to see a US Senator or Congressman on the links, or just as likely in the clubhouse bar.

When the club was built it was considered 'way, way out of town' in the empty desert, where land was very cheap at the time. As the metro Phoenix population mushroomed in the '60s and up to this day, the club was now, in 2004, centrally located in the middle of wealthy suburban developments. Just because the populace surrounded the club now, it didn't mean The Club welcomed the populace. The Valley Vista logo was a vintage Colt .45 pistol, barrel pointed up, surrounded by a circle of very sharp looking barbed wire. It was intended to invoke the cheery welcoming greeting: trespass here and we will shoot you. And we will believe you deserved it.

Observing the action from his favorite perch on the 2nd story casual dining room (an enclosed veranda) of the clubhouse was none other than Thomas J. Colt, retired professional golfer, one but perhaps not the most notable among the colorful and varied careers he enjoyed over his long and interesting life. He had played 36 holes at Valley Vista that day and now sat nursing a glass of the best merlot the club served, as he did most Saturday evenings.

Tom or Thomas or TC as he was variously known to his friends, had recently celebrated his 69th birthday. He had fought off the onset of old-er age with remarkable success. His face was tanned and etched with only a few lines from years out in the sun. When standing or walking, his posture was erect, his height 6'2", his physique still robust. His hair was thick, grey-blond, the grey courtesy of nature, the blond courtesy of his barber's magic.

He had blue-grey eyes. Keen eyes that never missed a detail. He smiled easily and often. His smile was the way he connected so easily and so well with his fans during his tournament golf career.

Tom, who still practiced golf every day, had his own exclusive spot on the driving range, with his name on a gold-plated plaque staked to the ground.

Tom lived in a modest-sized cookie-cutter condo, one of two dozen nearly identical ones lining the first fairway of the golf course. Even though Tom now owned the Valley Vista Country Club. "It's enough for me that I know I could buy a mansion if I wanted to," he would comment to people who asked.

The true reason was that Tom had to stay close to the game of golf. Golf was the one thing that connected all the strange and colorful threads of Tom's life, the triumphs and sorrows, the twists and turns, the thrill of unexpected new love and the sad good-byes.

The clubhouse had been built at edge of a stone outcropping, and blended in nicely to look like it was an extension of the everlasting rock. It was three stories high, with a second-story casual dining room that looked out over the 18th hole of the golf course.

Tom was alone in his favorite corner of that casual dining room, as most of the action was in the main dining room or the Gentlemen's Lounge on the first level (in other words, the bar room). Finding Tom alone at the club was an unusual sight. He was known all his life for his sociable nature. He had that ineffable quality called charisma: people were drawn to him. Tom had been the life of the party, any party since he was in his 20s.

Normally, he would be holding court, surrounded by admirers and buddies and those who just wanted to say they met this famous golf star, this local icon of the 1960s and '70s. This man who went head-to-head against Palmer and Nicklaus and Casper and Littler--and all the other greats of what he and many others regarded as the greatest era in golf history, when they were all in their glorious prime.

He was alone by choice, though. He wanted to savor his golf that day. In the morning he shot a 73, just one above par. Then came back in the afternoon with a strong 3-under-par 69. His playing partners, all much younger than he, marveled at the old-er man's undiminished skill—and will to win. In his days on the pro golf tour, he was known for the sheer power of his tee shots. The press even started calling the number one wood, the driver he used, the 'Colt .45'. A replica of that club from the 1960s is on display in the clubhouse. The original is in the World Golf Hall of Fame in St. Augustine, Florida. That's how famous his driving prowess became, even though he only won 6 tournaments on the professional tour in his entire career.

So Tom sipped the merlot and went over the highlights of his rounds that day, the most remarkable being an eagle 3 he scored on the longest par 5 on the course, the 580 yard monster 17th hole. As would be expected, Tom had lost distance off the tee down the years, but today he turned back the clock, hit a booming drive that caught the hard, sun-kissed fairway just right and bounded down the hill 325 yards. He followed that up with a perfect 3-wood that trickled on the green. And then he made a twisting, winding torturous 40-foot putt to cap off this perfect hole. All the young guys he was playing with could do was applaud. Tom always loved applause.

As he replayed that hole, he smiled to himself with great satisfaction. Golf, and the ability to play golf brilliantly, had been the one element of his life that had never changed--and the one that gave him the most joy.

***

My name is Brooks Benton. I am a writer, a golf journalist. I must humbly add that many consider me the premier golf writer in America today. Big deal, right. You're not impressed. I can tell. Tell you the truth, neither am I.

To give you a little background, I turned 50 this year, 2004. I was born in New York City, and my colleagues tell me I retain some of the abrasiveness New Yorkers are known for. So be it. What I like about how I look is my trim waist and strong arms; I'm a bit like a middle-weight pugilist. I like my dark, full, wavy head of hair. I don't so much like my acne-scarred face and bulbous nose. Or the fact I am only 5'6" tall.

My goal was to be an investigative journalist, mystery novelist or a golf announcer on TV. In my objective opinion, I have a wonderful sports announcer voice. I suppose I wanted to be like Mr. Smooth, TV broadcaster Jim Nantz. But the print guys never get promoted to be on-air personalities. We remain what we've always been: Ink-stained wretches. I should be flattered I suppose that I am so highly regarded by my golf writing peers. But it's just not enough. I want more from my career and my writing talent than discussing the challenges of playing Pebble Beach on a windy day. I want to be a seeker--and revealer--of more important truths.

For the last twenty years, I've been the Senior Writer for *Championship Golf Weekly magazine.* I've also been an occasional contributor to the *New Yorker, Esquire* and *Playboy.*

In 2001, when I joined the Valley Vista Country Club, in Scottsdale, Arizona, I met one of the most extraordinary and popular characters the game has ever seen. And for my money golf has had more strange, unusual and memorable characters than the other sports combined. It's a game of loneliness and individuality, which magnifies every quirk, foible and flaw of a player's personality, not to mention in his golf swing. Tom Colt was at the top of my list of memorable characters. Not because of his exploits on the professional golf circuit, which were spotty and overall just good enough to tease and then disappoint his loyal fans. Who were mostly female, I hasten to add.

No, it was off the course where this character was most vibrant. His life had been complex, dangerous, extraordinary--particularly in the often shallow world of the wealthy golfing set. A lot of his story has never been told. I am in the process of convincing him to share his life with the public, with your brilliant and talented scribe Brooks helping him get the story on paper.

I've been trying for two years—and he's rebuffed me over and over. But I'm making progress. Our friendship has been building. We play golf together regularly. Tom is beginning to trust me. I think. Anyway, wish me luck. I need it. Tom is one stubborn...

Right now I'm seated in the casual dining room of the club, on the opposite side of the room from Tom, who, for once is all alone, eating the same dinner he did every Saturday night: a medium-rare ribeye steak with garlic butter and a mushroom cap on top.

He is one of the most magnetic individuals I have ever met. Everyone wants to meet him, to be with him. Even young women thirty years younger than he. It's kind of crazy, if you ask me. As I sit and watch him looking over his scorecard for today, it strikes me that he has that rare quality of being 'cool' as they said about him, in his heyday on tour in the '60s.

So I think I'll put on my pushy journalist persona and go over and talk to him about my idea for a book about his life.

"Hey, Tom, can I join you for a few minutes?"

He looked up at me, a frown creasing his suntanned forehead. "I know what you want to talk about before you even sit down, but be my guest." He pulled a chair out and gestured for me to sit.

"I can get your story published with a major house in New York. I'd split the advance with you and then we could discuss how to share the royalties."

Tom waved that away. "I'm really too busy."

"You have a fantastic story to tell about the Golden Age of Professional Golf in the Sixties. You were there, right in the middle of the action. But your story is about more than golf...what a life you've had! My God, man, you have to get it all down on paper before you...."

"Croak?"

"Well, none of us lives forever. If you don't write it down now, it may be lost to the ages. You've told me some of what you got involved with as a private detective--it's hot stuff! High-society hijinks, shadowy government machinations, murder, sex scandals. And all those beautiful women you knew! James Bond could've learned from you."

He smiled. I knew this vain fellow loved being compared to James Bond.

Tom leaned back in his chair and latticed his hands behind his head. "You are right. It has been quite a journey." Tom cast a glance out the window toward the golf course. "See that table over there, between the 9th Green and 10th Tee? My mom used to bring the drinks out there to the golfers, when she waitressed here. Sometimes she had to work three part-time jobs when I was growing up."

"Now, you own the place."

"I do. The course, the clubhouse, everything down to the last bucket of practice balls on the driving range. I fell in love with this golf course the first time I played it in 1958, because Valley Vista is tough as hell, maybe the toughest course in the state. Some of the old fuds look like they're about to burst into tears when they come up the 18th fairway. I enjoy watching that. It's never too late in life to learn humility."

Tom drifted off to memory land a moment and then said, "And that condo on the 1st fairway over there, not far from mine. That's where my mom lived. I bought it for her. One of her last requests was that I never sell it, because she believed to her dying day that my father would come back to us."

I had Tom on the hook. Deep down, he wants to tell his story. I said, "Yours is a wonderful tale about social progress: The son of a waitress now owns the country club. You're The American Dream."

Tom leaned forward and recaptured his wine glass in his huge, rough hand--over time a golfer's hands get as tough as a farmer's--took a deep swallow then shook his head.

"I didn't think of it that way. It was an individual achievement, not a social one. I did it. I prevailed. I didn't do it for society, did it out of necessity. I feared poverty more than I feared death. After my father...was lost during the Korean War, we were so poor, my mom had to take a payday loan out from a church mouse."

I thought that was a lame joke, but of course I didn't tell Tom. "See, a great story, plucky young man prevails against all odds."

"But my pesky friend Brooks, I'm not a writer. I have no idea how to organize the story. Is this my autobiography? A novel? What the hell is it?"

Tom made a gesture of two fingers to the passing waitress, the beautiful Carmen Lopez. Every guy at the club loved Carmen. She only had eyes for, you guessed it, Tom.

Now, I was really making progress. He was buying me a glass of wine.

Tom continued: "A novel might be better. No one would believe some of the weird stuff that has happened to me."

"You just talk to me. I'll do the writing. I can send you questions to jog your memory. You can answer by email if it's easier. Your life has enough material for a dozen books. And I agree with you, I see this as a novel based on the facts of your life. I'll fill in gaps using third person narration. You tell me what you saw and heard in first person. I'll interview your acquaintances who are still alive."

Tom laughed. "I had no idea you were listening when I told those long-winded stories during our rounds of golf."

"The truly great journalists, like myself, have highly developed listening and memory skills."

Carmen brought out the wine glasses. She was a dark haired beauty, probably about 35, with marvelous long legs and a smile that set many a man's heart aflutter. Although with some of the old farts at this club, it may have been the onset of heart fibrillation pathology.

"Thank you Carmen," Tom said with his signature warm and reassuring smile.

Carmen patted Tom on the arm and smiled at him just as warmly. "I heard you were great out there today. A 69 from the back tees in that wind. Wow, just wow. You know, a certain major championship winner from the last few years played here two weeks ago and shot 75."

Tom said. "Well, he isn't the superior driver of the ball that I am. He sprays his tee shots like a crop duster."

"Dude was pissed. Double-bogied the last hole right in front of the members watching from the dining room. Wouldn't give me an autograph."

Tom took out a pen from his pocket. "What would you like me sign?" They kept smiling at each other for a few more long moments, forgetting I was even there.

I thought to myself, why do I want to write a book about this guy and make him even more popular and beloved than he is now? I don't think I even like him.

Carmen departed, finally. I took a discontented and slightly jealous slug of the wine, which was of course excellent. Everything at Tom Colt's Valley Vista Country Club was excellent since Tom had taken it over 5 years ago. The head greenskeeper had apprenticed at Augusta National. The chef had worked at one of Donald Trump's resorts. Tom even bought brand new Titleist golf balls for us to hit on the driving range. Not those dead rocks they set out at most driving ranges. I hate this guy. I really do.

Tom resumed, "If I were to agree to this collaboration, and I am not saying I will, I have no idea where to begin."

With Carmen's shapely and distracting legs out of view, I got fired up about the project again. "In my biz, we call it the 'inciting incident', the moment that gave your life purpose, a goal, sent you on your journey, changed you forever."

Tom reflected, then rose from his chair, walked over to the picture window and tapped on the glass with his index finger, pointing to the lights of the homes high on the top of distant Camelback Mountain.

"A party up there, in what seemed to me then the stratosphere of wealth, of achievement. Summer of 1953. At a really rich guy's house near the top of the mountain. The guy was Chairman of the Board of an oil company back east. He flew the Board of Directors in for golf and a party. It was one of my mom's first gigs after she started her catering business. I was helping her out that night, busing tables and such. When I took a break, I walked over to the pool area which looked down at the already rapidly growing city of Phoenix. I almost went into like a trance, lost in those thousands of twinkly lights. And I thought, with an 18-year-old's wild and impractical imagination, *All this will be mine someday.*" Tom's face was aglow with the pleasant recollection.

I very quietly took my Intrepid Reporter's Spiral Notebook out of my coat pocket and started writing.

He went back to the table and sat down. "Actually, there's a second incident years later, at the 1960 US Open in Cherry Hills, near Denver, that may have been even more impactful. When I played the best golf of my life and ironically realized I was never going to be a top-flight pro golfer, and I needed to find other ways of making the big bucks--to make all this mine."

I kept scribbling.

"No need to copy all this down, Brooks. I haven't agreed to the project yet."

I brushed that off without comment.

"Do you have any idea what year you want to start with?"

"1962, I think. A bunch of things came together in my life then, the people I spent my prime years with, or at least my early prime years, entered my life that year. And I began my unusual second career...as a detective."

At this point two attractive women walked up the stairs to the casual dining room. They were fashionably and expensively dressed and to me looked enough alike to probably be mother, about 50, and daughter, maybe 25. The mother was an attractive, high-class blonde, the daughter a cute, well-proportioned brunette with glasses.

Tom recognized them and waved. The mother saw Tom, her face lit up and she and the younger one hurried over to our table. Tom got up and she hugged him tightly.

I had the stray thought that I would enjoy spending the night with either one of these women.

She gave Tom a warm kiss on the cheek.

"You don't need to thank me like this every time we meet, Kathleen."

"Oh yes, Tom, I most certainly do."

"Are you having dinner tonight?"

"Yes, it's mother-daughter catch up on things night. Rosa is about to graduate from medical school!"

"Congratulations! I am so proud of you both, what you've done with your lives. Well, if you're staying, try the medallions of lamb. They are absolutely scrumptious."

Of course they are, I thought. *They're prepared perfectly in Tom's gourmet restaurant quality kitchen at Tom's perfect fucking country club.*

"Oh, Kathleen and Rosa, this is my golf buddy Brooks Benton. He is the premier golf writer in the USA."

"MMMM," Kathleen said. I had no idea whether that meant MMMM, that's exciting! or MMMM, how did this writer schmuck get into <u>our</u> swank club?

They went off to a nearby table and sat down. I asked him, "An old flame?'

"No, no. Just good friends. I was the one who solved her mother's murder back in '62."

"What???" I exclaimed, retuning my fallen jaw to its correct upright position.

"Poor Kathleen was only seven when her mother was killed. Actually, she didn't even know her mother then."

"What a story! Let's make that the first case in your book."

"That would be a great choice. If indeed we were going to write a book, which we're not." Tom looked away for a moment as though a jarring memory had come popping up.

"That was also the first time I got shot. Let me tell you, it hurts more than they portray in movies and on TV. He rubbed his shoulder for emphasis. "They let me keep the .32 caliber slug. I display it in a Plexiglas case."

"First time, you said?"

Tom nodded. "First of three."

I thought to myself, *I have a bona fide bestseller on my hands. This book is going to be huge. Tom doesn't know it, but I'll be able to get the publisher to put my name in larger type on the cover than his.*

"You know, Tom for someone who doesn't want to share his past with today's readers, my sources tell me you have a treasure trove of scrapbooks and mementos in your home."

"So?"

I thought it was time to provoke Tom just a little bit, "Did you ever wonder why with all your talent, you only won 5 tournaments in your whole career?"

"Six. And two on the Senior Tour. What's your point?"

"With your skill and strength you should have won more. You disappointed your fans."

"I had too much fun. We enjoyed ourselves on the pro golf circuit then. And I had other challenges in life than golf. It's not easy being a knight."

"You owe it to the golfing public, the fans who supported you all those years, to explain this to them, set the record straight."

"Bah. I owe them nothing. I made sure they enjoyed themselves as much as I did. Especially the female fans." He flashed that Smile of the Rascal he had perfected.

I had to quickly find another tack. "Well, then, the book will help them re-live all the good times."

I studied Tom for his reaction. He began drumming his fingers on the table, a sure sign of annoyance.

He said, "I don't want to talk about this anymore."

What a stubborn SOB he was! At that point, I was contemplating telling him to forget the whole thing. My time is too valuable. Why should I have to beg and grovel? I'm one of America's Greatest Living Sportswriters.

But I thought better of it and just shrugged, thanked him for the wine, got up from my chair and went into the bar room--which genteel folk call the Gentlemen's Lounge. I needed a stiffer drink than wine.

I couldn't completely get away from Tom Colt even in there. On one wall was an enlarged photo of Tom, in his youthful 20s, holding the trophy from one of his tournament victories. He hasn't really changed much, I thought. His hair was longer then, and sun-streaked blonde. The photo emphasized how muscular his upper body was: strong forearms, large hands. Either that or the trophies they gave out then were kind of small. A triumphant smile. A strong chin. A boyish, slightly thinner face than the Tom I knew. I could also see mischief in his eyes: there was that Look of the Rascal again.

***

Tom ate a ramekin of chocolate mousse for dessert and smiled when he thought of Brooks' tenacity. The club's General Manager, tall, slender, dour and prune-faced Nigel Hedgerow appeared and came over to Tom's table. Nigel was eerily identical to his father Basil, who had preceded him as Club General Manager.

"Excuse me, Sir. The Phoenix Police have arrived at The Club." Nigel raised a grey pencil-thin eyebrow. They asked for you. I escorted them to your office."

Tom looked puzzled more than alarmed. "Did they say what the problem is?"

"No, sir, I'm afraid not."

Tom thought he saw the shadow of a wicked smile on Nigel's face, which of course he was trying to conceal. Tom got up, tossed his napkin down on the table with evident irritation, put his scorecard in his sports jacket pocket and strolled to the elevator bank, then took a ride up to the third floor where his office was.

He walked through the door and saw a young woman in a nicely tailored suit and a young officer in uniform.

"I'm Tom Colt, the owner of The Club. How may I help you officers?"

"I'm Detective Elizabeth Thomas and this is officer Crowley." She observed the formality of showing Tom her detective badge. She looked tense. Tom wondered what had happened. His first thought was that one of his club members had been murdered--or had murdered someone. The officer was carrying a file box, one of those brown banker's boxes. It looked heavy.

"What did you bring with you, officer, the complete unabridged collection of my misdeeds?" Tom quipped. The officer remained stone-faced. *They must offer a class in maintaining stone faces at the Police Academy*, he thought.

And then inexplicably the female detective beamed. "Tom, I'm Det. Jerry Edward Mathers' granddaughter." She extended her hand.

Tom's expression showed how thrilled he was. "Great to meet you. So you followed in his footsteps. Do you work homicides, too?"

"Yes, I certainly do," she said enthusiastically, as though he had asked, do you have the coolest job ever?

Tom pointed to the box: "What did you bring me?"

"When grandpa died, he left all sorts of records about the cases he worked on. They were in a storage facility he had so much stuff. It's taken us two years to go through it all. This box is the material from the cases he worked on with you."

Tom looked happily surprised. "Really?" The young officer put the box on Tom's desk.

"In grandpa's notes he said he wanted you to have these records. He hoped that, maybe..." Her voice trailed off bashfully, for a tough young detective.

"What?" Tom asked as he sat down on the edge of the desk and opened the box.

"He had this idea that you might want to write about the cases you worked on together, tell the story of what you and he accomplished. He was so impressed with you and your detective skill, Tom. He said you had a better feel for cases than anyone on the police force at that time."

"Your grandfather was the finest man I ever met. Did you read the files?"

They both nodded. "Oh, yes. I loved how you solved the murder of that politician's wife, one of your first cases with grandpa. Brilliant work!"

To Tom's surprise, the shy young cop piped up, "Your solution was elegant in its simplicity, sir."

Tom, swelled with pride, made a mental note to contribute substantially more money to police charities.

"Why thank you, officer. Your kind words mean a lot to me."

Liz said, "You were more than a colleague to my grandfather, more than a brother, more than a friend."

Tom choked up. He busied himself at taking files out of the box.

He pulled out a folded-up green poster board, opened it into four large squares on his desk.

"Det. Mathers kept 'The Leaderboard'. How funny."

"What is that, sir?"

"It was an idea my sister came up with of how to organize information about a case. The lines down the left side are for the names of the suspects. Across the top we have motive, opportunity, why the suspect could have done it, and why it was improbable."

These were depicted with M, O, and an upward arrow, and a downward arrow.

"As Ed and I, I mean Detective Mathers and I, gathered information, we would move the names of the suspects up and down the Leaderboard, like in a golf tournament. Our prime suspect was listed first, the Leader in the Station House, we called him--or her."

"That is impressive Mr. Colt. What a fine crime solving tool."

"Thanks, officer." Tom took a few more mental victory laps. He turned to Liz. "I imagine you use this at Phoenix PD today…"

"Nope," Liz quickly replied, Tom thought a bit too curtly. Tom deflated. He was as proud of his crime solving exploits as he was of his golf career. Actually, the crime solving had been more successful.

Liz went back into bashful young woman mode—in the presence of Tom Colt, the man her grandfather described as one of the most heroic men he had ever met. And because, she had to admit to herself, he was still so handsome—and had an unusual quality she couldn't really describe, a way of putting you at ease like you'd been friends forever.

"Umm, Grandpa said if I ever had a case that was driving me crazy, I should contact you. Do you think you could help me sometime? We have too many unsolved-s, the Chief tells us on a daily basis in a harsh tone of voice. Some of them are murders involving the rich and powerful, like you and Grandpa used to solve."

"I would really like that. Call me anytime." Tom reached into his pocket and dug out his business cards, gave one to Liz, and just to be polite, to Officer Crowley. "This is my direct cell number."

Liz nodded with enthusiasm, put the card in her suit coat pocket.

Then she unexpectedly threw her arms around Tom and squeezed hard. Det. Liz was evidently a devoted member of a local gym, Tom quickly concluded, as the air was squeezed out of him.

"I miss Grandpa so much!" she said, finally letting go of Tom, allowing his lungs to re-inflate.

"I do too. My only regret about getting older is, too many of the people you loved are gone. And you find it impossible to replace them."

***

Liz and the young officer left. Tom returned to the casual dining room. After picking up a glass of cabernet sauvignon at the bar, he walked over to the window that looked out over his golf course.

He heard the popular swinging tune from the '60s, *Fly Me to the Moon,* being played by the piano player in the main dining room.

He quietly, and in a surprisingly good voice for a pro golfer/detective/real estate mogul, sang along.

He found himself starting to become emotional from the memories that song brought back. Thinking he was alone, he didn't fight the flow of emotion.

He didn't see the club's head waitress Carmen Lopez coming up behind him until he saw her beautiful reflection on the glass.

"Why so sad, Tom? It's such an upbeat song. Jimmy plays it every Saturday night. I sing along with it, too, until he begs me to stop."

"Just reflecting on my life. It's gone by so fast. My mother warned me that was how it would be. She was right."

"Well, you've had—you're having--a fantastic, amazing life-- and you're still going strong. That's what's important."

Tom smiled. "Truth is, I feel better than I did when I was 35. Probably because I don't party-hardy like I did when I was on the golf tour. I feel as though I've just rounded the turn and begun the second 9 holes of my life."

She nodded encouragingly. "Mind if I join you awhile? It's time for my break and I'd like to get off my feet. I had lots of tables tonight, even for a Saturday."

Tom pulled a chair out from a window table and said, "I would like that very much." Carmen sat down, Tom pulled out another chair for her to put her feet up, then sat down himself.

"Mr. Hedgerow forbids this. I'm not even supposed to be sitting here."

"You are one of our hardest working employees. And I own the chairs and the tables. Our General Manager Mr. Nigel Hedgerow can, respectfully, go screw himself. His father, Basil Hedgerow, total snob that he was, didn't even want me on the driving range giving lessons to non-members. Now I own the place."

"This club wasn't a fun place to work until you bought it, let me tell you."

"You look thirsty." Tom got up, went to a linen-topped sideboard and poured Carmen an iced tea, served it to her before taking his seat next to her.

"Thanks for always doing more than is asked of you here. You are appreciated more than you know."

Carmen took a satisfying drink of the tea, then, beaming, put her feet back on the floor, leaned forward and kissed Tom, softly and sweetly.

"I wish..."

"I wish, too, lovely Carmen. But you deserve someone young. Twenty years from now I'll possibly be an old man."

Carmen giggled. "But I love you, Tom."

"And I love you. I always will."

"I have a lot of mileage on me, too. Two hard break-ups and a disaster of a failed marriage."

"You look in pristine condition to me, like you've barely left the showroom."

"Then maybe you should take me for a spin."

Tom grinned.

"The dating scene is rough in Scottsdale. Too many poseurs. It's hard for a nice girl to find a Tom Colt."

"You were probably looking in the telephone directory under 'C'. I'm listed under 'K' for Knights."

She laughed. "I think you love that German lady Kat Stern the most. I see how she looks at you when she thinks no one is watching. I had no idea Germans could swoon."

"She's from the warmer part of that country. What I've learned is, the heart has many compartments and a nearly infinite capacity for love. And yes, I've loved my friend Katrina for forty years. But we'll never get married."

"So, to you, life is about love and golf."

"You have just discovered the essential truths of life, which were passed down to me many years ago by a remarkable woman 17 years my senior."

She turned her hand palm up and he placed his hand gently in hers. You could almost hear the crackle of electricity between them. It was a magic moment, for both of them, but one they had shared several times. A male-female attraction based on deep and enduring mutual respect. This stemmed from an understanding of where both of them came from and deep gratitude for how far they had come. A kind of Carmen-and-Tom against the rich snobs at the country club solidarity.

Even after Tom bought the Valley Vista Club property, he never felt like he was one of THEM, the sons and grandsons of the members who ran the club in the early 1960s when he was a near-penniless golf instructor there. Somewhere in the deep recesses of Tom's mind were recorded all the instances when those people looked down on him.

So why did he buy the place? He loved that beautiful, challenging golf course. He loved the stunning desert the course was set in, like a green jewel. He thought about buying the course and tearing down the clubhouse, but he needed the dues-paying snobs to support the maintenance of the golf course.

Carmen continued: "I overheard your conversation with Brooks Benton tonight. He's kind of a pompous jerk and always stares at my legs, but--"

"I look at you all the time."

"Mostly, you look into my eyes."

"Because they are a soft, muted brown that is unforgettable and express great warmth."

She turned up the warmth of those eyes. Tom's ever-strong heart beat a little faster.

"You are quite wonderful to say that. I do think, you should take Brooks up on his offer of writing a book about your life. I'd be the first one in line at Barnes & Noble to buy it. I'd love to learn more about you, to experience what you experienced."

"All right then, I'll do it."

"I won't even get jealous when I read about all the beautiful girls you've been with."

"I believe, Carmen Victoria-Marie Lopez, I saved the best for last."

Chapter Three
Brooks Closes the Deal at an Unusual Venue

Brooks Continues Our Story:

So, now you've met Tom Colt. He was, even at nearly 70, a hopeless romantic, a total optimist. The emotionally crippling afflictions of middle age, and then old-er age, didn't affect him. Things like encrusted cynicism, deep disappointment in life, the pain of losing loved ones, and especially the older person's typical envy of young people in the physical prime of their lives.

Truth is, Tom fervently believed he was still young--and the people he surrounded himself with heartily agreed with that belief. Just ask the young, strong, stud golfers he lifted cash from like hapless pigeons in big money matches on the golf course almost every day. Just look at how the lovely waitress Carmen Lopez responded to him and not to me, an internationally famous writer who is twenty years younger. Dammit.

One of the many lessons I took from my wonderful association with Thomas Jeremiah Colt was to not fear the passage of time, not even give it consideration. The one thing we can't do anything about is how old we are.

And fortunately for all of us, that seminal night at the Valley Vista clubhouse was not over.

After Tom and I had our falling out, I went to the bar, drank two scotches and tried to relax. I was mad at myself that I couldn't get Tom on board with this project. As a reporter, I was known as a bulldog. Tom was treating me like a yappy miniature poodle.

Eventually I had to visit the men's room. I took a position at the urinal and who should walk in but Tom. He nodded at me. I nodded at him. Then he found a spot down the line and we took care of our respective business.

I had an idea about how to close the deal with Tom, so I went for it like he does with a second shot over water on a shortish, tempting Par 5. "I took the liberty of coming up with a title for our book--'In the Shadow of Greatness'."

Tom turned to me and grimaced. "That's a crap title. Too artsy-fartsy. If we were to write such a book, and I'm still, I re-iterate because you don't seem to listen, not saying we will write such a book, I thought at first the title should be 'A

Swinging Time' because that's the way life was for a lot of us, on and off the course back then."

Did he say 'we'?

"But then I remembered in the '60s 'swinging' also meant wife swapping. Don't want to confuse our readers. So let's go with 'The Golf Club Murder'. It's clear. It's simple. The murder weapon was a golf club, a #1 wood. And the suspects were members of a golf club, this very Country Club in fact."

Did he say 'our readers'? I almost pissed on the floor with excitement, which would have resulted in immediate expulsion from The Club. "Great title. I like it. A lot. When do we get started? How 'bout we tee off tomorrow at say 10? You could dictate some of the story while we play. I'll bring my tape recorder."

"I still don't understand exactly how this works. I only know what I heard and did. Not what everyone else heard and did."

"I'll fill in part of the narrative."

"You mean make stuff up."

"Yes, if you want to put it crudely. Writing is a rare and magical skill, my friend. We're going to tell your story in a series of fictionalized biographies. And I'm--we're--going to be on the NYT Bestseller List."

Tom made a skeptical face. I don't know if I want you making up stuff about me."

"Making stuff up is how this works. Remember, it took a little added frog DNA to bring the dinosaurs back to life in *Jurassic Park.* Together, you and I can bring your fabulous era back. How fun is that!"

Tom sighed, with resignation, and said, "Fine. Ten AM it is."

The Old Bulldog, Brooks Benton, has prevailed again. I couldn't resist: "Probably a nice surprise to see Det. Mathers' granddaughter here tonight. Wonder how she found you."

"You bastard."

"You betcha."

Tom chuckled, washed his hands, dried them on one of the white perfectly folded washcloths provided, dropped it into the laundry bin, which had the club logo on it!, then departed. I was left to ponder life's imponderables.

This was definitely not how Fitzgerald or Hemingway got started in the world of literature, or even James Patterson, but what the hell. Tom's destiny was charted when he played in the US Open at Cherry Hills against Hogan, Palmer, and Nicklaus and many other golfing greats, had the chance to measure himself against the best. My writing destiny changed that night because I had to pee. Really, really had to pee.

The world provides different strokes for all of us very different folks.

***

The next morning I took my breakfast at The Club, early at 7AM, then got some practice in on the driving range for my match with Tom. I am one of the best golfers among the members of the media that cover our sport. I carry a strong travelling 8 handicap. The strength of my game is my putting, which rankles Tom because that is his weakness. If he could have learned how to make 10-15 foot putts consistently, he would have won 20 tournaments, and at least three 'Majors', I would guess.

At my locker there was an envelope addressed to me from Tom. I opened it. It was the names, addresses, and cell phone numbers of people he thought I should interview as background for our book. I chuckled.

When Tom commits to something, he goes all out, with great resolve. No dithering. Like when he selected a club during a tournament. He never changed his mind, put the club back, and took out another one, like so many indecisive pros do. He went with his initial gut feel of how to play the shot. He had the reputation as one of the fastest players on tour. Unfortunately, his gut feel let him down at key points in the final round of many tournaments.

It was a long list, maybe 30 names. Some of them surprised me. Prominent members of the business community, the sports world and the political crowd.

The first name on the list was Katrina Stern. Her address was a condo right here on the club grounds, not far from Tom's. His note said, "She knows everything. All my secrets. Great and wonderful friend since 1962."

I remembered her vaguely. She was a ladies tour player in the early days. I cranked up my cell phone and looked her profile up. Huh! Bit of a surprise. She won 12 tournaments, twice as many as Tom did on the men's tour. But who's counting. I'll be sure to bring that up today to needle him.

I looked at some pics of Katrina in her golfing heyday. She played on tour from 1960 to 1983. She was very tall, very trim. A runner's body. Great long legs and strong calves revealed by the shorts she wore. Her success on tour surprised me because tall golfers often have trouble keeping their balance and therefore their shot accuracy. You want your center of gravity to be around the groin. She had a steely glare when she was concentrating on the next shot. Her profile said she was born in Germany and emigrated to the US from Brazil. Brazil? German? Is there a story within the story?

There always is.

***

The 2004 edition of Kat Stern was very tall, still trim and with long beautiful shining black hair, not a hint of any grey. She wore blue shorts, a white sleeveless top with the club logo and white golf shoes as she supervised the junior golfers practicing that morning on the driving range. Her title at the Valley Vista Country Club was Director of Junior Golf.

Junior golfers, boys and girls between 10 and perhaps 14, were lined up on the driving range, hitting golf balls under Kat's watchful eye. I concluded after a few minutes of observation that Kat's teaching methods were one part golf coach and one part drill instructor. The pupils who were goofing around, as kids do, not focusing on their golf, were treated to Kat's steely stare until they re-focused.

Some of the kids' parents were there watching their little darlings' lesson. I had heard about her semi-controversial teaching methods from some of the club members. To build their strength, she would add weights to the bottom of their golf bags and of course make them carry their clubs when they played. As the group lesson session wound down, she had her little charges jog up and down the driving range.

It's a sad commentary on the American diet that so many youngsters are overweight. As some of her students began huffing and puffing from just this light jogging, I could see Kat muttering oaths under her breath. Finally, she blew the whistle that was around her neck and they came trotting back to her.

One of the parents, a Pudgy Dad who humorously matched his Pudgy Son, who was red in the face and wheezing, stepped forward and complained. "You're supposed to teach him golf."

"I do but as an added bonus, I teach him about life. If he keeps going as a junk food junkie, he'll be dead at 50. Is that the future you want for him?"

"Of course not," the father spat out.

"You are raising a generation of little tubby-wubbies, soft as bread dough, who will grow up with diabetes and heart disease and our healthcare system will eventually go bust trying to take care of them. So yes, I am going to make them exercise. Children don't need to ride in golf carts or use pull-carts. I'm 68 years old and I don't ride in a golf cart."

Pudgy Son said to Pudgy Dad, "She's some kind of exercise Nazi, Dad."

"Child, you have no idea how wrong you are," Kat said.

I watched this scene with amusement until the kids and parents went back to the clubhouse, then strolled over to Kat. I still had 40 minutes before my tee off time with Tom.

I broke out my most charismatic smile. "Katrina Stern! Ladies golf star. What a treat to meet you."

Kat looked at me warily, as she should. "I'm Brooks Benton, golf writer. I'm sure you've read my stories in the *New Yorker* and *Championship Golf Weekly.*"

"Oh, yes, of course," she replied. I could tell she had never read a word of my Collected Works.

But she extended her hand and I shook it. I explained my collaboration with Tom and asked to set up a time to talk to her. She suggested tomorrow. Great!

"One key piece of information I need is whatever became of Julia Wilkinson, the Judge's daughter. Tom is very tight lipped about it."

It's not easy to knock Katrina Stern off stride, but it seemed I did with what I thought was an innocent question. I thought wrong...

"I...can't tell you anything except what became of her didn't surprise me in the least." She tensed her lower lip as she said this. Interesting...

"I have to say, my investigative reporter instinct is aroused."

"You'll have to deal with your arousal when you're by yourself I'm afraid."

As I walked back to the clubhouse, despite her attempt at a witty brushoff, I was excited to be interviewing her. I had a little feeling Tom and Kat had been lovers back when they were young. Maybe they still were.

***

Tom was in his office when his cell phone rang. It was Katrina.

"So this annoying little man with a huge bulb of a nose shows up this morning and says you told him to talk to me for background on a book. What should I tell him?"

"Everything."

"Everything?"

"Yes, He's writing the story of my life."

"Scheisse, I'll be in it."

"You play a prominent, exciting, actually crucial role."

"But can I tell this annoying Brooks person all of our secrets?"

Tom mulled that over. "Except for two."

Kat mulled that over. There was a pause for silent mutual mulling. "Okay. Got it."

"I agreed to this book under duress. Brooks is like this little terrier who grabs you around the ankle and won't let go."

Kat laughed. "Is he an alkie or something? His nose is so red."

"Many writers are alcoholics. It must be a lonely, unpleasant profession."

Chapter Four
Tom takes Brooks back to the '60 US Open
Katrina and Tom Reminisce About the Mile High Club

Tom and I teed off at precisely 10AM. Sunny day, mild temperatures, not much wind. Easy conditions for Tom to shoot under par as he usually did on this course that he's probably played 2,000 times.

On the first tee I noticed Tom had a metal driver, not his legendary Colt .45 persimmon wood-headed driver. I asked him why.

"Can't swing that big old siege gun like I used to. Opted for this new technology. It's pretty good actually. No use holding onto the past."

This was an untruth. Tom positively cherished the past, as I would learn. But we all lie to ourselves, at least a bit.

He pointed out a condo on the left side of the fairway. "I bought that for my mom on her 65th birthday. She lived there the rest of her life, 87 years young. When I showed her the condo for the first time, the look on her face was one of the nicest moments of my life. I wanted her to be close by. She lived alone from the time my father disappeared in the Far East, or so the government said, when she was only 39."

I thought, *Fabulous! That story will be the basis of our next book!*

Tom said, "Brooks, are you listening? You checked out for a moment."

"Don't worry. I'm all yours," I replied.

"Okay, let me tell you about the 1960 US Open."

I could tell Tom was fully back there at Cherry Hills in '60. His face was alight from accessing the kind of rich and textured memories that only champion athletes know. I've seen the same look on Jack Nicklaus' face when he tells you the story of the 1986 Masters, his last Major victory.

Here's Tom's story, with some highly skilled editing by your humble correspondent:

The 1960 US Open Golf Tournament, played at Cherry Hills Country Club in Denver, Colorado, was the most amazing week of my life, a life-changing event for me in so many ways. I was 25, a moderately successful professional golfer since 1958, who up to that time had not won a tournament. But I was coming closer and closer. In the 1960 spring tour, I had 3 finishes in the TOP 10, including a third place finish.

I had easily qualified for the '60 US Open, which even through the fuzzy and ever-changing the lens of history is now regarded as one of the most exciting finishes in the history of golf. No fewer than 10 players had a legitimate shot to win in the final round. It was an amazing back and forth day. A treat for the fans but very nerve wracking for the competitors. You will probably remember the tournament as the one where the great Arnold Palmer made the most stirring charge to victory in his legendary career, coming from 7 shots behind in the final round to win. Of course, Arnold Palmer didn't just win, he blazed to victory. And a young--20 years old--but already celebrated amateur named Jack Nicklaus finished second, a precursor to the greatness that was to come.

Bitter disappointment visited competitor after competitor, including one of the greatest players of the last 20 years, Ben Hogan, who was attempting to win an unprecedented 5th US Open. The 17th hole was a par 5 with a pond surrounding the green. Hogan was tied with Palmer at that point. He hit what looked to be a perfect third shot to give himself a chance for a birdie and the outright lead. But, to show you how cruel this game can be, he hit the pitch shot <u>too</u> perfectly and it spun back off the green and into the pond and Hogan ended up with a bogie, not the birdie he needed to win. I read that Hogan still didn't stop thinking about that shot twenty years after the tournament.

That's why you don't see pro golfers attending horror films at the cinema. We don't need to, we lived them, and our personal horrors revisit us for the rest of our lives.

But there were many other story lines that week, including my own. In what now seems like a peculiar tradition, the final two rounds of the US Open were played on Saturday.

So there I was, in the last 9 holes of the final round, playing the best golf of my life—and with a chance to win the Open. It was like being in a maelstrom. In those days the scoring system was not as automated as it is today. We, the players, had trouble keeping up with who was leading, and what our relative position to the leaders was. I learned later that for a brief 10 minute period at around 3PM that afternoon, I actually was tied for the lead! Yes, me. Unknown Tom Colt from Phoenix, Arizona.

During the final round, the lead changed hands twelve times, and when the dust cleared all but one of those men were left muttering that they should've won.

In that 36-hole final day, I got lucky break after lucky break. To be honest with you, I hit several loose shots that could have spelled disaster. An errant drive hopped over a creek rather than tumbling into it. I chipped into the cup twice to save par. One of these chip shots I hit much too hard and it was barreling down the slick green toward the cup. If it hadn't hit the flagstick and fallen into the cup, it probably would have rolled off the green.

But that long tough day in the merciless Western sun also revealed all the flaws in my game that would continue to haunt me. My putting was pathetic as it usually was, but I managed to make gritty par after gritty par. I drove the ball all over the lot, left one hole, right the next. I also had difficulty concentrating for a full 18 holes, let alone 36 in the National Championship. My mind would drift off from the challenge of the next shot and I'd think of all sorts of extraneous things. Kat Stern always told me I had too active a mind to be a golf champion. She could cut out all distractions to the point all she saw was her ball and the target. I had extreme difficulty doing that. I was always wondering about...something.

And when I needed to summon my best shots on the back 9 the final day, I faded instead on the closing nine holes, and eventually finished 12th. The greens got more sun baked and faster as the day wore on. I three putted both par 3s on the on the back nine holes, or "the inward half" as the Brits say. On the same 17th hole that did in Hogan, I made the mental error of trying to hit that tiny green with my second shot, instead of doing the smart thing and laying up, then hitting a short pitch shot for my third. My shot splashed into the middle of the pond. I can still see that splash to this day.

I wanted desperately to finish in the Top 10, at least 9th in a major championship. That paid $1,950. Really could have used the dough from a Top 10 finish at that time. The winner, Arnie, pocketed a massive $14,400. Woo hoo! What's first prize today, like a million bucks?

That evening I couldn't calm down. I hung around the course and walked the back 9, replaying each shot in my mind. By that time the spectators had left. And most of the players, too. Some with a look of satisfaction at how well they played, others with the hollowed out look that spoke of what might have been.

No one in the gallery in Denver knew who I was, but I started to notice some fans actually cheering for me, following me from hole to hole in the last round. My caddie told me later that I was smiling almost the entire day. He said I never betrayed how nervous I was. I had climbed the very first mountain of my golf career.

As the years have gone by, flown by really, I have often reflected on that Saturday at Cherry Hills. I couldn't articulate this at the time, but I have come to realize and accept that the significance of that week was that I, on a subconscious level at least, realized that my lifelong dream of being a star player on the golf circuit had evaporated, was gone forever.

I had played my best golf, better than I had ever played. It shocked me how well I played. I even, for about 6 holes or so, entered that strange athletic universe, THE ZONE. The world seems to turn more slowly. Your thinking is calm and clear, your senses heightened. I was in the mix with current and future stars like Palmer and Nicklaus, as well as aging but still immensely talented and determined stars of the past like Ben Hogan and Sam Snead.

But the result of my amazing play was only a tie for 12th. I never finished higher than that in any of the US Opens I played. As it turned out, what I ended up becoming, was a journeyman who only won 6 events in his entire 20-year career (plus two Senior Tour events). And I must confess that each of those wins was a minor miracle.

In my young life all I had dreamed of and worked tirelessly toward was to be a champion golfer, probably since I was 11 years old and my father took me to my first pro tournament here in Phoenix, Arizona, The Phoenix Thunderbird Open. We moved here from Florida when I was ten. My dad had been stationed there when the War ended. The next day he bought me a set of junior clubs and took me out to a driving range for my first lesson. The magic of seeing the great players in action inspired me to want to play--not just play but to play well, at the highest level.

So, I have come to believe that strangely, my dream died that hot afternoon at Cherry Hills. But in another way, some new dreams were hatched that day, a realization that I would need to devise other ways to make my fortune in life. And for a variety of reasons, primarily because of the financial struggles my mother and I and my sister faced after my father disappeared, acquiring great wealth was extremely important to me.

Kind of a tough pill to swallow when you're only 25, your dream dying. Luckily a series of opportunities presented themselves and my life took these amazing twists and turns.

Brooks Continues Our Story:

Tom, despite his focus being on telling me that story, shot a solid 70 that day, two under par. Two things I noticed: he could still hit great tee shots with his Driver, that new metal-headed thunder stick of his. And strangely, his putting was better now that when he was a tour player. I tried to develop a theory for our book on why this might be, but couldn't come up with anything, except that Tom had found the secret to contentment in life. Wish I knew what that was.

My guess is that this guy who hid behind the happy-go-lucky playboy image wanted to win so much that he put enormous pressure on himself--and the pressure showed up in this performance on the greens.

You are probably thinking, thank you Dr. Brooks Benton, for that brilliant psychoanalysis. And please don't attempt it again.

***

I had created a binder with questions I wanted to ask Tom for our book. After we finished playing, I sat down on the bench by my locker and read through them.

Out of the corner of my eye I saw Tom coming out the shower stalls. *He can't be almost 70*, I thought to myself. Not any fat on the guy. And that build: narrow waist and broad shoulders just like forty years ago. His powerful arms and shoulders were the result of a night and weekend job he took after his father was lost in the Korean War. He worked at a produce packing plant, carrying 100 lb. crates of vegetables to delivery trucks.

He even had what they call 6-pack abs. I wondered if a trick was being played on me: this was an actor hired to play Tom. The real Tom was in hiding somewhere, maybe Palm Springs at some posh retirement village.

Tom stepped out of the shower, toweled off, then put on a soft robe with the club logo on it.

I said, "I looked at some photos of you from the early '60s. You had movie star good looks. A strong and handsome profile, kind of like a young Gregory Peck. That wavy hair, not too long, not too short. What a magnetic smile you had. No wonder the groupies loved you."

"What do I look like now?"

"Ah...an older movie star."

"How old?"

"Just slightly older. Like the difference between Gregory Peck in *To Kill a Mockingbird* versus in *The Omen*."

"I'm relieved. I thought you were going to say, I look like Mr. Peck in *Old Gringo*."

He went to his locker, pulled out a pair of boxer shorts, took off the robe, put on the shorts, and dropped down to the green carpet and proceeded to do 25 one-handed push-ups. I had heard, but doubted, that he and Katrina worked out in the Club's fitness center together nearly every day. Now I believed it. When he got back up he wasn't even winded. I got winded just watching him.

***

At 6PM Tom answered the doorbell at his condo. He opened the door, it was Katrina Stern. She swept past him into the living room. She looked, well, stern.

"What a long damn day with those spoiled little brats. I'm exhausted. Only one thing will revive me. You. Give me a moment to shower. The plumber is working at my place-- again. I need to talk to the guy who owns this Club about the shoddy workmanship in these condos. We need to import some skilled German craftsmen to Arizona."

"I wouldn't bother the owner. He's very busy."

"Busy golfing, or chatting up girls, I imagine."

She went into the bathroom. Tom heard the water running.

The floorplan of Tom's two-story condo was a master bedroom on the 2nd floor, with a balcony that overlooked the golf course. On the first floor were a 2nd bedroom, large kitchen and living room. Tom used the upstairs as an archive of his career and life. Him mom had saved every newspaper and magazine article featuring Tom. He also had a collection of photos from golf tournaments and parties and events he attended. Many of the photos showed Tom posing with sports and entertainment celebrities in the '60s and beyond.

He also kept some of his favorite golf clubs over the years, but very few putters, those tools of frustration and failure for Tom. After he quit playing competitive golf, there were articles about his blossoming career as a real estate developer, and then philanthropist. He sponsored a number of young players on the men's and women's tours.

Just added to the collection was the file box of the cases he worked on with Det. Mathers, which made the story of his life complete.

Tom didn't go up there and look at the stuff very often. So why did he keep it all? Had he secretly been waiting for a chance to put the story of his life on paper? Or was he saving it to share with the next great love of his life?

The first floor of Tom's condo was decorated in the Man Cave Deluxe style. Big screen TV, so Tom could watch a movie at least 3 times a week. He loved Westerns and, as you would expect, detective stories of all sorts. Twin leather chairs and sofas deep enough to fall asleep in filled out the room.

He had a stainless-steel griller/smoker unit about the size of a small truck on the porch. A decorator friend was on call to change the artwork and color scheme once a year or so, a recognition of Tom's forward-thinking view of life. He was always looking ahead to the next adventure. This year's theme was nautical, paintings of tall ships and colors like sea foam green. He had an urge to go sailing, or perhaps have an island adventure.

A few minutes later Katrina emerged, wearing a towel. "Could you get me a t-shirt. Mine was soiled today when one of the little monsters threw up his hot dog on me while I was taking him back to the clubhouse in a golf cart. He claimed he was too hot and exhausted to walk."

He followed her back into the bedroom, picked up a long-sleeved cotton shirt from a drawer. She dropped the towel, put on her panties, slipped on the shirt Tom gave her.

He always enjoyed looking at her lovely body. The lean, long legs, the still-smooth skin of her face, the gem-like green eyes. She was to this day still very much an athlete.

And of course Tom focused her smallish but pert breasts. Kat noticed this.

"The first time you saw my boobs you called them 'little beauties'. I'll never forget that. I wondered at first if it was a compliment. Or you were comparing me to Julia Wilkinson, Miss Knockers of 1962 herself."

"They're still beauties."

Kat put on her shorts and they walked back out into the living room. She noticed a painting on Tom's wall, of Pebble Beach Golf Links, was askew. She straightened it for him.

Kat said, "And you're not bad either. People who don't know who you are think you're about 50. So I guess you're one of my success stories. I had to get you to stop smoking, learn to work out regularly."

"If you hadn't, I wouldn't be here today. You and Gary Player were way ahead of your time when it came to working on being fit."

Tom thought a moment then added: "I was always grateful you never tried to get me to give up eating red meat."

"Even as a very young girl I was wise enough to not attempt the impossible. Any idea how many ribeye steaks you've eaten in your lifetime?'

"I wouldn't care to hazard an estimate."

"Remember how 'cool' you thought smoking was when we were young. You told me, don't worry about it, Katrina. John Wayne smokes. But I guess they all did back then. Even most of the big-name golfers."

Kat's laugh had a trace of bitterness. "And then I married Stan Barker, the Bratwurst Baron, purveyor of Barker's Fine Sausages, who died of emphysema and obesity twelve years later."

Tom wasn't sure what to say...

She paused and became wistful. "Your book project has gotten me all nostalgic. Our friendship has been so strange and extraordinary. It's like we've dated on and off for 40 years. "

"I remember lots of wonderful times we had," Tom said, brushing her damp hair away from her eyes."

"Sometimes aren't a lifetime, like we could have had. Oh, hell, I don't even know what I'm saying. Don't listen to me. I was out in the hot sun too long today."

"You're saying the words of a young hopeful person, like you were then and still are. What was your favorite of our dates?"

"That night in 1983 when we went to see a James Bond movie with that really romantic song, *All Time High*. And you surprised me by chartering a jet for us to fly to Vegas. We drank champagne and made love at 30,000 ft."

"Good choice. That would be mine, too."

"I had just retired from the tour. I felt so old and used up. I know that was stupid. I was only 44. You turned that night into a celebration of my career. You somehow knew I was hurting, and knew what I needed. It was magical. You were magical. I don't even remember where we spent the night."

"In each other's arms, I imagine."

Kat smiled. "Yes, I imagine so. Why did you pick Vegas?"

"Always had a soft spot for the place. I won my first tournament there, remember."

"Oh, right."

"Where was your first time?"

"Moline, Illinois, of all places."

They shared a laugh. "I'd always dreamed of winning at Winged Foot, or Merion or Medinah #2. And my first win was at a municipal course in the Quad Cities."

"You'll have to take me back there sometime and we can re-live your triumph."

"They closed the course years ago. It's a shopping mall now."

"Glory can be fleeting."

Tom could tell Kat had already migrated to another memory. "I'll never forget how bittersweet my wedding was. I couldn't help thinking that marriage wasn't going to work out for me."

She frowned as though from regret, then continued: "I loved Stan, my bratwurst man, I really did. And I knew you would never marry me. It's nearly impossible to domesticate a wolf. But still, I was conflicted on what was supposed to be the most wonderful day of my life."

"It was the best of times, it was the wurst of times."

"It was!" she softly laughed.

"I remember that day vividly. It was all I could do to not scream out, Don't Do It, Katrina!"

Kat took Tom's hand and squeezed it. "You should have. Marriage isn't for everyone. Walking down the aisle I felt suffocated. After I got married I needed permission from Stan to do anything. I hated that. I love my life now. I'm free. If I want to buy a sports car, I can go out and do it. If I want to fly to Brazil and visit my cousins, I do."

Tom nodded like he understood, then said, "You and Stan raised a wonderful daughter."

"We did. Didn't we."

"Always wondered why you kept your last name when you got married…"

"I had a bit of a brand name on tour by then. Stan was fine with it. We thought about hyphenating our last names but

Katrina Stern-Barker sounded like a very fierce cocker spaniel."

We grinned, then Kat remembered something important. "Wait, this is March 18. Our anniversary. Time to renew the vows. She went over to her purse on the marble top coffee table, took out a leather-bound book, 6"x9". She opened the book and began reading:

"We renew the vows we first took in 1962 to treat each other with kindness, loyalty and respect. And to be there for each other, whenever one of us needs the other, whatever the circumstances. For each of us, the other was and is the Special One. And one year from today, if we mutually agree, we will extend this pact again."

She set the book down. Kat said, "It's so extraordinary, our friendship has endured, even flourished down the years. No matter what happened to either of us. We've been apart for so many long stretches of time."

Tom took a pen from his pants pocket and signed his name in the Friendship Book. He turned the pages and saw some of the other 41 times each of them had signed. "I remember one year I was playing in a tournament in Australia and you had to air-mail the book to me to sign."

They returned to the bedroom. Tom put on a CD of songs from popular films, that included *'All Time High'*.

They made love, renewing and solidifying their pact, as they had on many of their 41 anniversaries.

Kat punctuated the glorious festivities by passionately exclaiming, "OOOOOOH, James," like the young women did in the love scenes in Bond films. Kat giggled and said, "I'm sorry. I just had the urge to do that."

"Don't apologize. I thought it was appropriate."

***

Later, they were outside on the first-floor porch of Tom's two-story condo. The porch looked out over the first hole of the golf course. Malibu lights gave a soft glow to the dark green grass. The course loomed in the darkness, inviting and mysterious, maybe concealing hidden dangers--appropriate for a game that can never truly be mastered--as all pro golfers will attest. They were finishing a bottle of champagne, a crystal glass in each of their hands.

Kat couldn't resist a bit of mischief. "So, what about that young waitress who's fallen madly in love with you. I didn't know you went in for spicy Mexican cuisine."

Tom was unfazed. "I've tried to sample as many tasty dishes as I could."

Kat laughed, sipped her champagne. "I'm sure you have. You've toured the world, so to speak."

Tom got up and turned on the stereo. "But just so you know, I think the modern term for Carmen is Hispanic. Try to stay up to date, be a hep cat, Kat. No sense living in the past. Who told you Carmen likes me?"

"The club members, especially the grumpy old men, spy on and rat on you all the time. I think they're jealous. Some resent the fact you now own Their Club."

The sweet, mellow tune *Moon River* came on, from the film *Breakfast at Tiffany's*. One of Tom's favorite songs, it captured this golfer's romantic view of life, well, to a tee.

Kat said, "Hah! '*Moon River*'. Now who's living in the early '60s?"

"I guess that means you don't want to dance with me, to this old, old tune."

"Don't make assumptions. I adore that song. " Kat got up, took his hand and lead him to the soft cool grass of his golf course. They were barefoot. They took each other's hands, embraced and stepped gracefully through the song.

"And I adore you," Tom said with great warmth.

"Not sure I can trust your adoration. You were enthralled with Julia Wilkinson--for years. And I never understood why."

Tom, who absolutely knew why, wisely said nothing and let the slow dance with Kat--which had been going on for 40 years--continue.

"What am I going to do with you, Tom...you still believe life is one romantic adventure after another."

"If not that, what is life about, then?"

Kat thought for a few moments. "I used to think life was all about achievement. Now I don't really know. And they always told us we'd gain wisdom as we grew older. They were wrong."

Kat let go of Tom.

"Time I make the long commute two doors down to my pad. Giving a group lesson at 7AM tomorrow to the Junior Girls, who aspire to be snotty society bitches like their dear mommies when they grow up. At least with my expert instruction, they'll beat the pricks they marry at golf. They show up for the lessons in these perfect little designer outfits that cost more than my first automobile."

Kat softened the harsh comment with her sweetest smile she could shine. She walked over and poured the last of the champagne into her glass, picked it up and walked toward her condo.

"And anyway, maybe you'll have a late-night craving for an enchilada." This smile was more wicked than sweet.

"No, I feel quite satisfied tonight."

"Of course you do. Goodnight Mr. Colt."

"Goodnight Miss Stern."

Tom watched Kat pass through the lights and disappear into the night. He had watched that confident prowling walk of hers, complete with her amazingly cute, firm backside, for more than 40 years, and he never got tired of it.

Club members, those gossips, speculated why Kat worked as Junior Golf Director at the Club, and lived in a modest condo, even more modest that Tom's, given that with the combination of her frugality when competing on the women's golf circuit, and the funds she received from her late husband's estate, her net worth had to be in the mid-7 figures at least. She could afford one of those vast, lonely desert palaces they were building at an alarming pace in north Scottsdale.

The answer was, like Tom, Katrina had to stay close to the game she loved so dearly. And ten paces from the fairway was just about perfect. She woke each day and enjoyed her cup of coffee on the patio, as the glorious Arizona sun brought the golf course to life. Some mornings, she daydreamed that she was again young Katrina Stern, just starting her professional golf career.

Chapter Five   2004 - Scottsdale, Arizona
Brooks Wants to Hear More About the Murder in '62
Tom makes him wait...

Tom was at his desk at Valley Vista CC poring over a short stack of spreadsheets when I walked in, carrying my tape recorder and several spiral notebooks.

Tom's office was neat and orderly. A desk, a cushy leather chair, a small round conference table. The walls had professional photos of the Valley Vista golf course at various times of the year. Even one photo of the clubhouse covered in snow after a freak storm in February. Curiously, no photos of his career as a pro golfer.

Tom's encounter with the daunting stack of numbers brought back memories of when he struggled with his own personal budget. Numbers still made him nervous. "Damn, it costs a lot to run a country club. The members demand the best of everything but piss and moan when I raise the club dues. My accountant extraordinaire Paige Lawson tells me we're barely breaking even."

One factor affecting the Club's bottom line was that Tom paid his employees much more than the current market rate prescribed. "It's a hard-knocks life, this country club life of yours," I commented.

"That reminds me. In one of our books we should include a story from Christmas 1980. Judge Wilkinson asked me to travel to Greer, in the mountains in eastern Arizona, to investigate one of his real estate partnerships. He suspected the managing partner in the deal was a swindler. Paige Lawson was there looking for her estranged father, who was dying. I helped her find him, but we got trapped in a blizzard and nearly perished together."

"So what happened then?"

"When we got back to Greer, Paige, with her financial forensic skills, helped me uncover the fraud the Judge thought was happening. Saved us all a bundle of money, not to mention trouble. And--"

"--let me guess. After saving the day, you and Paige had a brief but torrid holiday love affair amid the bright, new-fallen snow."

"That goes without saying."

All I could do is gaze heavenward. The hell of it is, I'm sure it happened just like Tom said. He exasperates me. He's somehow able to generate passion and joy from even the most perilous situations. I'll never understand how he does it. I've never met anyone like him.

Anyway, I set up shop at the small table a few feet from the desk. I flopped into a chair. I checked that a cassette was in the recorder and switched it on. "So tell me more about the murder in '62!"

"Not yet, my friend. You need to know more of the characters in my world at that time. Just be patient. Hope you brought lots of cassette tapes for that thing."

I rolled my eyes with frustration.

"I've already given you the story of when I found the nude, dead socialite, and I've even introduced you to the descendants of the deceased. I've read lots of mystery novels where the murder didn't even occur until the middle of the book."

"Okay, okay. Tell me about your life after the 1960 US Open..."

"I thought you'd never ask, Brooks-y. Well, I took my time driving back to Phoenix from Denver. I was on this incredible high, this US Open high. I stopped at a souvenir shop on Route 66 to get a six-pack of soft drinks and the woman behind the counter recognized me! Said she watched the tournament on TV. Sure enough behind the counter there was a tiny B&W TV with rabbit ears. Then she asked for my autograph. Do you have any idea what a thrill that was, the first time someone asks for your autograph?"

"No."

"It's intense, believe me. I was so pumped up I didn't even worry whether that old '53 Ford junker I drove was going to break down in the heat on the highway coming back. So I get back, and then it struck me that nothing really changed. I was still stuck in a dumpy one-bedroom apartment on 16th Street, with dirty beige shag carpet and a stove with only one burner that worked, and the delightful patio view of the warped, crumbling alley fence next door. I had almost no money in the bank, and in my heart of hearts I knew that at best I was going to be a journeyman on the professional golf tour.

What was my next move? I made a big, big mistake. Got married to a girl I had met only two months earlier. Her name was Mandy Davidson. She didn't really love me. She loved the idea of being married to a pro athlete, on the way up, who got his name in the papers every week, even it was just his name appearing near the bottom of that week's tournament standings.

She took a job with the telephone company. And we struggled, struggled the rest of '60 and into the 1961 season. Finally one day she came out to the course where I was practicing and said, sobbing at first but then with resolve and relief in her voice, that she wanted a divorce. I remember not being terribly upset. My career prospects looked bleak. She was a girl who really, really wanted money. Not just to buy things but to buy her a sense of self-worth, which was almost nil when I met her. But I only won about $3,000 the first four months of '61.

Mandy got her wish and married a rich guy less than a year later. He turned out to be a very rich, very dangerous mobster. But we'll talk about that later."

I was thinking, *Sheesh, our book has everything, even The Mob!*

Tom Continued: "My mom suggested I start giving golf lessons to the members here at Valley Vista Country Club where she had been a waitress until she started her own catering business. It turned out to be one the best pieces of advice I ever received.

She had been such a terrific employee that the Club president at the time, Wes Stoneman III, welcomed me, and recommended my teaching skills to the members, even though I no prior experience giving golf lessons. I spent the rest of '61 splitting my time between playing on tour and teaching golf. The members who signed up for lessons loved me. They thought I was the best instructor they ever had at the club.

I was booked up months in advance. About 80% of my clients were women."

I thought, *Golly, what a startling revelation!*

"I was so popular that I started getting invited to parties at the members' houses. They were so golf-obsessed that they were enthralled with my stories of playing in tournaments, and anecdotes about the great players I competed against. In retrospect, I think some of them thought they were doing me a favor, bringing an up-and-coming striver into their elite community. I took advantage of every opportunity to network, to meet influential people who could further my career.

My mom impressed upon me the importance of wearing the best clothes, so I spent a lot of my income on my wardrobe. "Always strive to look like you belong," was how she expressed it. It worked. In my new threads, I looked classier than I probably was at the time. Some of the members were convinced I came from 'old money' back east. I always had a graceful, easy way of moving. It demonstrated confidence, I hoped, even though I was not confident on the inside at all.

And the money I earned from teaching relieved the financial pressure I had been under, so I began to play better in tournaments. I nearly won the last event of the season. My putting, as usual, crapped out on the final holes. Two other guys slipped past me on the 18th hole and I finished third.

I opened my notebook and consulted it. "And that takes us up to the point you meet the people who changed your life."

Tom smiled with great satisfaction at the pleasant memories that were coming back to him.

"Yes it does. Phoenix was an exciting young city then, a small city with big dreams, growing by leaps and bounds, with all the positives--financial opportunity--and negatives--criminal activity--that rapid growth can bring.

People were flocking here by the thousands, beckoned by real estate brochures that promised all pleasures were there for the taking, all wishes could be fulfilled--except perhaps the dream of everlasting youth.

The newcomers were eager to shed their bulky winter coats and galoshes, excited by the prospect of being able to play golf in January, go swimming on the first day of spring.

It was also a place you could shed your old persona and re-invent yourself. Your past could be erased, forgotten. Each sunny day in the vast stunning desert brought the promise of a fresh start. We all felt that way, then.

The thrilling history of the Old West still lingered, with its tradition of rugged individualism and just as importantly, the tradition of neighbor helping neighbor. You didn't have to lock your doors during the day or install security systems in your home.

For young men and women with endless ambition, like me at that time, opportunity abounded. The only questions we grappled with were:

Who Do I Want to Be?

How Fast Can I Reach My Destiny?"

Chapter Six
Tom Meets Det. Mathers
Tom Gets an Irresistible Offer from The Judge

Tom asked me to reconvene at the practice putting green near the pro shop. All that talk of his early career made Tom want to have a golf club in his hand, even if was his least favorite club, the putter.

The putting green was shaded by hundred-year-old ironwood trees and towering eucalyptus trees. I brought over a patio chair and set up shop while Tom set down four golf balls and aimed for one of the 9 cups with tiny red flags that dotted the green.

Tom began:

I had an unfortunate stint in the National Guard in 1956, and learned that being in a military organization was not my thing, unlike my father. All I got out of that time was learning how to shoot guns, which turned out to be a helpful skill. I also developed a lot of respect for those who serve. I decided to offer a free golf lesson every month to a member of law enforcement, or the military. Wes Stoneman, the club president, thought it was a splendid idea to give the Club more of a friendly image. It was kind of a joke, though, because he made me give these lessons to non-members way off to the left side of the driving range, so the members didn't have to interact with them. Fearful of catching a dread disease from the riff-raff I guess.

Anyway, let's go back to August of '61. One hot, humid morning, I was waiting for a police detective to arrive for his free lesson. Out of the north the sky was an ugly purple color, like a monsoon thunderstorm was building.

The free lessons were awarded through a monthly drawing. People phoned in their names, we put them in a golf hat and drew one out. I often wondered what direction my life would have taken if I had drawn another name that month than Det. Jerry Edward Mathers.

I was waiting on the driving range for my new pupil to arrive. I had set out two buckets of practice balls and was hitting some wedge shots when I saw him approach. I had to stifle a laugh when I saw him.

He was of medium height, maybe 5'9". A stocky, nearly pudgy, guy. He had dark, thinning hair combed down in strands and held in place with what I recall was this greasy hair tonic called Kreml. He was carrying a beat-up canvas golf bag with mismatched clubs. I learned he was ten years older than I, 37. He looked older, as though his cop job aged him.

He had a rumpled, and awful, golf outfit consisting of lime green slacks, a cherry red shirt and brown and white two-toned golf shoes that hadn't been in style since the '40s.

Out of the corner of my eye I could see some of the club members who were practicing, with looks on their faces that said, "How the hell did this guy get in here?"

But what really stuck in my mind what how supremely happy this man looked to be here, at this beautiful country club, taking a golf lesson from a real-live Golf Pro. His smile was magnetic.

He dropped the bag and it clattered on the turf, extended his hand.

"Ed Mathers, great to meet you Tom. I saw you in the Phoenix Thunderbird Tournament this year. You were on fuego in the last round. Think you shot 67."

I shook his hand. His grip was very firm. "Great to meet you, too. Det. Mathers. And I believe it was a 66 I shot."

"I'm a little nervous. Never taken a golf lesson before. This layout is a beaut. I got here early and walked a couple of the holes. Some guy named Basil came out and told me I wasn't allowed to do that. I showed him my badge. Buddies now, Basil and Me."

I liked his attitude. "Why don't we get started. Let's warm up with some short irons. How about starting with a 7-iron."

He pulled out his 7-iron, a tool so old and worn the 7 on the bottom of the club face was faded. He took a few practice swings and then I set a ball down for him to hit. And then I was treated to the WORST GOLF SWING I had ever seen. It wasn't really a swing, more of a great, gouging effort punctuated by grunts and groans. The divot he took was huge, the ball went about twenty-five yards.

Det. Mathers looked very pleased. "Made solid contact on the first shot." He was grinning from ear to ear. "Usually I duff a few starting out."

I expelled some air. This was going to be a long 55 minutes. I looked over toward the storm clouds in the distance and tried to will them in closer.

But as I worked with him, I started to really enjoy it. I had never seen a really terrible golfer have more sheer fun with our game. I tried to introduce the proper technique slowly, so he wasn't overwhelmed. I could see he had the strength and coordination to rapidly improve. His grip was all wrong. Kind of a baseball grip. I showed him the Vardon Grip, placing my left hand on a club and then overlapping the right.

After a few awkward shots with the unfamiliar but proper grip, he hit a really nice 5-iron about 150 yards. He dropped the club and pointed at the ball he had just hit. "I'm a golfer!"

Well, not quite yet, I thought. *But if his joy and enthusiasm could be converted into diligent effort on the practice range, and he paid close attention to my instruction, he would be a decent player someday.*

We finished the two buckets of practice balls. He was hot and sweaty from all those swings in this humid weather. The thunderstorm had faded into the distant horizon.

"You know, Tom. I love this game so much! The night before I have a tee time the next day I can hardly sleep."

I liked this guy. I charged $7.50 per lesson in those days. I thought about offering him a discounted fee if he wanted to continue after today. But he must have been reading my mind.

"I'd like to come back next week for another lesson. At your regular rate. No more freebees like today. Getting something for free makes me uncomfortable. And at least let my buy you lunch."

"Sure, to next week's lesson and to lunch today."

We went in his unmarked police vehicle, a dark sedan. We headed back toward Phoenix. He selected the restaurant, The Sandwich Place on 24th St.

I like it when the name of a business tells you exactly what it does. I hate to have to guess before I walk inside.

On the way Det. Mathers got a message on his radio that police had been called to the robbery of a bank branch a few blocks away from where we were going. The dispatcher said the shooting of a guard and possibly a suspect were involved. We passed by and saw three squad cars and two ambulances there.

A fire hydrant had also burst open and Tom noticed the street behind the bank branch was a muddy mess.

We arrived there, at the restaurant, before the lunch crowd, at 11:45 and the room was sparse; only 4 tables occupied. The hostess took us to a window table. We ordered ice teas and studied the menu. He looked like a meat-eating guy, and I was right. He chose the double cheeseburger stacked with onion rings. That sounded good so I told the waitress to make it two. I'm convinced humans were meant to eat meat. In those cave paintings the ancient people left us, they're never hunting a salad.

"The business card you gave me said, Det. Jerry Mathers, but you go by Ed."

"Edward's my middle name. You ever see a TV show *'Leave It To Beaver'.*"

I didn't own a television set (I could barely afford to have a radio in my car) at the time but I nodded yes.

"The young kid who plays Beaver is named Jerry Mathers. His nickname is The Beav. So all my cop buddies started calling me The Beav. They have a great old time with this."

I chuckled but could tell the nickname was a thorn in his side. I offered him some hope. "TV shows don't last too long. Maybe it will go off the air and everyone will forget it."

My prediction was only partially correct. The show went off the air a year later, in 1963, to Det. Mathers' great relief. Unfortunately, the nickname lived on, the rest of his time on the Phoenix Police Force.

Our foot high stacks of meat, cheese and onion rings arrived. The waitress seemed to struggle under the weight of the plates. We tucked in like we both were starving.

Brooks Continues Our Story:

Between big bites, Tom noticed two men seated 5 tables down. Mathers' back was to them. Tom thought there was something odd about them. One of the guys, a small dark-haired weasel of a man, looked nervous; Tom noticed his hand shaking as he picked up his water glass. The other man, beefy and phlegmatic, was wearing a jacket even though the room was nearly stifling hot, the air conditioning barely working. Sweat beaded on his forehead.

Tom said, "How did you become a cop?"

"My dad was an electrician. He got me apprenticed into his union. I shorted out some old wires in the basement of a house and a fire started. He read the Police were recruiting. Marched me down to the Academy to enroll the next day. It's a good life. I love police work. Love golf, too."

"I could tell."

"I was the first in my family to take up the game."

"Usually people say that about the first member of their family to go to college."

"That would be even more of a first. Nobody's hardly finished high school in my family. I'm kind of self-taught. I read a lot."

Another police siren wailed as the car zipped past the restaurant. The nervous guy jumped about a foot in the air, then got up and went out down the hallway to the bathrooms.

"You know, Tom, the last time I came out to that country club was to arrest one the members who was suspected of killing his business partner. What I've learned is, you get enough of the very rich together, you're going to have shenanigans. Same with the very poor and the unemployed. Middle class is too busy working to keep their head above water, to get into much trouble."

Tom commented. "Glad I grew up middle class, even if it was the lower middle class."

"You hang out with high society crowd, know what I'm talking about. Amazes me what depth of sleaze they'll wade into just to make more money. When is enough, enough? Why can't they just relax and enjoy what they have?"

Tom reached into the pocket of his slacks and pulled out a Valley Vista course scorecard. "What is this for?"

"To keep score, to record who won."

"Exactly. I've found, that's what money is to the rich."

Mathers nodded thoughtfully.

Tom got up. "Restroom visit."

Mathers resumed chomping on the burger stack as Tom went into the bathroom. The nervous man passed him on the way out.

Tom got a strange feeling, a hunch as he had, randomly, his whole life. He went over to the waste basket, the cylindrical kind with a swinging door. He reached inside and pulled out a wad of paper towels--soaked in blood.

He knelt down and looked at the brown tile floor. Traces of mud were visible. Tom's expression turned dark. For a moment he didn't know what he should do. He took a deep breath to calm himself and walked back out to his table.

He sat back down, took the scorecard and a pencil from his pocket and wrote, "Please call for additional officers. NOW. I think we are in danger."

He passed the card over to Mathers whose brow quickly furrowed. He turned his hands outward, palms up, like, "What????"

Quietly, Tom said, "I have a bad vibe about those people behind you."

"A vibe? What are you, a beatnik?" Mathers read Tom's serious expression and got up, and feigning nonchalance, went out the back way past the bathrooms, went to his squad car, grabbed his service revolver and called for backup, which arrived, silently and down the block, in two minutes at the most.

The bigger of the two men got up to go to the restroom. Mathers noticed the tell-tale gun bulge in the man's nylon jacket. When he was out of the room, Mathers got up and walked very slowly over to the nervous man, who now was starting to look weak and wincing in pain.

In a gruff, authoritative voice Tom had not heard before, Mathers said, "Okay, Slick, this is how it's going to work. You are under arrest. Please step outside and do not say a word. The officers out there will take you in--and you'll be alive."

Tom learned that day if Det. Ed Mathers called you "Ace" or "Slick" you were probably going to be arrested.

The nervous man nodded. Tom could see the blood coming through his shirt. He got up and went outside where he was quickly cuffed and led off. The second man emerged from the bathroom, saw his partner was gone and scanned the room for information in that hyper-aware way that veteran criminals do.

The big man walked warily toward the door. He had his hand in his jacket pocket. Tom was frozen in place by fear. Mathers had moved to the side of the door. The other two tables of diners were oblivious to the drama taking place. This was the moment of truth. Time passed excruciatingly slowly.

The big man looked out the window, did not see the cops who were several steps down the sidewalk, firearms drawn.

Finally, Mathers said, "Do the right thing. Word is the guard you shot was only wounded. He'll be fine."

The big man swung around, startled, and saw Mathers had his Model 10 Smith&Wesson .38 police revolver with its robust 6" barrel pointed straight at his belly. Now the other two cops emerged and were visible through the window.

"Set the gun on the table," Mathers ordered.

The big man considered his limited options, deflated, complied, and all he could say was, "Shit." Perhaps he was describing what had just transpired in his jeans.

Just like that it was over. Mathers turned the suspect over to the officers outside. They had found the robbery loot in paper sacks behind the restaurant dumpster. Evidently the not-so-bright robbers stashed it there then were going to wait in the restaurant until the 'coast was clear' as not-so-bright criminals who have seen too many detective movies say.

Mathers looked at Tom with astonishment and gratitude. "How did you know what happened?"

Tom explained the combination of the nervous guy, the guy wearing a hot nylon jacket inside, the blood on the towel, the mud behind the bank and the mud in the bathroom floor. And then he added: "I just got this nervous, alert feeling."

"If the golf thing doesn't work out, you need to join the police force. You have the gift of observation and deduction. You can't teach that."

Tom, adrenaline wearing off, slumped into his chair and took a big swallow of cold tea.

"I'm gonna make sure you get credit for this. I'm a double dummy for not noticing any of that."

"Credit isn't necessary. And your back was to them, remember."

"Nope. I've read those detective novels. The cops always take credit for the gumshoe's brave work. I'm not going to let that happen."

Tom managed a weak smile. "I guess in this case it's the golfshoe's brave work."

Mathers grinned. "And I owe you big time. You cured my chronic banana ball slice in one golf lesson. Miracle, I say. I know in those golf magazines, like *Championship Golf*, they say you kinda suck on tour, but you're a terrific teacher."

"I don't really think they say I suck."

"Sorry, man, they do."

The *Arizona Republic* newspaper ate up the amazing story of the local golf pro who solved a crime and helped apprehend the perpetrators. Back at the Valley Vista Country Club, Tom's female golf lesson clients fawned over him more than ever. At the cocktail parties at the members' houses, Tom was asked to recount the heroic tale over and over, until it became a Local Legend.

To Tom, and to Det. Mathers, the most important thing was that they both made a friend that day, a devoted friend for life, as it turned out.

The newspaper stories of Tom and Det. Mathers' teamwork were devoured by Judge (ret.) Roy Wilkinson, 63, who read the morning paper each day by the swimming pool at his enormous North Phoenix estate, perched high on a mountain that looked down on the city. The Judge thought to himself,

Extraordinary. Like father, like son. He made a mental note to be sure to make Tom's acquaintance. He had found the 'fixer' he was looking for: the young popular man who could mix well in high society and had the analytical skills to help the Judge's friends out of the trouble so many of them unfortunately got into, in their pursuit of even greater wealth and pleasures, at a time when both were available in the exciting, emerging city of Phoenix in ever and ever greater measures.

***

Brooks with Tom – 2004
At Valley Vista Country Club

I said, "So, Tom, that takes us up to the end of '61?"

Tom Continues Our Story:

Yes. But there is one more key event to tell you about. It occurred in mid-November. Remember in those days, the golf tour was essentially over after the PGA Championship, the last major of the season. There were a few scattered events you could play in during the fall, to scrape in more cash, but a lot of pros just went home, worked on their games and got ready for the Winter/Spring tour.

I busied myself giving lessons at the Club. One afternoon the Club President, Wes Stoneman III, caught me after my last lesson while I was walking to my car. I was in a great mood. My last pupil was the lovely wife of a politician, Lisa Prentiss Luck. She had a beautiful body she displayed to perfection with a tight knit blouse and slim white slacks.

She was an eager student and quite athletic, limber and flexible. I asked her why she was so dedicated to being a good golfer. "I want to beat my husband," she said without hesitation and rather coldly. I didn't pursue it further. Turned out, I should have.

The weather was unseasonably warm that day, the sun very bright in a cloudless sky. Perspiration beaded on our foreheads; on Lisa, even sweat looked good.

"Tom, could I have a word," Stoneman said as I opened my car door.

"Absolutely. What's up?"

From Stoneman's level expression, I couldn't tell whether this was good news or bad.

"Judge Wilkinson would like to see you, as soon as possible."

I only vaguely knew who he was. A big mover and shaker in town, I gathered from the locker room conversation. Stoneman handed me a simple white business card with embossed black lettering that said, "Judge Roy B. Wilkinson, Private Equity. Followed by a PO Box and a phone number that said, Private Line.

"What is this about?"

"No idea, I'm afraid, but he was insistent I get ahold of you. ASAP. Here is his address."

Stoneman handed me a piece of note paper.

"Just a word of caution, Tom. The Judge is someone who can make things happen, and quickly, but nothing he does comes without strings attached. I know some guys who have been nearly strangled by those strings."

I didn't have any notion of what to make of Stoneman's odd warning.

All I could think to say was, "What does the B stand for?"

Stoneman chuckled, but not with mirth. "Bean, like Judge Roy Bean, the tough as nails frontier Judge in Texas."

Intrigued and I must admit frightened, I called the number and made an appointment with the Judge's personal secretary Marjorie for the next day.

***

November, 1961 - Phoenix, Arizona

Brooks Continues Our Story...

As Tom drove up the driveway to the Judge's mansion, a desert palace it seemed to Tom, fit for a Sheik in oil-rich Arabia, set on at least a 5-acre property, he felt smaller and poorer as each second passed. He thought maybe he should have borrowed a friend's newer car instead of rattling up the pebbled drive in his old, rusted Ford with its grumbling engine.

He was exactly on time, 10AM. He rang the doorbell and it opened quickly. A gracious woman of about 50 with merry eyes, wearing a long flowing skirt and silk blouse in southwestern colors, greeted him like an old friend and said she was Marjorie Cluff, the Judge's personal assistant. "Come with me, Tom," she said with so much cheer and warmth he felt silly at having been worried about coming there.

They passed down a quiet hallway until they reached an enormous room with dark paneling and high shelves crammed with books. Not just the law books that would be expected, but works of literature and non-fiction titles related to the acquisition of wealth.

A side door opened and the Judge himself stepped in. He was about 5'9" but seemed taller. He had short-cropped iron-grey hair almost in a military haircut. Tom had never understood what the word gravitas meant until that moment. The Judge clearly had it. He shook Tom's hand.

"I am so glad to meet you, Tom!" His smile was genial, but Tom accurately read that the friendliness didn't extend to his eyes, which were sharp and cold and hard. A formidable, brusque man putting on his most welcoming front, Tom discerned.

Marjorie excused herself and said to ring her if they needed any refreshments.

Tom took in the room. This was not a retired gentleman's lair. The room had two deep leather couches and a small conference table and matching mahogany desk. Stacks of real estate prospectuses, business plans, and newspapers and news magazines cluttered the table and the desk.

The walls were dotted with photographs of the Judge with entertainment and sports figures. He recognized Bob Hope, Jimmy Stewart, Mickey Mantle, Sam Snead, Vince Lombardi. At the time I thought it odd, given the Judge's prominence, that he didn't have any photos of political figures. But as I quickly learned, there was a good reason for this: the Judge hated politicians.

"Take a seat. I apologize for the mess in here. Lots going on right now."

Tom chose a spot on the couch and sat down. He had no idea what to say, so he started clumsily with, "What does 'private equity' mean on your business card?"

The Judge rolled his comfortable-looking desk chair around the desk and closer to the couch, sat down. "It means we move money around in the hopes of growing it. Rapidly and massively."

"Hmmmm," Tom said, still not understanding what that meant. Tom noted that the Judge was dressed casually, in grey slacks and a blue buttoned down short-sleeve shirt with little golf clubs stitched on the pocket. In this shirt pocket was a pack of cigarettes which he took out, removed one and lit it with a gold lighter he pulled from his pants pocket. The ashtray on the conference table was filled with spent cigarettes.

The Judge blew some smoke and began:

"I know you are a busy and popular fellow, so let me get right to why I asked you here today."

Out the corner of his eye, Tom saw an exciting blonde beauty hurry down the hallway like a whirlwind, "Bye, dad, see you tonight," echoed down the hallway.

"Bye Julia. Drive safely," the Judge replied. "My daughter. A lovely young woman and talented musician. She's off to what do you call it...a jam session."

Tom could tell that the Judge doted on his daughter. The cold eyes briefly warmed as she passed by then returned to flinty hardness.

"She and I live here by ourselves. Her mother died of cancer five years ago and my son died in a plane crash last year."

"So sorry to hear that, sir," Tom said, his mind on the blonde whirlwind.

The Judge puffed a few more times on the cigarette, got up and snuffed it out in the ashtray, sat back down.

"I am a fan of yours, Tom. I first saw you play at the Open in Denver last year. You almost won that damn thing! I've never seen a more exciting golf tournament. Nicklaus could've won it, Hogan almost won it, Jack Fleck almost won it, even that Amateur Billy Joe Patton. But you're the one we, Julia and a friend of hers were there with me, got all excited about. Phoenix's own Tom Colt. Great job, young man."

The part of the compliment that meant the most to Tom was, Julia got all excited.

The Amateur who almost won the '60 Open was Don Cherry, who oddly was also a professional nightclub singer, not Billy Joe Patton, the exciting risk-taking amateur who almost won the Masters in 1954. But I was in no position to contradict Judge Roy Wilkinson. Then, or ever.

"I know how tough the golf tour is. Financial struggles have snuffed out many promising careers. I would like to help you in that regard. I believe you have the potential to be a champion."

Tom didn't know what to say. No one had ever extended anything even resembling generosity to him before. He and his mother were used to the constant hard struggles of the lower middle class. At least in Phoenix, you struggled in warm weather.

So Tom said, "Sir, I don't know what to say."

"First of all, call me Roy. And I hope none of those jokers at the Club said my middle name is Bean like the hanging Judge in Texas. I'm not like him at all. I believe in a fair trial, then a hanging."

Tom smiled. He knew the Judge had told that joke many times before.

"Here's the deal. I have a splendid little guest cottage on this property. 2 bedrooms and its own pool, 1300 square feet. I want to invite you to live there rent-free and also provide you with $1,000 per month to cover travel expenses. We'll make this arrangement for 6 months, see how it goes and then possibly extend."

Tom was stunned. His mouth fell wide open. "That is, um, incredibly nice of you, Roy. But may I ask why you want to do this for me?"

"A host of reasons. I love the game of golf even though I'm a mediocre player myself. If I could help you, a Phoenix boy, take the next step, and be a winner, it would give me immense pleasure. Our young and growing city needs more winners. I also knew your mother when she worked at Valley Vista. What an...what's the right word...elegant woman she is. Always had a nice smile for every member she served, even if they acted like jerks. She would talk about how proud she was of you and how hard you worked to make your dream of being a golf champion come true. She would almost get tears in her eyes."

As the Judge spoke, Tom, who always tried valiantly to please his mother, was getting tears in his eyes. But a timely voice played a recording back to him in his head, "nothing he does comes without strings attached".

The Judge paused as if thinking whether he should reveal more. "And I knew your father."

Tom, his antenna up, waited for further details. None came.

The Judge smiled in a way that was clearly meant to shut off discussion. "Let's just leave it at that for now."

"Okay."

"But in return, I have small favor to ask." The Judge lit another cigarette and paced the room, puffing rings of smoke. He was a man who couldn't sit still for very long. "You have a very unusual skill set, that I could put to great use."

"I'm not sure I understand."

"Of course you wouldn't. I'm not expressing myself very well. Let me provide some historical perspective. In 1950 the population of Phoenix was just over 100,000. By 1960, it was 439,000. The rush of people moving here is going to continue--bringing with it fantastic opportunities for many of us to achieve great wealth. But there's a good way to grow, and a bad way."

If Tom were a dog, he would have been tilting his head from one side to another.

"I want ethical capitalism to succeed. There needs to be a group of us watching over the city's growth. Weeding out the bad capitalists, the crooks, the fast buck artists, the gangsters when necessary. Otherwise, the government steps in with its clumsy, inept, and invariably corrupt ways, and shits all over everything. And we must keep the Communists out."

More head tilting from Tom.

"Back to what you bring to the table, Tom. You move easily in the world of the wealthy set. You're a hit at their parties. They like you, they trust you, and I'll bet while you are giving them golf lessons they've revealed a secret or two."

"Yes, sir, they have. Golf pros are good listeners. Like psychiatrists."

The Judge nodded. "Great analogy. I completely forgot, would you like a cigarette? These are Pall Mall brand."

"No thank you, I don't smoke."

"Well, you should. It would relax you when you have a crucial putt to make in a tournament. Putting is the only serious weakness I've seen in your game, young man."

Tom nodded. And in a week, he took up smoking. Pall Mall brand, unfiltered.

"And I read about how you solved that bank robbery. You showed that, without even realizing it, you have detective skills."

"I may have just gotten lucky."

The Judge waved that comment away. "It was much more than luck." The Judge tapped an index finger to his right temple.

"From time to time, I will need your help to clean up unpleasant situations that arise among the rich, the kinds of things that can give the business community a black eye in the press. Wealth unfortunately gives people the idea they are invincible. You know how teenagers drive their hot rods recklessly because they think they are immortal. They play dangerous games like suicide chicken out in the desert. That's unfortunately how some of the very rich behave. In both their business and personal lives."

"So this is a janitorial position you are offering me."

The Judge guffawed—but Tom didn't think he was truly amused. "My goal for Phoenix is to make it the best run, most efficient city in America, where there is an ever-ripening potential for economic development and wealth creation. But we need a discreet way of cleaning up the messes that inevitable arise when high-velocity ambitions collide—and not involve the authorities or the press. To sum up, I want to run a clean city."

Tom felt as though he needed an interpreter.

"I'll let you in on a little secret. A lot of rich people are stupid. Intelligence, knowledge, wisdom, creativity don't necessarily lead to wealth. Many times sheer luck is involved, such as stumbling on a market that can be monopolized long enough to earn a fortune. But they remain stupid and make stupid mistakes that make the rest of us look bad."

Tom slowly blew air out through his pursed lips, as though he was totally lost.

"Do you have any questions?"

"Who decides who the bad capitalists are that need to be weeded out?"

The Judge registered surprise that Tom had asked such a perceptive question.

"That would be me." He smiled. "We have a small group of community-minded businessmen called the Founders Roundtable. I'm the de facto leader."

Tom reflected that he probably had already met some of the other members of the group, which until today he didn't know existed.

"And I hasten to add, along our journey together, I can show you how to achieve great wealth. You can't play golf forever."

"Quite a few of the golf writers think I can't play golf now."

"Fuck 'em. They're hacks. You're damn good." The Judge smiled. Then clasped his hands together.

"So what do you say, Tom. Are you with us?"

Times arose in Tom's life when he had no idea what choice to make, but was forced to make one anyway. This was probably the most critical of all the choices.

"I would say...that...I could probably move into the guest house on Friday afternoon. My last lesson is at 2."

No one could ever accuse Tom Colt of being indecisive. Impetuous, maybe.

The Judge happily banged Tom on the shoulder so hard that it almost knocked him out of the chair.

"I knew we could count on you."

As dutiful assistant Marjorie escorted Tom down the winding hallways back to the front door, the discomfiting thought uppermost in his mind was, *What did The Judge mean by 'We'*, but then he caught the lingering scent of Julia's sweet perfume in the hallway and banished all such concerns from his head.

Free rent and travel money. Dang.

Tom Continues Our Story...

On Friday I had asked one of the maintenance guys at the Club, Jeff Slocum, to bring a truck over and help me move my stuff to my new digs, the Judge's Guest House. I still had trouble believing this was actually happening. The son of a single mom who worked as a waitress doesn't usually end up living on a property called an estate. I had worried about money every day of my life. Even when I was a kid I worried--because my mom was constantly worried about being able to support herself and two children on a waitress' salary and tips.

Now, as day broke on this glorious, clear though chilly morning, I no longer had any money worries. I can hardly express how wonderful that felt. All I had to worry about was improving my golf game so I would be more competitive on the golf tour. And, completing those vague little tasks the Judge was going to ask me to do.

When I arrived at the Judge's home, I got a key to the guest house from Marjorie. The Judge was out looking at some property that was for sale on the west side of Phoenix, she said.

The design of the guest house echoed that of the main house. I guess you'd call it Southwest Modern. Dark red tile roof. White exterior accented by rust colored trim. I turned the key in the lock and walked inside.

The furniture in the living room looked brand new, comfortable, cushy and outfitted with blue upholstery--my favorite color. The one exception was the large green leather couch in the living room, a piece of furniture that would soon feature in memories I carry to this day.

The carpet also looked new, a nice soft caramel color, thick enough to walk on barefoot but not that hideous shag I had in my apartment—home to many different varieties of dirt and germs.

As I walked through the kitchen and then down the hallway to the bedrooms--both of which were huge, it struck me that it looked like no one had ever lived here before. I wondered why, or for whom, the Judge had built the guest house.

On the dresser in one of the bedrooms was an envelope addressed to me. I opened it. It was a check for $1,000, the first of my monthly checks to cover travel expenses. I held the check in both hands for a few moments, almost with disbelief. This was really happening! This was my pad!

The curtains in the bedroom were light brown, wood slatted. I pulled the cord to open them and saw that my bedroom looked out over a sparkling blue little swimming pool, a rectangle maybe 30 feet long and 20 wide. Beyond the pool was a putting green! I soon learned it had a surface as fine and true as those at the Club.

I was visited by a few stray thoughts that all this was too good to be true. But my sheer enthusiasm for the exciting direction my life was going, swept those discomfiting thoughts from my head.

The swimming pool was heated, by the way.

Chapter Seven
Tom Visits His Mom
Tom Gets His First Detective Assignment
...and a Magical New Golf Club

The only tournament I had left on my schedule for 1961 was a charity event on a course at a new real estate development between Phoenix and Tucson. The prize money was minimal but to show you how the Judge's kind gesture had inspired me, I finished second and won $300. So much of successful athletic performance is due to confidence, how you feel inside.

As I drove back to Phoenix, I began wondering when the Judge was going to ask for my help on one of his investigative projects. I hadn't heard from him in the two weeks since I moved in except for one evening when he strolled over to welcome me and see how I liked my new living space. He made a point of telling me to redecorate as I saw fit, to add my own personal items and make the place my own. He definitely believed our arrangement would continue on beyond 6 months. But what criteria would the Judge use to decide?

***

As the year drew to a close, I began to feel a small but growing sense of pressure, that I owed the Judge my best effort in every golf tournament I was scheduled to play in '62. I practiced 4 hours a day, which for me was a lot. I had never been known for a Hogan-esqe approach to practice. I found it boring, to tell you the truth. The rest of my day was devoted to giving lessons at the Club, which I really enjoyed. I was developing a knack for quickly diagnosing how to help a struggling amateur improve their game. It was fun, and rewarding, to see their eyes light up when they began hitting their shots crisply and straight. I especially enjoyed helping the female players. The younger ladies in particular.

In 1961, there were three big money winners on the pro golf circuit. Gary Player, who was only 25, (younger than me!) arguably the most physically fit golfer, led with earnings of $65,000. Arnold Palmer, rapidly becoming the most popular golfer on planet earth, was second with $61,000. Doug Sanders, a colorful and friendly pro with a quirky, shortish swing, bagged $57,000. From there it dropped off to the consistently excellent Billy Casper, $38,000, and Jay Hebert, whose brother Lionel also was successful on tour, with $36,000.

I should mention that sweet-swinging, genial Gene Littler also had a super year, winning the US Open and $29,000 for the season. The '61 season will forever be remembered as the year Arnold Palmer won his first British Open, which sparked a tremendous revival of interest in the game's oldest championship. Gary Player won the Masters. The PGA Championship had one of its oldest winners ever, 45-year-old Jerry Barber. Barber was like the golfing inverse of me. Short off the tee but a demon with the putter.

How did I do in '61? I wasn't invited to play in the Masters, of course. I missed the 36-hole cut in the US Open (by 1 stroke!). No way I could afford to fly over to the British Open and I tied for 49th in the PGA.

For my dogged efforts that year I won $9,200 in prize money in 17 events. I also made $8,000 giving lessons at Valley Vista. *There were so many more promising players to choose from*, I thought. *So why again did Judge Wilkinson want to sponsor me?*

***

December 27 was my mom's 48th birthday. I happily took a break from my practice routine and spent the day with her at her home in a modest neighborhood in what is now south Scottsdale, near Thomas and Scottsdale roads, which was then the center of the city. Since that time the tremendous crush of population growth has spread north and east, gobbling up vast sections of what had been pristine desert when I was a boy. My dad used to take me hunting for javelina (sorta like wild pigs) in an area that is now the 101 Freeway corridor. Progress, they tell me. I'm not so sure.

My mom's house was the one my sister and I grew up in. It was a bungalow-style house, only 1100 sq. ft., grey exterior with teal accents on the window frames and door. The property had a charming wrought-iron fence around it, covered in vines. My mom loved to grow colorful plants. Outside the front door were two beds with red and yellow lantana plants. Pots with seasonal flowers were suspended from the porch roof. Every time I visited her, I can't believe the four of us lived in that tiny place without getting in each other's way.

My mom never even considered remarrying because she didn't really believe my father was dead. "I know he still walks the earth," she often told me.

In the driveway there was a maroon van that said COLT CATERING on the side. Parked there also was the same blue Ford sedan she had since 1950. My mom's catering business began one Easter weekend when the Head Chef at the Valley Vista Country Club called in sick and the Assistant Chef was on vacation. My mom, without hesitation, stepped in to feed the guests. "I can cook, don't worry," she said to the panicky and skeptical club General Manager, Basil Hedgerow.

She took a quick look at the Club's pantry and refrigerators, and made a huge batch of Cioppino with fresh baked garlic bread, and then on that very day invented her signature lasagna. All the members who dined there that day raved about how good the food was. Ladies started calling my mom to cater their parties. When the Head Chef returned, a haughty Frenchman named Claude (we pronounced it Clod), instead of thanking her for pulling his ass out of the fire, he merely said, "Ze luck of Ze be-gin-eer."

It was a mild day for December with watery sunshine peeking through the clouds. My mom left the front door open. I opened the screen door and stepped inside, announcing that I was here. I was carrying a small box with her birthday gift. Given our perennially scanty funds, the gifts we exchanged were quite modest. This year with my positive change in circumstances, I splurged. I set the present on the table in the foyer.

My mom swept in from the kitchen and we greeted each other in the same fashion we always did, an almost fierce hug, a kind of recognition of how we hung together during all the financial struggles we had after my father disappeared while serving in the military. "I am so glad you're here!" she exclaimed as she squeezed me.

Laura Colt was a petite, trim woman with soft, dark red hair, which she wore in a short bob style. She had a warm, reassuring smile. She worked so hard at her catering business that she always seemed slightly weary. She punctuated conversations with heavy sighs.

When you endure the terrible financial struggles she had, actually all three of us did, and survive them and then prevail, only your balance sheet completely heals. The emotional damage is permanent. That's why I knew she would work her little tail off for the rest of her life. At least she got to work at something she loved: cooking for people and making them happy. Many strugglers toil at jobs they hate.

And it was also why I knew I had to discover a way to become wealthy.

Her three passions were her children, her church, and her catering business, in that order. I'm a bit biased but to me she was the best Italian cook in Phoenix.

My father had left her with virtually no cash, few assets and two precocious, squabbling teenagers with genius level IQs. She prayed for strength several times a day, every day.

We released each other. She noticed I had a new blue blazer over my grey trousers. "You aren't spending all your winnings on clothes, I hope," she said only half-jokingly. Frugal was her middle name.

"That's some of the good news I have for you. My money situation is much better than the last time I was here."

"So glad to hear that. I worry about you from the time I get up in the morning to--"

"I don't believe you will have to worry from now on."

"Well, sit down. I'll get you a glass of wine. I have an interesting new Merlot to try."

"I should be serving you. It's your birthday." I really didn't care for red wine back then.

"No need to make a fuss. I have one every year. Lately it seems like every 6 months!"

While she was getting our wine, I went down the narrow hallway to my old room, which was now a kind of shrine to my golfing career. Every trophy I had ever won, back to my days as a junior golfer, was on display on lighted shelves. Every article ever written about me in the sporting press--the favorable ones at least--not the recent article in *Gentleman Golfer Monthly* that implied I was an underachiever who partied too much--were framed and on the walls. She even had my very first pair of golf shoes--ugly brown and white saddle shoes--under a glass case. At least she didn't have the damn things bronzed.

I smiled, went back out to the living room and she handed me a sturdy tumbler of red wine.

"Take a sip. I need your opinion. I'm serving this at a client dinner, the VonEssen's 30th anniversary party, next month."

I had no real talent for evaluating wine vintages, but of course the secret is, to act like you do. I sipped, furrowed my brow in concentration and announced: "Excellent. Do I detect apricot notes in the bouquet."

"Nice try. But there are no such notes. Plum would have been the correct answer. Would you rather have a beer?"

"Yes, ma'am," I said gratefully. She went to the fridge and got me a Pabst Blue Ribbon.

I could smell her glorious, signature lasagna dish bubbling away in the oven. The dish featured two secret ingredients of her own design; I'd tell you what they were except she had me sign a non-disclosure agreement when I turned 18 and could enter into valid contracts.

She sat back down, expelled an exasperated breath, puffing out her lips. I do the exact same thing after missing a five-foot putt for birdie. Must be hereditary. I wondered what was troubling her.

"Your sister," she said and slugged down some wine.

Those two words were weighted down with so much emotional baggage.

My twin sister Caroline, born 10 minutes after me, could be beautiful. She had lovely long brown hair and an attractive figure. She had the same pale blue eyes I do, but less of a prominent, strong chin, which I'm sure she was glad of. Her mouth curved up at the corners, making it look as though she was smiling with secret knowledge available only to her.

Now, at just 27, she was rail thin and looked older than me because of a lifestyle that, I suspected, included drug abuse. She got into frequent arguments with both me and mom, usually over trivial issues. My sister is very emotional, dramatic—with I suspect lots of bottled-up rage. Our mom says Caroline lacks the coping mechanisms that keep the rest of us upright.

Caroline was nearly always broke. She's probably smarter than me, and got better grades in school. But she fails over and over at jobs, mainly because she has trouble showing up on time. Yes, my sister was a mess. And I couldn't help thinking it was partially my fault. But I couldn't explain why.

My mom said, "I just can't give her any more money. She never makes an attempt to change her life in a positive way."

"She does, but then falls back into bad habits."

"I don't approve of how she sleeps around."

"I've been known to play the field, too."

"That's different. You're a man. And also, being sociable is part of an aspiring golfer's job. You want to build your female fan base. Your sister is just a tramp."

Her logic escaped me, but I chose not to comment.

"I'll go see her next week. But I'm not sure what I can do. To change your life, you have to want to change your life."

"You'll have to wait a few weeks. She's driving down to Puerto Penasco to do God knows what with God knows who."

My mom's intense frown accentuated the worry wrinkles on her forehead. "Don't you give her money. You work too hard for it." She even wagged a motherly finger at me.

She got up, clenched and unclenched her fist to get rid of frustration and walked back to the kitchen. In a loud voice she said, "I hate this because I have no idea how to reach her anymore, how to help her."

The bell on the oven rang just in time to close out this dreary discussion.

Mom said it was such a nice afternoon, we should eat on the back patio. Phoenix is often called a pools and patios community because we spend so much time out there, having our meals or cooling off in the swimming pool.

She served me a huge plate of lasagna and a fruit and lettuce salad with walnut and herb dressing.

We set down our plates and wine glasses, sat down and toasted her birthday.

I took a healthy forkful of the salad and said with mock seriousness: "Hmmm. I detect notes of basil and fennel."

She laughed, finally breaking the tension from our Caroline discussion.

"Just hush up about ' notes' already and eat!"

So I did.

"You told me you had some good money news to share with me."

"Do you know a member of Valley Vista named Roy Wilkinson, a retired Judge?"

As I was driving home and reflecting on our conversation that day, I wondered why there was a noticeable pause before she said, "Yes, of course. He's quite prominent."

I told her an abridged version of the Judge's generous offer, my moving into the guest house and his proposal that I help him deal with delicate matters from time to time.

"Why, that is surprising and amazing," she said, but her tone did not indicate surprise--more like concern--and her smile seemed forced.

I finished the last bite of lasagna and then summoned the courage to ask the difficult question: "The Judge said he knew Father. Is that true?"

She looked away from my questioning eyes and gazed out toward the thriving grape vines near the back wall of her property. Did I mention she produced her own wines?

"He wants you to gather information for him, is that it? I'm not sure I understand."

"He wants to keep messy situations involving his business associates from getting messier. I'm in a good position to gather information. While I'm giving lessons to them, or in the locker room, the members tell me things about their lives I really don't need to know. They've taken me into their confidence even though I don't belong in their set."

"Just be careful. Wilkinson was a man who intimidated some of the other members."

"You don't mean, like he's a gangster."

"Not in that sense, nothing sinister like the man your ex-wife Mandy married. Now, he's a gangster."

Thanks for reminding me, mom, I thought.

"Roy was and probably still is, someone who could open doors for people in business deals. And some of the members...sought to curry favor with him."

She saw the concern on my face, tinged with confusion.

"Just be careful. I'm glad Roy wants to sponsor you. You deserve a chance to succeed."

I sensed that she wanted to tell me more, but was holding back. I also knew that it pained her not to tell me everything. It struck me as significant that she called him Roy. She looked nervous.

"I think he had some involvement with the government. That may have been how he met your father. Yes, that must be it."

She got up rather abruptly and began doing the dishes. I went to the hallway and retrieved her present. Now back in the living room, she opened it. It was a travel voucher to attend the Bing Crosby Invitational Tournament, informally known as the Crosby Clambake, in Monterey, California, along with tickets to a big-time culinary festival that was being held the same week.

She was thrilled. She set the present down and gave me another of her patented squeeze-hugs.

After she let go, I said: "You haven't seen me play in a tournament outside of Arizona in ages. Remember the Crosby Clambake is in the California wine country. You'll be able to collect some new vintages to dazzle your clients. And, I thought you need a vacation."

"Do you think I could meet Mr. Crosby? I love his music! And his movies! What a fine actor he is!"

"I think that could be arranged."

"I'm so lucky to have you for a son."

"I would totally agree."

"You always were such a confident boy."

If she only knew that my confidence, especially on the golf course, was mostly an act. Damn good one, though.

***

Brooks Continues Our Story:

On Mondays, when Tom was home and not travelling to a tournament venue, first thing in the morning he would sit down at the dining room table and (attempt to) pay his bills. His thinking was that it was best to take on that nasty chore first thing each week instead of allowing it to hang over him.

It was unusual for Tom to be able to accumulate more than $500 in savings after he met all of his monthly obligations. The nomadic pro golfer had to in effect pay for two residences: his home base in Phoenix and lodging wherever he stayed when playing in tournaments.

He sat down, took his checkbook out, and took a deep breath.

He had a strict budget, which he kept track of in a ledger book. That morning, when he opened the book and examined the major expenses in his revised budget, it finally hit him:

Rent expense - 0

Electricity - 0

Water - 0

Home Maintenance - 0

Thanks to his arrangement with Roy Wilkinson, he would be earning a cash surplus every month. He could, for once, accumulate a significant amount in savings. It wouldn't be long before he could afford a new car, a long-held dream that seemed so distant just a few weeks ago.

Tom was almost giddy at this realization. A very poor dancer he was, but he got up from his chair and mimed leading a beautiful woman across the dance floor. He could afford to take a date to a fine restaurant!

Tom already had enough life experience to know that happiness isn't something that is delivered to you, like an anxiously awaited package. Achieving it involved removing each of the unpleasant, tragic, worrisome and unwholesome elements of life, until what you are left with is a condition of bliss.

The doorbell chimed. He let go of the imaginary, gorgeous dance partner and went to answer it. Tom was surprised to see the Judge there. He was carrying a tall, slender rectangular box and a 9"x12" envelope.

The Judge was wearing jeans and a grass-stained white sweatshirt. For reasons Tom didn't understand, Roy still mowed his own lawn. But Tom had already seen that rich people have earned the luxury of being eccentric.

"Judge, c'mon in."

"Why don't we step over the lawn next to the pool. I have a surprise for you."

Tom retrieved his sandals, put them on and followed the Judge to the guest house lawn. He handed Tom the box.

"Open it."

Tom pulled open the top of the box, and removed THE BIGGEST DAMN GOLF CLUB he had ever seen. The club look formidable, special.

Tom dropped the box and took his golf stance with the club. He waggled it a few times, feeling the relatively light but very stiff shaft and the massive clubhead.

"Is this legal, I mean for tournaments?"

"Of course. I would never have you participate in something illegal. I met this old German clubmaker, quite an engaging fellow, and told him I had a supremely talented young protégé who had trouble keeping his tee shots straight. He fashioned this beautiful club himself in the shop in his garage."

Tom stepped 10 feet away from the Judge and swung the club over and over. It felt great.

"I can't wait to try this out. How much do I owe you?"

The Judge smiled. Lit up a cigarette. "Nothing. It's a gift."

Tom was ecstatic. The last person to buy him a golf club, other than himself, was his late father, 11 years ago. The Judge picked up the envelope and handed it to Tom.

"And I have your first assignment under our little arrangement. Please look inside." Inside was one typed sheet of paper. Tom read it:

Thomas, I need you to follow Missy Gould for the next week. See where she goes during the day when her husband Sterling is at work. He suspects Missy may be stepping out on him. He has noticed 5 large cash

*withdrawals from their bank account over the last 10
weeks. By large I don't mean $50,000. They were for
$1,500 each. Perhaps I should have termed them
unusual cash withdrawals.*

"I don't know sir. It sounds like a job for a private eye who
can be invisible. People around town know me, what I look
like."

"We'll get you a disguise. Moustache. Panama hat like the
tourists wear. Some hideous white patent leather shoes."

Tom cringed. He had just purchased a pair of those hideous
shoes and paid a full retail $3.75.

"This is important to us, Tom. Sterling is investing in one of
our real estate syndicates and the last thing we need is for his
assets to be tied up in a divorce action."

The Judge took a drag on his cigarette.

"We have the chance to acquire 250 acres along the corridor
where the new Interstate will be, but we have a small window
of opportunity."

Tom hadn't heard anything about a proposed new
Interstate and wondered how the Judge knew.

Tom asked, "Why doesn't he just ask her where the money
went?"

The Judge chuckled, condescendingly Tom thought. "He has
no moral basis to do so. You see, Sterling cheats on her all
the time. If he caught her doing the same, he would divorce
her on the spot."

This was all a new world to Tom. His head was spinning.

"So, are you in, young man?"

"Yessir," Tom said, thinking: *like I had a choice.*

"Good fellow. You can meet the happy couple at the New
Year's Eve party at their home."

"But I'm not invited to that."

"You are now."

Amused, Tom just shook his head.

"Get out to Valley Vista and try out that new--very
expensive--driver. I took the liberty of naming it for you, The
Colt .45."

Tom grinned. "That's awesome."

The Judge knew that Tom was a big fan of Western movies
and a student of Western history, facts Tom had never
revealed to him.

The Judge started back to his estate. Tom asked, "Roy, why
do you still mow your own lawn?"

The Judge turned and looked at Tom not with amusement, but with the cold stare that originated in the Judge's murky, dangerous past. "To remind me how hard I had to work, and must continue to work until the end of my life, to get all this-- and keep it forever." He swept a hand over the vista of his estate. Then he walked out of view.

That morning Tom learned that the Judge believed 'all this' was the purpose of life. Tom, almost infinitely poorer and vastly less experienced, already knew better. Tom thought to himself that the Judge had paid too high a price for 'all this', even though as yet he did not know all the sordid details of just how high that price had been. But that would soon be revealed.

Tom had assured himself since he was a teenager that what he wanted was essentially what the Judge had--wealth, power and the security afforded by them. But at that moment, he clearly saw that he wanted something more.

In 1961, he could only vaguely define what that something was. He knew it was something more than winning golf tournaments, although that was definitely important to him. The something more had to do with the opportunity to help others.

He was immodest enough to believe that at age 27 he had it together in his own life and was in a position to have a positive impact on others' lives. Did that mean through entertaining the fans with his tremendous golf skill? Sure, but only partially. Did it mean helping Det. Mathers pursue the course of justice? Maybe. But he wasn't certain he really had true, professional detective skills. Or did it mean rescuing damsels in distress? He scoffed at that notion. There had been an extremely important damsel in his life who needed rescuing, and he had to date been a dismal failure at it. His own twin sister.

No longer burdened by pressing money worries, Tom was allowed to ask himself, What do I really want from life?

Chapter Eight
Sleuthing At a High Society Party
We Meet The Fabulous Jilly Flannery

Tom Continues Our Story:

The invitation to the Goulds' New Years Eve Party said, "Please dress casually. I envision an informal get-together of dear friends to celebrate the joy of a new year. I'm sure 1962 will be a memorable one."--Missy

I usually just drink at parties rather than envision at them. And I wasn't confident enough back then to just throw on jeans and a sweater and go. So I chose powder blue slacks, a dark blue long-sleeved shirt, and a beige linen sport coat. The casual part was the penny loafers I wore.

The Goulds' life revolved around the Country Club, and as I walked into the party I saw this reflected in the assembled guests, all club members save one or two. The odd thing was I spotted none other than Sen. Richard Luck and his lovely bride Lisa, one of my golf students, there. From what little I knew about politics then, Sen. Luck belonged to a different political party than most of the members of Valley Vista. I could only assume that perhaps the rich and connected put aside their rancorous political differences one night each year.

The Goulds' house was an imposing, majestic turreted grey castle, with a high-ceilinged Great Room that looked out over rolling lawns complete with a man-made pond with a fountain. The home was furnished with what I learned were priceless pieces of furniture inherited from Missy Gould's family. They looked like museum pieces to me, but please never rely on my decorating advice. Everything there smelled kind of old, and I don't mean just the guests.

Our host, Sterling Gould, came over to welcome me to the party. He was 70, sturdy and handsome in a rugged, weathered, outdoorsy way, with a shock of silvery hair. His enormous bulging belly was only partially hidden by his expertly tailored suit and probably a girdle. He had the searching eyes of a big-game hunter, but the game he was best known for going after was the attractive female over the age of 30 but under 50.

I found out right away that my mini-celebrity status from helping Det. Mathers foil the bank robbers was still current.

"Tom, welcome! It's an honor to have a celebrated golfer/detective at our humble soiree." His voice was clear and strong, almost like a radio announcer.

I thought saying it was an honor to have me was kinda stupid, but I smiled as best I could, and attempted to look like someone bestowing an honor. However that looks.

"I was so surprised to get your kind invitation, sir. But no free golf lessons for your guests tonight."

I know, that was a strange thing to say, but this crowd was not my scene and I was starting to sweat already even though it was December 31.

Sterling looked at me like I was an idiot, cleared his throat and said, "Well, ahem, enjoy yourself, Tom." He hurried off to the guests that really mattered.

I strolled over toward the buffet table, but oddly was intercepted by Sen. Richard Luck, whom I had never met.

Sen. Luck looked and acted like Kennedy-lite. Handsome features, noble even. A strong chin, great posture, thick dark hair with a wave of two to make it interesting, sincere smile and brilliantly white teeth. I knew he was a state senator running for the US Senate, but not much else.

I knew virtually nothing about politics. I voted for Eisenhower in 1956 and Kennedy in 1960. I was one of the millions of young voters who were swayed by Kennedy's calm assurance vs. Nixon's sweaty nervousness in the televised debates, even though we knew little about their respective competence. A naïve approach to voting, to be sure.

Because of subsequent events in 1962, I would soon be well-schooled in the brutal game of politics on the national level.

The Senator clasped me on the back and said, "Tom. I'm so glad to finally meet you."

I was not so naïve as to believe this was sincere.

"Same here. How's the campaign going?"

"Super. We're gaining momentum by the day. It helps when your opponent is practically a fossil."

I recalled that my mom had left work early and stood in line for two hours to vote for that particular fossil in three consecutive elections.

"If you'd like to join our movement, we'd love to have you on our team. You are very popular here in Phoenix. We need to carry Maricopa County to have any chance."

I must have involuntary grimaced, for I was thinking that almost my entire golf lesson clientele roster were people registered in the opposition party.

"I have no idea what your political views are, Tom."

"Neither do I."

Sen. Luck laughed.

"Politics is not your bag. That's OK. I wanted to ask you a favor."

I smiled blandly and waited, fearing the worst, like he wanted budding sleuth Tom to gather dirt on his opponent.

"I'm working 24/7 on the campaign, and I feel like Lisa is alone too much. I worry that she's getting bored. She loves taking those golf lessons from you. She's always talking about what a great instructor you are, how patient you are, how encouraging."

"That's very gratifying."

"I wondered if you could give her some playing lessons, take her out to the course for 9 holes, several times a week. The fresh air is so good for her."

I had to chuckle at how self-possessed politicians are. He was in effect saying, too bad if you have to miss that little tournament Bobby Jones puts on in Augusta, Georgia, in April. I want you to play golf with my rich, bored wife instead. I had taken an instant dislike to Sen. Richard Luck.

"How much do you charge for playing lessons?"

"Twenty-two dollars is my normal rate."

A number I had pulled out of the air, right then. I'd never been asked to give a playing lesson before.

"That's perfectly reasonable. I'll have her call you to set up something for next week."

"Look forward to it. Lisa has game."

Whatever I said touched a nerve because he gave me an urgent, penetrating look that seemed to say, "What the hell do you mean by that?"

The moment passed. The Senator's politician-fake-smile bloomed again on his face and I saw he noticed more important people than I that he needed to schmooze.

Wonderful, I thought. Now I'm a dime-a-dance girl, cheering up the bored, neglected and lonely.

He clasped me on the back again, said, "Great!" and hurried off.

I scanned the room for Lisa Luck. She was seated in a high-backed chair near the fireplace, by herself. Lovely, bored and even a bit sad, like a lost child. She held up her champagne glass and watched the firelight reflected in the crystal, as though trying to read her future. I thought about going over and offering her some company. Her political glory-hound husband was obviously ignoring her, but I remembered why I was there and decided to observe our happy host couple, the Goulds. Time to head to the back of the room, make like a potted plant and watch for signs of stress fractures in their marriage.

As I walked Lisa saw me and waved, with an enigmatic but friendly smile. I waved back, the suave golfer/detective that I was.

My next encounter was with Les Levine, who I heard was the Luck Family attorney. He was a short, slight of build man with thick glasses over small darting eyes. Nearly bald except for tufts of greying hair that clung to the sides of his head. At the Club Levine had a reputation for being cheap, mean and short-tempered with both the caddies and the service staff.

His demeanor suggested to me someone looking to pick a fight, an argument at least. Maybe that's what lawyers do. I'd never needed an attorney, so I couldn't tell you for sure. He was carrying a large and smelly cigar.

"I know you," he said, or more precisely, sneered. "Tom Colt. Had a rough go on tour this year, didn't you. Not even one tournament win."

I was not going to take the bait. "Glad to see you follow the golf tour. I did okay this year. Lotta good players out there, you know."

"They say you can't putt for shit."

I wanted to tell this rude, sleazy little man to go to hell. But I couldn't afford, for a variety of reasons, to make a scene there.

"You're very perceptive, sir. Putting is my weakness." I tried to smile and walked off as fast as I could, muttering curses.

I saw the Senator over by the fireplace, looming over poor Lisa. Instead of the politician's fake smile, he had a genuine, dark and stormy frown. He picked up her champagne glass and walked away. Lisa fell back further into the plush chair, maybe hoping to disappear.

So far that evening, I had seen no evidence of any marital discord between Sterling and Martha (Missy) Gould. On the contrary, she looked devoted to him, bringing him snacks and drink refills as needed, laughing in an exaggerated fashion when he told a joke.

Perhaps she was just a superior actress, I thought. But then she appeared behind me and even that flimsy theory was shattered. Missy was, I heard, a beauty queen in her twenties, and at 51 retained her beautiful figure. Her stylish silver-frosted dark hair was in the pixie Audrey Hepburn style. She was an expressive, vivacious woman, whose personality could fill a room. And a damned good golfer.

"Tom, dearest Tom, I do hope you're having a splendid time."

She was beaming, glowing with happiness at the success of the party--and sincere.

Dearest Tom replied, "Missy, your party is one of the best I have ever been to. I can't thank you enough--"

"This is such a wonderful night! I bet '62 will be the greatest year ever, for all of us, all my friends, including you, one of my newest."

Missy's sunshiny optimism would of course be tested later in the year when the Soviet Union built missile launching facilities in Cuba, aimed at, well, us.

She put a friendly hand on my shoulder, perhaps too friendly. I felt the weight of her huge diamond wedding ring.

"I think you're right. No, I'm sure you're right!" Gushing while trying to seem sincere wasn't in my social skill set at that time.

She took her hand from my shoulder and squeezed my hand. Hers was very warm, an outward sign of inner serenity. I know this because my hands turn to big fat icicles on the first tee of every big tournament.

"Well, Ta, Ta."

Yes, these society ladies really said 'Ta, Ta' in the '60s.

"And a terrific, Ta, Ta, too, to you."

She laughed and danced off toward the kitchen. As she left, I resumed simmering over what lawyer Levine said to me. My parents taught me to never let anyone insult or belittle you. I decided to confront him after all. How many US Opens had that little shithead qualified for?

But my plan was derailed by a strange incident near the glass doors that opened up to the patio and the beautiful lawns and gardens beyond.

Sen. Luck looked like he was about to come to blows with Devin Hughes, campaign manager for the Senator's opponent. Hughes was a skinny guy with small pointy black beard, small almost girlish frame and small, delicate hands, all of which were contrary to his reputation as a cutthroat political operative.

Their words could probably be heard in most parts of the Great Room where most of the party attendees were.

Hughes, seething, said, "You run a dirty campaign, Senator, and starting now, we are going to respond in kind."

"From what I've seen, you aren't running much of a campaign at all. Total incompetence."

Devin was not backing down. "You go to hell, Sen. Luck!"

"Hope your candidate enjoys retirement. Shoulda been retired by the voters years ago."

They stared daggers at each other a few moments, then broke off, and as they say in boxing, retired to separate corners.

A few gasps of surprise had erupted in the room as this ugly scene unfolded. As high society folks would say, this simply isn't done at a swank party. Something bothered me about the whole thing. After I reflected a few moments, I couldn't help thinking the argument was faked. I couldn't explain why I thought that, though. It was just one of those feelings I get sometimes.

I needed to visit the restroom. I was told by a waiter to go down the corridor with the family portraits on the wall until I came to a door with a gold handle. Unfortunately, it was occupied. I heard the unmistakable sound of someone throwing up. And then a female voice I had never heard before: "You are nothing but an embarrassment to the Senator. You are destroying what we've worked so hard to build."

I turned and quickly went back to the Great Room. The chair Lisa had occupied was now empty. I sat, actually slumped, into the chair, my head spinning with all the strange things I had seen and heard that evening. The lower middle-class parties I was more familiar with seemed so much less fraught with drama. We just drank, ate and had a few laughs.

Lisa finally re-entered the room. She came back over toward the fireplace. I got up to let her have the chair back. Sterling Gould was following her. As she reached the hearth, he took her hand and said, "Lisa, I hope you are feeling better. Can I get you anything?"

She pulled her hand away. "Like you care, Sterling. Just go away."

He did.

Lisa saw me and momentarily rallied. She walked over close to me. "I'm leaving. I've had enough. Could you give me a golf lesson tomorrow? Or maybe a life lesson. I clearly need both."

"See you on the practice range at 10AM. And Lisa, I think your game is coming along nicely."

She tried to smile, but couldn't. It was only when it was much too late did I realize how significant were her words, "I'm leaving. I've had enough".

At this point, I was getting very irritated with these people. They can't even take one evening off from political and financial machinations, or call a truce on their messy personal lives. I thought I might feel better if I told Les Levine off. I saw his weasel-ly little profile reflected in the patio window. He was outside. I had to steel myself--remember I in no way believed I was equal to these people--and strode to the door, which Missy had left open to let some cool air in evidently to combat the overheated emotions in the room.

Levine was talking to someone I couldn't see. "Everything's under control. Smooth sailing to election day. I delivered our proposal in person--tonight."

I backed away until the second person came back inside. It was Sen. Luck.

Shit, I thought as I returned to the safety of the chair by the fireplace. I haven't solved the mystery I'm being paid to solve, but seem to have uncovered five more. Our hosts seemed like happy rich folks to me. I was having zero fun at this party, and getting nowhere with my assignment.

But then fun personified arrived at the front door and changed all that.

Her name was Jilly Flannery, a bubbly, supremely happy, chatty divorcee, 44, who loved to dish about everyone's lives. She didn't walk into the room, she kind of effervesced. She wore a red strapless cocktail dress, about knee length, held up by the awesome power of her cleavage, with a faint image of a scary dragon that ran diagonally across it. The really short skirts of the '60s had not made their appearance at the fashionable stores yet. But they were worth the wait.

Jilly also wore red sandals--yes, sandals in December. Her glossy brown hair was cut in a short bob, with cute curls on the sides and gold highlights. The overall effect of her hairstyle was that of an elegant lampshade.

In today's world, we might call Jilly a cougar. In 1962, I just called her a hell of a lot of fun. She took golf lessons from me. I knew she was a close friend of Missy Gould's. They often partnered in team golf events at the Club. I needed to talk with her, but had to wait for her to make her way through the meet and greet rituals as she passed through the crowd. I went back to the buffet.

It was really bad: cheese squares on toothpicks and meatballs in some kind of bland watery marinara sauce. Dry crab puffs (I couldn't detect much crab, mostly just puff). And tiny, greasy smoked sausages. Why didn't Missy ask my mom to cater this party? Yikes.

I finished some sharp cheddar and felt a small but firm hand on my left buttock. It had to be Jilly, and it was. She managed to seem tipsy even though she was just starting on her first drink. Her personality was naturally tipsy.

I gave her my brightest smile. "I was hoping you'd make it."

"I didn't think this was your kind of scene. Thought you'd be back at your pad poring over *Ben Hogan's 20 Newly-Revealed Secrets to Golf Perfection*. Probably by candlelight 'cuz you struggling golf pros can't afford electricity." She sipped what looked to be a Manhattan.

I ignored her needlessly cruel comment.

"Actually I moved into the guest house at Judge Wilkinson's estate."

Jilly, of course, knew this already. "Oh yes, I heard something about that. Have you met the Judge's darling daughter yet?"

"No I haven't."

"Guess not. You're still alive! Ha!"

I had no idea what she meant, but part of Jilly's personality was dropping the occasional conversational bombshell, just to see your reaction.

"I have a question to ask you." The small firm hand remained in place.

"The answer is, yes, of course we can go upstairs and make mad, young love. Missy lets me use the bedroom overlooking the pool."

I think I sputtered. The small firm hand grabbed mine and I felt myself being swept away toward the stairs.

I don't remember much about the bedroom she took me to, other than the bed was a robust four-poster and the brilliant white cotton sheets were very soft.

By the time I carefully removed my new beige sports jacket, she had shucked the dress, the sandals and wriggled out of her pale blue panties, then untethered herself from her pale blue bra.

"Nice tan," I commented when I noticed every inch of her skin was beautifully bronzed by the sun.

"Just got back from the Caribbean," she effervesced. "Friend of mine from Scottsdale owns an island there. Very private. No need to bother with swimsuits."

My eyes still on luscious Jilly, I removed and carefully placed on a chair the slacks I had pressed earlier that day.

She said, "Hurry up and get undressed, sweetie. We don't want to keep the guests waiting. That would be bad social form."

"I was focused on your amazing form."

She flashed her bright, confident smile.

She was extremely curvy, resembling one of *Playboy's* centerfold girls (I knew this because I had been a loyal subscriber since '57). She twirled around confidently like, "take a look at this!"

She took her golf stance and mimed a perfect little swing.

"I've been exercising. You said I needed to get stronger legs to hit the ball further. As usual, you were right! She placed an index finger on her rear end. My derriere has never been tighter!"

"I understand a tight ass is a requirement for membership at Valley Vista."

It's hard to strike a scornful pose when you're nekkid, but she did her best.

"If you hate us so much, why do you so desperately want to be like us?"

I had no answer to her sage observation. She brightened again when she noticed the bulge in my underwear. Her uncovered beauty was having its intended effect. She came over to me, softly kissed me on the lips and then lightly stroked the bulge. Jilly had skills. I was feeling warmer, breathing faster.

In my romantic youth, I had believed that tender feelings of love lead to great sex. But with Jilly, great sex led perhaps not to love, but to being enveloped in a soft, fragrant mist of near-love. A temporary, overpowering bliss. Nothin' wrong with that.

There was no physical awkwardness or emotional uncertainty; we twined around each other like we already knew each other's body, like we'd been lovers forever. She was eager to have me inside her, as eager as I became to enter her paradise. We tumbled, explored, enjoyed each other to the max. I could feel with my entire being that she wanted to satisfy me as much as I wanted the same for her. As our passions rose, we both came to know that we cared for one another, on some level, as unlikely as that might seem.

She was also a vocal lover, and as she cried out with the joy of full completion, we quite clearly heard, coming from downstairs, 5-4-3-2-1 being counted down. And then cheers erupted.

We leaned back and laughed, both of us thinking: *We were that good?* It was midnight. The New Year was here. Jilly slipped her soft fingers down my warm, moist chest, all the way to her ultimate destination.

"Fabulous way to start 1962, don't you think?"

I replied, "Oh, yes. Going to be a memorable year."

She giggled softly. "We talk about you in the ladies' locker room."

"What? Why?"

"What do you suppose we girls talk about? Knitting? Our children? Hell no. We talk about our handsome hunk of a golf instructor."

"What are you going to say now, after tonight?"

She put a finger to her lips. "Absolutely nothing. Tonight belongs to just you and me. Most of those stuck-up dames hate me anyway. One of them told me I should have been a Flapper in the 1920s. What does that mean?"

We shared quiet moments under the cooling sheets. Then Jilly sat up, propped herself on a pillow, letting the sheet fall away. The bubbly-Jilly persona fell away, too, and she spoke in a soft, sincere tone--almost filled with wonder.

"I love my life, Tom. Look at us tonight. We came together, and it was like we left the earth and traveled across the galaxy as we embraced. I forgot where I was and who I was--you and I were the only ones in the universe, two perfectible beings looking for that perfection in each other. Two incredible bodies, two warm, sweet hearts, totally in tune."

That was so beautiful I didn't know what to say. She continued:

"Sometimes when I am golfing and I hit a near-perfect shot, it's like every muscle in my body knew exactly what it needed to do to create that perfection. The moment the club makes contact with the ball it feels like if you can create near-perfection in this impossibly difficult game, then no dream is out of reach."

I never cry, not even at funerals, but she captured the essence of our game so splendidly, I almost did that night.

She finally broke out of her reverie, returning to the light-hearted woman she presented to the world. "Well, I share all this deep, personal philosophy with you, and the whole time you were staring at my bare chest."

"But I was listening. You said that golf and love are the building blocks of a happy life."

She looked amazed, like I was some kind of savant. "Yes, that's exactly what I was trying to say."

She leaned over and kissed me.

I said, "And you have a gorgeous body. It would be a crime not to look."

"I suppose that's true. I'm glad you're enjoying yourself then," she said, then asked, "How long have you been giving me golf lessons?"

"A little over five months, I think.

"In that case it's taken me four months longer to get you into bed than I planned. Maybe I'm losing my sex appeal."

"And maybe the sun will lose its warmth."

"You are so sweet!"

And maybe the sun will lose its warmth. Did I really say such a sappy thing out loud?

We became very quiet, almost sleepy. "You said we shouldn't be gone from the party too long," I commented.

"I did? You changed my mind." She gifted me with another sweet kiss. "I believe you said you had a question for me."

I thought, *Wake up Mr. Hotshot Detective. Why are you here?*

"Oh, yes, right. In the Men's Locker Room, I overheard a rumor that Missy may be having an affair. The gossip was something about Sterling finding unusual withdrawals of funds from their bank account."

Jilly sat bolt upright. "Pish tosh. Gossipy old farts in this Club! Missy is totally devoted to that bastard. By the way, it's Sterling who's the busiest tomcat in the alley. And I can tell you what his wife, my best friend, spends extra money on. She donates to a dog shelter in Scottsdale."

She became so intense it worried me. She saw that and reached for my hand. "I'm not mad at you, lover. I hate these old boys with nothing better to do, sitting in the so-called Gentlemen's Lounge sucking down martinis all afternoon, that make up lies about people."

The shameless shamus needed more details.

"A dog shelter?"

"Yes. She was brokenhearted when her Gordon Setter, Beauregard, passed away. She wanted to get another dog, but

Sterling wouldn't hear of it. Beau, it seems, had chewed his brand new crocodile-skin golf shoes from Italy."

No world traveler I, I really didn't know there were crocodiles in Italy. Gotta stay out of those canals in Venice next time I visit.

"Can't blame the dog," I said. "Probably tasted good. Like chicken."

"Missy volunteered at a dog shelter so she can play with as many pups as she wants, any day she wants. Generous soul that she is, she became one of their top donors. If I ever find out which of those old farts was spreading these lies..."

I cleared my throat. "Glad to hear that all is well in the Gould Household. Sterling can concentrate on his investments."

She bounced up from the bed and began dressing to return to the party. Back in her bra and panties, she calmed down and smiled seductively at me. "Maybe we could do my next golf lesson in the nude."

"Let's take things slowly. I just got the Club President to relax the rule that ladies must have collars on their golf shirts."

She laughed, padded over to me in bare feet, stood up on tip toes and kissed me. "You are so much fun! And I deserve fun."

***

Next morning, I drove out to the dog shelter and looked around the place. Sure enough Missy's gold metallic Mercedes was in a parking spot labeled, Donor Parking Only. "Case closed," I said out loud, with authority and rather idiotically. From the nearest pay phone, I gave the Judge a ring.

"I have the information you requested sir."

"Already? I only gave you the assignment a few days ago."

I explained the harmless activity Missy was up to.

"Dog shelter," he harrumphed. All Judges, even retired ones, enjoy a good harrumph. "I would have never guessed that. Outstanding, Tom. How'd you make the discovery?"

I was thinking to my 27-year-old self, *HOT DAMN I'm a real detective!*

"I put several pieces of information together, one from a confidential source who came forward (I didn't add, a buck naked confidential source). The solution became obvious. As Sherlock Holmes said 'When you have eliminated the impossible, whatever remains, however improbable, must be the truth'."

"Yes, well. Excellent work."

"You can proceed with your real estate transaction, sir."

"Glad to hear I have your blessing, Tom," he said rather tartly.

The conversation ended. When I got the check from the Judge for February's expenses, a $1,675 bonus was included. No idea how he arrived at that calculation.

***

As the first event of the 1962 pro tour season approached, I nearly chained myself to the practice range, attempting to master my secret weapon, the new driver the Judge had given me. It was an incredible club. I began to hit consistently straight tee shots for the first time in my life. Not absolutely straight. The shots had a glorious, ever so slight draw--right to left flight--that added distance. I was consistently hitting 280-320 yard drives! *Just give me the Player of the Year trophy now*, I thought. I never believed in the Magic Club theory of golf. But this club certainly boosted my confidence.

On Wednesday afternoon I saw in my lesson scheduling book that one Jillian Flannery was booked for 2PM. Jilly's golf swing, after 5 months of lessons with me, was sweet, a thing of near beauty. Her swing had a slow, deliberate rhythm that built to a powerful, exciting climax when she made contact with the ball. Sometimes she even emitted this sharp little noise.

The major thing I worked on with Jilly was staying under control. She had a tendency to overswing and get off balance because she wanted to knock the snot out of the ball, especially on tee shots. She told me her key swing thought was imagining her most recent ex-husband's head perched on the little wooden tee-peg.

I was already on the practice range when I saw her emerge from the Ladies Locker Room, dressed all in pink today. I was concerned that it might be awkward giving her a lesson after we slept together the week before.

She walked up to me, put her arm around my back, pulled me in and kissed me on the mouth. "Hello there, sweet lover. Ready to give me a good workout? Or maybe a golf lesson?"

Guess I needn't have been concerned.

Her swing looked really, really good that day. So did she. She focused mightily on making each shot perfect, and to a large extent, succeeded. I believe she wanted to impress her fabulous instructor. After about 20 shots we paused for a few moments.

Jilly said, "I know I'm a hundred years older than you are. But what does it matter. Age is just a number. I'm prettier than I was when I was 20, and I feel terrific inside and out."

I wasn't sure what was going on. Did she want us to go steady?

"What was the first thing you thought of when you saw me without my clothes on, upstairs at the party."

"Spectacular."

"Super! No hesitation."

"I'm imagining you without clothes right now. Do I have a great job or what?"

She smirked. "I may take lessons from you forever, you cad."

"I think we are taking lessons from each other, but I'm the only one getting paid."

"Were you always such an old soul?"

"Even as a toddler."

She burst out laughing.

I said: "Let's get back to work. How about a few 5-irons..."

She took that club out of her bag and hit a ball that I had placed for her on the ground.

The Club General Manager, imperious Mr. Basil Hedgerow, walked onto the driving range with his caddie. The remarkably observant Jilly noticed me scowling when I saw him.

"You look at ghoulish old Basil like you want to punch his lights out."

"I do. My mom hated working for him when she waitressed here. One day she almost quit it got so bad."

"Sounds like irresistible Club gossip. Do tell."

"There was a table of drunken old men at the bar near the end of her shift, the only ones there. One of them asked her, 'How big a tip would we have to leave for you to serve the next round of drinks without your top on'?"

"Oh, my."

"My mom tried to shrug it off and laughed. Next thing the four old men take out their wallets and toss money on the table, like she was a stripper. They laughed and laughed as the money piled up. She said it looked like $500—a month's salary. One of them grabbed her and said, 'C'mon, Laura. Show us what ya' got.' They threw down more money. My mom pulled away from him and ran off in tears, she said."

Jilly was watching my retelling with rapt attention. She also looked angry.

"Even worse, Basil had watched the whole scene, from the door to the kitchen. Didn't make a move to come to her aid. As she ran out, he caught up with her. He said, 'What would it have hurt to give the members what they wanted?' My mom was so mad she couldn't even speak. He went on, 'Do you know how much money those four have among them? They could put Tom through college.' My mom got her voice back and said, 'I don't need their help. Tom and I will work together and get him through school'. My mom said Basil laughed at her."

Jilly squeezed my hand in a gesture of comfort. "Well, what can I say. I'm sorry sweetie, but this doesn't arrive on my doorstep as news. Rich old men can be pricks. Remember, I divorced one and buried another one."

I hadn't meant to burden Jilly with this story. I had never told it before, to anyone.

She smiled and said, "That's why, from now on, it's only horny young guys for me!"

"On behalf of the Young and Horny Men of America, we thank you for your confidence in us."

We both laughed. She knew exactly how to make me feel better. We got back on track to our favorite subject, golf.

"I wanted to wish you luck in the Phoenix Open Invitational. I'll be in the gallery every day rooting for you."

"You won't be rooting for Arnold, like everyone else."

"Arnold has enough fans. I want to be a Charter Member, make that the Founding Member, of the small but growing Tom Colt Fan Club. Wait 'til you see the initiation rites I have planned."

"Don't I initiate you?"

"Precisely. But I select the rites."

She was a nut. But I really liked this woman. A lot.

She got back to practicing, this time with her 3-wood. She stopped again, though, after three shots.

"I have an idea, Tom. How about if I go on tour with you this spring. You could play golf all day and we could play all night."

I felt a dog collar snap around my neck, the lock closing with cold finality. And then a rough hand attached a leash to the collar, a rather short leash.

I thought, *gotta come up with something quickly, boy.*

"I'd love that. I get lonely out there. (A bit of a fib, on my part: gorgeous groupies including film starlets and fashion models flock to every tournament). But I'd hate for you to miss all the ladies events you've practiced so hard to compete in. You and Missy can win the State Ladies Best Ball Tournament this year, I'm sure of it. I don't tell you enough how impressed I am with your progress. Your game is ready! I believe in you."

She hit her best shot of the day, a soaring 3-wood that sailed down the practice range about 180 yards. She turned to me with a wicked gleam in her eyes.

"Very well played, Thomas J. Colt. You managed to turn me down flat and make me feel absolutely great about myself at the same time."

"You and I both got game, girl."

Chapter Nine
A Visit with Tom's Twin Sister
John Wayne Saves the Day

My sister Caroline lived in a blighted midtown 2-story apartment building, the kind of building you see too often in Arizona unfortunately, carelessly put together with chicken wire, stucco and spit. The swimming pool in the building's atrium had unidentified but clearly toxic green slime growing around the perimeter, and the building manager somehow never had time to clean it. But be 1/2 day behind in the rent and he camps out on your doorstep with his shotgun and his beefy ex-con cousin Wade.

I stepped across the dry weedy yard that led from the parking lot and found Apartment 13.

I knocked quietly. No answer. I knew Caroline was there because I saw her beat-up Oldsmobile in the carport. I knocked again, this time louder. Still nothing stirring.

I noticed a gap beneath the door big enough for rats to run in and out, depending on their preference. If I were a rat, I'd vote for out.

I tried the loose, rattling doorknob. It turned. I opened the door and heard deep, loud snoring. I walked inside. Caroline was there on the old rust-brown couch. She had a camisole top on and panties. Her mascara had run as though she'd been crying. There was a weird, new bruise on her shoulder. It was 11AM, which was a few hours before dawn, Caroline Time.

"Caroline, wake up, it's me."

After several iterations of this greeting, each marginally louder, she stirred, cracked open one red eye, frowned and said, "I'm sorry. I didn't order a golf instructor today. My game is under control. But thanks." She closed the eye. Caroline's voice had a dusky quality, as though her vocal chords had been very lightly sandpapered.

I walked over and flopped down on the couch, which made her sit up. The last year or so I've been shocked at how thin she was getting. Her face, though still pretty, looked unnaturally thin. Her lifestyle, if you want to call dissipation a lifestyle, was aging her rapidly. And to be honest, she didn't smell very good. Her hair looked stringy and dirty.

Caroline, tragically, had found relief from life's inevitable disappointments through using drugs, both the recreational variety and prescription drugs.

Her purse was better stocked than many local drug stores.

What a shame, I thought. In high school the boys thought she was, as they put it then, CHOICE.

"How was Mexico?" I asked as cheerily as I could given my concerns at her appearance.

She yawned. "Very Mexican. Good tamales, great tequila, excellent weed and an eager guy on the beach named Pablo, or was it Paco?"

"Just so you had fun."

"Oh yes, my life is one amusing episode after the other."

I got up, went into the kitchen to make coffee.

"Nice of your boss to let you take time off from work so you could go."

"Boss," she chuckled. "No such boss. I lost that crap job two weeks ago. Setting out vegetables at the local grocery store turned out to be too challenging for yours truly. Mr. Pelligrino said I was sloppy and didn't care about my work. So he fired me."

"Sorry," was all I could think of to say. This was just another piece of an unfortunate pattern in Caroline's life. After a period of uncomfortable silence, the coffee was ready. I found two mostly clean cups and poured, took one over to her.

"Good," I really need this today." After a few sips, she began to wake up, which produced a full-face frown. "Why the visit, bro?"

"I thought we could spend the day together, maybe do lunch and then a movie, like we used to."

She made a chortling sound, like angry gargling.

"Since when do you have time to take the day off from being Mr. Popularity to hang out with your loser of a sister? I haven't seen you in months."

"First of all, you are not a loser. No matter how hard you try to be one. And I'm hardly Mr. Popularity. Just a struggling golfer."

"Not what my friend Lisa says. She says all the country club chicks, young and old, 20 to 70, fall all over themselves to take lessons from you. Tom, says she, is like the most wonderful-est golf instructor ever. I bet you sleep with all of them."

"Not all, no. Who is this Lisa?"

"Duh. Lisa Luck, the Senator's wife."

I must have looked too surprised.

"Yes, she's my friend, idiot. I met her that year our wonderful bitch of a mother sent me to reform school."

"It was a Catholic school."

"Same difference. Each cheery school day began with a Nun saying: You are a sinner young lady. Repent now. This is your last chance."

She got up and refilled her coffee.

"The kids at reform school thought we were an odd pair. Lisa was prim and proper, and came from money. I was, well, me. I love her to death, though. She never looks down on me 'cuz I'm po' folks."

I wandered around the room, sipping my coffee. I noticed a stack of bills on the dining room table. Based on my own considerable experience, I judged them to be delinquent. At one point I was even able to sniff the presence of dunning notices in the mailbox, like those dogs that can find drugs in luggage.

"Do you need a little help with the rent? I'm doing better myself. I'd be happy to—"

I saw from the red light of anger in her eyes, the caffeine had kicked in and she was fully awake. Her voice was just below a scream.

"No. I don't need our help. I don't want to have lunch with you. I hate going to the movies. I want you to get the hell out of my apartment."

"Okey," I said, not knowing what else to say.

She went into the bedroom and slammed the door for emphasis. I heard the shower being turned on. It's an odd thing to fight with your twin. It's like fighting with yourself. She's about 75% Caroline and 25% me. I'm 75% me and 25% Caroline. When we played golf as kids, I was better with long shots, she was better with chipping and putting. In school, I liked to sit in the back of the class and observe. Caroline loved to get up in front of the class and perform.

I knew exactly what she was feeling before she expressed it. She was mad I found those overdue bills. She may be losing her youthful good looks, but she still had her pride. And she was right, our mom was a bitch to her, and I never really understood why.

But it didn't take a semi-brilliant golfer/detective to figure out that the key to Caroline returning to the beautiful, popular, confident woman she was when she was 18 involved changing how our mom reacted to her. Not my area of expertise, though.

It's a lot easier to correct a reverse pivot in an amateur golfer's downswing than to reverse 10 years of nonstop, bitter conflict in a family.

I sat back down, my mood sinking into despair. I felt like cooties were climbing out of that crappy old rust-brown couch with the funky smell. I must have stayed there 10 minutes clouded over with gloom and helplessness.

Wearily, I got up and went to the door, opened it. Then I waited in the threshold a few moments. I don't know why.

The bedroom door was flung open and Caroline rushed out wearing a lovely bright sunshine yellow dress, her hair still damp.

She ran to me, pulled me by the hand back into the room. Then pulled me to her and began to cry, deep anguish coming from deep inside her. We didn't say anything. Didn't need to. The regret she felt was clear in her reddened, wet eyes.

"I'm so horrible to you. I don't know what gets into me sometimes."

I thought, *I think they're called illegal drugs.*

"Forget it. We can still have a nice day."

"Are there any John Wayne movies playing at the Kachina Theater? Daddy always took us to see John Wayne."

The budding but sometimes dim detective, me, thought to himself, *I just received a clue. But what does it mean?*

***

The Kachina Theatre, an impressive film palace in downtown Scottsdale owned by local impresario Harry Nace, was indeed showing an excellent John Wayne western, *The Comancheros.* I took Caroline to lunch at Bob's Big Boy restaurant, where we had huge cheeseburgers and shakes. I wanted to get some calories in Caroline, who looked much too thin, almost on the verge of collapse.

We went to a 1PM matinee. The theater was nearly deserted on a Wednesday afternoon, so we could sit in the back and talk softly without disturbing the other patrons. The theater was always very clean and had seats comfortable enough to take a nap in, should the film be boring. It even had a "smoking loge" area for those who couldn't last two hours without their nicotine fix.

Caroline asked: "How many times did Dad take us to see Westerns?"

"We saw '*She Wore a Yellow Ribbon*' four times at least. I come here by myself sometimes in the afternoon, and imagine Dad is sitting right there next to us. I even talk to him. I'm telling you, sometimes I can feel his presence."

Caroline didn't register any surprise at this. She just nodded. Perhaps she felt his presence that day as well.

"Next time you come here, don't go by yourself. Take me with you."

"Sure thing, Pilgrim."

The film had lots of action and snappy dialogue. John Wayne was super, of course.

We watched the movie and munched our popcorn for an hour or so, until Caroline said, "I did a bad, bad thing."

"Oh," I said with probably not enough surprise in my voice.

"I took that magazine article that said you were an underachiever over to Our Mother's house and read it to her."

Caroline managed to say Mother like it was a mild cuss word.

I shook my head in mock agony. "How did mom react?"

"She gave me that hot, angry look like she did when I was 10 and naughty and she was fixin' to spank me with that heavy brass metal ruler she always had handy."

"Why do you do such things?"

"I was mad at you because you never take me out anymore. And to piss her off. I was mad at her because she wouldn't loan me any money."

"But you didn't want to take money from me..."

"No. Absolutely not."

"Why is that?"

"I don't really know. You're the boy who likes to solve puzzles. Bet ya' can't solve me."

"Maybe I can, if you give me a chance. From now on, let's get together at least every two weeks."

"Deal." She paused a few moments, then said, "Did that article hurt you?"

"Not at all. The golf writers are mostly dumb asses. There's a few talented ones like Dan Jenkins and Herb Wind, and of course Jim Murray at the *LA Times*, but not many."

Her popcorn cup was empty. I offered her some of mine and said, "Dad always taught us that if you do your absolute best each day, the only opinion about your work that matters is your own."

Caroline sighed. "I've definitely not been doing my absolute best. I don't know why. I guess I don't even know what I should be doing, to do my best in."

We watched the movie another 5 minutes until the film ended. As we walked out the door, she said, "Tom if you ever get so serious about a girl that you want to marry her, which I completely doubt, ask her if she likes John Wayne."

I chuckled. "Why?"

"Because if she doesn't, she could never really understand you."

All our adult lives, whenever we got together, whether the two of us laughed, or cried or fought with one another, Caroline always left me with something to think about.

Chapter Ten
The Circus Comes to Town
Tom is Left Holding the Bag

Brooks Benton Continues Our Story...

I knew that, once we got Tom talking, this book would be a breeze to write. Tom, like all people who have been in the limelight, have heard the addictive sound of applause, dearly love to talk about themselves. Athletes are performers, golfers are sorta athletes, and all performers are narcissists. All I have to do is keep the tape recorder running.

I've written about golf for 25 years, and the best way I can describe the pro tour is that it is a traveling circus. It goes from town to town, sells tickets, sets up refreshment tents and bleachers for spectators to watch the action, puts on a 4-day show, then packs up and leaves for another town. Some of the golfers soar to great heights like trapeze artists, others fall tragically to the ground, eliciting groans from the spectators. Tour life isn't real life. It's all about putting on a show.

The pro golfers in their own minds even separate their tournament life from their other life, at home. They refer to the tour as "out here" as though it were a separate universe.

The golf circus doesn't have clowns, although some of the golfers, particularly the great ones, would argue that's the role we sportswriters play.

And just like the circus, the saddest thing is to walk around the golf course after the tour has packed up and left. The almost unnaturally perfect dark green grass is trampled down from all the foot traffic of the spectators, littered with paper cups, cigarettes, and snack wrappers. But the saddest part is the eerie quiet. The colorful characters called tour pros have departed their stage, the high-spirited cheers have dimmed to echoes whispered on the wind.

Tom Colt began the winter golf tour with sky-high expectations, even though he's never been able to afford a ride on an airplane. But the weakness in his game, putting, caused him continued frustration and disappointment as the '62 season began.

Tom skipped the first tournament of the season, the LA Open. His first start was in San Diego, where he achieved only one of four rounds under par and won a whopping $176.50. Next came one of the pros' favorite events, the Bing Crosby

National Pro-Am in the gorgeous Monterey Peninsula in Northern California. Pro golfers and entertainment industry celebrities, singer Crosby's friends, mingle and socialize--and play some golf--for the entire week.

This was the tournament Tom had purchased a travel voucher for his mom to join him. The week was more successful for her than for Tom. She had a blast at the Culinary Festival held there, picking up lots of recipes, ideas and vendors offering gourmet food to delight her catering service clients. Tom missed the cut, by the excruciating margin of one single stroke, but at least got to spend more time with his mom. Sadly, his weekend was free.

Tom fared better at the first tournament in February, the Palm Springs Golf Classic, which would later be known as the Bob Hope Desert Classic, when the legendary entertainer assumed duties as tournament host. Tom played 4 solid rounds, 69, 71, 67, 68. The tournament was won by Arnold Palmer, on the fast track to becoming an American Legend--it was already his 28th professional victory. Tom went home with $721. Food and lodging in Palm Springs and gasoline for his car cost him $298, so Tom earned a small profit.

Tom continued to give lessons at Valley Vista CC, despite the Judge sponsoring him on tour. He didn't want to abandon his students he had been working with for a year, and besides he really enjoyed teaching.

Next up was the Phoenix Open Invitational, at that time played at Phoenix Country Club, a layout built in 1921 that was located right in the heart of the city. An errant drive on some holes could bang onto the hood of unsuspecting motorists driving by on Osborn Road. The downtown location made it easy for businessmen to sneak out of the office for a long lunch on Thursday or Friday and catch some of the golf action.

The Phoenix Open was organized by a local civic booster group, the Phoenix Thunderbirds. Most of the prominent businessmen in town belonged to the Thunderbirds, including Tom's new benefactor, Judge Roy Wilkinson. At the Pro-Am event preceding the tournament, the Judge made it a point to introduce Tom to as many of these business leaders as possible. At the time Tom didn't understand why, but the Judge was paving the way for Tom's future success in business. Then as now, it's all about who you know.

***

Tom Continues Our Story...

The favorite to win the Phoenix Open was understandably not me; it was Arnold Palmer, fresh off his victory in Palm Springs. I competed against him for 20 years. The Arnold Palmer I knew in the '60s and '70s was a superbly conditioned athlete with a trim waist, the powerful hands and arms of a prize fighter--and a fierce, and I mean fierce, will to win that was unsurpassed by any golfer playing at that time. Any.

He had a repertoire of gestures, unique to him that fascinated his fans and the media. He would hitch his pants before choosing a club. He would casually drop his cigarette on the ground as he sized up his next shot. The cigarette manufacturers saw how cool he looked doing this and hired him to appear in their advertisements. After swinging, he would anxiously follow the flight of the ball with a canting of his head. These gestures, when I experienced them first-hand the few times I was paired with him in tournaments, demonstrated a kind of frenetic nervous energy, and outward expression of a competitive fire that burned inside of him, raged actually. Damn, he wanted to win, and win and win.

Arnold Palmer also had a quality that the men who play heroic roles in cinema have--he caused the fans to bond with him, to want to be like him, to want him to succeed. He was their ideal. And this applied equally to male and female fans, young and old. Children particularly adored him.

Although I competed against him, I am not ashamed to admit I was a fan, too. His popularity and amazing ability to express the ups and downs, the challenges and frustrations of our wonderful game--in the brand-new medium of television--caused the popularity of golf to soar. In the '60s, it finally became possible for many of us pros, not just the superstars, to earn a fine living from playing golf.

The 1962 Phoenix Open began on Thursday, February 8. I didn't get off to a good start.

I felt extra pressure playing in my hometown. And the Judge was front and center in the gallery on the first tee. I had finally figured out that to Judge Roy Wilkinson, I was just another of his investments, not a young person he was lending a helping hand to. I had become part of his portfolio of assets. The question on my mind was, what sort of Return on Investment did he expect?

On the first hole, I hit a wicked hook off the tee that rattled into the trees on the left, setting me up for a sloppy bogey 6 on this relatively easy par 5 first hole, that most of the pros expected to make a birdie 4 on. I shot a dismal 75 for the round, four over par.

The leader was, Guess Who? Arnold Palmer with a brilliant 7-under-par 64. He birdied 6 of his first 7 holes to start the tournament. If that sounds familiar, that was precisely what he did to ignite his 4th round charge to win the US Open in 1960.

Besides the struggles with my game, I had trouble during the round with my caddie, Old Georgie. He was a wizened little man with a humped back and a scraggly beard. A cigarette was perpetually dangling from his lips. I thought I smelled alcohol on his breath when we teed off that afternoon, and he made at least two serious errors in the yardages he gave me for my second shots during the round, which resulted in bogies on both holes.

When I arrived at the practice range the next morning for the second round of the tournament, the Founding Member of the Tom Colt Fan Club, one Jilly Flannery, was waiting for me. She kissed me and with the sunniest of smiles, said, "Don't worry, today's your day."

I was bolstered by her confidence in me and by the low-cut, rose-shade frilly blouse she was wearing, with her shapely legs clearly defined by tight white stretch pants. Jilly had a way of making sexy look classy.

I waited a good 10 minutes for my caddie to bring my clubs. Finally he arrived, sweating already, despite the crisp temperatures in the 50s. He looked unsteady. Oh, crap, I thought. He's drunk. Sure 'nuf he was.

I stood there a few moments, then lost my composure, unusual for me, and in prima donna fashion, said: "How can I build a first-class career with third-class help. You're fired."

This didn't seem to register as significant in his life. He dropped my golf bag; it clanked on the asphalt cart path. "Fuck you, underachiever," was all he said as he walked away.

So there I was, 90 minutes from my tee time and I was without a caddie. I sat down on my golf bag and pondered what to do. My sister Caroline surprisingly appeared from behind me. I stood back up. She was wearing a funky outfit of red Keds, one of my old college golf team sweatshirts and two-toned leggings, the two tones tragically being pink and lime green.

"I saw what happened. Bummer."

"I think it's slightly beyond bummer. I'm hosed."

She mimed a few golf swings. "I could caddie for you today."

My expression must have been a mix of surprise and horror.

"What? You don't think I'm up to it? Dad taught me how to play the game, too, you know, including the rules and the propah etiquette."

I had to weigh the fragile state of my sister's psyche versus the fragile state of my golf career.

"Okay. The bag is yours."

She grinned then set the bag back upright, lifted it. "Heavy son-of-a-gun."

Caroline opened the zippered pockets and began pulling out the items I took with me every round--rain gear, a metal thermos with either cold or hot lemonade, a first aid kit and other stuff. Yes, first aid kit. Golf is a rough sport.

"What are you doing?" I enquired.

"Lightening my load. Does it look like rain today?"

She found a piece of beautiful of quartz I collected on a desert hike. It was said to emit positive energy. "You carry rocks? Good Grief, Charlie Brown."

"Some of those things are my good luck charms."

"Evidently they don't work."

She finished tossing things out and lifted the bag. "Better."

I went about my warm-up ritual, hitting several shots with each club, which went well except Caroline made thumbs-up or thumbs-down gestures to judge the quality of each shot, which the fans gathered there thought were very, very funny. I heard lots of chuckles and giggles.

"Do you have to do that?"

"Don't like it, find another caddie."

We proceeded to the practice putting green. I got out my Achilles heel, the seemingly harmless little putter, smallest club in the bag, and 3 balls and worked on gaining confidence in my stroke. Fat chance.

I didn't notice Caroline wandering off to the other side of the green, where, to a round of heartfelt applause, none other than our beloved Arnold Palmer had arrived. Caroline was quick-frozen in place, about 5 feet from him.

She reached out a hand toward him, as though to confirm he was real.

"You're...you're...Arnie."

Palmer's mastery of the game extended to mastering the art of dealing with, shall we say, unusual star struck fans.

He smiled in his boyish, disarming way. "Yes, I am."

I recovered from my own mortification and gently tugged at Caroline's sleeve to bring her back to my side of the green. "Sorry," I said back to him. He was already focused on his own practice routine. Ah, if only I could focus like the great players do.

On the first tee, I boomed a drive 265 yards, 'straight down the middle' as Bing Crosby croons in that song. Caroline was mildly impressed. "Your tee shots have finally improved. Cool beans." She was chewing bubble gum and making huge bubbles that popped loudly, sounding like gunshots to my jittery competition nerves.

I hit a stellar low draw with a 3-wood for my second shot, which stopped just 20 yards from the putting surface. A good chip and putt and I would start with a birdie 4. I did just that. A nice chip that rolled to within 5 feet of the hole, leaving me with a simple uphill, straight putt which I made. *Good start, Tom*, I thought.

And then to my dismay Caroline's natural performing instinct emerged from hibernation. I'd forgotten how much she enjoyed starring in high school plays.

She walked the perimeter of the green, clapping her hands and saying, "Put your hands together, people. That's my brother!"

The little gallery laughed and applauded. They were all smiles. It was a though they discovered the price of the tournament ticket included a bonus show starring Caroline. I looked at my playing partners, one of whom was scowling, and shrugged sheepishly.

I made 5 pars in a row. On the 7th, I had a 10-foot putt with little or no break, for birdie. I left it a foot short. Pathetic effort for a professional golfer. My little gallery groaned. I tapped the ball into the hole for a par.

Caroline took center stage after replacing the flagstick. She put her hands around her throat and said, "Choke, choke."

I gave her the putter and muttered, "Don't say that, it's rude."

"Don't miss easy putts and I won't."

On the par 5 eighth, I rammed in a 30-foot putt for birdie. It had a wicked break that I read--guessed--perfectly. Caroline punched the air with her right fist and exclaimed, "YESSSSS!"

"Just so you know, I think the player is supposed to punch the air with sheer joy, not the caddie."

"Sorry. I was overcome with sheer amazement that you actually made a putt."

By now, my playing partners thought she was kinda humorous. They were both playing crappy that day, so I think they appreciated the distraction.

On the back 9, I knew I needed at least one more birdie to be assured of making the 36-hole cut and playing on the weekend--and getting a paycheck. I felt tight on the 10th tee and faded my tee shot into the rough. I took a cigarette out and lit it. The Judge's advice was correct, it did calm your nerves.

Caroline looked cross. "Didn't know you took up tobacco."

"Judge Wilkinson said it might help me calm down during the round."

"Judge says castrate yourself to improve your short-iron play, you goin' do that?"

I crushed the cigarette out with my heel.

At this point, I noticed my sister was running out of energy. She began dragging the golf bag down the fairway instead of carrying it. Her party-like-there's-no-tomorrow lifestyle was taking its toll on her health.

On the 16th tee, I told her we'd share the bag-toting duties the rest of the way. She nodded wearily. For my third shot on this par 4 I had a delicate little chip shot from the fringe--the short grass that ringed the even shorter-cropped putting surface. Also known as the frog hair. Yep. Frog hair. No idea who names these things. Evidently sports reporters like Brooks Benton with too much time on their hands.

I surveyed the shot carefully, then chipped it in to the cup for a birdie!

The fading Caroline sprang back to life. She mimed a golf broadcaster holding a microphone and then with that impassioned radio sports announcer voice, said: "And Tom Colt goes to 3 under par for his round. This fine young player is really on his game today!"

The gallery, which had doubled in size as we neared the clubhouse, laughed and applauded.

Then she whispered to me, "Can you please carry the bag the rest of the way. I'm beat. Somehow I've gotten out of shape."

I gave her a little hug. "Sure."

On the 18th hole, I had an 18-foot putt for another birdie. I decided to give it a good run. I'd already made the 36-hole cut. I stroked it beautifully and it slammed into the back of the hole, popped up like it might escape the hole, rolled around and then dropped in. My fourth birdie of the round!

Caroline put two fingers in her mouth and generated a jarringly loud whistle. Given the rigid decorum of professional golf, I should have been upset by her antics that day. But I wasn't at all. I was proud of her. We had fun together and as a result I played much better. I had shot a 67 in the second round for a two-round total of 142. I would have been even more excited if I hadn't seen the scoreboard: the Leader, Mr. Palmer, was still a massive 10 strokes ahead of me, at 132.

After I signed my scorecard, I found Caroline dozing in a metal lounge chair by the practice range. The poor thing looked so worn out.

Before I left that day, I had to find someone, anyone, who could caddie for me tomorrow. I went into the caddies' room and was penning a note to post on the bulletin board with my name and phone number, when I noticed this mountainous, but forlorn figure seated in a corner. I nodded at him. He waved back.

I walked over to him. "Are you a caddie?"

"Like to be sir but no one's hired me."

I sized him up. He was mid-thirties. Had a slightly crooked nose that looked like it had been broken--several times. He wore his sandy hair in a bristly crew cut. He had to be at least 250 pounds. His arms were enormously muscular. He looked absurd sitting in the narrow plastic chair.

"What's your name?"

"Sheboygan."

"That's a place."

"I go by Sheboygan." There was annoyance in the way he said that. I had to make a decision.

"If you're here by 9AM, you're hired. My name is Tom Colt."

The big man's face lit up with gratitude.

"I know who you are, sir."

I left, put my clubs in the trunk of my embarrassing old car and went to retrieve my drowsy sister Caroline.

"Do you have your car?"

"No parking nearby. Took the city bus."

"You can come home with me. We'll grill some steaks and you can see my new place."

"Red meat. You're buying. I'm there."

She kind of sleepwalked to my car and fell asleep, complete with loud snoring, on the drive uptown to my place. Uptown. That sounded so good to me, to say that.

Three glasses of wine and medium-rare tri-tip steak revived my energy-depleted sister. We sat on the patio and chatted. For once, we had a non-confrontational evening.

I said, "You saved this week for me. Because you were there, I remembered this game should be fun."

"And I got to meet THE MAN, A.P."

"I'm sure he will remember meeting you."

"I work hard at being memorable."

***

I slept great and got up at 5:30. It was still dark when I stepped outside and retrieved the morning paper. Yes, I admit I wanted to see if there was any mention of my hot round in the sports pages.

I poured myself a cup of strong coffee and opened the paper to the sports section. I saw the golf columnist had indeed included...us.

> *Local favorite young Tom Colt rebounded from a dismal first round with a crisp, nearly flawless 67 to easily qualify for the final two rounds of the Phoenix Open Invitational. He was greatly assisted by his new caddie, a cute, leggy, demonstrative young gal who became a crowd favorite from the first tee on as she exhorted the gallery to cheer for her boss. This duo put on a great show for the patrons, one and all.*

Caroline padded in on bare feet, desperately in need of coffee. She was still wearing my college sweatshirt as a nightshirt. The sunshine and fresh air from the previous day seemed to have done her some good. She displayed the beginnings of some color on her face, not her usual vampire-ish child of the night pallor.

She sat down with her coffee. "Mornin'," I said.

"I am sore in places I didn't know I had."

I handed her the paper. "Read the sports column."

She did. She smiled. "Our act got good reviews. He said I was cute and leggy!"

"You are. The newspaper editor evidently took out the 'pain in the ass' part. Space constraints and all."

She grinned, then frowned. "But what is this shit at the end. You're not my boss."

"Focus on the cute and leggy part. And you enjoyed entertaining the fans."

"I really, really did. I felt like...me."

As for myself, I simply felt pumped up, more hopeful than ever. I was convinced the worst was over for my sister. Her life would be on the upswing from now on.

I was wrong.

***

When I arrived at Phoenix Country Club for the 3rd round, I was relieved to see my new caddie Sheboygan waiting by the pro shop, smoking a cigar, still looking morose, though.

That day I was not quite as sharp as in the 2nd round--I hit two loose shots that led to bogies on the front 9. Sheboygan did just fine as my caddie. He was a taciturn fellow to be sure. I don't think he said two words the whole afternoon. But he understood the etiquette of pro golf, the little things like when to remove the flagstick from the hole, where to stand when a player is putting. He didn't seem to know the course very well, though, and didn't help me read the break in the greens. Fine by me. I don't need a caddie for that. I can read the greens incorrectly and miss critical putts all by myself, thank you very much.

Sheboygan was certainly polite, but terribly subdued, almost beaten down. Several times I glanced over at him and he had an anguished expression on his face. I wondered what his story was, the origin of his apparent demons.

On the 14th hole I noticed an enormous throng of people, buzzing with enthusiasm, marching down the adjacent hole. It seemed like 10,000. This could mean only one thing in 1962--Arnold Palmer was playing that hole. His fans were so numerous and loyal that the press eventually gave them a name: Arnie's Army.

I estimated about 75 fans were following my group. No worries. I always preferred quality over quantity.

My group had to wait a few minutes on our tee because the group in front of us featured two of the most notoriously slow players on tour. We nicknamed them Sloth and Slug. While I watched the crush of enthusiastic spectators around

Palmer, I could think of only one thing: money in my pocket. This man was causing a boom in popularity for our sport, or our game as some insist on calling it. Trust me, it's a sport.

My score for the day was still respectable, an even par 71. But it was an up and down day, 5 birdies and 5 bogies. If I'm ever going to win out here, I have to keep The Bogey Man away. He visits me much too often.

When I finished, I told Sheboygan that he did a fine job, and asked him if he could caddie for me next week in Tucson. His reaction was peculiar, to say the least.

He almost started to cry. In a breaking voice, he said: "Thank you so much sir. I am so grateful sir. Yes, sir, I will be there."

As we parted ways, I saw him take a white handkerchief out of his pocket and wipe his eyes. Odd duck, this Mr. Sheboygan.

I saw my sister and her apparently new best friend Jilly Flannery, coming happily down the cart path toward me.

Jilly beamed at me, "Another nice round. Good work, Tom!"

"Okay, Tom Colt Fan Club members, what did I shoot?"

Caroline cast a sly glance toward the scoreboard but she's a little nearsighted and had to squint. Ha! Busted, Sis.

"A smooth effortless 71," she said.

"Smooth, eh? Actually I had a roller coaster round of 5 birdies and 5--"

Jilly burst in, "Oh, Tom you should've seen the 5-iron Arnie hit on the 9th hole. It was like quail high, bored through the wind, moving inexorably toward the defenseless flagstick."

I had my hands on my hips. "Inexorably. Wow."

It was Caroline's turn to gush, "The ball landed on the green twenty feet past the hole and then backspin pulled it down 3 feet away for an easy birdie." She mimed a yo-yo snapping back. "His iron shots have been spectacular this week."

"You are so right, girlfriend," Jilly gushed.

Then the most annoying part: they both giggled like schoolgirls. I was getting pissed. Or was it simple jealousy? The Fan Club finally picked up on this.

Jilly said: "We were just cutting through his gallery and happened to see the shot. Shortest way to the refreshment stand."

Caroline said: "The hot dogs the Thunderbirds serve here are the best."

I couldn't really be mad at them. Sometimes when my round was finished, I went out and watched the truly great players, too. I liked to study the graceful swings of Sam Snead and the Old Smoothie himself, Julius Boros. Watching them helped me focus on better rhythm in my own swing, which tended to get choppy, even wild, when I was under tournament stress.

Jilly said she had to be off. Party at the VonEssen's tonight.

Caroline stayed with me. "I like Jilly," she announced. "She knows words like 'inexorably', as in Tom Colt's ball headed inexorably for the water hazard on the 13th hole. She's a clear upgrade over the usual blonde ditzes you sleep with."

I must've looked peeved.

"No denials. I'm your twin. I know everything."

She gave me a conciliatory hug. "I'll be in your gallery tomorrow for sure. You're only 10 strokes behind the top golfer in the world with 18 holes left. You can do it, kid!"

"Oh, just shut up."

I could tell she was still giggling as she walked to the bus stop.

I had one more agenda item on my list for that day. Call it scouting the opposition. I wanted to watch a tour rookie whose debut had generated an incredible amount of hoopla, a 22-year-old from Ohio named Jack Nicklaus. I was able to catch the last four holes of his fourth round that day. He was a chunky, serious-looking young guy who wore his blondish hair slicked back. I had never seen him play. Nicklaus had one of the best amateur records in history, but his college career began after mine had ended.

I could see what the buzz was about. He had an enormously powerful but controlled swing. I had never seen more leg power in a golf swing than he was able to generate. But what really impressed me was that he didn't have that tentative, uncertain look most rookies have. (Hell, I still have that look at times).

There was clear purpose to everything Jack did on the golf course. He was a man who was out there to win and believed he would win. As he finished his round, I, Tom Colt, pronounced Jack Nicklaus THE REAL DEAL. I'm certain had he known this, he would've been terribly excited.

In the fourth round the next day, I played well but got a few bad bounces on the fairways and a few too many near-misses on the greens. My score was 72, one over par. Rain began to fall on the back 9, and I faded a bit with two bogies. I won $608.

Young Jack Nicklaus finished second that week, a fine finish for a rookie, to be sure. But Arnold Palmer won by a truly amazing twelve shots, finishing with a fabulous 4th round 66 despite the steady rain. For now, it was Arnold Palmer's world. And lesser pros like Tom Colt were just lucky enough to be along for the sweet ride that was to come.

***

For my part, I was glad my hometown tournament was over. Too much pressure playing in front of everyone you know. I was invited to an after-tournament party at a local restaurant. I was dog-tired and thought about begging off.

But in the end, I went ahead and showed up. It always sobered and even scared me when I reflected upon how seemingly small decisions like whether to attend a party or not can completely change the direction of your life.

Chapter Eleven
Tom Makes a Successful Singing Debut
Love Blooms at the Tiki Lounge

An after-tournament party, one of several around the city, was held in the lounge, called the Tiki room, at the Islands Restaurant on 7th Street. This was a hugely popular Polynesian-themed eatery. When I walked in, I thought, *whoever designed and decorated this restaurant was a wizard.* You felt as though you are at the real beach. I half-expected to find sand in my shoes when I got home.

That's why I loved my home city, Phoenix. So much about it was new, exciting and unexpected. The weather and many of the girls here were gorgeous. Now, if I could just learn to consistently make 10-15 foot putts, my life would be perfect.

That night, I anticipated a meet-and-greet style party with maybe a buffet set up. Instead it was a sit-down dinner, the invited guests seated at cocktail tables dispersed around the room. The entertainment was to be provided by an all-girl band, *The Loose Impediments.* I'd heard of them; they performed at the hotels and bars at the golf tournament venues across the West. Lots of guys raved about how good the band was. We shall see.

The hostess put me at a small table near the stage. I felt oddly self-conscious being there by myself. The melancholy thought crossed my mind that I hadn't had a steady girlfriend since the break-up of my marriage to Mandy. Oh well. And neither member of the Tom Colt Fan Club could join me that night.

I ordered a teriyaki steak kabob entree and of course a draft beer. I saw a few of my fellow golf pros there, but none of the top-5 finishers in this week's tournament, in keeping with the old golfing adage: Winners Tire, Losers Don't.

I saw that two tables over from me were Sen. Luck and his bride Lisa. Neither looked too happy. So why were they there? One of my gifts, or perhaps curses, was a superior sense of hearing. In a crowded room like this one I could overhear conversations five tables away from me.

Sen. Luck got up and walked over to where Carter VonEssen was seated, sans his wife Babs, but with a young woman I didn't recognize. The Sen. turned on that fake-politician smile he excelled at. "Carter, just wanted to thank you for that contribution. Much appreciated. I've been facing an uphill battle with my campaign."

Carter looked furtive as he said, "Glad to do it, Senator." Sen. Luck returned to his seat. This conversation seemed odd because Carter VonEssen was a stalwart and top contributor in the opposition party.

I also noticed, to my surprise, seated in the back observing was my ex-wife's new husband, Marco Greene. He was reputed to be what they called at the time "an organized crime figure." He sure looked the part. Tough guy with short wiry hair, steely eyes, pock-marked complexion, either from raging youthful acne or very small caliber bullet holes. No matter his chosen occupation, he seemed to take very good care of my ex-wife Mandy, which I was grateful for. She needed more financial security than I was able to provide her.

My steak kabobs arrived. They were pretty good, except their version of teriyaki sauce was far too sweet. I'm sorry to be such a harsh food critic but my mom was, her catering clients agreed, the best cook in the entire world. If I could golf like my mom cooks, I'd win every tournament I entered.

Eating the food was an excellent cover for my observing other goings-on that night. I saw the odious little lawyer Les Levine leaning over our Club President Wes Stoneman's shoulder. They were in a quiet but intense conversation.

I was eating too fast; a holdover from childhood when I wasn't sure when our next meal would be. I stopped and sipped the beer. Lisa Luck got up and went over to a table where three young men were seated. She hissed at one of the men, "Not another dime." I later learned that young man was her brother-in-law, Jordan.

I visited the rest room and when I returned and passed by the Luck table, Lisa gave me a friendly little wave. When I got close enough she said, "Great tournament, Tom. And thanks for helping me so much with my game."

I nodded and smiled. "The pleasure is all mine," was all I could think of to say as I wondered, What exactly is her game?

I returned to my table. The band's gofers--or I guess what they are called, roadies--were setting up for the performance to come. I moved to another chair at my table so I could see the stage better. My back was now to the Lucks. The Sen. had the kind of voice you remembered, through much practice I'm sure he sounded authoritative but sincere and approachable. He was sincerely and authoritatively pissed off at poor Lisa.

"Oh, now the golf pro is one of your conquests," he barked.

That be me.

She purred: "Tom does like a hands-on approach to teaching."

For reasons I could not fathom, lovely Lisa told a fib. I'd never laid a golf glove on her.

She clearly enjoyed baiting her husband. I started to look at things from his point of view and wonder why he stayed with her. Then it became clear: a divorce would tank his campaign. I hoped she would stop asking me to teach her the great game of golf. The Luck family, as a whole, were not folks I wanted to associate with. I couldn't explain why at the time, but I thought they were dangerous people, emotionally if not physically.

When the band, *The Loose Impediments*, took the stage, I forgot all about these unpleasant individuals. Because the lead singer was, to my joyful surprise, none other than Judge Wilkinson's daughter, Julia. The crowd seemed to know her: they cheered enthusiastically when Julia stepped up to the microphone stand.

When a man sees an extraordinarily beautiful woman for the first time, his reaction can be centered in one particular organ. Or his entire body can become animated with renewed energy, quickening hopes. For me, it was definitely the latter. Seeing Julia up close for the first time, I felt almost feverish.

She had wavy blonde hair styled with an exciting flip where it kissed her shoulders. It was actually rose-gold colored hair that shone exquisitely in the lights above the little stage. She was wearing a soft white turtleneck sweater, without a bra, to the delight of the gentlemen in the room. Her breasts were, well, awesome, with a bounce that matched the rhythm of her songs.

She had deep blue, expressive eyes. Her face was perfectly proportioned. High cheekbones. Lush lips. I saw no flaw worth mentioning except a small scar on her chin. Her dark blue skirt was well above the knee. Her legs were as lovely as the rest of her.

A cute touch for this all-girl band was that they wore golf shoes with the spikes on the soles removed.

She also had that performer's ability to take command of the stage. She drank in the generous applause. "Thank you so much! My name is Julia. On the keyboards we have Kristen. Sara is our fabulous lead guitarist with Gracie doing double duty on the guitar and the tenor sax."

I imagine the other girls were attractive. But I saw only Julia.

Her first song was a country standard about a young woman who laments her true love is gone too much because of his love for his rodeo career, but she pledges they will soon be together. Oddly for a country song, there was no mention of trucks, beer, guns or dogs in the lyrics.

She sang the song looking directly at me. My little fever continued to grow. Julia had a surprisingly strong voice, no problem with any note on the musical scale. But it was the combination of her vocal quality and her repertoire of emotive facial expressions that kept everyone's attention riveted on her. She acted out the stories in her songs with tremendous passion, like she had lived them.

The song ended and the audience cheered for a good thirty seconds. She smiled with humble appreciation. *The Loose Impediments* performed four more songs in their first set, then the lights went dark and they took a break.

A waitress came by and asked the band members if they wanted anything. "A Jack Daniels on the rocks," Julia said.

Impressive, I said to myself. This was a very healthy, very confident All-American girl of the exciting '60s. During the break I went outside to get some cool, fresh air. Doctors Hospital had just opened on 20th Street and Thomas Road, with state-of-the-art diagnostic equipment and each room outfitted with TV, radio and intercom. I wondered if they had a ward to treat hopeless romantic cases like me. I had fallen in love with Julia in a matter of 27 minutes.

I returned and so did the band. As I took my seat, I saw Julia writing something on a small piece of paper. She performed several beautiful ballads in the second set. For the last song of the set, Julia said, "As you *Loose Impediments* fans know, I like to invite an audience member up on stage to sing a duet with me."

The audience got very quiet, serious stage fright breaking out.

"Hmmmm...whom to choose," she said as she scanned the crowd.   She looked at me. "We have our very own Tom Colt in the audience tonight, fresh off a great finish in the Phoenix Open Invitational."

A voice in the back shouted, "Colt finished 16 strokes behind the winner!" Some chuckles broke out. I knew that voice. One of my fellow tour pros, Rodney Burkett, a sourpuss golfer from England. He was a dick to be paired with in a tournament, a dick to the fans, and a dick to his lovely wife. I have no info on what his dog felt about him.

Julia came to my defense. "Thing is, golf is a difficult game. I don't play the game myself, but I love to watch." She ran her tongue lightly over her lower lip, then over her upper lip. The effect on the men in the audience was quite extraordinary. There were cheers and catcalls, like might be heard at a strip joint over on Washington Street.

"Come on up, Tom!" she reached out her beautiful, ring and gold bracelet bejeweled hand and I stepped on stage. A few people applauded, but just a few.

Curiously, I was not in panic mode. Looking into Julia's eyes removed all doubts I had, about anything.

"I'll bet you know the words to *Fly Me to The Moon*, sung to perfection by Miss Peggy Lee."

I said, "One of my favorites. I've played it a hundred times." How did she know I have that album? Had she been in the guest house when I wasn't there?

To the band, "All right then, on 3. 1, 2, 3."

I leaned into the mic and sang with her. I have no idea whether I had a good singing voice or not. I did that night. What I will never forget is when she took my hand, we looked into each other's eyes as we sang. For that brief time, it was as though Julia and I were the only ones in the room.

Too soon, the song was over. The crowd actually applauded and cheered--us. I had the same feeling I get when I sink a 75-foot putt for an eagle. Julia and I, still holding hands, turned toward the crowd and took our bows. She let go of my hand, took the piece of paper out of her skirt pocket and pressed it into my hand.

She looked over at me. "Hey everyone, an extra round of applause for Tom Colt. A name to remember. And doesn't he have a nice singing voice?"

And then I blurted out, "You are unbelievably talented and gorgeous."

Not missing a beat, she turned to the audience, and in a May West-y voice said, "I like a man who knows what he likes and likes what he sees in me."

More laughter and applause. "Thank you, Tom." Julia gave me a chaste kiss on the cheek and I sat back down.

I opened the folded paper she had given me and read it: "I'm in Room 212 at the hotel across the street. Would love to get to know you better. I'll be there 30 minutes after the show."

Get to know you better, I repeated to myself. No need for me to supply a vivid description of the glorious images that passed through my 27-year-old mind.

I slugged down the rest of my beer. Being a singing star, even a local one, makes you thirsty.

The band played a half-dozen more songs. Julia sang several love ballads to me. Only to me--as I innocently believed. If the note from Julia had told me to put my golf clubs in the dumpster out back and come backpacking with her across India, I surely would have.

Their performance ended. *The Loose Impediments* got a standing O from the crowd as they left the stage. Julia and the other girls beamed. They had as much fun performing as we did listening to them. We all paid our dinner tabs and the crowd slowly dispersed.

I went outside, puffed on a cigarette, unsuccessfully trying to look cool doing it, especially when I coughed a few times. I asked myself why Julia spent the night after a gig at a hotel rather than just driving the 30 minutes or so back to her family manse. I speculated that she might be too wired after performing to just go home and go to bed. I already knew the Judge was an early-to-bed, early riser. Many mornings I heard his car roar by at 6AM or earlier, on his way to fresh business conquests.

I don't remember walking through the cool night air, finding the hotel, then the elevator and going up to the second floor. My memory starts when the elevator door opened and I saw Julia, walking in bare feet from the ice machine, carrying a bucket. She had changed into a t-shirt and short shorts.

She looked extremely happy to see me. "Tom, you're here! I needed some ice to cool myself down after the show. They keep this hotel way too hot, don't you think."

"Hot," I agreed. I was pleased I wasn't the only one sweating. One might have concluded I was falling in love with her. Wouldn't that be silly of One.

She opened the door to her room, stepped in and I followed her. It was a suite, with a living area and a bedroom/bathroom in a room to the side. The suite was fresh and new and decorated in that generic mid-century modern mundane hotel style.

"Have a seat. Like a drink?"

"Anything cold."

She had a second bucket with ice and drinks chilling. She pulled out a bottle of Blatz beer and gave it to me along with a bottle opener. She made herself another Jack Daniels on the rocks and sat down next to me on the couch. I recalled that when she was onstage she barely took a sip of her drink. She just liked the flavor, I guess.

"Here's to neighbors becoming friends," she said. It was still hard to believe I was living next door to this perfect young woman. I clinked my bottle to her glass.

I hadn't any idea what was going to happen that night when I came up the elevator. I felt such passion, such warm emotion when we sang together. I wondered what she felt. But then when I saw her in the hallway, something extraordinary occurred: I realized and I believe Julia did, too, that we had made a connection that night. We already understood each other, already were friends. This wasn't exactly a date, to be sure, but there was none of that first date awkwardness between us.

So what did we do that night? We stayed up to 3AM. Talking. Yes, talking.

After she got me a second beer, she noticed I was uncomfortable in my wool slacks and sport coat. "I'm sorry I don't have anything cooler for you to put on. Probably wouldn't fit you."

"Wait here. I have a suitcase full of clothes in the trunk of my car."

She laughed. I loved the melody of her laugh--full, vivacious. "You golfers are such vagabonds. You carry all your worldly possessions in the trunk of your car."

"We have to. A tournament might break out at any time."

That melodic, seductive laugh again.

I retrieved a light cotton sweatshirt and my gym shorts from my car, changed in her bathroom. "That's much better," I said, as I sat back down.

"I've wanted to get to know you since you moved into the guest house. My father is quite taken by you."

"It was a wonderful thing, what he did for me."

Her sunny expression seemed to darken for an undiscernible reason. "You'll have to learn to tell him 'no' sometimes. He's used to ordering everyone about, including me."

"He hasn't asked me to do anything illegal," I joked, but Julia winced when I said it. I decided to change the subject.

She picked up on my wish and put music on her record player.

She got up off the couch and gently tugged at my hand. We danced and sung to the song we had sung together just two hours earlier: *Fly Me to The Moon.* Sung much better by Sinatra when he recorded it in '64 than Tom Colt did in '62. But then again, I'm the one with Julia in his arms, holding her as close as I could except for the natural barrier of her large breasts.

"They've been that way since 10th grade," she commented.

"I knew I went to the wrong high school."

We danced to several more tunes, soft romantic ones, holding each other in a warm embrace. I felt as though I was visiting heaven.

Then we went back to the couch and talked some more. At 1AM we ordered cheeseburgers. She went after her burger like she was starving.

I told Julia my life story. She told me hers. She began to cry when she talked about her brother's death, but quickly rallied out of it. I saw she was a woman of great emotional strength.

She pulled her feet up and under her on the couch. "You are so different from the other men I know."

"Better looking probably," I said.

She smiled. "You seem grateful--grateful to my father, grateful I invited you here tonight, grateful for the fans who cheer for you at the tournaments."

"I guess it's because I am. Things I've worked hard to achieve are starting to become possible."

"I watched a little of your round on Friday. You seemed so happy to be entertaining the people."

"You were there!" I said with much too much excitement.

"I do wish you'd tone down your caddie a bit. Father doesn't approve of that kind of behavior on the course."

"I've been trying for 27 years. She's my twin sister."

"Ah. Just stay as you are, stay grateful. I've dated so many men who take everything for granted, including me."

"I can't imagine taking you for granted. I feel like we have begun a friendship already, starting when we sang together tonight."

She smiled, but it was an enigmatic smile. I wasn't sure she agreed.

I made a visit to the bathroom. When I came back out, Julia was lying on the king bed, pillows fluffed up against the headboard. I joined her. She seemed to be getting drowsy, maybe coming off that performer's high they speak of.

"Stay the night, please. I don't want to be alone. And you make me feel...safe."

Don't have to ask me twice. I sat next to her on the bed. We leaned against each other and talked some more. She asked me what I dreamed about for my future. I desperately wanted to tell her that my dream had arrived that night, but I pulled back and said, "I don't have just one dream, I have a bag full."

"How big a bag," she said as she snuggled closer. "Like the huge golf bags the pros use?"

We both laughed contentedly and started to fall asleep. Maybe I just imagined it, but I thought I heard her say, very softly, "Make room in your dreams for me."

One of us got up, sometime during the night and shut off the lights in the hotel suite. It was a perfect evening, except I so wanted to kiss her, it almost hurt.

***

When I got up at 6:30, Julia was dressed and nearly packed. She gave me a quick, and I thought, weak smile. "So much to do today! A radio interview in an hour, we have rehearsal at noon. I need to look at new costumes."

I took the hint and quickly dressed.

"Last night was so much fun, thank you, Julia."

She nodded. She seemed so cool this morning. Did she regret last night?

"I guess I will see you at home," she said, levelly, without much enthusiasm.

And so I left. I walked back to my car in a befuddled state. I stopped at a pancake joint and loaded up on bacon, flapjacks and syrup. Julia is a complicated woman, I concluded as I finished the last bite. Not the most brilliant deduction by the young detective.

***

For a golf pro, Monday could be a travel day to the next tournament, or for me this particular week, it was a day to prep for the short drive to Tucson on Tuesday afternoon. I knew the course so well--it had been a venue for a number of my collegiate tournaments--I didn't need to go down early to practice. I would get in a practice round on Wednesday.

I drove down to Goldwaters department store in Scottsdale and picked out two new outfits to wear on tournament days. Yes, that store was owned by the same Goldwater family that included Sen. Barry Goldwater, who ran for President in 1964.

My only criticism of the men's clothes selection there was that they came in colors that were too muted. I suddenly had the urge to add more color to my wardrobe, to stand out more. I made a mental note to ask Doug Sanders where he bought his clothes. He and Jimmy Demaret were known as the most colorfully dressed golf pros. You have to work at being snazzy.

My favorite brands at the time were Munsingwear 'grand slam' golf shirts and IZOD/Lacoste shirts. Wearing new, classy clothes made me feel like, almost like, I was worthy, I belonged on the professional golf tour and at the fine country clubs where many of our tournaments were held. But it was odd it took Penguin and Alligator logos on my shirts to help me feel that way. What an insecure lad I was back then. Maybe I still am. Do we ever really change?

I also did an equipment check. That didn't take long. We're not skydivers or mountain climbers after all. I mainly removed dried sweat and dirt on the leather grips of my golf clubs. Guess which of my clubs had the most sweat on it? The putter, of course.

I also replaced all of the critical items that Caroline had tossed out of the bag. Nothing wrong with a grown man having lucky charms in his golf bag, Dear Sister.

Golfers are known to have peculiar superstitions regarding equipment. I always carried exactly 7 golf balls in my bag to begin a tournament. I believed it was a lucky number. I also began each tournament with a brand-new white golf glove. Being right-handed I wore the glove on my left hand. On the morning of the last round of the tournament, I tossed that glove away and put on a new one. This reminded me that the final round of an event was when we earned our money. I needed my focus as sharp as possible.

On Monday night I sat on the patio of the guest house and took stock of the last week. All in all, not bad:

-- I now had a Fan Club albeit a tiny one. Palmer has Arnie's Army. I have Tom's Terrific Twosome.

-- I had solved one of the two thorny problems I had with my game that kept me from winning on tour: consistently accurate tee shots.

-- I made a new...friend, unlike any woman I had ever met before.

As thrilled as I was with my relationship with Julia, I tried to be realistic. She probably would not be seriously interested in me. We came from different worlds. Being socially successful in her world required lots of money. Sorta eliminates me as a suitor for Julia Wilkinson.

I pulled my putter out of the golf bag, took three balls and went out to the little putting green by the pool. The porch light was sufficient for me to get some practice time in. I was too young to have the dreaded putting disease golfers call "the yips", but I had a variant of it. I never felt comfortable when I was faced with a putt of 10 feet or less.

Good golf at the professional level is partially a matter of overcoming embarrassment--your flubs and mistakes are there for the world to see. I've tried to self-diagnose why missing a short putt caused me the most embarrassment, and therefore put the most pressure on me when I got ready to hit the putt. I couldn't reach any conclusion that would help me solve the problem. We didn't have golf psychologists in those days. Couldn't afford 'em, anyway.

I was musing over this, which led to thinking about the larger issue of how so much of life involves struggle, striving, failing, falling down, picking yourself back up, struggling some more, praying, hoping--but once in a glorious while everything you've ever dreamed of finds you, walks up your path without you even having asked.

On this chilly (for Arizona at any rate) late winter night, down the serpentine pebbled concrete path that led from the main house, came a barefooted Julia. She was wearing a purple gauzy nightgown. As she walked through the little lights that lined the path, and the gown swayed in the soft breeze, I saw flashes of her perfect legs.

Julia was carrying a bottle, Jack Daniels I would guess. She didn't look the least bit cold. I imagined that she was warmed by her tremendous enthusiasm for life, her desire to experience every adventure available to her.

Seeing this beautiful and confident woman coming up the path to see only me, wasn't the best moment in my life, but it was in the TOP 5.

"Thought you might like some company," she said as she arrived on the putting green.

"You were right."

She led me inside. Opened a cabinet, selected a record album from my small collection and started up the record player.

The couch in my (I mean the Judge's) living room was a large, green leather one. Julia sat on it, then leaned back and pulled up her nightgown.

"I want you Tom. Right here. Right now."

My heart began to pound when I saw the glimpse of rose-gold between her legs. Almost as though she planned it, the beckoning glimpse was illuminated by the kitchen light.

I was never one to ignore an urgent beckoning. This magnificent girl and I, my girl I boldly and foolishly asserted to myself, made love. Nice and easy alternating with hungry and passionate. She modulated effortlessly between tender and fiery, softer and cooler. We prolonged the ultimate moment until the last possible moment, then she looked at me with soft, deeply contented eyes. I imagine I looked at her with wonder.

On that evening we were both in the exact physical prime of our lives, but we exhausted ourselves.

"Glad I came over tonight?"

"I don't know. What do you think?" I brushed a damp strand of hair from her eyes.

She laughed softly.

Maybe at that moment there was a yellow caution flag somewhere in my head, but I didn't notice it. I reveled in the runaway feelings of ecstasy the two of us had created that night.

We got off the couch. She adjusted her flowy nightgown and went into the kitchen. She quickly found glasses in the cupboard and poured us each her favorite drink. I thought it strange she didn't ask me if I wanted it. I was never a whisky drinker. My putting stroke was shaky enough without strong booze.

I watched her admiringly, perhaps trying to memorize how she looked that night. In case the moment didn't last past this night.

She handed me the glass and walked over to the window overlooking the pool. She took a sip of her scotch on the rocks. "Imagine the fun you and I can have out there when the water warms up in April."

"I do. And I have an active imagination." I walked closer to her and leaned against the wall. Maybe I was feeling a little unsteady. "I believe we started something special tonight, something we both were looking for."

"MMMM," she purred as she sipped her drink, then put the cold glass against her cheek.

What I had said was the kind of hopeful idiocy that comes out of a boy's mouth after sex with a dream girl. I wish I could go back now and edit that premature ejaculation of true love. But once you say something aloud, the words live on forever.

Julia's eyes ranged over me, searched me. I got the horrible feeling that she was deciding whether I was good enough for her.

She took my hand and led me outside. We parted on the path that led her back home. A last kiss for the evening.

"Sweet," was all she said. I watched her walk back through the soft lights of the winding path, until Julia finally disappeared into the darkness, like a mirage.

I went back inside, flopped down on the now-legendary couch and thought, *the calendar hasn't even turned to spring, and '62 is already a helluva year.*

***

The drive down on Tuesday gave me a chance to reflect on my brief but emotionally powerful time with Julia. She seemed a little cool, a little distant when she went home on Monday night. With my characteristic insecurity, I wondered if she regretted coming over. I tried to banish such unhelpful thoughts. But she hadn't said anything about being available to see me in Tucson, where her band had another gig scheduled for Friday and Saturday nights.

I'd never stayed out late while competing in tournaments, but I'd never had a chance to stay out late with Julia Wilkinson before. I was in a new world, even though I wasn't quite sure how I got there.

I checked into my hotel, a motor lodge style place near the freeway. Many of the B-list pros stayed there. It was reasonably clean and CHEAP. Just how I like my hotels. The lock on the door even worked. That wasn't always the case in these '60s motor lodges, which often had more resident roaches than paying customers.

I unpacked and went down to the tiny lobby to get some ice. The desk clerk saw me and said, "Mr. Colt, an envelope just came for you."

I opened it. A note in a feminine hand: "No, no, no. You're not staying in that dump. That's where the caddies stay. Come over to my suite at the Desert Star. I promise you will be more comfortable. The more comfortable you are, the better you will play. The better you play, the happier my father will be." The note was signed with a flourishing, abundantly confident J.

"Golly," I said out loud.

"Everything all right. Sir?"

"Oh, yes, but I'll be checking out. Now."

And I vowed that was the last time I would check into a dumpy motel. I wasn't at the top of the mountain yet, but my climb was gaining traction. I felt more sure-footed every day, in no small measure because of remarkable Julia.

I saw the evening paper being delivered to the check-in desk and fished out a dime to buy one. I took it up to my room and re-packed. I noticed something at the bottom of the front page that caught my eye. A dead man had been found, shot to death, on the farming land south of Tucson. The article said he was a Mexican national. The property where he was found was owned by the Lucato Family Vineyards, whoever they were.

Sometimes in the sheltered world of sports we forget it's a dangerous world out there.

***

I knocked on the door to Julia's room at the newer, much spiffier, grander hotel where she was staying. "

"Who is it?"

"Your neighbor. I wondered if I could borrow a cup of sugar."

I heard her laugh. "Are you sure one cup will be enough?"

She turned the knob and opened the door. She was wearing a man's large sized light blue dress shirt, buttons open and white panties. The coolness of our parting on Monday was gone. Her smile, which reached all the way to her large, deep ocean-blue eyes, was almost aggressive in its brightness.

"Isn't this better?" she said, indicating the room, but that was only part of the reason for my enthusiasm at being there.

I stepped inside to a large room decorated in the color palette of the Southwest, orange, yellow, sienna, turquoise, rose. The bedspread, curtains and wallpaper carried the colorful theme forward. The furnishings were sturdy, elegant yet rustic, fashioned from wood native to the desert. It was a hotel room for an Indian Chief who was having a prosperous year in the cattle business.

She and I kissed, a sweet and warm pressing of the lips.

Julia asked: "Are you hungry, tired, thirsty?"

"No, no and no."

"Good because I've been thinking about us, and nothing but us, since we parted. What an unforgettable night we had!"

I was overwhelmed. It was like a guy who grew up eating canned beans now was offered his first platter of filet mignon. Even at only 27, I had gotten used to my dreams not coming true, coming apart at the seams instead. But here was the most beautiful, classy woman I had ever known shedding her shirt and panties and leading me to her bed.

I may have torn several buttons off the light blue cardigan sweater in my haste to remove it and all my other clothes. We jumped into bed and kissed like hungry lovers who had been parted for far too long. What followed was scorching, voracious lovemaking, an eagerness for us to share our youthful bodies. But it was not desperate or fleeting. The communication I got from Julia was that we would be enjoying each other for many, many nights.

Cooling down afterwards, both of us spent by our efforts to please, perhaps to enchant, each other, I said, "What can I tell you. Golfers are athletes."

"So are singers," she added. And I couldn't disagree.

Julia got our energy levels back up by ordering steak sandwiches, cottage fries and ice cream sundaes from room service.

We topped off this splendid evening with Julia running a bath in the enormous tub in the bathroom, setting candles around the edge and inviting me to join her. She dimmed the lights and I sat there contentedly, looking at this incredibly beautiful woman in the flickering candlelight.

"You seem so happy when you look at me."

"It's because you are perfect. And perfection is a rare thing in this world. It's like if I went out tomorrow and birdied all 18 holes."

"My body reminds you of a golf course."

"I didn't express that too well."

She laughed. "You say the oddest things sometimes. But I love our conversations. You can make me laugh, which I appreciate so much. The other men, some make me cry."

"Do you think your father would object to finding out we were..."

"Screwing like there's no tomorrow."

"I was going to say, enjoying the splendor of each other's bodies."

She moved over and leaned against me. I put my arms around her.

"In case you haven't noticed, this is the 1960s, not the Fifties. I am a grown woman who can do whatever she wants, with whoever she wants, whenever she wants."

I thought but did not express, *'cept you still live at home with your dad.*

There was cold irritation in her voice. She didn't like my question at all. It was an attack on the wall of independence she tried to erect around her. But this quickly passed and she said: "Do you think you would be able to splendor me once more tonight?"

***

Later, when I was in the bathroom by myself, I noticed two prescription pill bottles on the counter. I had an urge to look at the labels, but didn't want to snoop. She seemed so healthy (understatement), and in '62 it was unusual for a young person to be taking prescription drugs.

***

The next morning I woke to an empty bed. I threw on my undershorts and walked into the living room. I saw Julia by the front door dressed in a smart-looking navy-blue travel outfit. Was she going to the airport? In those days we dressed up to go on an airplane.

Her suitcases were packed and by the door. She saw me, hesitated a moment and then said, "Change in plans. Sorry. My father called and said a dear old friend of the family is coming to visit. Father wants me to be there. He's sort of been my Godparent."

"What about your band and the weekend gigs?"

"No problem. The bar owner already got a back-up band to fill in."

I must have looked crestfallen.

"Such sad-puppy eyes. I don't like this either. We were having an amazing time. But I'll see you in a week or so."

"A whole week?"

"We may go on a little trip with my father's friend. To Denver."

The melancholy silence that ensued was interrupted by a timely bellboy rapping on the door. Julia opened it, the young man took her luggage and she smiled at me in a way that shattered my disappointment into insignificant little splinters.

"A week goes by fast. See you soon."

And she was gone. I got dressed and ready for the week's work on the links. Something puzzled me, though, and I have a zeal, perhaps a borderline obsession for puzzle solving. I didn't hear the phone ring in the suite that night. The only phone in the suite was on a side table by the bed.

Brooks Continues Our Story...

Tom was lacking two vital pieces of information as he prepared to tee off in the Tucson Open Invitational. Julia was not leaving to see an old friend of her father's. A long-time boyfriend, Derrick Rhodes, scion of a vastly wealthy mining family in Colorado--whose mining claims dated back to frontier times--was flying to Phoenix to see her and take her back to Denver with him. Derrick was a jet-setter before that term came into use. He flew his own plane, searching the country for mining operations to acquire for his family's corporation. He had pursued the elusive rose-golden Julia since 1958. She thought he was a bore, but kept him on the string because she loved the idea of being with a man who had more money than her father.

In a strange coincidence, he and Julia attended the 1960 US Open at Cherry Hills. They even saw an obscure pro named Tom Colt play a few holes. When Julia remarked how handsome Tom was, Derrick gave her a stern reminder that she should have eyes only for him.

She laughed.

Tom also did not know that the prescriptions in Julia's bathroom were issued by her psychiatrist. She had a condition that we now call bi-polar disorder, fortunately a mild case, but it was largely unknown in 1962. In the '50s, sufferers of mental illnesses were given grim treatments such as lobotomies or electro-shock 'therapy'. The prescriptions the Doctor gave Julia were for two new medications just approved to be on the market. He hoped to hell they worked.

***

Dottie Petersen, speechwriter and campaign coordinator for Sen. Richard Luck, was staying in the same hotel as Tom and Julia. But Dottie wasn't there to enjoy the golf tournament. Golf wasn't her sport. Dottie's father, whom she disliked immensely, had taught her golf when she was a teenager and had shown athletic ability.

Her father thought Dottie, tall, gangly, and slightly horse-faced, might benefit from learning a social game like golf. His real concern was that she would never meet a suitor and therefore live with him and her mother FOREVER.

Though she showed promise as a player, Dottie disliked golf as much as she disliked her father. The game, to her, was too slow. She preferred sports with faster, more physical action, such as basketball and racquetball. Her chosen profession reflected this preference. What moves faster and is more hard-fought than a political campaign?

Dottie was in Tucson to address a group of women voters about why Richard Luck would make the greatest US Senator the state ever had.

That day was also her birthday. But no time for celebration. The pace she set for herself was non-stop, exhausting. Every successful campaign has that person who is the driving force and Dottie P, as her friends and colleagues called her, was that person for the Luck Campaign. The other members of the campaign team revered Dottie P--even though she drove them as hard as he did herself. They shared a sense of being on an important mission.

The phone rang in the hotel suite. She answered it. "Happy Birthday, darling!" her mother Stella exclaimed. Dottie brightened hearing her mother's voice. Just as Dottie was Sen. Luck's most devoted and enthusiastic supporter, her mother was to Dottie. Stella, a fine athlete herself, was a physical education teacher at Scottsdale High School.

"Thanks, mom," Dottie said. "I'd almost forgotten what day it was."

"Well, I sure didn't. And I want to wish you a very special day and tell you how proud of you I am. Those speeches you write for Richard are brilliant. He always seemed like a shallow bumbler to me. But with your words coming out of his mouth, he sounds like JFK. You make him shine."

"You underestimate Richard. He's a born leader. I'm honored to be able to help the cause."

"I'd say a born used car salesman, but I didn't call to argue with my smart and dedicated daughter. Please take some time today and have fun."

When the phone call ended, Dottie thought, I have fun every day. *Who has a better job than mine? Or a more wonderful man to work for...*

***

Tom Continues Our Story...

My tee time for Thursday's first round of the Tucson Open at El Rio Country Club wasn't until noon so I had time to recover slightly from spending Wednesday night with Julia. I didn't expect much from my golf that day, but with passion-fueled adrenaline I shot a fine 65 and trailed the eventual winner Phil Rodgers, a tour rookie having a fine season, by only 1 shot. I was pleased when I followed that up with a 68.

On Saturday though, I ran fresh out of adrenaline and deep fatigue set in. I shot a crappy 73, which was really bad on this easy—and boring—course. I rallied on the last day with another 68 but my paycheck was a paltry $120. But something far more important happened: I was certain I had found the woman I was destined to fall in love with.

Chapter Twelve
A Bumpy Landing in Phoenix
A Secret Crush is Revealed

One of the limitations I faced until the Judge generously decided to provide money for my travel expenses on tour, was that I couldn't afford to fly to tournaments. The golf tour circuit ranges across the entire US. The winter tour started in California and Arizona, then moved across the country to Florida and then Texas. Later in the year, we had tournaments in the Midwest and Northeast. Driving long distances to get to events was exhausting. The result was that it limited where it was feasible for me to play, financially and timewise.

But as I began to shed my cheapskate ways I decided to enter a tournament in Florida and take my very first plane ride there and back. Flying was exciting, an event, then. Not the crowded bus- ride-in-the-sky experience with surly, sweaty strangers it is now. No slobs in rumpled t-shirts, baggy shorts and flip flops.

Julia and the Judge didn't come back the following week. That old family friend must be a fascinating fellow. I thought I saw the Judge's car go by a few times, but that could have been Marjorie or the housekeeper going out for supplies.

The tournament I entered was the Pensacola Invitational. Surprisingly, my putting perked up and I finished in a tie for 11th. The grass on the greens in Florida is much different than the grass on the Southwest courses. For some reason, I putted much better. The winner was colorful and popular Doug Sanders, with a great score of 18-under-par 270. He had four rounds in the 60's—three straight 67s and a 69 in the last round.

I shot 70, 69, 69, 70 for a 278 total. I was thrilled to finally be able to play 4 solid rounds in a row. *I can win out here*, I declared to myself as I boarded the plane to return to Phoenix.

As far as my first experience with air travel, I was nervous on the takeoff and landings, but I was proud that I didn't lose my ham and cheese sandwich I ate in the airport before I boarded the plane. At one point the wing dipped noticeably, and the pilot announced in a relaxed fashion: "Just a little turbulence folks, nothing to be worried about." Gripping the armrests tightly seemed the right thing to do. During the flight the co-pilot invited some of the youngsters up to the pilot's cabin and presented them with a pin that said, "Junior Pilot Wings". That was a nice touch.

On landing, I was hoping for a pin from the cute brunette stewardess with the dimpled chin and lively, friendly eyes, named Pauline. Perhaps one that said, '*I Survived My First Plane Ride!*'

All in all, flying was kinda fun. I might try it again in a couple of years.

When I got back to the Wilkinson's, I parked in the driveway of the guest house. As I approached the front door, I heard the sound of laughter coming from the pool behind the house. It sounded like young female laughter. I put my suitcase down by the front door and walked around back.

Playing touchy-feely in the heated water, the steam rising from the surface on this chilly night, were a very naked Julia and a naked guy, a dark haired, hairy chested fellow who looked to be about 10-15 years her senior.

Julia saw me and emitted a squeaky shriek, or maybe it was a shrieky squeak. I hoped she didn't swallow too much pool water in the process. And then, of all things, the guy tried to cover her naked breasts. His small hands weren't quite up to that formidable task.

My initial reaction was stunned, but sadly, not surprised. When the elements of your life so perfectly align that it seems too good to be true, it usually is. I was making birdies in bunches in my life, but eventually, the Bogey Man caught up with me. He always did.

"Tom," Julia exclaimed. "You're back early. Thought it would take a few days for you to--"

"There's this new invention called the Aer-O-Plane."

The guy, who I could tell through the lighted water was starting to shrivel, said, "Who is this, honey?"

"Derrick Rhodes, please meet Tom Colt. He's my father's protégé, who's staying in our guest house. Father sponsors him on the pro golf tour."

The message she wanted to convey was delivered with bull's-eye accuracy. I'm a poor boy getting financial assistance from the Judge. In this fellow's pecking order, I was now placed just above the gardener and the maid.

Then, I could only laugh when the guy piped up with, "You'll kindly avert your eyes from Julia's nakedness."

What kind of pompous asshole talks that way? The answer, a very rich pompous asshole.

I flashed back to something perceptive, savvy Jilly Flannery said, "Then why do you want so desperately to be like us?"

Why, indeed.

My existence on this earth had filled a temporary but apparently powerful need for Julia: she hated to be alone. That was all there was to our 'relationship'.

I said with an ease and levelness that surprised me, "You kids have fun. I'll bunk out tonight."

I remembered the great Ben Hogan would call someone "fella" to make the point that he didn't remember the guy's name.

So I said, "And fella, this time of year the pool water's too cold to advance your cause."

Thanks Mr. Hogan, I thought.

Julia started to sputter some weasel-y words of explanation, but I had no time for it, no interest in it. I walked away, tossed my suitcase back in the trunk of the car, and drove away, not knowing where to go.

Where I went was a lighted golf practice range, open until 11PM, that had just been built between Phoenix and neighboring Tempe, the home of my alma mater, Arizona State University. The glory days of my college team placing second the NCAA Golf Championship seemed like a century ago. I pulled into the parking lot and unloaded my clubs from the trunk.

I was desperately in need of ego boosting. I thought of calling an emergency meeting of the Tom Colt Fan Club, but Jilly Flannery was visiting her sister Janie in Florida, and I had no idea where Caroline was. Sometimes I didn't know whether I had a sister or a cat.

I felt of course like a colossal fool. But I had a haunting feeling that I half-expected something like this to happen with Julia. I'd been building castles in the air and installing Julia in the tower as my Princess. It appears I rescued a witch instead, and she wasn't too happy about being trapped in the castle.

I bought two buckets of practice balls from the young, pimply and disinterested attendant in the little shack at the entrance to the driving range. A cold front was moving in. I felt a light, cold mist falling as I set my golf bag on a stand, laced my golf shoes and put on my glove, simple acts that somehow gave me reassurance that my world was still turning.

Six other people were out there that night, dispersed down the half-moon shaped line. At the far end was a young woman. Watching the various swings, I could tell she was the only accomplished player in the lot besides me.

I hit the first 15 balls in the bucket. It was remarkable how much better I felt. Throughout my life, whenever something disappointing, sad, depressing or unfair happened to me I could find solace with a golf club in my hand. Not just solace but a kind of emotional repair. I re-established my special place in this world when I hit one perfect golf shot after another. My golf skill was not a talent from birth, far from it, but the sum of all the work, all the study, all the sheer exercise of will, of more than a decade. I created my golf skill. It belonged only to me. As the golfers sometimes say, I dug it out of the ground.

What happened tonight at the Wilkinson's Guest House--I would never again refer to it as my pad--quickly was reduced to an absurdity that was retreating from my emotional landscape. I was wrong, actually goofy, to think a girl like Julia from a wealthy family, who enjoyed a privileged upbringing, would ever be seriously interested in a guy from my background. After my father disappeared, my mom and sister and I were so impoverished at times that people like Wilkinson father and daughter would have classified us as poor white trash.

This magical skill I have to hit a golf ball better than almost anyone in America had raised my social standing, but I was still on thin ice, I feared. I had been dropped into the middle of the wealthy and powerful set, without a map or compass.

The time would come, I decided, when the girls from Julia's background would treat me as a potential life partner. As I hit a booming drive that bored through the gloomy night air, I wondered when that day arrives would I still want someone like Julia. Maybe I should marry a woman who understands that life is hard work, and then even harder work, like a waitress.

The mist was thickening into light rain. The other dedicated, though I could tell, not very skilled golfers packed it in for the night and left. I was alone with the woman with the nice swing.

I loved watching other good golfers practice. I often picked up little nuances in the golf swing from watching others. A golf swing is like a patchwork quilt that is never finished.

Thirsty from my practice session, I walked over to the soda machine on her side of the range, to get a bottle of Pepsi-Cola. I found the necessary 5 cents in my pocket. I drank it down and watched her hit a series of very accurate 3-irons. It dawned on me that I knew this tall, slender woman. She was Katrina Stern, who went by Kat, who played on the woman's golf team at Arizona State around the time I competed on the men's.

Her swing was economical, smooth, no wasted motion. She had great control over the ball. Kat was almost Hogan-esque in how she could place her shots on the correct side of the fairway or on the green in a place that gave her the best chance of making the putt.

I had read in the golf weekly and monthly publications, for whatever they're worth, that Kat had won several tournaments but was not a star on the ladies' tour. Writers speculated that she was too cautious--she took the safe, careful route to the green every time. To win a tournament, you have to banish your fears and execute shots that you aren't sure you can carry off successfully. We all have to talk ourselves into believing in ourselves.

Kat's other weakness was lack of length off the tee. In college she was into physical fitness--weight training, stretching, running. But somehow the training didn't translate into generating superior clubhead speed. Watching her that night, her swing seemed a little tight. In a way she was the polar opposite of me. My swing was sheer power. I swung with abandon at times. But my accuracy was suspect, to say the least. That's why I was so excited about how superbly my new driver, #1 wood, was working out.

Kat was dressed in a grey windbreaker and black slacks, now shiny from the mist. She had a pretty face, could've been prettier if she didn't frown so much. I recall she was a very serious girl in college, as both an excellent student and a college golf star. Her long black hair was in a ponytail pulled through a black baseball cap.

I walked a few paces from the soda machine toward her. She finally noticed me. That was another thing I remember about her from college: her focus, her ability to shut out distractions and concentrate was amazing. Another contrast between Kat and the easily distracted, scatterbrained Tom Colt.

"I was just admiring your ball flight, Miss Stern."

She smiled, crossed one foot over the other and leaned on the 3-iron in that cool way golfers do and said, "That's the best opening line I've ever heard, Mr. Colt."

I walked closer to her. "Thank you. I do my best."

"I've heard that about you," she countered, a twinkle of mischief in her unusual green eyes.

She had the trace of a German accent. I remembered she was from Brazil but her family emigrated there from Germany in 1945.

"Working hard, as usual," I said.

"People think the pro golfer's life is all about adoring fans, playing at swank country clubs, the chance for fame and fortune and to be on the cover of sports magazines."

"You mean, it's not?"

"Maybe on the men's tour it is."

"You forgot the parties and the endless parade of hot chicks."

"I wouldn't know about hot chicks."

"I'm glad to hear it."

"What I was getting at, between bouts of banter with Mr. Popularity himself, was that they don't realize success actually comes from dragging your ass out on a cold wet night in February and hitting about a thousand golf balls, because no matter how good you get, it's never good enough."

"Very well said, Miss Stern."

As she spoke, I was thinking, *why are people calling me Mr. Popularity? Is there an article about me I haven't read? I hope the writer said nice things. I wonder what magazine it's in...*

"I know you try for this happy-go-lucky façade, but I remember you from college tournaments. You're just as dedicated to this game as I am."

I tried a quizzical look, with goggle eyes.

"I am? That's good to know."

She flashed a cross look at me.

"Are you making fun?"

I took out the only paper I had in my pocket, my airline ticket from earlier today, scribbled my phone number on it and gave it to her.

"I enjoyed seeing you again. Those college tournaments were a blast! If you want to have dinner sometime, call me. I think we'd have fun talking shop, in this case talking golf shop."

I offered her the paper. She took it without hesitation. "I will give your offer serious consideration."

"Goodnight Miss Stern."

"Goodnight to you, Mr. Colt."

I walked back to my spot on the driving range thinking, *I double doubt this golfaholic gal ever takes time out for a nice long dinner and fascinating conversation with a guy like me. She probably just has vital nutrients injected into a vein and then gets back to hitting golf balls 'til the sun comes up.*

***

Brooks Continues Our Story...

Tom was off the mark on that one, but we might excuse him because of the rough night he had. Katrina Stern had a serious, dreamy crush on him since their college days and kicked herself for never letting him know she was interested in him. He wasn't Mr. Popularity then, far from it. He was kind of shy and unsure of himself and his place in the world. He only seemed confident when he had a golf club in his hand-- except the putter of course.

He didn't have the courage to ask her out back then, either. Years later, Kat had read an interview with Tom in *Championship Golf Weekly* that said his life changed when he played so well in the '60 US Open at Cherry Hills, against two generations of the best players in the world. He began to believe in himself.

After Tom left the driving range, his opinion of the high society life suffering a serious downgrade earlier that evening, he checked into a cheap motel near the Phoenix downtown. Not realizing how exhausted he was, he slept 12 hours. Just before nodding off he made a mental note to ask the Judge's gardener to please drain, sanitize and refill the pool at the guest house.

He'd leave the fellow a $10 tip—of the Judge's money.

Chapter Thirteen
Sheboygan Calls Tom on the Carpet
Tom Draws Four Aces in Vegas

I decided a hiatus from interacting with females would do me a world of good. The next tournament was in a town I'd never been to and where I didn't know <u>any</u> women, Las Vegas.

The tournament was a brand-new event on our schedule, The Vegas Winter Fling Invitational. I thought the name was appropriate given what certain notorious married men are known to do when on a business junket to Vegas, and their wives are left at home.

My inscrutable caddie Sheboygan and I drove to Vegas in separate cars. I still didn't know anything about this guy except that he was an excellent caddie. I had booked us rooms in an inexpensive motor lodge a few miles of from the center of the action in Vegas, the Casinos, or as they were called then Gaming Halls.

When I checked in on Tuesday evening the desk clerk apologized profusely that because of the golf tournament, they had accidentally overbooked the hotel. There was only one room available, for both of us.

When Sheboygan rolled up to the motor lodge, in an ancient Cadillac of all things, with the noisiest engine I had ever heard except at construction sites, he took the news with a shrug. We put our luggage in the room, walked across the highway to a diner-style restaurant.

The big guy devoured a plate of BBQ ribs and ordered a second one. I had a petite filet mignon. This may have been a restaurant in the middle of the empty, dust-blown desert, but the food was excellent. The cook even put a mushroom cap sautéed in garlic butter on the top of my filet. Nice touch. I made a note to tell my mom about it.

I ordered a beer, Sheboygan a Pepsi-Cola. I had never dined with such a non-conversationalist. It made me a little nervous to sit there in silence and listen to a large, muscular creature gnaw on bones.

"You are a fine caddie, Sheboygan."

He gazed at me over the pile of ribs.

"'preciate it."

"You never talk about yourself. What's your story?"

He ripped some flesh off of a rib and looked warily, or was it menacingly, up at me.

"Not much to tell."

"Try me." I sounded insistent.

Now he was definitely irked bordering on angered. Some cave men do not like their gnawing on bones to be interrupted. The clever detective knew this by the emphatic way he tossed the bone back on the platter.

"Played football in college. Was an All-American. Blew out a knee. End of football career. Didn't have anything to do. Hung out with the wrong crowd. One night, police came. I found out my crowd was dope dealers. They arrested me too, just for being there. Did three years. I wasn't Mr. Innocent. I did drugs and alcohol, got in fights."

I didn't know what to say. He continued:

"Tried construction work, but I got knocked in the head so much playing football that the heavy physical work gave me awful headaches. Took up caddying. Toting a golf bag is easy for me. Golfers are strange folks, though."

He took a swallow of Pepsi. "Could we talk about something else? My life isn't very interesting, even to me."

He finished his meal first, went outside and lit up a big stogie. I nursed a cup of coffee and a piece of cheesecake. Telling me his story clearly upset him. I thought he supposed I was now going to fire him because he was an ex-con.

As we walked across the deserted, tumbleweed tossed highway, he turned to me and said, "I knew it was wrong to hang out with that trash but you get injured, everyone forgets you." He paused, puffed. "What really hurt was when they took my All-American Trophy out of the display case while I was doing time. Think the Athletic Director tossed it in the dumpster."

We walked in silence a few moments.

"Would you have hired me if I told you this story that day at Phoenix Country Club?"

"Yes. The young lady caddying for me that day, my twin sister, has been arrested for prostitution."

"You're a good man, Tom. Most people don't like to give you a second chance."

"My father always said, for most of us, life is a series of mistakes. If we're lucky, we survive them." I thought, but did not add, *My dad disappeared in the war when I was 17, so maybe he didn't survive that last mistake, in a country far away.*

Back in the room, Sheboygan went into the bathroom to brush his teeth and clean an amazing amount of encrusted BBQ sauce off his face.

I took my putter and 3 golf balls out of the golf bag along with a putting aid, a metal disk that had a hole in the center about the diameter of a regulation sized hole on a green. And little metal louvers that flipped down and let the ball pass into the cup with a satisfying metallic sound.

I was working on 10-foot putts when Sheboygan came out-- in black and white striped pajamas. He looked like a morbidly overweight zebra. He sat on one of the twin beds I was so thankful our room was outfitted with and watched me. I saw out of the corner of my eye he was shaking his head.

"Yes?" said I.

"You hold the putter too tight. It's not an ax. You aren't chopping wood."

"Uh huh." I hit another ball. No satisfying metallic sound. The misbehaving ball rolled under the bed.

"Caress the ball like a beautiful woman. Think of a busty blonde."

He didn't understand why I then clenched the putter as though having a nervous seizure.

"No, Hoss. Gently, gently."

He stood up with surprising agility for someone who had just eaten 20 lbs. of ribs, took the putter from me in his massive hands and showed me. Three balls into the metal cup, 1, 2, 3.

"You don't read the greens right, Hoss. You stand behind the ball and look down the line to the hole. Best way is to stand in the middle, between the ball and the hole and look both ways, like our mommas said to do when we crossed the street. Second half of the putt, the ball slows down and it breaks more, takes the slope of the green."

"Do you ever play?"

"Some."

"What do you shoot?"

"Around par."

"Really." My voice was dripping with skepticism.

"On days I'm not playing well." He grinned. First time I'd seen him smile. He was missing two lower teeth.

We both slept well that night. We went to the course early at Sheboygan's insistence so I could practice my new putting grip and greens-reading instructions. I was desperate, willing to try anything to improve my putting short of voodoo rituals or taking those new mind-altering drugs I'd read about.

When I stepped to the first tee and the starter introduced me, I had this unusual feeling, one I had never felt before at the beginning of any round of a tournament. I was totally without nervousness. Totally ready to play great golf. The Legends of the game would call it confidence, something I was unfamiliar with. The elements that caused this change were:

1) I was doing great with my new #1 wood; 2) My encounter with Kat Stern reminded me of the importance of maintaining focus for a full 18 holes. NO admiring the pretty scenery, or chatting with the pretty girls; 3) On the practice green that morning, I made putt after putt, from 20 feet on in. Thanks, Sheboygan.

I went out and shot four consecutive stellar rounds of 68, finishing the tournament at 16 under par. It was amazing, like drawing 4 Aces in a card game at the gaming hall next to the course. I drove the ball better than I ever have. I only missed two fairways per round. And my putting! I rolled them in from all over, 40-footers or five-footers, I made nearly everything I looked at.

The 18th hole in the final round was one I will never forget. It was a long par 4, a dogleg left that measured 460 yards. I hit my now usual strong tee shot, 285 yards with a slight draw that bent around the dogleg perfectly. But I'd forgotten about the sand trap that was diabolically placed at the bend in the dogleg. My ball trickled into the sand.

I had a reasonably good lie for my second shot, 175 yards to the hole. I selected a 6-iron, took my stance, digging into the sand for balance, and swung. I made clean contact, perfect contact, picking the ball off of the soft white sand. The shot soared high across the bright blue sky, plopped onto the green.

And rolled into the cup for an eagle 2, two under par!

"We won, Hoss," Sheboygan commented in his economical way. Up to that time this had been the most he had said while we were on the course.

The galleries that had come out for this brand-new event were not huge, but when my ball went into the hole the cheers were huge, some of the fans jumping up and down.

My playing partner was a grumpy old pro, about 50, who was just playing out the string of a career that began in the '30s. I looked over at him for his reaction. He just sniffed, snorted and sneered, like "Lucky shot." Well, screw him. I am the Champion.

Walking up that last hole to the ongoing, enthusiastic cheers was a surreal experience. I knew I could win out here, but was starting to think I wouldn't. The people around the green looked so happy for me. I hadn't really understood until that moment how popular I was with the golf fans. It was like they were waiting for me to win, so they could cut loose. I laughed when I thought about how the Tom Colt Fan Club might grow beyond the current two members.

Golfers and other athletes sometimes break down in tears when they win, particularly if it was unexpected. I had no such emotion. I knew my mom would cry when she got the news. My predominant emotion was relief. Getting that first win had been much more difficult than I expected. As I reached the green I tried to smile at every one of the fans gathered there, especially the lovely women, of whom there were many. I decided my period of abstinence had gone on long enough.

A crowd of about 20 autograph seekers, still buzzing from the exciting conclusion to the event, gathered around me after I signed my scorecard. I was thrilled to see them there, and signed every scrap of paper, every golf hat, ever pairings sheet that was thrust in front of me.

I felt something being inserted into my back pocket. When I was by myself I removed it, a small perfumed envelope. Inside was a small photo of a pretty young woman at the beach—topless. My close inspection revealed that the photo was taken on a cold but sunny day. Her smile was sunny as well, her ample chest thrust out with great pride. On the back of the photo was a phone number and a name, Patti.

What a wonderful life I have!

Since this was a brand-new event, the prize money was modest. My winner's share was only $2,150. At the trophy presentation, it occurred to me that on a per hour basis, I was earning far more working as a detective for the Judge than I was competing on the golf tour.

A small crowd gathered around the green for the trophy presentation. The Tournament Director gave a boring little speech. He was an affable fellow with an impressive head of grey hair and perfect white teeth. That's pretty much how every single Tournament Director looks. They only vary by height.

As the gentleman spoke, I noticed a strange, mousy little man in a rumpled brown suit who was shifting from foot to foot. Everyone's attention was on the Tournament Director except for this guy's. I noticed that the cuffs of his jacket were worn, slightly frayed. He was wearing crepe-soled shoes.

In the Old West days, thieves wore those shoes so they could sneak up on their victims on the plank sidewalks of the frontier towns. They were called foot-pads.

The Director handed me the trophy. I don't remember the probably boring little speech I gave. I was still overwhelmed by the moment, by winning. For all I knew, I talked about how good Lombardi's Green Bay Packers football team was going to be that year.

I do remember Sheboygan firing up a big stogie when they gave me the check for my winnings.

When the ceremony concluded, a portly bespectacled man wearing a huge gold wristwatch exclaimed, "My wallet's gone. What is this!!!"

The tournament officials rushed over to him. I noticed the man in the brown suit silently backing away, on little cat feet as the poet says. I said to the Tournament Director, "I think you want that man," and pointed to the brown suit, who had turned and was hurrying away.

"Stop him," hollered the Tournament Director.

A police officer, serving as tournament security, stopped him immediately. The portly man's wallet, thick with currency, was in the brown suited man's jacket.

***

The AP wire service dispatch printed in newspapers and delivered around the world the next morning said, "Colt Hits Miracle Shot, Wins Vegas Tournament, Captures Thief."

A nice summation of my Sunday afternoon. When I purchased the newspaper (my mom would want a clipping for her scrapbook in her Tom Colt Museum), the hotel desk clerk handed me a stack of telegrams from, I guess you could say, well-wishers:

Don DiMarco (my college golf coach): "Finally."
Kat Stern: "Dinner's on me. Congrats.--Katrina M. Stern, ladies golf professional who has won three more events than Tom Colt."
Judge Roy Wilkinson: "Celebration at my castle upon your return. Rack of Lamb and a bottle of Chateaux Margaux."
Jilly Flannery: "Sweetheart, I am so proud of you! I'm going shopping to celebrate!"
(War with the Soviets could break out and Jilly would still go shopping, probably thinking it's her patriotic duty)

Caroline: "My brother, a Winner on the Pro Tour. Who'd a thunk it."
(I get such wonderful support from my Fan Club)
Det Mathers: "How to go, guy! Get back soon. And conserve those detective powers. We've got crime in Phoenix too, you know."
Lisbeth Stirdivant *(my High School English teacher)*: "I taught a future celebrity! I know you'd go places, Thomas."
(Then why did you give me a C+ on my essay about Fitzgerald's use of color in 'The Great Gatsby'? Sometimes a green light is just a green light, you know)

***

Success is so bizarre. People raise their estimate of you, substantially, but you're the same person. Even so, success is vastly preferable to failure. I've known both.

Consider what happened on the 18th hole. I hit a golf ball up into the air, as I have done a million times in my life. The 8mph wind currents cooperated by guiding the ball on a path directly toward the flagstick. The ball landed on the putting surface, took an odd, fortuitous bounce toward the hole. The ball rolled over all the imperfections in the grass, including ball marks, worm casts, and spike marks from golfers' shoes, without veering offline, until it hit the flagstick and dropped into the hole.

I was only involved in Step 1 of that process: hitting the ball into the air. But now The World viewed me as A WINNER.

And even this early in my career I was wise enough to not get an inflated ego from winning a professional tournament. I did not suddenly believe I had discovered the secret to Great Golf. The problem with putting advice like Sheboygan gave me is, it doesn't last. It's magic dust that inevitably blows away and dissipates. That's why you see the scores of even the best players fluctuate so much, over the season or even in one tournament. What the unknowing golf journalist refers to as a golfer being in a slump is really just an interim period when he's trying to find more of that magic dust. Somehow, somewhere.

Checking out of the hotel I flashed on something that had been in the back of my mind. I walked up to Sheboygan, who was waiting for me in the lobby.

"Midwestern accent. Nickname Sheboygan. Played college ball at a high level. Too small to be a linebacker but too big to be a running back. You're Jeremy MacLane, played fullback for the University of Wisconsin."

He said, "Well, ain't you the hot shit detective."

Everyone has to be a wise guy these days. Caroline got a huge kick out of that story when I shared it with her. She always enjoyed being entertained at my expense.

I handed Sheboygan an envelope with $215 in it, his 10 percent share of my winner's purse. "Do you want to count it?"

"Nope," he said, picked up his suitcase and walked outside.

Chapter Fourteen
A Dinner Party in the Twilight Zone
Lisa Luck Reaches Out to Tom

When I got back from Vegas on Monday and checked my messages, I had five urgent requests from my students to book a lesson with me "as soon as possible." It was as though I had discovered the formula to great golf and they hoped I would share it. My favorite was from colorful Det. Mathers: "Hey guy, you're really crushing those tee shots now. Read in the *Arizona Republic* fish wrap that you hit a 300-yard drive in Vegas. Can you teach me to do that?"

Not likely, buddy, but I'll give it my best shot.

I was enjoying a beer on the back patio of the guest house when who should breeze in but dear sister Caroline. She was carrying a duffel bag. She dropped it on the patio, grabbed my glass of beer and quickly drained it."

"Ahhh, I needed that."

"What's up?"

"Need to crash here a while. Landlord and I had an unpleasantness concerning the rent. He preferred I pay it. I preferred I didn't."

I chuckled. "Put your stuff in the spare bedroom. I'll get you a beer. Or more precisely, get me one."

As we relaxed on the patio with our beverages, I told Caroline the strange tale of my mini-romance and embarrassing break-up with Julia. Confession is good for the soul, they say. Caroline was her usual understanding self.

"Oh, crap. You banged the Judge's daughter. Why, Tom, why? I love visiting you here. It's so new, so clean. Smells nice. You'll be back at that rat-infested apartment, where I didn't feel safe to spend the night."

She reflected a few moments, frowned. "I thought you liked my friend Jillian."

"Great. You two are buddies now. Just what I need."

"Deal with it. We're your Fan Club. We're all you got."

She made a sour face. "Julia? Really? And to think I'm the one mom sent to Reform School."

"It was Catholic School. Do you want me to grill you a steak?"

She leaned back in her chair, stretched and yawned. "I've been waiting patiently. The service here is substandard."

***

An hour later, I walked up the path to the Main House as the Wilkinsons call it, with apprehension, more like dread. I thought about how much had changed since Julia walked down the same path to my little guest cottage just a few weeks ago. I still felt like an idiot for all the fantasies about Julia that had blinded me to the true situation: I was an amusing sidebar in her excitement-driven life. Her approach to life was very much like how she approached eating the juicy cheeseburger we ordered from room service our first night together. She didn't savor it, or even particularly appreciate it. She simply devoured it. And when she was done with a meal, she was done.

The back entrance to the house was now in view. I shook off the gloom of unpleasant memories and rallied myself by remembering this was a dinner party in my honor at the home of the city's most influential person. As Caroline would say, Who Woulda Thunk It.

Marjorie spied me walking up the path and opened the sliding glass door. Her smile was bright and welcoming. I had finally realized that she was Judge Wilkinson's mistress, not his secretary. I was learning about how their world worked. Slowly.

"Tom! Welcome! And a belated congratulations. How does it feel to be a Champion?"

I stepped inside and she hugged me. Her question was too complex for a quick answer, so I said, "I've never felt better."

Marjorie led me to the living room, which was approximately the size of the guest house I was staying in. The space was open, uncluttered, gracious and unpretentious. Three long, sleek low-backed sofas dominated the room. They were upholstered in a rich royal blue fabric that looked like velvet. The carpet was a muted lemon color. The coffee tables and end tables were glass-topped with chrome legs. The paneled walls were stained dark green.

Although I suspected the decorator of the space was the tasteful but thoroughly modern Marjorie, the décor also reflected the Judge's desire to lead us charging headlong into the future. The room looked as 1962 as 1962 could, almost like all the pieces had been manufactured the day before and delivered that afternoon.

The Judge was standing by the white marbled bar area, mixing a drink. He saw me and raised a glass: "Hail to the conquering hero." He had an odd smile: his lips stretched out like a curtain opening and revealed two rows of perfect, though small teeth. It wasn't a smile that conveyed mirth; it was not a smile that came from the soul.

I walked over to him. "Thank you sir." I suddenly realized that I had just been admitted to The Club. I don't mean Valley Vista Country Club. I mean The Club of Fabulous People Going Places in Life, in the amazing city of Phoenix, AZ, in the 1960s. Judge Roy Wilkinson was President of that Club. He was only a member of the Board of Directors at Valley Vista.

Marjorie had disappeared into the kitchen. She brought me a tall ice-cold glass of Blatz beer. It tasted like Victory to me.

The Judge said, "Sit down, Tom. I am so pleased you could make it tonight. Tell us all about your triumph." He indicated an Eames reclining chair, upholstered in dark leather. Apparently, the Guest of Honor chair.

When the Judge summons you, you go. I dropped down onto the Eames, they each chose a couch to sit on, and I gave them a quick synopsis of my victory week in Vegas, along with colorful anecdotes like the sight of Sheboygan in his pajamas, and of course my last round heroics.

Remember, there was no TV coverage of most golf events in those days. And definitely no channels devoted to sports. Golf enthusiasts had to rely on brief newspaper reports of the tournaments. I realized Marjorie was a golfer, too, because she was even more enthusiastic in her comments than the Judge was.

This was all new to me: I had never believed what I was doing was notable enough to tell other people about. I think it was my Protestant upbringing: stay humble, be quiet, don't seek attention. Do your job and shut up about it. But this was fun: I felt calmer and more confident as I told the story of my miracle shot on the last hole, and the vignette about catching the pickpocket.

When I finished, Marjorie actually clapped her hands. The Judge sat there and smiled. I imagined it was the smile a wealthy person has when one of his investments unexpectedly pays off, or maybe when a prized horse wins a race.

"We have a special dinner planned for you. Marjorie, let's check on things in the kitchen and I'll pop down to the wine cellar and fetch that incredible bottle of Chateau Margaux."

The part about the wine was meant to impress me, but I had no idea why. From the shaky high school French I recalled, I translated the wine as 'Margie's House'. What's the big deal?

"Can I help?" I asked.

Marjorie waved that away. "You just relax. Guest of honor."

I wondered how'd they react when I win the Masters. See, my self-confidence was soaring that night. I didn't say to myself, *IF I win the Masters.*

My hosts stepped out of the living room. I sat back and looked out the expansive windows. Even though we were in the desert, the landscaping at the Wilkinson chateau could have been from an English country garden. It was serene. Balanced. Proportional. I took a moment to feel...satisfied with all aspects of my life.

I heard a door from the garage open and a familiar female voice said, "I'm so sorry I'm late. Traffic was bad. This town is getting way too crowded with stupid tourists, if you ask me."

I heard the Judge say as he came up stairs from the wine cellar, "Tom is already here, in the living room."

My serene, satisfied feelings quickly evaporated, replaced by a rising nervousness. I didn't think Julia would have the nerve to be here tonight, at a party for me, whom she made a gigantic fool of. I stood up and waited, with the urge to flee.

Julia swept into the room like a fragrant and welcome breeze, swept toward me and threw her arms around me. "Tom, I missed you so much."

She held me tight for a few moments, as I cursed myself for thinking how wonderful she felt in my arms, and then let go.

I stood there, stunned.

She bubbled on: "I am so proud of you! You won! And in such dramatic fashion!"

High praise from this girl, I thought, *who definitely knows how to execute a compelling drama.*

Her smile was bright and utterly convincing. Then she grabbed me again, as if magnetized, and kissed me on the lips—the passion of the kiss was equally convincing.

What was going on here? Either Julia had a serious problem with short-term memory loss, or she saw nothing wrong with her behavior the night I interrupted the tryst at the guest house pool. I was starting to feel light-headed.

Marjorie, bless her, arrived just in time to announce that dinner was served. We sat down at the very formal maple wood rectangular dining room table, with place settings that you see at prestigious banquets. Gold sconces adorned the walls, not so much to provide illumination but to express sturdy pride. The Judge and Marjorie sat opposite each other on the long end, Julia and I next to one another on one side. The food was excellent. Rack of Lamb, as promised, medium-rare. I ate too much, but hacking on pieces of meat gave me something to do with my hands besides attempting to strangle myself.

The conversation was light and merry. Julia punctuated her light and merry stories by touching me on the hand. I hated that every time she did so I felt a powerful electrical charge.

Later, over brandy served in short, glittering crystal glasses, back in the vast, glittering living room, it was Julia's turn to offer a toast. "To Tom, our new friend who has brought so much excitement and fun into our lives."

"Well said," said the Judge. Of course, he was such a doting father that she could have puked brandy onto the fine blue cloth of the sofa and he would have said, "Well done."

His keen and infinitely experienced eyes had been studying Julia and myself all evening. He was pleased, even tickled, I could tell, that Julia was, seemingly, enamored of me.

In 1959, a seminal television series debuted called *The Twilight Zone*. As I sat there with the Wilkinson clan that night, I heard Rod Serling's distinctive, edgy voice saying:

> *Consider Thomas Colt, a golf professional of growing fame who thought he was attending a dinner party in his honor. Instead, the short walk up the path that night was a journey from the reality we know, to the place we call, 'The Twilight Zone.'*

Next, Julia gushed about my role in capturing the would-be thief at the tournament. You'd have thought I'd slain Count Dracula with a wooden tee-peg.

The Judge took a thoughtful sip of brandy and said, "It's high time we formalize your detective work, Tom. At the very least, you need a business card that we can hand out to those who might require your services."

I was thinking, *Can't I just play golf?*

Happy, happy Julia said, "Oh, yes, and he needs a proper title."

"Right-O," the Judge said. "Sherlock Holmes called himself a 'Consulting Detective'. I like that title."

Julia shook her head, animating the lovely waves of rose-gold hair. "Oh, Father. That is so old-fashioned. We need something modern, hip. This is 1962, after all."

Marjorie said, "Let's describe the services you want Tom to provide his clients."

The Judge swirled his brandy. "Defuse difficult situations without attendant publicity."

Julia looked at me, "He means clean up the mess when Father's friends fuck up."

The Judge laughed, that throaty laugh born of a million cigarettes. "Sometimes Julia dear, you are too blunt. But you're correct, that's the idea."

Marjorie said, "Who will be your target clients?"

"The wealthy and important people, of course," the Judge said.

"I've got it," I said. "Confidential Investigations and Upscale Janitorial Services." I was trying to make a joke of it. They took me seriously. Good grief!

"That's it!" Julia said with her glorious, melodic laugh. She leaned into me and put her silky head on my shoulder, like a girlfriend might do. At least my buddies with real girlfriends tell me that's how it is.

The Judge chortled, "Love it! Marjorie, have 500 biz cards made up right away for Thomas J. Colt, our resident detective."

"I will tomorrow. Now, if you'll excuse me, I need to do the dishes. Tuesday is our housekeeper's day off."

Julia popped up. "Let me help you."

The women left. I was surprised, as with the Judge mowing his own lawn, that these vastly wealthy people had no issue with doing routine chores themselves. Self-reliant people, these Wilkinsons. Or perhaps when you are so rich you know you can hire people to do any and all of your chores, they don't seem like chores anymore.

The Judge leaned toward me, his hands folded together in front of him. This had the air of a pre-planned speech.

"My daughter is extremely fond of you," the Judge began.

I recalled when she hiked up her gown on the green couch that night, guessing that qualifies as fond. I made an involuntary chuckle at that, which the Judge didn't notice. His expression was serious, even grave.

"And more importantly, from a father's standpoint, is that you are good for her. You are...solid. You have a will to succeed that reminds me of myself at your age."

I said nothing, because I no longer had any idea who I was or where I was. Help me, Rod Serling.

"I don't really know how to tell you this. Julia has issues we've been dealing with for some time. The best way of expressing it is…volatility. She swings like a pendulum, and we don't know why or what triggers these changes."

"I don't understand."

"We all have to patient with her, I believe. But she's getting better."

I thought, *was he trying to tell me Julia had an illness? She seemed healthy enough to me.*

The Judge stood up, so he was towering over me.

"The other thing is, she will need to choose a husband who is a wealthy man. She is used to living very, very well, and must continue to do so. I will insist on it. Her music career is barely a break-even proposition. It's more like a hobby where you on occasion get paid."

Like my golf career up until Las Vegas, I thought.

The Judge strolled with a serious face over to the bar, refilled his brandy. He held up a glass for me. I shook my head, no. The path back to the guest house is winding, with treacherous creatures like bunny rabbits, road runners and horned toads. I needed my wits about me to ensure I got home safely.

"So, if you have romantic intentions regarding Julia, and I would never put pressure on you in that regard, by the way, I will need to teach you how to become rich."

"Is that even possible?"

"Absolutely."

Before I could enquire further how this might be accomplished, Julia and Marjorie re-appeared. We chatted for a few more minutes and then I thanked them for a lovely evening, bid them good-bye at the glass door that opened to the back yard and the path back to the guest house. After I'd walked a few yards, I looked back at them, this strange little family. The Judge and Marjorie waved. Julia blew a dramatic kiss my way. I continued on down the path.

Cue *The Twilight Zone* theme music.

***

The next morning, over coffee and a cheese Danish, Caroline asked me how the dinner party went.

"Well, I'm not sure, but I think the Judge is going to teach me how to get rich so I can marry his daughter."

Coffee sputtered out of Caroline's mouth. "What the hell sense does that make?"

Then she hummed *The Twilight Zone* theme. That's why having a twin sister is such a hoot. Or at least, it can be at times.

***

My schedule for the day was a full slate of lessons, starting with Det. Mathers, then a playing lesson with Lisa Luck. Mathers wanted a putting lesson, so I met him on the practice putting green at Valley Vista. I know, I know, me giving putting lessons is like the Borgias opening a cooking school, but I try to give the client what he or she wants.

"Morning, tournament winner," he said affably. "You aren't going to charge me more now that you are famous."

"Not unless I win the US Open."

"I got nothing to worry about then."

Here's an *Important News Bulletin*: I had asked for and was granted a major concession by Valley Vista General Manager Basil Hedgerow. I was now permitted to have my non-member golf lesson clients join me for lunch or a beverage. BUT ONLY if we sat at a tiny bistro table set up at the far, far end of the practice range, out of sight of any club member who might be practicing. Progress my friends, progress.

Mathers and I sat there and sipped our lemonades. "Are we still on Club property way out here?" he inquired.

"I doubt it. I think we're on the outskirts of Tucson."

We finished and walked over to the practice green. It was a hike.

I found it fairly easy to help Det. Mathers improve his putting stroke. His technique was, of course, awful. He had the ball way too forward in his stance, which would have served him better in the sport of curling than the sport of golf. I gave him Sheboygan's tip about not gripping the putter so tight, and he immediately started to sink short putts from 10 feet and in. What I enjoyed about teaching him was that every improvement we made in his game, no matter how minor, made him so happy. I never thought of police detectives as being happy people before. In the movies, they are usually dark, tortured souls.

He drained a twisty 20-footer, grinned and turned to me. "Where did you learn all this stuff?"

"Oh, I pick things up here and there."

Mathers liked to chat about his job during the lessons. It was flattering that sometimes he would ask my opinion on a case he was working on. That day, the dead man who was found on the grounds of the Lucato Vineyards was the topic.

"Strange one. The guy was shot once in the temple, probably instantly fatal, then a second time up the ass."

I made a grim face. "Why would a killer do that?"

"Only seen it once." Ed knocked in two more putts, from 15 feet. I'd never met anyone who could focus so well on golf while discussing a grisly murder. Cops are a breed apart.

He continued, "Anyways, the killer was making a statement. It's a mob-style hit. Mob does everything for a reason. That's why it's called organized crime. They don't kill guys and dump bodies willy-nilly in school playgrounds and parks."

"Is the message meant for the cops, the newspaper, or for the owner of the vineyard?'

"Bingo, Tom. That's what we got to find out. Ed stopped putting and looked intently at me. "You picking up anything?"

I laughed. "Ed, I'm not psychic."

"I know, but you get those vibes, you call it."

"Can you be more specific as to which frequency I should dial into?"

"My cop instinct, for whatever it's worth, says something explosive is about to rock our community."

He missed a putt of 4 feet. He picked up the golf ball and examined it closely, as if to check for proper roundness, just like a pro does. It's never the fault of the guy with the club in his hand.

"You heard anything unusual—you know, shenanigans of the rich?"

"Lots of strange threads of party conversation, but nothing like you LEOs look for." He liked when I called him a LEO. Made him feel like a roaring lion, he said.

"Just be extra aware. It's funny as hell to me that you can learn more by chatting with these people at a cocktail party than I can by hauling their ass in for interrogation."

"That's because I don't threaten anyone. I am, after all, merely a relatively impoverished golf pro."

Ed grunted at that one. "And Einstein is merely a guy who writes numbers and symbols on a chalk board."

At that moment, Lisa Luck, glum and gorgeous, strolled onto the practice green and approached me. I checked my wristwatch. It was time for my playing lesson with her, which involved 9 holes of actual golf on the actual course, not just hitting balls on the practice range.

She was wearing blue and white houndstooth checked shorts and a tight, dark blue sleeveless top, a few buttons strategically left open, to make available the promise of the lovely view within. Her golf shoes were white with dark blue tassels.

Months later, when Ed and I talked about that morning, it struck both of us that it was perhaps the first time in law enforcement history that a future murder victim, and the detectives who were destined to solve her murder—one professional, one amateur—met on the green at a country club and chatted breezily about what a lovely day it was for golf.

"Lisa Luck, I'd like you to meet another of my students, Det. Ed Mathers."

"Pleasure to meet you, Mrs. Luck."

At being called Mrs. Luck, she got a bemused smile. "Thank you Det. Ed. Tom is a terrific teacher, isn't he."

"Yes he is," Ed agreed enthusiastically. "My game is sweet now, because of this guy. I mean, I've always been a jock, but Tom's fine-tuned my game."

I thought, *SWEET! Not quite yet, pal. Merely not hopeless and pathetic anymore.*

Lisa offered, "Tom has this way of showing you things without talking down to you."

Suddenly, Lisa wasn't glum anymore. She flashed a bright smile at Detective Ed. And I filed away a piece of information about Lisa: she identified as one of US, not one of THEM, the country club snobs who were ostensibly her people. Other Club Members I introduced my Detective buddy to looked at him like he had no right to trod their sacred turf.

"Ready for your playing lesson?"

Lisa nodded, smiled, "Let's go," she said happily.

Then a dark cloud seemed to envelope her and she turned to Mathers. "Could I have your business card, Detective Ed?"

He quickly dug one out of his pants pocket, handed it to her. She looked oddly relieved. "Thank you."

We got in our Cushman electric golf cart, introduced at the club in '58, and zipped over to the first tee going at least 7 miles an hour. Call me a stodgy traditionalist, but I always preferred having a caddie holding the bag. An electric cart can't bolster your spirits after you hook a drive out-of-bounds.

When we got out to the course, those burdens Lisa was carrying immediately lifted. She loved the "smack" sound of the golf club on the ball. She loved the entire experience our great game offered. The beautiful scenery, the fresh air, the solitude.

On the 3rd hole, she asked me if she could take her golf shoes off. She said she loved to walk barefoot on the cool turf. "Fine," said I. I thought it funny that Lisa, a Club Member, asked me, the part-time employee for permission.

She picked up on my ironic expression. "You're the Golf Pro, like the Constable of the Course."

She removed the shoes. I could tell it made her feel like a carefree young girl again. She had pretty pink nail polish on her toes.

On the 5th tee, we stopped to get cups of ice cold water from an orange jug placed on a stand. She sat on a bench and laced up her golf shoes. Enough of being a wild bohemian woman for that afternoon, I guess.

"I enjoyed meeting your friend, Detective Ed. It was refreshing to be with two men who have actual jobs."

"I imagine being a politician is a hard job."

She snorted. "I should have said men who had honest jobs."

On the short par 3 eighth, which had its tee perched high up on a knoll, the highest part of the course, actually, Lisa hit a beautiful shot down to the green, a 50 ft. drop from the tee. Her ball ran up 3 feet from the hole.

She smiled briefly at her accomplishment, then said, "Your sister Caroline is wonderful. She's been like a sister to me. I feel as though I can tell her anything, no matter how dark. She never judges me."

I tossed a ball down on the tee, selected a 7-iron, made a smooth, easy swing. The ball almost went into the hole on the fly, stopping a foot away.

"Show off," she said. She stuck her tongue out. We both laughed. It was good to hear Lisa laugh. It didn't happen too often. I wasn't sure why. The sporty way she dressed indicated a capacity for fun.

"Caroline told me you have, like, a side business as a private detective. Could I have one of your business cards?"

I took out my wallet, removed a card and gave it to her. She saw my silly slogan and laughed softly. Then became serious again.

"Call me anytime," I offered, and meant it.

That didn't provide solace so much as remind her that whatever danger she faced was closing in.

I said, "Which service do you need, Confidential Investigations or Upscale Janitorial Services?"

"Definitely the latter. I already know who the bad guys are. Nothing to investigate, really."

She didn't amplify on that cryptic remark. As we rode up the cart path to the 9th green, she said, "I just hope I don't drag you into something that—"

"Don't worry. Just call. Day or night."

"Okay. Thanks Tom. I really mean it."

We finished out on the 9th hole. I gave her a summation of the golf tips we worked on that day, although today's playing lesson was probably only 1/3 golf, 2/3 psychotherapy. She nodded abstractedly as I went over what I taught her.

She said, "You know, Caroline speaks of you like you're the Atlas that holds up her sky."

"She might tell me sometime."

"She doesn't need to. You already know."

And that was the day's most important lesson.

***

Brooks Continues Our Story:

At 5PM, in the Ladies' Locker Room at Valley Vista CC, Jilly Flannery was shedding her sweat-soaked golf clothes, anxious to take a cool shower after practicing golf for two hours in the blistering afternoon sun. In the desert, 4PM is often the hottest part of the day.

She was the only one in the locker room, she thought. But she became alarmed when she heard muffled crying from the shower stalls. Still in her bra and panties, she walked to the shower room.

The crying voice sounded familiar. "Missy?" Jilly said loudly enough to be heard over the running water in the shower stall.

"Oh, Jilly!" It was Missy Gould. The crying intensified.

Jilly opened the shower stall door. Naked Missy was slumped on the floor of the stall, her legs splayed out, the water running over her head like she was trying to drown herself. Jilly wondered how long Missy had sat there crying. A long time, she speculated.

"Honey, what happened?"

Missy pointed weakly to a folder that was on the bench next to the shower stall.

Jilly picked it up and read it for thirty seconds.

"What the hell!" Jilly exclaimed.

"I found this in Sterling's desk. Please don't tell anyone. It's too humiliating."

Jilly angrily tossed the folder down, stepped into the shower and helped her soaked friend to her feet. Jilly thought how small Missy looked, as though the contents of that folder had diminished her.

"I won't tell a soul. I promise. Not even Tom."

Jilly grabbed her friend's hand and held on tight until Missy was able to stop crying.

"This has to end," Missy said in a clear voice. "It's killing me."

***

In the shower at the Men's Locker Room, as Tom let the warm water roll over him, he remembered something significant. Lucato was the original family name of Sen. Richard Luck. His father, Dominic Lucato, was the owner of the vineyard where the shot-up body was found.

Chapter Fifteen
Tom Earns Fame, a New Car, and Wisdom
Jilly Has a Shock in Store for Tom

Katrina Stern danced around her apartment in her underwear, as she got ready for her dinner date with Tom Colt. She had Bobby Darin's jazzy tune *Beyond the Sea* playing loudly on her record player. She set out three different outfits to choose from, of varying sexiness. One suggested a casual dinner date with a buddy, another a stylish outfit for dinner with a valued colleague, the third a little red dress for a hot night with a potential love interest.

Each of these outfits was a birthday gift from her prosperous older sister Ingrid, a business planning consultant. Kat hated shopping for clothes and was careful--tight, actually--with money. Her wardrobe consisted solely of her "work clothes", golf outfits.

Her roommate, Pauline Kramer, a glamourous brunette who worked for Pan American Airways, came out of her bedroom and said, "Let me guess, a date with a guy you're really interested in tonight. Who might it be with?"

"It might be with golfer Tom Colt."

"OOOOOh," responded Pauline.

"What does OOOOOh mean?"

"It means OOOOOh, lucky you. I haven't seen you this excited since you made a hole-in-one at the LPGA Championship."

Katrina met Tom at Guiseppe's Pizza Palace, on 7th Street, which was actually owned by a savvy entrepreneur named Guillermo. Smart marketer, that one. He didn't think people would go for Sicilian style pizza baked by a guy named Guillermo.

Kat, ever cautious and conservative, had selected the cream blouse and aqua slacks. The stylish outfit for dinner with a colleague. But when she saw Tom walk in, her heart fluttered, not like it does when you see a valued colleague. When Tom saw her, his heart fluttered a bit, too. He was wearing an aqua shirt, cream-colored slacks and loafers. No socks. Tom Colt, the Rebel of the '60s.

Katrina had ordered a pitcher of German draft beer that was the specialty of the house. Very multi-cultural for 1962, this Guillermo. After they exchanged greetings, Kat poured two glasses and offered a toast to the recently crowned champion.

"Your first victory. I was so thrilled when I heard."

"Many thanks. It was...a miracle."

Kat raised her glass. "Then, here's to the miracles to come."

They smiled warmly at one another and enjoyed the first sips of the ice cold brew on this unseasonably warm spring evening.

"Sharing German beer with an authentic German girl. This is nice."

Kat unexpectedly giggled. "Look at us. Our outfits are identical but opposite. Either we have a lot in common or we are very different."

Tom said, "Here's to finding out which it is."

They ordered a 15" pizza with as much meat—sliced steak, pepperoni and Italian sausage—as the chef could pile on. Neither of them had to worry about gaining even an ounce of weight—the blessings of being a fit young athlete.

Between large bites, Kat said, "This is a treat for me."

"Dining with a tournament winner?"

"No, I can dine alone and do that. I meant going to a restaurant. We girls often cook for each other at the tournaments to save money. I'm one of the best of our golfing chefs. Not that many people know how to cook real German cuisine."

Tom thought, *this is probably a good thing.*

"I get tired of eating out on the road. So many restaurants are terrible," he said.

"You're lucky you can afford it. Our prize money is so much less than on your tour, it's really unfair." Kat had the kind of mobile face that clearly displayed when she was irritated.

Tom had to navigate around an apparently touchy subject. "I think it's a matter of more people wanting to see the men play. Our tour sells more tickets, hence more prize money."

"Why would that be?"

"I don't know. I love watching the lady athletes play. Especially you. I've admired your game since our college days."

"You have?" Kat felt that heart fluttering again. She didn't like this, the feeling of not being totally in control of her emotions.

"Absolutely. You had the soundest swing and by far the cutest ass of anyone on the Women's Team."

Kat felt herself blushing.

Tom thought, *she looks even cuter tonight than she did in college. I like this girl.*

Looking at Tom's warm smile, and the total package of Tom's good looks, his newfound aura and popularity as a successful pro golfer, and the confidence he had gained since college, she thought, *I like this guy.* But fighting against these exciting new feeling was a tiny but insistent thought that a relationship with Tom would be...trouble.

"Do compliments make you uneasy?"

"No. It's just..."

"Just what?"

Unfortunately and unexpectedly, surprising even her, Katrina's cautious nature came to the fore at just the wrong moment, and shut her down emotionally before she could tell what she was really feeling, which was: "It's just I wanted this evening to be 6 years ago. I dreamed of going out with you when we were in college."

But what came out of her mouth was instead, "I can't do this."

Tom shrugged like he didn't understand.

"This. You and me going out on a date."

Tom had a puzzled look on his face like, *"What is the matter with you?"*

"You have a bad reputation now. Everyone in the golf world knows that all the hot, beautiful women that follow the tour chase you. I never chase men."

Tom was stunned. He thought they were having a good time. They were.

"I'm sorry. I didn't mean to..." Then he thought, *Why am I apologizing? She insulted me. And not all of the girls chase me. Only about 25%.*

He said, "What you said is unfair and actually, you're the one who invited me out tonight."

Katrina looked away. "I know. I made a mistake."

Tom got up from his chair. "All right then. Enjoy the rest of your pizza." He walked to the cashier's table, gave the waitress $4 for the pizza and $4 tip, then walked out.

The waitress, one of those care-worn veteran food servers with the weary eyes and the full figure you find at many eateries, and of course the beehive hairdo, walked over to Kat's table and put her large hands on her large hips.

"What you told him was the biggest load of hooey I've ever heard. You really like the guy. I don't even play golf and I know who he is from the newspaper. Mr. Popularity. He's a great catch."

Kat's face was alight with the first signs of impending fury. "This isn't any of your business, but I don't care how handsome he is. Or popular. Or charming. Or how he can make me laugh. Tom Colt is a notorious love 'em and leave 'em crying guy. I don't want to be hurt, you see."

"So the bottom line is, you're scared. Maybe he's just never met the right girl. Maybe you're the right girl."

Kat made a show of wiping the napkin across her face, where there was some very unbecoming garlic-infused tomato sauce on her chin. "You're so wise, for a waitress."

"Thank you. Remember that when you leave the tip."

"Tom already gave you a hefty tip. I saw you pocket it."

The waitress shook her head and walked off.

Tom, on the drive back, reflected on how he seemed to be attracting female psychos these days. He tried to drown out these discomfiting thoughts with the car radio.

Glad to be home, he went inside the guest house, poured himself another beer, domestic, not German, opened the sliding glass door to the patio, and sat outside, finally able to enjoy part of the evening. He kicked off his shoes, got a putter that was leaning against the patio wall, and went out to the little putting green to practice.

The night air was sweetly aromatic from the lovely flowers the Wilkinson's gardener had just put in for spring, and there was renewed warmth, the hint of the warmer weather that was inevitably on its way to the desert.

Tom thought he heard a car drive up, but paid no attention. His putting was so much better now he actually enjoyed practicing on the green. He didn't hear the soft knock on the door or see Katrina coming around the corner.

She stood silently for a few moments and watched Tom. Admired Tom. Wanted Tom.

I am a dummkopf, she thought to herself.

He stopped putting and looked at her.

Katrina took a deep breath and opened with, "I just want to win, Tom. Win, and win and win. I don't have time for broken hearts or hurt feelings or even passionate distractions. I'm at the top of my game—mentally and physically. I'm there. Can you understand what I'm saying?"

"Kind of."

"It's nothing to do with you. It's true confession time. I've had a gigantic crush on you since college. But sometimes it's better not to act on our crushes. Just keep them warm and glowing in our hearts for a rainy day."

Tom dropped a golf ball, effortlessly sank a putt from 20 ft.
"I dunno. We could just play golf together."
"Golf?"
"Yes. It's a great new game I've just taken up. You try to hit
a small ball with a small club toward a distant target."
Kat made a cute frown.
"Ass," she said.
"I like ass too, but probably like golf more."
Then she laughed, finally.
"I have to go. Long drive tomorrow to our next tournament.
Three of us packed into a '57 Chevy, golf clubs strapped to
the roof. I hope those two girls bathe before we leave. Oh,
joy!"
She deliberated a few moments.
"But, I...like you a lot." When she said that, it made her own
heart flutter.
Tom dropped the club and walked toward her. Extended his
hand. She extended hers and accepted Tom's. "When you get
back in town, let's play."
"We will definitely play."

***

Tom got a surprise the next day that totally pumped him up.
He received a phone call from the Senior Editor of
Championship Golf Weekly, a newspaper-style magazine that
as its name suggested, came out each week and covered the
most recent tournament results. The editor said he wanted to
do a story about Tom winning his first tournament, complete
with photos.

The editor apologized about the lack of notice and asked
him if he could be available for a photo shoot at a studio in
Phoenix the next day. The interview portion would be over
the phone, and if all went well, the article would come out the
following week. The editor asked him to bring his #1 wood,
his driver, to the photo shoot.

All did go well. On the newsstands the following Thursday
was Tom on the cover of *Championship Golf*, wearing an Old
West lawman's long black coat and a sheriff's badge on his
shirt. The headline read: "The New Sheriff in Town: After
Years of Struggle and Determined Striving, Tom Colt Gets His
First Victory."

When Tom saw the magazine, he thought, *not that many years of struggle, really.* But that's always how we feel about a long struggle, once it is over.

Tom was over the moon about being on the cover. He recognized, finally, that he belonged on the pro golf tour. He still was not sure he belonged with the high society crowd he was now immersed in. He retained the suspicion that continued immersion might lead to drowning.

After he mailed a copy of the magazine to his mom, Tom decided it was time he rewarded himself with a symbol of his newfound success—besides buying spiffy new togs to wear at tournaments.

Perhaps it is not as true today, but in the late 1950s and early '60s a young man was defined by his 'wheels', the kind of car he drove. Back in the '40s most vehicles were boxy looking. In the late '50s and beyond to the new decade, they became longer, sleeker, and some even sported fins. Autos looked as though something heavy had been dropped on them and flattened and elongated them.

Autos were designed to be bigger, roomier. The more chrome and metal you owned, the cooler you looked. A zesty new vocabulary was even created to describe our experience with cars: burn rubber, souped up, playing chicken, peel out, brody. Driving was a way we got our kicks, and not just on Route 66. Teenagers cruised down Central Avenue in Phoenix every weekend night--just like they did on Hollywood Blvd. in Los Angeles. And gas was 31 cents a gallon.

And OH! the power those cars had, the acceleration. Vehicles weren't burdened with all the emission control gadgets they are today. Driving was to experience a feeling of commanding an awesome force.

The vehicles we drove at that time perfectly reflected the image of a country that was growing, expanding in all directions, and were perfect for people who were more prosperous than ever before and ready for more adventures than ever before.

This was also the era when the travel trailer became popular. This was the ultimate extension of the trend toward bigger vehicles--now you could take a home with you when you hit the road. Of course, these 'tin can tourists' as they were called, were not cool to the younger generation. A big, bright, powerful, sporty-looking car was cool.

So Tom, always striving mightily to be the cool guy, took a deep breath, stopped by his bank and asked for his balance, which had swollen like the dry desert river beds when the summer rains finally come. He had $4,970!

He could hardly believe it.

He took another deep breath and went to a Ford dealership and paid cash for a red Ford Thunderbird. A real beauty. A two-door hardtop coupe with a V8 engine. Bucket seats, red vinyl interior in front and in the rather small back seat. It had a swing away steering wheel that could be moved to the right so the driver could exit more easily. And YAY! The T-Bird had air conditioning. No more sweltering in the desert heat, with your clothes stuck fast to the vinyl seats.

Tom's mother had drilled into his head that you should never go into debt for any purchase except a home. So Tom was not quite ready to abandon his careful approach to finance. Although the auto looked brand new, it was actually 9 months old, having been driven, the salesman said, by an elderly gentleman who seldom left his carport in Mesa and now was checking into an old folks' home and wouldn't need the car. Tom got a good deal on the T-Bird: $3,375 off the lot.

Tom had of course never owned such a beautiful vehicle before. His first sporty car. He could have sworn the T-Bird still had a new car smell. And fortunately the elderly gentleman was not a smoker. When Tom got back to the guest house, he stayed in the car for thirty minutes, and enjoyed that special feeling of owning a great machine.

When he went into the guest house, the phone was ringing. He picked up the receiver in the kitchen. It was Julia.

"Far out!!!" she screamed into the phone. "I have in my hand the latest issue of *Championship Golf Weekly*. What can I say, Tom: you are awesome!"

"I'm only about a quarter way to awesome. All I've done is leave mediocre behind."

Julia continued, talking so fast she was breathless. "And Father got home and said he saw a red Thunderbird in your driveway. He said it was fine, it was cherry."

Tom was pleased his little deception of buying a used car worked. Even Judge Wilkinson was impressed.

Julia said, "I think we simply must go out on the town and celebrate, in your new car."

Tom was perceptive enough even at 27 to know that his value as measured in the peculiar currency of the upper-class female, had never been higher. He was a winner, had earned national publicity, and now had a hot new vehicle, such a fine machine that even Julia would not be embarrassed to be seen in it. He got the impression she thought he was finally ready for her to show him off to the wealthy young set in the Phoenix real estate community.

He mused a few moments about how enticing, how irresistible her offer would have been just a short time ago. But growth in knowledge in life does not occur in uniform little steps at uniform intervals. Many times 5 years of experiential growth can be packed into eight weeks, as it had for Tom in 1962.

His response shocked even him, but left Julia temporarily without the ability to speak.

"I don't think it's a good idea, Julia."

Her voice returned. "It's my friend Derrick from Denver, isn't it? I know it must have looked bad to you."

Tom thought, *No, you looked great naked in the pool. It was your mining tycoon drilling core samples on you that caused me some concern.*

"It's hard to explain Derrick and me, Tom."

Tom thought her explanation was probably going to be, *I wanted to show him how nice the guest house pool was, but suddenly all of our clothes fell off and a wind blew us into the water. It was so weird.*

Julia said, "He's just someone I've known a long time. I have a much better time with you, Tom. You have to believe me."

"That's really nice of you to say, that you enjoy being with me. But tonight isn't good."

"I see. You're so popular now, you have a date. Anyone I know?"

"No, I don't have a date. I need to relax. So much has happened I'm kind of worn out."

Julia was nothing if not relentless in pursuing her pleasures. "How about I come over and then we relax together."

More firmly, Tom said, "I'm sorry. Not tonight."

There was an ominous pause.

"You know, Tom, one word from me about you to my Father, and you'll be out of the guest house."

Tom had come too far and worked too hard, to be intimidated, and he was enormously disappointed she would say something that ridiculous—and childish.

"I don't think so, Julia. He has his own relationship with me, now, independent of you. And I am...valuable to him."

What Tom said must have stunned her, because there was more silence on the other end of the line.

Julia started to sob. "I didn't mean to say that. Please forgive me."

"I've already forgotten you said it. Goodnight, Julia."

She added in a few significant snuffles and then hung up.

Yikes, Tom thought. He could feel her fear of being alone come through over the phone line. But he could not ignore what had happened that night by the pool. If what she had done that night with Derrick was unimportant, he reasoned, then so was the glorious time she spent with him in the hotel room.

He thought, *It would have been easy to invite her over for another hot session on my couch. And we both would have loved it. Our hearts had become entangled—no doubt. But when the sun came up the next morning, I still couldn't compete against a man who flew his own plane and owned silver mines.*

Tom knew that being a successful athlete in '62 was cool, but it wasn't silver mine cool.

What Tom couldn't articulate at the time, or perhaps admit to himself, was that Julia had become the most important person in his life at that time. But she was also the ultimate frustrating puzzle, a mystery he had no capacity to solve. And he could not deal with the obvious reality that she was much more important to him than he was to her.

***

Tom Continues Our Story...

The next day, after a blessedly good night's sleep, I had pure fun on my calendar, watching my student and friend Jilly Flannery compete, with Missy Gould, in the Arizona Ladies Best Ball Challenge tournament. Sixty-four ladies from around the state of Arizona were entered in this event, played over five days on four different courses. The semi-finals and finals were held at our very own Valley Vista CC.

Best ball is a game in which teams of 2 compete against each other, head-to-head. The best score of the 2 team members on each hole is counted as the team's score. Lowest score wins the hole. The team that wins the most holes wins the match.

I was excited that Jilly and Missy had made the semi-finals. I decided to watch their match that morning. The finals would be in the afternoon.

Jilly asked me to watch her warm up on the practice range. She was dressed completely in lavender—shirt, pants, shoes, hat. Quite a vision she was. She explained: "Gary Player wears all black because it makes him feel stronger. I thought wearing all lavender would calm me down. I'm a bundle of nerves over this match. We're playing two fat women from Prescott. They both hit the ball a mile."

I watched her hit a few shots. She was uncharacteristically nervous. I told her, "Tempo, tempo, tempo. That's what I want you to concentrate on during the match today."

"Got it Coach," she replied, trying but not succeeding to appear cheerful and confident.

I thought, *This is why golf is the greatest game of all. It reduces each of us to a quivering mass of nerves when the pressure to perform is on, no matter how well we have played in the past or how large our bank balance is.*

Jilly must have picked up on what I was thinking. "All the shit I've been through in my 44 years, and I fall apart over a little golf match."

So I revealed my 'quivering mass' theory to Jilly.

"How do you deal with nervousness, Tom? You play in way more important tournaments than this, in front of thousands of people."

I shook my head pessimistically. "I don't deal with it. Typically my nerves get to me and I collapse at the critical moment in the final round that decides the match."

"My, you're being helpful. Thanks a bunch, sweetie."

"Tempo, tempo, tempo," I repeated. "Focus on that, not on how nervous you are. I know you are going to win."

"Thank you!" she said, this time with slightly greater confidence in her eyes.

I strolled back to the clubhouse, looked through the mail that had come for me at The Club. I was starting to get fan mail! Later, I got an iced tea from the kitchen to bring with me as I followed Jilly and Missy in their match that morning. I ran into both of them in the hallway, coming out of the Ladies Locker Room.

Jilly said, "I need a hug, Tom. I am so nervous!"

I set my glass down, embraced her and whispered in her ear, "Tempo, tempo, tempo." When I let go, she looked bucked up, to some extent.

Missy said, "I'm scared too, can I have a hug."

So I repeated the process with her and whispered in her ear, "Slow and easy on the backswing, slow and easy."

Jilly frowned. "You're holding onto Tom a bit too long there, Partner."

Missy let go of me and they marched resolutely out the doorway, off to war.

The golf professional's job involves many strange tasks and wondrous challenges.

No other word for it, Jilly and Missy were terrific in the morning match, cruising to a 4&3 victory, meaning they were 4 holes ahead with only 3 holes to go, so the match was concluded. I didn't watch the Finals match in the afternoon, until the last hole, which Jilly and Missy won in dramatic fashion. The match was square—tied—after 17 holes. Jilly made a beautiful, slick, twisting, 35 ft. birdie putt for the win. Then it was Jilly and Missy's turn to embrace.

I can tell you Jilly didn't learn how to sink clutch putts like that on the last hole of a tournament from Tom Colt. Maybe I should ask Jilly for a lesson in performing when it matters the most.

Jilly asked me out to dinner to celebrate her victory, and belatedly, mine in Vegas. We went to the Red Dog restaurant in Scottsdale, known for their great prime rib. The restaurant had a dance floor and a decent band that played—but I had a feeling she and I would be dancing under the sheets later that night. The energy level Jilly had always amazed me. She played 36 tough holes of golf that day and looked like she could stay up all night.

She was always bubbly, but that night, still flush with the thrill of victory, she talked nonstop. I smiled periodically and consumed a gigantic serving of prime rib, 16 oz. at least. Something told me I was going to need my strength.

Jilly said, "I had a delightful time with Caroline yesterday."

"What's my Fan Club up to now?"

"I took her clothes shopping. She dresses like a hobo, the poor thing."

"She's cultivated an individualistic style."

"Hobo isn't ever a style. I bought her 8 new outfits. The great thing about divorcing a real estate magnate is that you end up owning at least 2 shopping centers, more if you have a sharp lawyer like I did."

She paused long enough for a bite of prime rib, then continued, "I took her to 6 or 7 boutiques. She was so thrilled. She gave me a hug that was more like a football tackle when we put the packages in the car."

"In a bizarre way, you're a super role model for her."

"She tries to act all dark and gloomy, but deep inside she's all light. She just needs to be encouraged to show the light."

"You are an extremely perceptive and sexy young woman."

I loved the way Jilly smiled at me. She simply sparkled.

***

Brooks Continues Our Story:

Later that night, Jilly was on top. And that's not a metaphor. Back at her house she straddled Tom on the ocean liner sized bed in her master bedroom.

She said, "Tempo, tempo, tempo, Tom. That's what I want you think about tonight."

"What a goof you are!" he said with an excited laugh.

She giggled and then they focused on their furious passion they had for each other, built on relentless fun and the thrill of helping each other succeed in their lives. Afterwards, they lay close together and Jilly said, "You have just about a perfect body. I know, because I do too so it works out well."

"As I said at dinner. You are a perceptive and sexy young woman."

"And you are, well, my Young Prince, the best thing since department store charge cards."

"Tell me about that putt you sank to win the final match. I've had that same 35-footer probably 10 times over the years and never made it."

With her index finger, she softly, slowly traced a sinuous line on his chest.

"The secret was to not over-read the break. It's a lot straighter putt than it looks. And of course I'm a fabulous golfer. A champion, now, just like you." She demonstrated this by tracing a line down Tom's abdomen until she found what she wanted.

He said, "I think you wandered off the fairway."

"Sometimes it's more fun in the rough."

Tom spent the night. At daybreak he felt a hand gently stroking his manhood. He opened his eyes.

"An early riser, I like that," Jilly said with a giggle. The woman even woke up happy. She kissed Tom where her hand had just visited. They began the new day the way they finished the previous one, with exuberant lovemaking-- laughter, passion and joy.

They had breakfast in her bright and modern kitchen, exactly the kitchen you'd expect a bright and modern—and wealthy—woman to have. She made scrambled eggs with gruyere cheese, accompanied by thick sausages. "They're a new brand," she told Tom. "Barker's Fine Sausages. Really good. The spices they put in these are unusual."

Tom gobbled down three of the sausages and said, "Barker's...I'll have to get some."

They finished their breakfast, which included really strong Mexican-style coffee and fresh-squeezed orange juice, picked right off the trees in her small but spectacular back yard. Jilly's yard was a metaphor for Jilly. Every inch of the space was tightly packed with life: flowers of all colors, vegetable beds teeming with healthy produce and trees full of bright fruit with sweet juice.

"Great morning feast. Thank you."

"Don't worry, I'm not trying to win your heart with my cooking. I know where we stand."

"It's not just where we stand, it's where we lie down I enjoy."

"Me too! That's why I'm Founder of the Tom Colt Fan Club."

She smiled. Tom smiled. They were both having equal measures of unbridled pleasure with each other. And it was more than Tom making Jilly feel younger. She made Tom, who carried many silent burdens he did not readily discuss, feel more optimistic as well. Jilly was a furiously positive woman.

"I do have one serious topic to talk about," Jilly said as she got up from the table and put the dishes in the sink.

Tom sipped the strong coffee and said, "What's up?"

"I met this fascinating woman the other day, Felicity Greyhawk. She was a film actress--she must have done quite well--and now lives here."

Tom rolled his eyes. "Not her. She was married briefly to my uncle."

"Really. She's your aunt?" Jilly lifted one curious eyebrow.

"One side of my family is very wealthy. Just not my side unfortunately."

"Anyway, Felicity is a psychic."

"So she says, to anyone in earshot."

"Don't be skeptical. She and I have the exact same concerns. More than concerns. I thought I'd share them with you."

"I would of course want to hear about anything that's worrying you."

"I think something wicked, something horrible is about to happen in our peaceful little golf-y community. And so does Felicity. She brought the whole subject up when we had lunch at Camelback Inn last Tuesday."

Tom perked up and not just from the strong Mexican coffee. He remembered Det. Mathers saying almost the exact same thing.

Tom sipped the coffee. "Please go on. You have my attention."

"You even sound like a detective now. Thank you, Lord Peter Wimsey, I shall continue with my narrative."

She sat back down at the table.

"It think, as does Felicity, that things are going to get thick around the Luck Family. Everyone knows the Senator's campaign is in the toilet. Lots of people, mostly out of state I have heard through the grapevine, have ponied up big bucks to back him, and they are not happy."

She poured herself more coffee. "I mean, what did they expect? Sen. Prescott Vance is an Arizona legend. And the Lucks---aren't even from here originally. They're from California." She added with a hiss, "Their real name is Lucato, you know."

She forgot I'm half-Italian, one generation removed from Tuscany. She must have been making love to my Irish half.

"What do you and Auntie think is going to happen?"

"Well, as she put it, the epicenter of the crisis is Lisa Luck. Everyone knows she goes to Mexico and parties without the Senator. You can confirm that with Caroline. She's been down there with Lisa--and they get into trouble together. You don't even want to know the rumors I've heard. That's why I'm taking Caroline under my wing--she needs to change. Lisa Luck is not a good influence for her."

Tom winced, sipped more coffee, shook his head wearily. "Caroline."

Jilly looked intently at Tom. He knew she was deciding whether she should tell him something more, something alarming. He prayed it wasn't about his sister.

"I've heard this from three different people, but I have no idea whether it's true. Lisa, 7 years ago, stayed in Mexico for the whole spring and summer, March to September. I mean, who does that? People in Phoenix with money go to San Diego or San Luis Obispo for the summer, not bloody hot Mexico."

"So what was the rumor?"

"She went down there because she was carrying a child--fathered by a member of a prominent Mexican family. The child, a girl, was born there."

Tom looked just as intently at Jilly. He saw no uncertainty in her eyes.

"Damn." Tom leaned back in his chair, drummed his fingers on the table. He wished there was golf club in the kitchen he could grip and re-grip, Tom's equivalent of a child holding his security blankie.

He said, "I don't know what to do with all this--"

"I don't know either. Neither does Felicity."

Jilly reached over and took Tom's hand in hers. "I'm telling you this because you are rapidly becoming one of the most significant people in our community. You're becoming one of US."

Of all the revelations Jillian Flannery shared with Tom Colt that morning, the last one was what frightened him most.

Chapter Sixteen
Trouble in Paradise Valley Revisited

Tom Continues Our Story:

Everyone, it seemed, thought that the epicenter, as my daft Aunt Felicity termed it, of the impending catastrophe was going to be Lisa Luck. But nobody did a damned thing to prevent what did happen.

Lisa was dead. I found her body at her home, in the back yard by the swimming pool, after she sent me an urgent message that she was in danger.

By 7PM that evening, the cast of characters around the swimming pool area was growing. The County Coroner had come. Two more police investigators where there, combing the house and the grounds for evidence. An artist was busy sketching the crime scene and the locations of pieces of evidence. And a police photographer was taking pictures of Lisa's body from all angles, as well as other spots in the crime scene.

Sen. Luck had been notified of his wife's death and was rushing back, with his entourage, from a fund-raising event in Flagstaff. His arrival was estimated for 8PM.

I wasn't sure why Det. JB Leeves insisted I stay. I had told my story of what happened, and my non-relationship with the deceased.

Thankfully, Det. Ed Mathers arrived on the scene. He was wearing a tuxedo of all things. This being my first time at the scene of a brutal murder, I wondered it that was the standard protocol for the Lead Detective in charge of an investigation.

He was getting funny looks from the other cops. He said, "I was at a wedding reception for my niece. Came as quick as I could."

He saw me, nodded rather formally, then huddled near the door to the bedroom and got a report from JB Leeves. Several times, Leeves pointed at me which I did not take as a good sign.

Mathers put on latex gloves and then did a quick 360 around the body. He gave the Coroner permission to take Lisa away. She was placed on a stretcher to take the final journey from her home.

Mathers chatted briefly with the Coroner. Then brought Det. Leeves over to me.

"Colt admitted his fingerprints are on the murder weapon."

Mathers sniffed. I think he was allergic to the flowery landscaping, mostly plants non-native to his beloved desert, around the pool. "Where were you at 4PM this afternoon, Tom?"

"Giving lessons at Valley Vista Country Club."

"Any witnesses?"

"A whole driving range full. And the locker room attendant who let me use the phone to call for my messages--when I received the message from Li...the deceased."

"You hear that, JB?"

JB shuffled like my airtight alibi disappointed him greatly.

"Give me your first impression, JB."

"Looks like a sex crime to me, for certain." JB was almost leering. I was disgusted.

Mathers said, "I wouldn't leap that far just yet. What is evident is the anger the killer displayed here this afternoon. The woman was killed near the bedroom door then dragged, probably on that bath towel on the pool deck, over to the pool chair. I'm sure we'll find blood on the towel, but our lab can confirm."

"Why go to the trouble of posing the body?"

I felt like a kid in a classroom who knew the answer to the teacher's question but was wasn't sure whether he should raise his hand for permission to speak. *The answer,* Tom thought, *was that the killer wanted to display her in an indecent way. It was a commentary on her loose morality.* He recalled how his own reaction to seeing her, before he knew she was deceased, was that she wanted to bring him there to seduce him.

"All right, JB you take a preliminary look around the house for anything that seems unusual. The uniform guys can continue searching outside. The sprinkling system was on sometime today and the flower beds are wet. Might get lucky on footprints."

JB, now clearly in the subordinate position, strutted off to the house. "Anything you say, Beav," he said very quietly.

The Coroner reported to Mathers that Lisa had been struck with multiple blows from behind. The first may have knocked her out and the second one was most likely the fatal one. Mathers made a motion with his hands as though wielding a golf club. "Even though the club was a right-handed one, the killer could be left handed. There are many ways to grip a golf club, after all, right, Tom."

I nodded. I wasn't sure what my place was here, so I thought it best to not talk unless absolutely necessary. I had several moral dilemmas churning inside me, the biggest one being whether I should share with Mathers the information from Jilly about Lisa's rumored child in Mexico. I decided not to, not immediately. It may be just malicious gossip after all.

Mathers motioned for me to join him in a secluded part of the yard, away from the crime scene. We walked to edge of a sidewalk that wound around to the side of the house, which I now saw was a giant L-shape with the pool, patio and small lawn in the center.

Away from his colleagues, Mathers went back to being the buddy I knew. "Don't pay any attention to Det. Leeves, Tom. At Police Academy, they give everyone a personality test and his came back negative."

I smiled. Relaxed, slightly.

"You spent time giving her golf lessons, Tom. Any insight on her emotional state?"

"Frightened of something that was a tangible evil, in her mind. Angry and depressed at times. Also on the verge, of a big change in her life. She asked me for my business card, my private detective card. And remember, she asked for yours, too."

Mathers looked distressed, like he had to say something he really didn't want to. He said, "I have to ask you this. Don't take offense. You weren't romantically involved with her..."

"Nope. She never even made a pass at me. I was just there. To listen. And because she loved to play golf. Being on the course seemed to relieve her worries, at least for a while."

"Excellent. The reason I had to confirm what I already knew—you are much too smart to mess around with her--was because I'll need your help to get whoever did this. These rich people will talk to their beloved golf pro but shut tight like clams when Detective Mathers shows up. I want you to get out there and stir the conversational pot. The solution may rise to the surface."

"Anything you need, just holler."

"Believe me, I'll holler louder than Tarzan."

Mathers paused, the wheels turning in his mind. He was coming up with a strategy. "Your first homework assignment, Junior Detective, is to think long and hard on the choice of murder weapon, the reason for it. It seems like a statement the killer was making. Someone had to go to the trouble of stealing the club from Valley Vista and bring it here."

"Seemed odd to me, too. Whoever took it was probably spotted. This was Men's Day at the Club. Every part of the place was crowded."

"You said the other day you were hearing lots of party chatter that seemed unusual to you. Anything relevant to the case?"

"Yes." And then I told him my observation that the way the body was posed may have been a commentary on her loose morals. I hesitated, thinking how much to disclose, then said, "Lisa is reputed to have slept with a number of men, married and single, from the Country Club, and also during trips to Mexico."

Mathers pondered that a few moments.

"This case is irksome, Tom."

"Irksome?"

"Irksome and personal. The dead lady reached out to both of us—and we did nothing to help her. Det. Leeves said both of our business cards were in her purse."

"I don't think she was ready to tell us anything. I think she didn't...expect to die."

"No. Sure didn't. Her and the hubby have separate bedrooms and in hers two suitcases of women's clothes and accessories were packed and ready to go."

I just shook my head. This tragedy was absolutely personal to me, too.

"Now," Mathers said in a sharp tone. "I want you outta here before Sen. Luck and his minions get back from Flag--and the shitheads in the press slither in. You are my secret agent so to speak. Don't want them to know you are on the case."

"I'm gone. Okay if I stroll through the house on my way out? I might see something you need to know."

"Make it a quick stroll. I'm serious. Go!" He pointed angrily at his wristwatch.

One of the investigating cops had discarded a latex glove, probably by mistake, on the grass. As I walked back to the house I picked it up, put it on my right hand. I took one last look at Lisa. Just a few short hours ago, she was a living being. Now the law enforcement officers referred to her as 'the body.'

I had never seen the result of a violent death before. The finality of it, how quickly life can end, made me for the first time in in my life, wonder how long I was going to live. When you're young, you just assume you are going to go on and on.

I walked back to the Senator's bedroom. Not hard to spot. His room had a large framed photograph of himself making a speech that nearly covered one wall.

I opened a few drawers. And then did my first unethical act as a Private Eye, which in reality is how you get nominated for the Gumshoe Hall of Fame. 'Best Ethical Bending' is one of the categories. In a top drawer of a dresser, I found a key with white tape on it labeled 'Warehouse'. I don't really know why I picked the key up and put it in my pocket.

I just had a feeling.

***

When I finally got back to the guest house, I got a beer from the fridge, and drank half the bottle in a few deep gulps. I was totally worn out and dehydrated. I held the cool bottle against my face, which was so hot from the high emotions of the day that I felt feverish.

I noticed an envelope on the dining room table.

I opened it. It said: "Tom, please come over as soon as you get home. I need 15 minutes of your time but it's urgent." It was signed, Roy.

As I walked up the familiar path to the main house, I tried to guess what the Judge wanted to tell me. I was certain he had received word of Lisa's death.

When I knocked on the patio door, a subdued Marjorie smiled wanly and said hello, then led me without further comment to the Judge's office.

The Judge was standing by a framed map of the state of Arizona. His face was oddly reddened, as if from anger. He was wearing a long-sleeved white dress shirt and dark trousers.

"Come in, Tom. Sit down. Thank you for coming so quickly. You too, Marjorie." He indicated the chairs near his desk. We took our assigned positions. The Judge sat behind his desk. It took on the aspect of a CEO addressing his subordinates about a crisis. He toyed with a heavy glass paperweight on his desk, palming it from hand to hand. This went on, in silence, for probably 30 seconds.

Finally, he put the paperweight down and slammed his fist on the desk. I swear the walls of the room shook. In a growl a grumpy bear might make, he said, "Dammit! I know something like this was going to happen." He slammed his fist down again. His face was getting redder.

The Judge seemed like someone always in control of his emotions. I glanced at Marjorie, who was just as shocked as I.

The Judge was direct, demanding, even conniving, but here, now, he was livid. I could see a vein pop out on his neck.

"I detest these people. They come to our state with the worst of intentions and the lowest of morals. All of the sudden they mysteriously had the money to mount a campaign to unseat arguably the best Senator the state has ever had."

He swiveled around and poured himself a drink of water from a pitcher on the credenza. He didn't offer Marjorie or me any.

"These Lucks, or Lucatos or whatever the hell they're called--no one even bothered to check out who they really are when they got involved in politics. Great job our local press does."

He picked up the paperweight again. I had the terrible notion that he was going to throw it at my head. But why? What had I done?

"So now his wife, his tramp of a wife, dies and guess what-- this sleazy Richard Luck will play the sympathy vote for all its worth. Mark my words. He might even win in November."

Marjorie started to speak. The Judge held up his hand to stifle her. "They may even stoop so low to insinuate someone on our side killed her."

I said, "How do we know that's not what happened?"

Sharply, the Judge replied, "I know."

The Judge always had difficulty sitting still. He rose from his chair and paced the room. I was glad to see he left the paperweight on his desk.

"This kind of scandal can be ruinous. It makes us look like frontier bumpkins all over again, to every important member of the business community around the country. We want investment capital flowing here. We <u>have</u> to have capital flowing here or our big plans for the city are dead. Hell, Tucson could surpass us. How shitty is that."

Marjorie was finally allowed to speak.

"Did the police tell you anything about what happened?"

"I talked to the Chief of Police. And he was very close-mouthed. Only would reveal that the Luck woman died from a blow to the head."

So, I thought, the Judge knows the Chief of Police. Not surprising, I guess. I was learning how exciting it is to be on the inside, to know things others don't.

I said, "Lisa died from multiple blows to the head. They think, from a golf club that was the property of Valley Vista CC. She was killed around 4PM."

The Judge opened his eyes wide with surprise. I was surprised with myself that I could have this effect on a man who believes he runs the City.

"How did you find that out, young man?"

I was aware that he was putting me in my place.

"I was the one who discovered the body. Lisa left a message for me to come to her home because she believed she was in danger."

The Judge looked at me in a new way. I wasn't the malleable little protégé anymore. He wasn't sure what I had become, though. He walked over to me, loomed over me. I was uncomfortable, which was his intent.

"You knew the Luck woman?"

"I taught her golf. She taught me to watch my back around the rich and powerful. They are capable of anything."

The Judge looked at me curiously, as though wondering whether he was one of the rich and powerful I was wary of.

He was.

"The Chief, my friend of 30 years, James Flannery, told me that the lead Detective in the investigation would be your acquaintance Ed Mathers. This provides us with an opportunity. He confides in you. You've even solved a crime together. You will be our means of staying on top of this investigation--so we can get out in front of situations before they create trouble."

He smiled for the first time that night, but there was nothing cheerful about it. "That's why I needed to talk to you. My own in-house detective so to speak."

I found myself enjoying sparring with the Judge. It was fun to know things he did not. I was probably still pissed from the dinner party when he said I'd have to be rich to be worthy of his daughter. After I reflected on that a few days, I thought it was bullshit. He should be more concerned with making his flighty daughter worthy of me.

Time to play the trump card.

"Det. Mathers already asked me to assist Phoenix PD as a kind of informal agent, gathering information by talking to people at the Club, which I do every day."

I had no idea how he would react to this. He laughed, a big bellowing laugh. "Great work, Thomas. As usual."

Marjorie inexplicably cheered up as well. She had a beamy smile.

The Judge walked back to the map of Arizona. He tapped the glass of the frame. I couldn't interpret why he did that other than he looked like a General planning a military offensive.

"I will call Chief Flannery and request that Det. Mathers come here for a breakfast meeting tomorrow. I want to share my ideas about who may have committed this horrible crime. I trust you can be available, Tom. 7AM sharp."

"Thank you, sir, for including me."

"You are...valuable to me, Tom." He said that with a knowing twinkle in his eyes. Did Julia repeat what I said when I turned down her invitation?

"Just one more thing, Tom, and I'll let you go. You must be exhausted after the day's events. Seeing your first dead body can be traumatic." He went over to his desk, leaned against it, casually. And finally, took a cigarette out and lit it.

"Your buddy, Det. Mathers. Can we trust him?"

I waited a few long moments, as he puffed furiously on the cigarette, before I answered, "Who's we?"

He stubbed the cigarette out in the ashtray. He turned to me, his expression hard.

"Who I decide it's going to be. Always make certain, Tom, that you are part of the We."

***

The full impact of Lisa's murder didn't hit me until Judge Wilkinson's temper exploded during the meeting in his office. Their little golf community—I didn't view it as mine—had its share of petty jealousies, disagreements and even mild conflicts—but there now had been a cold-blooded murder, most likely committed by a member of the Club where I work. I was eager to help Ed Mathers solve the crime, but I felt at sea. This was beyond my shallow, amateurish investigative skills. Also, I must admit I felt conflicted: the golf tour was in full swing, I was playing well, and hated to miss the tournaments I was scheduled to enter.

I went into the kitchen and picked up the stack of mail that had accumulated over the last week. Nothing of interest except a letter with no return address and a small object inside the envelope. I opened that one. It was from Lisa, postmarked 2 days ago. The small object was a short, wide orange key, like for a storage locker. The letter was written in longhand. The uneven lettering and sentences that wandered over the pale blue stationery suggested her agitated emotional state.

> Dear Tom:
> I have to leave. I don't know when or if I will return. Enclosed is a key to a locker. The contents of the locker are photos I received from an anonymous source. I hate to put you through the task of discovering where the locker is, but I need time to get away before the photos are revealed. And you are so honest and conscientious, I was afraid you would give them to Det. Mathers before I could get to safety.
> The locker number is 27D. I trust you will know how to proceed.
> And Tom, our friendship means more to me than you know. I may have started out as just a golf student to you, but you were something more to me, and I hope you felt the same. I'm sorry I wasn't better company when we golfed together, but when you see the photos, you will know why I was so upset and anguished. It is a horrible feeling to be trapped.
> At times over the last few months, I felt as though you and Caroline were my only friends in the world.
> Yours, Lisa Prentiss

The letter cleared my mind considerably. I knew I had to help Det. Mathers find who killed Lisa. I meant something to her; she meant something to me—and especially to Caroline.

The phone in the kitchen jangled. I picked the receiver up. It was a Phoenix Police Officer named Farrell. He said Caroline was at Encanto Park, an urban park west of the downtown area, drinking wine out of a paper bag, and appeared intoxicated. When he questioned her, she handed him a business card with my phone number.

I had been concerned how Caroline would react when she got the terrible news, and now I knew. She fell apart, again. To myself I said, "Hell," to the officer I said, "What part of the park?"

He replied, "Bench near the lagoon."

"I'll be there as fast as I can. Thank you, officer."

"She's very upset about something, sir."

I brought a thermos of coffee with me—the strong Mexican brew that Jilly shared with me--and drove there as fast as I could. I found her where the officer said she would be. The wine bottle was on the bench next to her. Her head was tilted back as though she was sleeping, or passed out. She stirred when she heard my footsteps on the path.

She was wearing one of the new outfits Jilly bought for her. Beige slacks and an emerald green top. A gold pendant hung from her neck. She looked like the most stylish wino in the history of wine.

I sat down next to my sister.

"They killed her, Tom." Her speech was slurred.

"I know. Why did you leave the guest house and come out here?"

"When I got the news, I started to wander down the street. After a few miles, there was a bus stop."

I lifted the bag with the bottle. It was empty.

"Lisa was such as good person. I don't understand..."

How it came out was, "Leesha wa sush a goob persum. I don unnerstan."

"Ed Mathers and I are going to find out who did this horrible thing and why. But we'll need your help."

She looked startled, like she didn't hear me correctly. I opened the thermos and poured coffee into the cup that serves as the top. I handed her the cup.

"Drink this, please."

Giving an inebriated person strong coffee doesn't restore their motor skills, but it does snap them around enough to carry on a lucid conversation. She understood this and drank two cups without complaint.

And then Caroline delivered one of the worst gut punches I have ever received. She said: "The last time I saw Lisa, she told me she was going to book out of here—and swore me to secrecy. Then she said, 'I wonder how differently my life would have turned out if I had found a wonderful guy to marry, like your brother Tom'."

I had to turn away for a moment, because hot, angry tears began to well up in my eyes. We sat in silence for a couple of minutes. I got up from the bench, as did she.

We walked a few steps, she tottered and fell onto the grass. She said, "I'm sorry."

I shrugged, picked her up and carried her to my car. "You'll get your pretty outfit all grass-stained."

In the car, she said, "When I was on the bus, an older lady with a big floppy straw hat said how nice I looked."

"You do look nice. Stay with us, Caroline. Hang tough. Nothing can happen to you. You're too important."

***

Back at the guest house, to revive Caroline I made her a gigantic Tom Colt-style Reuben sandwich with extra slices of corned beef and Swiss cheese, coleslaw instead of sauerkraut which she disliked, and my own sweet chili sauce instead of the traditional Russian dressing. My sandwich making skills came courtesy of the summer in college when I worked at a popular deli in Scottsdale. Put on 8 pounds that summer.

I know, my answer to everything is food; it beats drugs and alcohol as a remedy. Caroline quickly devoured the sandwich. I bet she hadn't eaten all day.

We listened to records for a while, but all the songs seemed gloomy, even the upbeat ones, so we turned the record player off and Caroline went to bed.

I was too keyed up, too restless to sleep so I went outside and walked the silent, softly lit lawns of the Wilkinson estate, my home that wasn't really my home. I tried to absorb some of nature's peace into my troubled soul.

After maybe a half hour, I saw a figure coming down the path from the main house. After the events of that day, my first thoughts were alarm, but then I saw it was Julia, barefoot in shorts and a thin, white cotton top.

I walked toward her. I realized I wanted to see her. I had no emotional choice in this. We embraced, held onto each other in silence for many moments. She felt glorious in my arms. Was I stupid? Hopeless? Yes, but I didn't care.

Julia said, "I had to see you tonight. Please take me to the guest house."

I shook my head. "Caroline is sleeping in the spare bedroom. She took the news of Lisa's death very hard."

Julia nodded, thought a moment. "Come with me, then."

We crossed though the gardens, past a stream with a little waterfall until we reached a gazebo sheltered by sprawling eucalyptus trees. We went up the two steps and sat down on a couch-sized iron bench.

Wordlessly, we began kissing, an unbroken series of lovely warm kisses. There was a surprising feeling of fresh acquaintance in each meeting of our lips. Her eyes shone with a warmth and tenderness I had not seen before. I felt as though I had finally met the real Julia.

I needed those kisses. I was hurting more than I could admit to anyone, probably even myself. I believed, perhaps foolishly, that I could have saved Lisa, if I could only have gotten her out of there. That night I couldn't console myself with the impracticality of my belief. How would I have rescued her? And would she have gone with me? Of course not. She had too much honor to put me in danger.

Feelings are very different things than logic or reason. But on the day when cruel and unexpected death visited us, I was grateful to be with the most alive girl I knew. Each kiss was filled with a vitality that gave me strength for the battle that I knew was to come.

She said, "Please be careful. Forget what my father said. Let the cops deal with this. I've never seen my father more...frightened than he was tonight. He never loses his temper. These people are dangerous." She kissed me again, then added, "I can't lose you. You're too important."

I smiled and she didn't know why. She had echoed what I had said to Caroline earlier in the evening.

Perhaps violent death reminds us of the significance of each day of life, and to give full value to the people who are the best part of our lives.

"I promise, Tom, to never hurt you again."

Even I was not so much of a fool to believe her. Julia's unquenchable thirst for experience would lead her to make a fool of many men over the years, reducing many solid fellows to useless rubble, not just me. If anything, she treated me much better than the others.

The quality she admired most in me was resilience. No matter what happened, I never lost my enthusiasm or optimism. That is why, for that night, I could forget the pain she had caused me.

Each kiss repaired the part of my heart she had broken. I wondered what each kiss meant to her.

She moved slightly away, took my hand in hers.

She said, "Please don't try to lay claim to me, Tom. No one can. My father would love it if you put a ring on my finger. He would buy us a cute little house, where we could get right to work producing 5 grandchildren for him—he wants more heirs."

"But I need to be free. That's the only reason I put up with Derrick. His airplane gives us freedom. One afternoon I said

I'd love to see the sun set on the Pacific Ocean. He flew me to Santa Barbara and we did! How magnificent it was! But I could never be with him. He's too controlling, can be cruel, and he's a bore."

She leaned in and we kissed again. "You, on the other hand, are simply the best." We resumed the soft, tender kissing.

No need for us to have intercourse that night. We had left sex behind about 100 kisses earlier and were already on the threshold of a kind of spiritual bonding.

My girl said, "I just want to have a good time. I want to swing with the music that's playing in my head in this modern year of 1962."

One last kiss, which we held for long moments, like the last notes of an unforgettable symphony. And to think I can't even read music.

Brooks Continues Our Story...

In the shadows 50 yards from the gazebo, stood an enraged Derrick Rhodes. He puffed madly on a Camel cigarette, as though nicotine was the only substance keeping him alive. *The bitch*, he whispered. He had made an unexpected stop in Phoenix to get his plane serviced at Sky Harbor Airport, decided to come by and see Julia. He had seen her walk down the path and followed her.

What angered him the most was how Julia kissed Tom: the tenderness, the satisfaction of deep mutual hunger was all too obvious to him. She never kissed Derrick that way. He had never been hungry in his life. *That bitch, he repeated. After all I've done for her—and with that dead-broke golf bum whose mother was a waitress at the Club that my father helped build!*

That night, Derrick Rhodes ceased to be Julia's lover and became her stalker, his once-loving thoughts for her transformed into ugly, monstrous imaginings. *Nobody treats me this way*, he muttered under his breath.

***

Tom Continues Our Story:

On the path back to the guest house, after one of the strangest days of my life, I reflected on how I, who lost his father in 1952 at a time when a young man needs a father the most, had in 1962 cobbled together a strange little, mismatched family:

A stressed-out, fragile twin sister; a sexy complicated rich girl; a wacky, but even sexier, older rich girl; a quirky cop with an addiction to golf; a dangerously powerful retired judge; a near-perfect mom; a way too serious golfer girl who thinks love might mess up her game; and an ex-con caddie named Sheboygan.

Well, I thought, levelly and with surprisingly great hope, *it beats the shit out of being all alone in the world, like so many other people are.*

And then I looked up at the stars on this crystal clear desert night and wondered which of the twinkly lights was Lisa Prentiss Luck. "I will figure out what happened, I promise," I said to the stars, with all my resolve. Which was a hell of a lot of resolve, even when I was only 27.

Chapter Seventeen
Let the Investigation Begin...

At 6:59AM I knocked on the back door of the main house. The Judge himself let me in. He was dressed in a power-business suit, dark blue with a light blue shirt and silver and blue tie. I was of course in a casual golf outfit.

"Come in, Tom. Right on time! Excellent," he said affably. We chatted lightly about what a lovely spring morning it was, as though yesterday's angry outburst was a distant and insignificant memory.

The front doorbell rang. The Judge said, "Buffet breakfast in the dining room. Grab a plate and help yourself." He hurried off to answer the door.

The housekeeper had set out a fine spread on the buffet table in silver serving trays heated with Sterno. Who doesn't relish a breakfast warmed with a petroleum product?

The breakfast spread looked particularly appetizing that morning, although I'm almost always hungry. Scrambled eggs with smoked salmon, banana-nut muffins, cottage fries and an array of bacon and sausages including those Barker brand sausages Jilly acquainted me with. They were becoming really popular all over town.

As I filled my plate with as much as it could hold, I heard Det. Mathers saying, "The famous Judge Roy Wilkinson. I don't know whether to shake your hand or genuflect."

Mathers sounded feisty, even frosty. This breakfast was going to be fun.

"Kneeling before me will suffice, Detective," the Judge said without skipping a beat. "Welcome to my humble home."

Mathers was wearing a hideous cardigan sweater with wide vertical alternating maroon and tan stripes. I had no idea where he buys his clothes, and I hoped I never find out. He wore new black jeans--and expensive looking cowboy boots. Our Det. Mathers was a multi-faceted guy.

I put my plate on the dark red dining table and sat down. Mathers and the Judge picked up plates and served themselves.

Mathers said, "I truly enjoy arresting rich crooks in big houses like these."

The Judge smiled as he tong-ed two of the fat Barker's sausages onto his plate. "I equally enjoy making sure that doesn't happen."

The two men sat down and regarded each other with obvious dislike.

We each took a few bites of our breakfast. Mathers looked satisfied with the food. And I knew how much he loved food.

"Good stuff, Roy," he commented.

"Thank you, Ed. It means the world to me that you're enjoying it."

I think in tennis they call that a nice volley.

The Judge pulled a folded piece of paper out of his suit jacket and slid it over to Mathers. "I took the liberty of compiling a list of suspects in this terrible tragedy."

Mathers opened the page and read it. The Judge's business card was inside. "Okay, thanks," he said blandly and stuffed the paper into his jeans pocket.

"Detective, I want to impress upon you the need to keep me in the loop as the case progresses."

"Not possible. You'll have to wait for our press conferences and learn about our progress like anyone else."

"That's not acceptable, Detective. Who would you like me to call? The Chief of Police, my friend James, or the Mayor of Phoenix, the Governor of Arizona, or how about the former Vice President of the United States?"

Mathers said nothing. Just kept chowing down, staring at his plate.

The Judge ate a piece of sausage with visible satisfaction. "These are good."

I thought how fun this sparring match was to watch.

"I don't have to impress upon you the need to solve the case quickly."

"What does that have to do with you?"

"You confide in Tom. It would be courteous if you do the same for me."

"The difference being, Roy, on the golf course, I take direction from Tom. On a case, he takes direction from me. You're not a person comfortable with taking direction, are you Roy?"

The Judge shook his head.

Mathers got up and helped himself to more eggs and two more sausages. He stood by the buffet table and ate them.

"So, Roy, you can call JFK for all I care, but I'm running this case, and I won't tolerate interference of any kind."

The Judge ruminated over that, then pushed his plate to his left and sat back in the chair. "All right. We'll do it your way. But I'm available for consultation."

"Dandy," Mathers said, "If I need ya', I'll call ya'."

Mathers finished the eggs and sausages, picked up a glass of orange juice and gulped it down.

I had to admire the Judge for not showing visible evidence of the outrage I'm sure he was feeling.

Mathers said, "Thanks for the lovely meal. I have to get back to the station: At 8:30 Sen. Luck is holding a press conference, and I want to watch it with the other guys I've picked to solve this case."

"I'll walk you out," I quickly volunteered.

On the Greek-pillared front porch, I said, "That went well."

Mathers smiled, "About as I expected. He's afraid we'll nail one of his buddies for this and wants a heads up to do damage control. That ain't happening."

I took a folded piece of paper out of my pocket and handed it to Mathers. "These are the notes and impressions I've gathered that may have a bearing on the case."

Mathers' brow furrowed at first as he read it, then he cheered right up. "Now we're getting somewhere. The Judge's list was bullshit. Just the names of every person connected to the Luck's family business and the campaign." He finished reading and said, "Great work, buddy. I'll make a cop out of you yet. Whether you make a golfer out of me remains to be seen." He thought a moment then asked, "Did you share this information with Wilkinson?"

"Nope."

"Good man! Let's talk again tomorrow."

"I'll keep digging."

He gave me a friendly but manly slap on the back and headed down the driveway. He didn't get far.

The front door opened and Julia came running out, barely covered with a thin white tee and panties with little hearts. She put her arms over my shoulders and kissed me. And what a nice kiss it was.

"Sorry I missed breakfast, but I couldn't sleep last night. All the ugliness that's happened..."

She let go of me and finally noticed Mathers there. He walked back toward us.

"Oh, hi!" she said.

"Detective Ed Mathers, this is The Julia Wilkinson."

"Nice to meet you." He seemed fixated on the nipples poking delightfully through the thin shirt, as though they were significant clues—to something.

"It chilly out here. I better go in and see if Marquita can make me a quick bite."

She smiled at me, fluttered her fingers "bye" and ran back inside. Ed enjoyed looking at her wiggly chassis as she went.

"She has beautiful...hair," Ed commented. "Unusual color."

"It's rose-gold."

Our detective walked to his car saying "Rose-gold" several times as though it were another clue--to that mystery with no solution.

I went back inside. Since I didn't own a TV set, I was going to watch the Senator's press conference at the Judge's house.

You've seen I was known as a risk taker in golf tournaments, and this attitude on occasion bled over into everyday life. Today's BIG RISK was inviting Caroline over to watch the Press Conference. You never knew, not even me, her twin, what words might come out of her mouth. My thinking was that she may spot an inconsistency in what the Senator says about Lisa.

I heard a soft knock on the patio door. It was Caroline. I let her in. We smiled at each other, me a bit nervously.

She looked...lovely. The picture of health. She amazed me how quickly she could recover from a raging hangover. You'd never know the bad shape she was in--wasted--last night. Maybe it's like golf, you get better with frequent practice.

She was wearing another of the outfits Jilly bought for her. A black pencil skirt, a gold knit top and a string of black pearls around her neck. The pearls looked real, from the South Seas. I thought, *Jilly, don't spoil the kid.*

But Jilly's generosity was as much a part of her personality as Julia's flightiness, or Kat Stern's ever-present seriousness. Each of us has a dominant personality trait, I suppose. My predominant trait was that I really, really loved girls. That may have been my fatal flaw as well.

With pride I took my beautiful sister inside. Caroline might have been, the way she looked that morning, an up-and-coming career girl in the city, if only we could discover which career, and which city.

The Judge was still sitting at the table, reading yesterday's afternoon newspaper, *The Phoenix Gazette*. He stood up to greet Caroline.

"A pleasure to meet you. You definitely resemble Tom, though of course much, much prettier."

"And I have heard such amazing things about you from Tom." I realized just how much she loved that guest house.

I'd never heard her suck up to anyone in my life until that moment.

The Judge smiled, almost a grin. Even millionaires hunger for compliments evidently. "Help yourself to breakfast," said he.

She brightened, got a plate and quickly filled it. I poured myself more coffee. The Judge sat back down and resumed paging through the paper. He looked up and said to Caroline, "Please fix up the spare bedroom any way you want it. New furniture, bedding, draperies. Whatever you need. And send me the invoice. I want you both to feel welcome."

"Thank you, thank you!" my sister gushed.

What a conundrum Roy Wilkinson was. As tough as nails in business, even mean-spirited at times, but also a sweet, caring soul to those he deemed his allies.

At 8:29 we were seated in the room the Judge called The Den. It had stuffed oxblood leather wing chairs, an equally stuffed sofa, and the largest television console you could buy at the time--a massive, heavy thing that seemed to take up half the room.

When those who could afford them got television sets, the TVs were revered objects in the home, something to impress guests. The TV wasn't referred to as the 'Boob Tube' until much later.

I sat in one chair, Marjorie appeared and sat in another. The Judge and Caroline took places on the couch. Julia had gone back to shower and get dressed.

The news conference was in the ballroom of the Adams Hotel a Phoenix landmark that dated back to before Arizona was a state. Everything about news gathering in 1962 was bulky--the cameras, the microphones, even the electric cables. You couldn't set up an instant news conference like you do now.

The room had chairs for about 50 set up. I had no ideas there were 50 news reporters in our little town of Phoenix.

At 8:37, a somber Sen. Richard Luck took the podium. The room went silent.

"Yesterday, ladies and gentlemen, I lost the love of my life, my partner, my best friend. And our great state lost one its finest people, a young woman with so much to live for, so much to contribute."

I looked over at Roy and Caroline. They had identical expressions: both shaking their heads. Caroline rolled her eyes.

"Barf!" Caroline blurted out.

"I couldn't agree more, young lady," the Judge said, with a growl.

On TV, the Senator paused, as though to regain his composure.

"What a fucking actor!" Caroline said. "He's glad she's gone."

"I was thinking the same thing," said the Judge.

The Senator resumed. "I want to assure all my supporters, our numbers growing by the day, that our campaign will go on. We will rise above our grief and carry on with courage and determination. They think they can stop us, but they are wrong. And my campaign is not funded by wealthy business interests. My family and I are the biggest contributors to my campaign--because they believe in what we are trying to accomplish for the people of our state. Lisa was one of my most enthusiastic supporters. Let us use my beautiful wife's death as a call to action--and a call to victory in November. Thank you, for all your support, and your words of encouragement you have sent us since we got the horrible news. They mean so much to me. Again, thank you."

The Judge switched the TV off, sat back down. "What a smarmy loser of a little man, already trying to capitalize politically on his wife's death."

I said, "I've only met the Senator a few times, but I agree Judge, he's as sleazy as they come." I had no real basis for that conclusion, except my rising loyalty to Lisa which took shape when I read her letter to me.

Marjorie just made a disgusted noise like, "AAAHUGGH," and fled the room.

Caroline was still staring at the dark TV screen. Finally she turned to the Judge and said, "He killed her, Roy. Maybe he didn't whack her on the skull with a golf club, but he caused her death. I knew Lisa. She was about to rock the Senator's world, big time."

The Judge nodded thoughtfully and put a compassionate hand on her shoulder. He got up, seemed to grow in stature and became THE JUDGE. "I can promise you, our wonderful new friend Caroline, that I, we, will not let that bastard Richard Luck get away with this."

***

As if the conclusion to our breakfast meeting wasn't sobering and dramatic enough, when I checked my messages a few hours later, there was one from Det. Mathers: "Tom, that stuff you wrote up for me is outstanding. Gives us lots of avenues for investigation." A long pause... "I wanted to tell you, this is about to get real nasty--as soon as we start poking about their hornets' nest. These are serious bad guys and there are more than one. If you don't own a handgun, go out and buy one--today."

Unfortunately, I didn't own a gun. But during my dismal year in the National Guard I was taught how to be a competent shot. Never in a million years did I think I would need that skill.

When I hung up the phone, my hand was shaking.

***

Brooks Continues Our Story...

After the press conference concluded, Dottie Petersen, Richard Luck's speechwriter and campaign coordinator, walked over to him at the podium.

"That was wonderfully done, Richard. Just the right tone, I thought."

Luck was a clever enough politician to not smile with the reporters still watching there, and with him supposed to be in his period of mourning. "Thank you. I wasn't sure I could get through it. I was so glad to see you arrive at the fund raiser last night. I know you have a million details to contend with in this campaign. But you hold the whole thing together. You're my rock."

Positive comments from her boss always thrilled Dottie to the bone. "I really appreciate that..."

"How was the meeting in Winslow?"

"The whole northern part of the state is breaking our way. We just need to secure Maricopa County."

He nodded like he realized this was a difficult task.

Dottie didn't know how to express her condolences about his wife's death. She wasn't good at warm sentiment. She decided to try to write a note to him later that day. She had met Lisa a few times, but did not know her well.

***

Also watching the press conference that morning was Monty Cummings, at his photography studio in Tempe. A corpulent, sour-faced man with thick lips, Cummings grew livid when he watched Sen. Luck on TV. "That's the guy!" he boomed out loud. He switched the small black&white TV off and paced his studio, thinking. *"Fucking Greene only paid me for my time. I think I deserve a bonus,"* he thought.

***

Tom Continues Our Story...

I spent the afternoon and evening visiting locksmith shops in Phoenix, trying to match the key Lisa gave me to a locker somewhere in town. Eight of these visits produced nothing of value. The key was unusual, 5 of the store proprietors repeated, as my frustration mounted. I tried Sky Harbor Airport and the Bus Terminal downtown. Nada.

Lisa was depressed when I knew her, but she was sharp as a tack. It seemed likely the key had a two-fold purpose--to give me access to these apparently bombshell photos and to give me investigative avenues to pursue. For a relative beginner, she naturally took a strategic approach to golf; probably did in her life as well. I wondered why she couldn't find a way out of the terrible situation she was in.

I quit detecting for the day and went looking for a handgun. For some reason, I didn't want a new gun, I wanted one with some history, a real Private Eye's type gun. You know, a Sam Spade type of gun. I found a pawn shop uptown, at the edge of a strip shopping center. I went inside and found the gun I was looking for in about 15 seconds. It was a beauty: a snub-nosed Smith&Wesson .32, which looked in such good condition it was probably manufactured just a few years ago.

The elderly pawnbroker, with tufts of white hair and a bit of a stoop as he walked, took it out of the case and let me hold it. "A fine, fine, piece," he said, in an undetermined foreign accent. The barrel could have fallen off while I held it and he still would have said the same thing. But I had to agree with him. A nifty firearm.

"You wonder why anyone would get rid of such a nice gun," I said, stalling a bit as I looked around at other handguns.

"Perhaps it held some unpleasant memories," the old man said, smiling with surprisingly perfect teeth.

I filled out the necessary paperwork and bought my very first handgun and ammo for $19.95. The pawnbroker put my purchase in a handsome wooden case with green felt inside.

As I was leaving, he said, "I thought you might be looking for a Colt .45." He grinned and laughed.

I smiled back. It's kinda fun being kinda famous.

***

Brooks Continues Our Story:

Carter VanEssen and Sterling Gould played a round of golf that day. They had the course almost to themselves. It was late Wednesday afternoon. Wednesday was 'Ladies Day' at Valley Vista, which meant women were allowed to tee off between 9AM and 10:30, and were expected to be off the course by 2:30, so The Boys could have their course back for the rest of the day.

Ladies Day was a relatively new concept for Valley Vista CC, instituted in 1959 when many of the old guard still resisted the idea of allowing who they termed "broads" on their course at all.

The two men were vastly successful in business, vastly inferior on the golf course. They were what skilled pros like Tom and Katrina called duffers.

Carter and Sterling's round had been a subdued one. They both had troubled, distracted minds. Carter was shorter and much thinner than portly Sterling. He had a florid complexion and was well-muscled. He had a large, blocky head like Fred Flintstone. He was a harsh, unsmiling man, tightly wound. He wore his hair long, like a silver mane.

On the 12th hole, an easy, straightaway par 4, Carter hit his tee shot and then turned to his friend of nearly 50 years.

"You and I attended the same prep school in Massachusetts, went to Yale at the same time, came out here and built successful businesses at the same time—and now we share something else: we both fucked a young woman who has now been murdered."

Sterling walked over to the teeing area, bent over with significant effort, put a tee-peg in the ground and placed a ball on it. He began his swing ritual with several shaky and ineffective waggles of the club, paused a moment and then took a choppy swing at the ball, his right arm barely clearing his wide gut on the downswing. The ball popped up in the air and traveled maybe 145 yards. Sterling seemed pleased with the shot.

"I wouldn't be surprised if you killed her, what with that bad temper of yours," Sterling said.

Carter sniffed in a dismissive way. "You know I'm not capable of such a vile thing," Carter said.

"Who know what any of us is capable of when the heat becomes unbearable."

"So maybe you did the deed."

"No, I kind of loved that young woman." Sterling thought a few moments. "You know who has a worse temper than you...your wife."

"That's for certain," Carter agreed. "I wish I could remember why I married her."

"As I recall her Greek papa put up 20k of seed capital for you to start your company."

"A lot of grief over thirty years for 20k."

***

Tom Continues Our Story:

I arrived home to the unwelcome sound of the ringing phone. I hardly ever got good news from a phone call. It was Judge Wilkinson. He sounded tired.

"Thank you for bringing your charming sister over this morning. Her insights were immensely helpful to me. She confirmed suspicions I had. I admire Caroline's spunk. Please relay this to her."

"I will, sir."

"And one more thing, Tom. My daughter loves you."

I didn't know what to say. But I wished with all my heart it was true. I went with: "We are learning more about each other every day, and growing closer every day."

"I know. And it pleases me. Julia isn't a person who is easy to make happy. She always seems to be searching for something. I have no idea what it might be. Her late mother didn't either."

"Aren't we all...in a way?"

I could hear the sound of the Judge puffing on a cigarette. "I guess we are. Anyway, you and Caroline have as good an evening as you can, in these difficult times."

He hung up. I stood there with the receiver still in my hand, thinking, here's this mighty man, who apparently runs an entire city, and he finds strength from talking with my emotionally frail sister, who views herself as a complete failure, a washout. I put the receiver down.

I still couldn't call him Roy, like Caroline did with such ease and directness. She gets to be the wild child, the loose cannon. I've always believed it was my role to stick to the strict rules of behavior set down for people who started where we did in life. Near or at the bottom.

Maybe it was time I changed.

***

Lisa's funeral was a private family-only affair--no business associates, no friends, no press. This surprised me, given a politician's need for a constant infusion of publicity to sustain their campaign. Mathers' idea was that a large public gathering might give ace detectives, like Mathers and Colt (mainly Mathers), a chance to observe the conflicts among the business associates and friends that may have led to her death. It may sound cliché, but sometimes the killer does show up at the funeral.

After a few days had passed, my spirits began to rise. We had a team effort in place to catch Lisa's killer--and unorthodox team to be sure--but who knows, it may turn out to be effective.

Caroline was invited to watch the hugely popular TV show *Gunsmoke* at the main house, with the Judge and Marjorie. He watched every western on TV, and that time there were quite a few. Some television programs became so popular back then that it seemed everyone with a TV set tuned in to watch them each week. *Gunsmoke* was one of those shows, and it ran for 20 years.

Caroline was in the bathroom getting ready to walk over and watch the show. I noticed she was putting on new gold earrings. Very sparkly. Guess who bought them for her?

"I never knew people lived in such beautiful houses," she commented as she walked out of the bathroom. The place we grew up in was such a dump."

"It seems so small when I go back and visit mom."

"You know in the Wilkinson's kitchen they have a gas grill. They can grill a steak right there. Don't have to go outside in the July heat. Remember that rusted, crappy charcoal cooker we had in the back yard?"

Tom laughed. "Yes. It had that crank on the side so you could raise or lower the grill to control the temperature."

"Roy says I can come over and watch Westerns with them anytime. How nice is that!"

"I think you need a dad."

She treated Tom to a dramatic theatrical pose. "And Sherlock Holmes astounds us with another brilliant deduction. How does he do it?"

"You might want to get going. Show starts in five minutes. It takes 3 minutes to walk up the path. How's that for a deduction?"

"You mean, it takes Julia three minutes to walk down the path and hop into your bed. Amazing she can move so fast weighted down by that chest of hers."

"Don't worry, little girl. You'll grow breasts someday."

"Why wait for someday. You can go to hell right now." She laughed, grabbed her purse and sailed out the back patio door. "I love you, Tom," she hollered back as she went.

***

I had committed myself to put all my efforts into helping Det. Mathers and Phoenix PD solve Lisa's murder. I made the painful decision to withdraw from the next tournament, and erase the notes I had made in my calendar book to enter the two tournaments after that. I would miss the entire Texas/Oklahoma swing of the golf tour, including the Houston Classic and the Colonial Invitational, held at magnificent Colonial Country Club in Ft. Worth. I felt like I would win again this year, so this was difficult to do. But, I thought, it was the right thing to do.

The next tournament was The Masters in Augusta, Georgia, which I was not yet eligible to receive an invitation to. I had dreamed of the day I would be invited to Augusta, for as long as I could remember. The invitation I did receive was from the Judge, for me and Caroline to watch the final round on his TV. Not the same as being there.

I sat at the kitchen table and reviewed the notes and observations I had shared with Det. Mathers. I didn't write down one name that I considered as a suspect. I wasn't ready to share it with Mathers: Judge Roy Wilkinson. He was so angry the night of Lisa's death. He truly hated Sen. Luck. It was like the Judge was protecting his kingdom, his people, from barbarian invaders. I didn't for a moment think he killed Lisa himself. But why was he so concerned that the Luck crowd would try to pin the crime on one of his associates? Was there a reason to be concerned?

The notes I did share with Mathers were:

- Devin Hughes, Sen. Vance's campaign manager, arguing with Sen. Luck at the New Year's Eve party. "You run a dirty campaign."
- Lisa had reportedly given birth in Mexico to a child fathered by a member of a prominent family down there.
- The Luck's marriage had disintegrated into bitterness, obvious acrimony.
- Lisa asked for my help, not as a golf pro but as a private detective. She was clearly afraid of something or someone.
- Les Levine and Wes Stoneman, Valley Vista Club President, had an intense conversation at the after-tournament party. A legal issue?
- Lisa's conflict with Jordan Lucato, the brother-in-law. "Not another dime." Blackmail? Why? An affair? Or did J. Lucato have other information that could damage her?
- Dominic Lucato, the Father. A dead body was dumped at his vineyard. Must be a connection. Possible mob hit, per Det. Mathers. Winemaking isn't usually a violent activity.
- Carter VonEssen, staunch member of the opposition party, made a significant campaign contribution to Sen. Luck. Makes no sense to me, but the rich always have a strategic reason for where they place their money. That's how they get richer, while most of the rest of us don't.

I made some notes on whom to talk to and what questions to ask. Mathers said he would take care of interviewing the political writers at the state's newspapers, which I thought was a splendid idea.

In the afternoon I went to Valley Vista and hit practice balls on the range. Something was nagging at me, lurking in the back of my mind. I thought I might remember what it was if I let my mind drift while I engaged in my most joyful activity-- hitting a golf ball with near perfection.

But unfortunately, no such luck. No pun intended. Whatever was nagging me chose to remain hidden.

Chapter Eighteen
What Wine Pairs Best with Red Herring?

120 men had tee times at Valley Vista CC the day of Lisa Luck's murder. It was Men's Day at The Club. I traced the path of the driver—the apparent murder weapon—and found out it was set out in the morning on the driving range, was brought back in the afternoon and set inside the back door of the pro shop—which opens onto the hallway that leads to the locker rooms. Virtually anyone walking down the hallway could have seen it and taken it. The pro shop doors were left open during the day.

The men's locker room attendant, LeRoy Boggs, had a clear view of the exit from the locker rooms to the parking lot. He said he didn't see, as he put it, any of 'his gentlemen' carrying a #1 wood, a Driver, out the door that afternoon.

But, he admitted he left his post periodically for tasks such as setting out fresh towels in the shower room or polishing a member's golf shoes.

I thought, *it's not easy to walk out with an object as large as a driver and not be seen. But it was also not out of the ordinary for members to be carrying a club with them into the clubhouse or the locker room.*

The assistant club pro did a brisk business re-gripping golf clubs whose leather handles were showing signs of wear. My concern with whose fingerprints were on the club—such as mine—were unfounded. The assistant, who brought the future murder weapon in from the driving range, immediately cleaned the club's grip. Mathers' team found no prints on it at all.

I reviewed the roster of Men's Day golfers. It became just a blur of names. No one unusual stuck out. They were all men of wealth and prestige. I couldn't see any of them taking a driver from the clubhouse, sneaking over to Lisa's home and bashing her in the head. I could see no motive. They hire people to do their dirty work. The staff would have noticed a stranger wandering the hallways of The Club that day.

I had a quick phone conversation with Mathers and told him what I had learned. "120 suspects is just as bad as no suspects, my friend," Ed wisely commented.

***

The sand was flying everywhere...

No, I wasn't visiting an archaeology dig that afternoon. The flying sand was the result of Carter VonEssen attempting to practice sand trap shots. I kept my distance until he saw me and ceased his furious excavations.

I was there to give him a lesson in how to the get the ball out of the sand trap and safely onto the green. Amateurs tend to struggle with these shots because it is the one instance in golf where you don't hit the ball. You hit the sand behind the ball, which pops it out of the trap and onto the green. You take a fairly long swing with these shots, given the short distance you want the ball to go. This is where the Amateur's fear kicks in: if they accidentally hit the ball first, it will go screaming over the green and the poor hacker will find himself in even more trouble and great embarrassment.

One of the secrets of the truly great players is that they refuse to be embarrassed, and stay focused, no matter what strange and unfair things happen on the golf course. Jack Nicklaus was a master at this.

Carter was making the other fatal error in sand play: hitting so far behind the ball that he barely advanced the ball at all. The mean little sphere stayed in the sand trap, mocking him. If a golf ball could only talk...it would probably use quite a bit of profanity.

"Hey, Mr. VonEssen," I said.

He was red in the face from frustration and the exertion of pounding a steel club into hard sand twenty times. He took his sand wedge and with kind of an overhead lumberjack motion, slammed it into the tender turf at the edge of the sand trap. The turf was soft from spring rains. The blade of the club embedded about two inches. The club stood upright, not so much like the Sword in the Stone but the Tool of the Fool.

It always angered me to see someone damage the turf at a golf course. Golfers have no idea what pains the greens keepers take to keep the course looking beautiful for the players. Respect the game, or get lost, was my motto.

I never could tolerate displays of temper on the golf course, anyway. The game was designed by the ancient Scots to be difficult, frustrating and unfair. Their thinking was that golf would make the other aspects of life seem easier and benign by comparison.

As my father once told me when I caught a bad break while playing in a junior tournament, which kept me from capturing the trophy: "Tom, in golf as in life, you have to take your punishment like a man."

I let Carter catch his breath for a few moments, and the angry crimson fade from his face. I delicately removed his sand club from the turf, patted the grass back in place and hoped it wouldn't leave a scar.

I thought, *Detective Tom finally picked up a clue: VonEssen has a bad, almost uncontrolled temper. His wife Babs was worse. When she hit an errant shot, she was known to heave the misbehaving golf club (always the club's fault) as far as an Olympic javelin thrower.*

I showed him that if you hit 8 inches behind the ball, like he was doing, it was impossible to generate enough force through the sand next to the ball, to drive the ball up and out of the hazard—no matter how long a swing you took.

Carter looked at me with a puzzled expression. Like many successful businessmen, he had the approach of bludgeoning everything and everyone that got in the way of his success. That's doesn't work in golf. The little white spheroid is not impressed with any of us.

I showed him, for I believe the fifth time, that if he struck the sand two inches behind the ball, it would magically come out of the sand and onto the green.

Later he asked me to join him for a cold beverage at a table on the clubhouse patio. He chose a table where we could be by ourselves.

"I know you sometimes assist the local constabulary, Tom."

I nodded, wondering where this was leading.

"I wanted to give you a piece of information and let you decide whether it might be significant."

"Fine."

"The Lucks and the Goulds and ourselves share a gardener. He just started working for us two weeks ago. He's been working for the other two for some time. His name is Mondo Gonzalez. He does a damn good job. A real wizard at growing things. Fellow takes great pride in his work."

He sipped his lemonade, then brushed some sand from his sweater, rather nervously I thought.

I sat quietly. Det. Mathers shared with me a technique of his to let the person you are interviewing talk as much as he wants. Don't interrupt or lead them. Many times they will be so relaxed, because you aren't pressing them, that they will divulge more than they intended to. There is also the compulsion some people have to not let there be even a moment of silence in a conversation. That works really well to mine key info.

Carter cleared his throat. He fidgeted in his chair. He ran his hand through his luxuriant grey locks. Guy had more nervous gestures than that young New York comic Rodney Dangerfield.

"The thing is, I had him checked out. I don't like strangers wandering around on my property. The lower classes are full of envy. They steal. Almost can't help themselves. Maybe it's genetics. Who knows."

"So what did you learn, Sir?" It galled me to call morons like Carter, Sir, but that was my social position at the time.

"This Gonzalez has a rap sheet, I think you call it. He's a criminal, Tom."

"That's too bad."

"The worst of it is, my chauffeur Henry overhead him talking to one of his lawn crew about Lisa Luck's murder."

"What did he say?"

"He said, 'I'm glad she's gone. No one will miss her'. Imagine the bloody gardener saying such a thing about his employer. It's outrageous."

More thoughtful nodding from Super Sleuth Tom Colt.

"This is what I need you to share with your friend Det. Mathers. And please don't tell him this came from me."

No nodding from the sleuth. I certainly wasn't going to agree to that. Carter kept going anyway.

"The day of Lisa's death, this Gonzalez worked at the Luck Estate. His shift was from 9AM to 3PM. He was there, Tom. Maybe he bashed her head in with a shovel."

My first thought was, *what wine goes best with Red Herring?* But I had vowed to keep an open mind. "I really appreciate your sharing this with me, Mr. VonEssen."

"Call me Carter, please."

You notice when the rich want me to do an unpleasant errand for them they allow me to call them by their first name. How generous.

"Envy. It breeds hate like a swamp breeds mosquitoes."

"I will definitely check this out. Thank you for coming forward, Cart--

--Sir."

***

When I went into the clubhouse to grab my daily hamburger, I checked my messages. One was from a locksmith I had visited. He told me after I left his shop, and idea occurred to him. Early in his career, when he worked for a metal fabrication shop, they had lockers for the employees to store their personal gear. The key looked very similar to the one I showed him. I thanked him, but wasn't any further along. How many industrial lockers are there in a city the size of Phoenix?

***

I was starting to feel overwhelmed with information, probably much of it useless. I needed something to visually keep track of the suspects in the murder of Lisa Luck, and rank order them, from the most likely suspect to the least likely. I called in my incredibly artistic sister Caroline, told her what I had in mind.

"You need a Leaderboard," she immediately said.

"Right! I got a notepad and scribbled while I spoke. "We need name, motive, why they could have done it, and why it was improbable."

"Don't forget 'opportunity'."

"Of course."

Caroline's brow furrowed (just like mine did) as she pondered how to design this. "I know what we need. You hang loose. I'll beat feet to the art supply store and snare the goods."

I guessed she had said, You stay here. I will hurry to the store and back.

She came back in less than an hour with two large shopping bags and smiled. "No sweat." She disappeared into her room.

An hour later she emerged with a 3' x 3' stiff poster board. Across the top, in beautiful calligraphy-style lettering, she had printed LEADERBOARD. Next there were four columns labeled, motive, opportunity, and an upward arrow for why they were likely suspects and a downward one for why they weren't. On the left margin were 8 brackets that ran down the board vertically, apparently for the TOP 8 suspects' names. In each of the four columns there were brackets big enough for 3x5 cards with the information on each suspect.

Proudly, she handed me a bundle of white index cards and a package of felt-tipped markers of various colors. I looked it over. It was brilliant.

"Outta sight!" I exclaimed.

Caroline took a bow. "Thank you, thank you. But Tom, don't try to use cool lingo. Your charm with women comes from being both attractive and square. You're very 1950s. It a good decade for you to stay in, I think. You manage to be a bad boy who's non-threatening. It a marvelous balancing act you do. You're like a combo of James Dean and Roy Rogers."

"You come up with these brilliant insights about me. Maybe you should analyze yourself."

"I know enough about me already."

"Hey man, I can dig it, hipster sister."

Caroline looked up at the ceiling, then shook her head. "I really do not understand what the Wilkinson girl sees in you. It must be difficult for a young, rich, beautiful chick with tits as big as Idaho to get a date in our little town."

Caroline was joking, but what she didn't know was that Julia in fact spent many nights alone. A number of eligible, affluent young men in Scottsdale were simply afraid to ask her out on a date. Maybe I was braver than I thought.

***

Brooks Continues Our Story:

As night fell, Les Levine was drinking a perfect martini prepared by the supposedly grieving Sen. Luck. They were in the living room of the Luck home. Les was seated on a couch, the Senator standing at the native stone fireplace.

"You know how hard this was on me, Les?"

"You were a saint to put up with her."

The Senator looked to be getting emotional. "I did my best." He recovered his composure amazingly fast. "I have to know, Les, did you kill her?"

"No."

"Did you cause her to be killed?"

"No."

"I didn't think so, but I had to ask."

"I don't resent your asking at all."

"Who was responsible for her death?"

"I'm afraid it was someone on our team."

"Who?"

"I thought, perhaps...I was concerned your father Dominic might have done it. He is so protective of you and your ambitions."

The Senator reflected on that a few moments, looking outside at the lights by the patio, by the pool deck where Lisa was found. "I hope not, but I could understand why. Lisa was slowly but surely sinking us, sinking us all."

"I took a precaution against possible trouble from the police."

The Senator turned back to Les, eager to hear what the precaution was.

"We've had a problem with a prowler in the neighborhood. Remember, I only live a half mile from here. He's a drunk who breaks into houses to steal money to buy booze."

Les finished his martini, set it down on the table and stood up. "I came over that afternoon to try and talk Lisa out of filing for divorce, at least until after the election. I found her on the patio. The blood was fresh. The killer might have just left."

"So what did you do?"

"I got out of there as fast as I could and I saw the neighborhood bum passed out in a gully, sleeping it off. It gave me an idea. I took his shoes and went back here, put them on and made prints in the soft soil in the flower beds near Lisa's bedroom."

The Senator chuckled. "You are pure evil, Les. But you are also my most loyal friend. Dominic, or whoever it might be, is off the hook."

"Yes. The really great thing is that the old drunk may not remember what happened that afternoon anyway."

"I wondered, though, Les, if the killer might be one of our opponent's many allies."

Les shook his head. "Why would they get rid of their ticket to victory in November? Can you imagine what would have happened if Lisa filed for divorce right now. We need the conservative Catholic vote to have any chance. I mean, all the rednecks in this state love Sen. Vance."

Sen. Luck nodded. "I should have never married her. But she was so damn beautiful. And came from a classy family. I couldn't resist her. And I was good to her, Les, I really was. We couldn't have children, but that's not everything. The Doctors said I was 'shooting blanks'."

Les Levine really did not want to hear about the Lucks' personal/sex life, but Sen. Luck continued: "And she hounded me to adopt a child, but it wouldn't be a Lucato, you know. So why bother. And then she made that horrible, unforgiveable mistake in Mexico."

"It's over now. Don't let it be a burden to you. Rise above all the trouble she caused you."

"It's not easy to do that, Les." The Senator let out a deep sigh. "One more thing before you go. Our unexpected supporter Carter VonEssen told me that the golf pro Tom Colt is poking his nose into this. Do we have anything to worry about?"

Levine, though diminutive, could swell up into a bullying pose. "No, but if Tom Colt fucks with us, he surely will. I'll take care of that myself."

"Carter told me he sent him down the wrong trail. Colt seemed to buy it."

"Of course he did. He's an idiot golf pro. Don't give him a second thought."

Les Levine, who took immense pride in knowing everyone's secrets, and leveraging his and Sen. Luck's position as a result, had absolutely no knowledge of the secret that would very soon shake their foundations like an earthquake.

Tom Colt held the key to that secret. Literally.

***

Missy Gould was having lunch at her golf partner Jilly Flannery's house. Jilly's maid served club sandwiches on fresh-baked 7-grain bread, iced tea brewed in the intense Arizona sunshine and homemade vanilla ice cream on the patio that overlooked Jilly's beautiful back yard.

Missy and Jilly were going over the ladies' amateur tournament schedule for the remainder of the year. The duo was on a roll as a golf team.

Jilly was always a dedicated golfer—particularly now with Tom helping her so much as her coach—but Jilly had noticed that Missy was more determined than usual that they succeed as top amateur golfers of the country club variety. Missy was spending half her time on the golf course and half working at the dog shelter. She spent very little time at home with Sterling. Jilly suspected a rift had opened up between husband and wife.

Missy had looked the other way with Sterling's philandering in the past. Jilly knew that Sterling had ended a brief affair with Lisa Luck right before the holidays last year. At the New Year's Eve party, Missy was more upbeat than ever, probably relieved that Sterling had come to his senses, silly, fat old fool that he was.

Amid the light conversation about upcoming tournaments, Jilly couldn't help wondering if Sterling really had ended the affair with Lisa Luck. And if not, did he have to kill her to end it? The thought made her shudder with chills even though it was 85 degrees on the patio. Then Jilly had a thought that positively mortified her. She looked across the table at her wonderful friend. Could Missy have killed Lisa Luck? How well do we really <u>know</u> the people we know?

Jilly's assumption had been that someone in the Lucato organization had murdered Lisa. They were dangerous people, she knew. Dangerously ambitious.

Missy noticed Jilly staring at her. "Everything okay, Partner?"

"Absolutely." Jilly did her best to smile.

Chapter Nineteen
An Afternoon with Heroes
Mathers Visits His Nemesis, The Press
Tom and Katrina Finally Hook Up (On the Course)

Tom Continues Our Story:

On Sunday afternoon, Caroline, Julia, the Judge, myself and Marjorie took some time off from murder and mystery and gathered around the TV to watch the final round of The Masters Tournament.

When Arnold Palmer made a truly epic shot on the 16th hole for a birdie--holing a 40-foot, slick as glass chip shot--Caroline and Julia both sprang to their feet, applauded and cheered. In those days, Palmer always seemed able to summon a miracle shot when he needed it most. Up to that point in the final round, he had been having a rough day, losing the lead he held after three rounds. Two pros at the top of their game, gritty competitors both, Gary Player and Dow Finsterwald, had caught him.

I reflected on how we all need heroes, and then thought about who were mine. My father and John Wayne were the two I settled on. Since my father had been gone so long, and John Wayne was still here, going strong, maybe the two had merged into one image.

Caroline, her self-confidence increasing by the day, said, "You know, Julia, I met Arnie at the Phoenix Open, when I was caddying for Tom."

Julia looked incredulous, like her social order had been turned upside down. "You did????"

"Yes, indeed. We had a friendly but brief conversation about golf and life."

"You did????" Julia repeated. Then Julia turned to me, "Tom, your sister is very cool."

"She amazes me each and every day," said I.

The girls got even more excited when Palmer birdied the 17th hole from ten feet. "Arnie is unreal!" Julia exclaimed.

I thought, *we are the first generation to have the opportunity to get totally jazzed about watching a golf tournament on TV. I knew who to thank for that.*

We didn't get the satisfaction of seeing who won or being able to watch famous Green Jacket ceremony, during which The Masters winner is presented with a green sports jacket with the tournament's crest on the pocket; the previous year's winner helps him put it on. The tournament ended in a tie among Gary Player, Arnold Palmer and Dow Finsterwald. An 18-hole playoff would be held on Monday.

The Judge asked me, "So who's going to win tomorrow?"

"Palmer," I said with assurance. The Judge nodded in agreement.

The Judge said, "The way Palmer is going, I bet he wins 25 Major Championships."

I shook my head. "I doubt it, Sir. This game wears you down. It taxes your nerves to the limit, which shows up in your putting sooner or late. Look at Mr. Hogan. Sometimes it takes him 30 seconds to draw the club back on a short putt. It's painful to watch. If not for his putting, he would have won the US Open in '60 at Denver by 5 strokes."

"Not sure that's the best example. Hogan was nearly killed in a car wreck back in, what, 1949."

"But he recovered and had one of his best years in '53. He played great in major tournaments, especially the US Open, all through the Fifties. Also, we've never had so many great young players at the same time. Every tournament is a fierce battle."

"Hard to believe, Tom, that these formidable golfers are brought to their knees by the shortest shots in the game-- putts."

Caroline simply had to chime in. "That's where Tom has an advantage. His putting's been lousy all along, so he has nowhere to go but up."

Julia didn't care for that remark. "You be nicer to him Caroline."

"Someone has to be the realist in the family," my sister replied.

How did it feel to watch a tournament on TV that you've always dreamed of playing in, at a time when your game is strong enough to compete on that extremely challenging course?

Shitty. Absolutely shitty. But I tried my best to be a congenial guest that day. I wanted to go outside and scream.

In the 18-hole playoff for the Masters title on Monday, Arnold Palmer won his third green jacket, making one of his most heroic back nine charges to overcome Player and Finsterwald.

Heroes. Gotta love 'em. Gotta have 'em.

***

Brooks Continues Our Story:

First thing Monday morning, Det. Mathers paid a visit to David Breer, the senior political writer for the *Arizona Republic* newspaper. It was a hot day, the afternoon temps climbing into the 90s. Mathers wore a brown suit and was perspiring heavily as he made his way through the mass of cubicles until he found Breer's tiny corner office.

Breer was a balding, pale, rumpled looking guy, about 60, Mathers guessed. Actually, Breer was only 52. The newspaper biz is rough. His office was, well, a mess, with files strewn everywhere, even piled on the floor. Two steel grey filing cabinets, a beaten up desk and two chairs were the only furniture. The most striking aspect of the office were the numerous framed journalism awards that nearly covered one wall.

Mathers sat down. "Thanks for seeing me, Mr. Breer."

"No problem, detective. I thought you might pay a visit."

Breer took a mega-pack of Wrigley spearmint chewing gum from his desk, selected a piece and put it in his mouth. "Trying to quit smoking."

"The best way to quit is to never start," Mathers said with an air of superiority, not knowing why except that journalists made him nervous. They worked hard at making the police look bad.

"Very true."

"So tell me about the race for the United States Senate."

Breer laughed, leaned back in his chair and put his hands behind his head. "It's more of a crawl than a race. I've been covering politics since Roosevelt's first victory in '32, and I've never seen two more inept campaigns."

"Really."

"It's like neither of them wants to win. I didn't think this Luck character would get anywhere. He's just a pretty face. He's done nothing of any consequence except get pictures of himself and his lovely late wife in the society pages. Quite the party boy, this Sen. Luck is. Off the record, I think he's a puppet on a string. Just don't know who the puppet master is. There are rumors of rich industrialists in Mexico, but nothing I've been able to confirm."

"You said both campaigns are inept."

Breer popped in another stick of gum. *Trading an addiction to tobacco for an addiction to sugar*, Mathers thought.

"What surprises me is Sen. Vance's campaign. His long-time manager Rod Banks retired, so they brought in this hotshot from LA, Devin Hughes. Guy is supposed to be a genius. But he's doing everything wrong. He doesn't attack Luck on his do-nothing record in the State Senate. He doesn't stoke the rumor mill about Luck's wifes's well-known promiscuity. They overwork Vance at campaign events so he comes off as old and tuckered out, which he probably is by the way. But politics is an art of deflection and distraction. To sum up, Devin Hughes has lost the magic touch. I have no idea why. Even the slogan Hughes came up with is lame: 'Don't Take a Chance, Stay with Vance'. What a joke!"

"So who's going to win?"

Third piece of spearmint. *Glad my only addictions are to golf and red meat,* Mathers thought.

"Mathers, it all changed with Lisa Luck's demise. Sympathy is one of the most powerful forces in politics. The next polls come out in a week. I bet Sen. Luck surges, big time."

"You know my next question, David. Did politics play a role in Lisa Luck's death?"

"I knew you'd ask that and I wrestled with the question all morning."

"And..." To Mathers' surprise, he really, really had a craving for a stick of gum.

"And...I'm not sure. I mean, this case must be a cop's dream. It has sexual lust, lust for power, revenge--remember the dead body at Luck's Old Man's vineyard--and I would add shady business dealings."

"How do you mean?" Mathers asked eagerly.

"Luck makes this big deal about having a family-funded campaign, not being owned by big business interests and real estate developers like Sen. Vance is. But where did the money come from?"

Mathers' face showed he liked the information that Breer was giving him.

"As far as we can tell, Old Man Lucato runs a marginally profitable vineyard/winery operation and has some sort of import-export business with Mexico. It doesn't add up to wealth."

Mathers drove back to the station with renewed vigor. He loved to uncover corruption, which was rather easy because as he once told Tom, in his view 90 percent of wealthy business people, not to mention the politicians, were corrupt.

Over the years Tom learned that Mathers didn't really believe that inflated estimate of 90 percent. It was Mathers' way of reminding himself to remain alert, that people were seldom what they appear to be. Even the seemingly upstanding, upscale members of the community.

In any case, he was glad he lived the less complicated life of the middle class, honest cop. But darned if he didn't wish nearly every day that he could afford to play golf at Valley Vista Country Club. *That place is like heaven must be*, he thought.

***

Tom was in fact playing at the heavenly golf club at that very moment. He had invited Katrina Stern, and she quickly accepted the invitation, guided by that fluttery but perennially lonesome heart of hers.

On the first tee, Kat announced, "I don't mind playing from the men's tees." Which were further back, making the course longer and more challenging. "It's a good training tool. I have to keep improving, Tom. I really do."

Tom admired Kat's burning intensity to be a champion golfer. And her powers of concentration. All she saw was the target in front of her.

If this were a date, and Tom was pretty certain it wasn't, it was an unusual one. Kat said very little except to express her admiration for how hard he hit the ball. She insisted they carry their own bags, so they didn't even ride in a cart together.

"A gorilla would have a hard time out-driving you," she said in near-awe after he drove the green in one stroke on the 310-yard par-4 5th hole.

He swung the club with such ferocity, such abandon, it almost seemed primitive to Kat. He reminded her of a cave man bashing an antelope to take home for dinner. In her mind's eye, she pictured herself romping through the savannah, her female parts barely covered by a thin animal skin. Kat being Kat, she mentally pulled down the hem of the prehistoric garment for modesty reasons.

Kat's game was a mystery to Tom. She was so long-limbed, so flexible, with great muscle tone, she should have knocked the damn cover off the ball. But she didn't. The golf instructor in him came out as early as the 7th hole; he couldn't help himself.

"You know, you have the flexibility to swing back much further. You'd add 20 yards to your tee shots."

"I'm too tall. I'd just get off balance swinging back that far."

Tom demonstrated: "Brace your right knee more as you take the club back."

"Let me show you why that won't work." On the 9th tee, she executed both of his suggestions. She clobbered the ball; it went nearly 240 yards.

"Incroyable!" she cried out. "I mean, incredible. I speak French when I get excited."

"You have much more athletic potential than you are using."

"I know," she bowed her head like she was ashamed. Then she looked up at him and smiled. They shared a moment, but Tom couldn't tell whether it was a "thanks, buddy" moment or a "after the round, let's take a shower together" moment. It was a hot day. They were both sweaty. A boy can hope.

Kat continued busting out long drives all through the back 9 holes. She only got off balance once, on the 15th. She topped the shot and her ball dribbled down the fairway only 110 yards. On the 16th, she came right back and blasted her tee shot only 20 yards behind his. He smiled reassuringly at her.

Tom said, "When I won the tournament in Vegas, I was thinking of you the whole time, how you focus, shut out distractions and give each shot your best effort. My victory was due in part to you, Katrina."

Kat flushed with excitement. Her inner voice said, *Kiss Him! You want to with all your heart. The waitress in the restaurant was right: he could be THE ONE.* And again, she backed away from a wonderful moment. Her reasoning was, how do I know he feels the same way?

How does anyone know, Kat?

And here's what Tom was thinking: *Look at those sweet, full lips of hers. I bet her kisses are amazing. I wish this lovely girl wasn't so opposed to romance.*

The lovely girl chose to force all romantic thoughts out of her head and they finished their round of golf in 'golf buddy' mode. They ordered iced teas on the clubhouse patio and sat in friendly silence for a few minutes--save for the insistent beating of Katrina's heart, which she was sure Tom could hear.

Finally, she said, "How do I get the fans to like me, like they like you?"

Tom became animated: "You want to be Miss Popularity!"

"I wouldn't go that far. I just want to be noticed. There are opportunities for product endorsements and guest appearances at corporate outings, for the most popular players."

Tom normally wouldn't get drawn into a conversation like this--filled with land mines--but since she obviously didn't view him in a romantic way, he plunged ahead. "I can give you some ideas, but you have to promise you won't get mad at me."

"I promise. Unless the suggestions are stupid."

Tom took a big gulp of the cold tea, for strength. *Okay, here goes.* "Try smiling more. You make frowny faces when you're playing. The fans think you're frowning at them."

"I don't even see them, Tom."

"Well you should. When they cheer for good shot, wave at them and give them you're brightest smile."

"That would break my concentration."

"Look, you only have to focus your concentration for about 3 minutes before each shot."

"I've seen you in tournaments. Sometimes you get so involved with chatting with your adoring female fans that you forget it's your turn to hit the ball!"

"I admit I lose focus at time. But interacting with fans can help you break the tension."

Kat said, reluctantly, "I see what you mean."

"My next suggestion is to let loose out there. Don't play so cautiously. Let the big dog hunt, is what we say on my tour."

"I play the percentages. I chart every shot the night before a round. Your style of play leads to hitting the ball in the water hazard or out-of-bounds."

"Or it leads to making an eagle on a par 5 that takes the spectators' breath away. I mean, you carry more than one ball with you when you play."

"Let loose," Kat said. "Not sure about that one. Any other advice?"

"Let's talk wardrobe."

Kat's face twisted into that pretty pout.

Tom continued: "Guys like to look at attractive girls. And trust me, you're just about the most attractive one out there. You move with such grace. Your long dark hair is gorgeous. And you have those mysterious green eyes framed with lovely dark lashes."

Kat blushed with excitement again.

"But you look like you buy your golf clothes at the Army Surplus Store. Drab colors, baggy outfits."

"Pardon me, but I don't have lots of money to spend on clothes like you do. I heard Judge Wilkinson pays you an allowance, like you give a child."

"It's called having a sponsor. You're full of excuses."

"That's not true! I'll tell you what it is. When I first started on tour, I was so unsure of myself, I just wanted to blend in. If I could have found them, I would have worn clothes the same colors as the trees." Now, Kat made her famous frowny face--at Tom. And folded her arms together.

"No need to hide now. You're a champion, and in 5th place on this year's money list. I checked this morning."

Kat nodded graciously at the compliment, then said, "Also, I'm crappy at shopping."

"Well, do not worry. My friend Jilly Flannery is the most celebrated shopper of our era. Let me tell her to call you and you can go out clothes shopping with her."

Kat surprised Tom by saying, "Okay, I'll do it. But I don't want to look like a pin-up girl out there."

"Put yourself in Jilly's hands. Because of her fashion sense, my sister went from looking like a bag lady to looking like a confident young career gal on top of the world."

That night, when Tom called Jilly to set up the shopping date, her first perceptive question was, "Are you and Katrina lovers?"

"Not at all. Barely friends. She isn't interested in me as a boyfriend. Just doing a favor for her because she and I were on the college golf team at ASU. She needs help with her image."

"Okay then. I need to buy a few new things for me, too. But I don't want to give a boost to my competitor's sex appeal."

"No matter the boost, she'd never compare to you."

"My, my. I'm feeling rather warm. Let's get together on Friday night."

"Great. You can take off some of your brand new clothes."

***

Jilly took Katrina to 3 stores in Scottsdale known for their fashionable, trendy sportswear. Jilly got Katrina prepared for the experience by remarking, "Katrina, you dress like a guy. But don't worry. I'm here to help."

Jilly selected a goodish pile of shorts, slacks, tops and sweaters for Kat to try on, and of course an equally goodish pile for herself. They went into a changing room that had plenty of space for them to try on clothes together. They both stripped down to their underwear, Jilly going one step further. Kat wondered why Jilly had to take off her bra to try on pullover sweaters. Things became clearer when Jilly remarked, "You have a wonderful athletic physique, but you are so skinny. Tom likes curvy girls." Jilly preened, her chest thrust out.

"Tom and I are just golf buddies, not boyfriend-girlfriend or anything." She didn't add, *Because I keep chickening out--ever since college.*

Jilly thought, *look at that beautiful young thing. And she's a better golfer than I am. This is not good!*

Kat began trying on the colorful, coordinated outfits Jilly had selected. She was impressed. Jilly's taste in clothes was excellent.

Jilly said, "You are so trim. Lucky you! But I thought German girls like to eat--pork shanks, sausage, potatoes, sauerbraten."

"I do have a weakness for bratwurst."

A light bulb appeared above Jilly's head. She was also an accomplished matchmaker. "At a food expo, I met this very handsome, up-and-coming sausage company owner. And very single. His name is Stan Barker. His bratwurst is delicious-- large and juicy. When I saw it, I just had to take a nibble. Let me introduce you two. Who knows, you may hit is off."

"I'm not sure..."

"I forgot to mention, he loves golf. And he grew up in Milwaukee. That's almost like Germany, isn't it. He went on and on about this marvelous country club his family belongs to there, Blue Mound CC. Said he terribly misses being able to play there. Made the place sound like the Elysian Fields with water hazards. Stan's a total golf nut. As if I should talk!"

An hour later, Katrina with an armful of pretty new clothes and a potential date with a sausage tycoon, went to the cash register to complete her purchase.

Jilly came up behind and said, "No, no. My treat."

"I can't let you do that. I like to pay my own way."

"Let's do this: let me pay half. Tom and I are such good, I mean close, very close, friends it's the least I can do for an old college bud of his."

The total cost for Kat's new threads was $119. Kat opened her wallet and pulled out three twenty-dollar bills. Jilly laughed, took out a charge card for that store from her wallet. "You need to get with the modern age, girl. Cash is on its way out. Credit cards are the thing of the future."

Kat looked doubtful. "I've heard those things make you buy more than you should."

"Absolutely! That's the future."

After they paid and were walking out of the store, Kat thought, *So Tom likes girls with bodies like Jilly's.* She had a beautiful new wardrobe, but went home crestfallen. Later, at her apartment trying on the new clothes, she rallied. *I don't care what Jilly said, I know Tom likes me,* she thought. *Why can't I tell him how much I want him? Why can't I bust loose?*

She unbuttoned the top two buttons of her new turquoise golf shirt. It was a start.

Chapter Twenty
A Confession in the Shower
The Body Count Rises
Brunch with Mandy and Marco

Tom Continues Our Story:

5PM at Valley Vista CC. I was showering in the deserted locker room. Jilly told me one time that in the Ladies Locker Room, there were individual shower stalls with doors. The men's side had gang showers like an athletic team's locker room. I wondered if this was because men like to compare anatomy.

Why did Jilly share that tidbit? She had a fantasy of making love with me in one of the Ladies' shower stalls. I reminded her that she had a perfectly fine, spacious shower in her master bathroom at home we could use. "Where's the danger in that?" she replied.

I said, "Well, Danger Girl, if I were seen in the Ladies' shower room, General Mgr. Basil Hedgerow would immediately fire me."

She said, "Are you kidding, sweetie? Club Management messes with you and the Ladies of Valley Vista CC would riot."

So far, I have not taken Danger Girl up on her fantasy.

Back to the men's side where I was showering that afternoon, Sterling Gould stepped under the shower head two spaces down from me. Without their perfectly pressed shirts, silk ties and expensive tailored suits, the rich old men like Sterling typically looked repulsive. He had enormous rolls of fat around his midsection that jiggled obscenely as he moved.

I hoped, no I pledged, that when I'm 70 I will have a much better physique than that.

Sterling, looking preoccupied, took a bar of soap and slowly rubbed it with a washcloth with the Club's gold logo on it, until soap was dripping onto the floor. Finally, he said, "I have some things to tell you, Tom," he said.

Washing my hair, I thought, *what a strange place for a meeting.* But I said, "Fine. What ya' got?"

"Ummm...last summer and into the fall, Lisa Luck and I were..."

"Intimate?"

"Great word! Precisely. We were for a time passionate about each other. She told me that she was meeting with a divorce attorney shortly before she...died. I had recommended the firm to her, Hastings & McCandless. Poor young thing was miserable."

I rinsed the shampoo out. Still seemed like a strange venue for this conversation. The young detective in search of The Naked Truth. I stifled a laugh.

"That's important information. I'm glad you came forward."

"The cops..."

"Don't suspect you at all in her death."

His entire girth shook with relief, all the quivering rolls of belly blubber. "Thank heavens. I could never hurt Lisa. I was worried because she was quite put off when I ended the affair, just before Thanksgiving."

"You have nothing to worry about, as far as I know."

"There's more, I'm afraid. Missy and I threw a New Year's Eve party."

"I was there, yes."

He looked startled, like he couldn't recall my being there that night, or understand why on earth I would have been invited. And here I thought I was the life of the party.

"Yes, well. This Les Levine person handed me an envelope toward the end of the evening. It was a proposal that Sen. Luck would grant Lisa a quick divorce if I would agree to divorce Missy and marry Lisa before the November '62 election."

Now it was my turn to look startled.

"The whole thing was written like a binding legal agreement. I read it over and thought Levine was completely daft. I had no intention of leaving Missy. We have a good arrangement. I'd never divorce her unless she cheated on me."

I had already learned to not comment on these people's weird moral code.

"The kicker was that the agreement included a 90K payment, a dowry, I suppose they called it in the old days."

I said nothing. I knew more was coming.

"Cash is a little tight right now. The development projects I'm in with Roy Wilkinson have me tapped out. But I can't pass them up. The payoff will be in the hundreds of millions of dollars someday. We're buying the best acreage all over the state. Our children and their children will be set for life."

"How would Les Levine know you were cash-poor?"

He soaped up his chest, snorted like a big ol' walrus. "That little weasel has his ear in every keyhole."

I turned the temp down on the shower water. This meeting was making me hot under the collar, even though I wasn't wearing one.

"Sterling, would you describe Lisa as a slut? As promiscuous?"

"Not at all. She was monogamous with me, I can tell you. A lovely girl but a lonely girl. I shall miss her."

He grew wistful, and smiled as though remembering the sweet and sweaty details of being intimate with Lisa.

He said, "When I was with Lisa, I was a remarkably robust lover. It's like the years fell away."

I narrowly avoided barfing.

Evidently the business portion of the shower was over. I put my head under the water spray to cool off. I noticed Sterling glancing over at me, specifically at the package below my waist.

"No wonder the ladies, young and old, like you so much. You're the most popular golf pro in the history of this Club."

"I thought it was my wit and charm."

"Perhaps so. It would be difficult for them to like you for your money."

Their go-to insult was always about money. *Well, pig man, someday I'll have more money than you.*

Sterling laughed at his little joke, the fat rounds shaking like pasty pale jello. I turned the water off and left the shower room. As I was dressing, I thought, *Les Levine. What a piece of work. Tried to ship Lisa off like an unwanted piece of furniture. All she was to them was an attractive backdrop to the Senator's campaign. To hell with these people. I admired that girl.*

***

Brooks Continues Our Story:

Tom got a phone call when he was dressing to leave the Club that evening. It was Det. Mathers:

"We can move Jordan Lucato down the Leaderboard. Officer Rudy confirmed with two sources that Lisa gave Jerry money because she felt sorry for him. He wasn't blackmailing her. Richard made his brother grovel for every last dime. Richard was the eldest of the Lucato sons, so he controlled the purse.

"Lisa was softhearted."

"Evidently. Unless another motive emerges, Jordan isn't our guy."

***

The front door to Cummings Photographic Studio opened and a man walked in. It was just after sunset. Monty Cummings heard the door. He was in the darkroom. "Be with you in just a minute," he said.

About 5 minutes later the door to the darkroom opened and the wide-bodied Cummings waddled out.

The knife plunged into his throat. He staggered forward and held his hands to his neck. Blood spurted out between his fingers.

"Who are you?" he said, gurgling out blood.

The fastidious killer backed up so none of Cummings' unpleasant, messy blood splattered on him. He was wearing black gloves.

Cummings, rapidly bleeding out, collapsed face down on the linoleum floor. The killer quickly got to work looking through every file cabinet, every drawer in the desk, and the usual 'secret hiding places' people put things which seldom turn out to be completely secret.

The man came up with nothing. Angered, he looked over at Cummings, who clearly had expired.

He slipped out quickly, and unnoticed. He had the gnawing feeling that his mission that night was a complete failure. The photographs were already in others' hands.

***

The next morning, over eggs benedict perfectly prepared by his devoted wife Mandy, Marco Greene scanned the newspaper in between bites.

Mandy was a perfectly proportioned young woman with exciting curves, and a pleasant face with cute dimpled cheeks that appeared when she laughed. But, she didn't laugh that often these days. She had convinced herself that she was getting fat, which spawned a fear that Marco would one day wake up to the fact she was blimpy and dump her, probably for his floozy of a secretary with the dagger-like fingernails, Eliza.

Her solution was to become an expert cook, to please her food-loving husband. She took cooking classes in Scottsdale, and practiced new recipes when Marco was at the office, until she perfected them.

Here's where communication is so vital to any relationship, even a Mafia marriage. Marco thought Mandy was a tad too thin, but was afraid to tell her.

Marco finished his eggs, and smiled contentedly at his lovely wife. She loved it when he loved her cooking.

Marco noticed the small article about the death of local photographer Monty Cummings.

"This is what happens when you get greedy, when you don't live up to the business agreements you make."

Mandy stopped cutting her egg and English muffin and looked up at him, clueless. "What do you mean?"

"Never mind, darling. It's not important. I was just thinking out loud."

What was on his mind were some very dark thoughts indeed.

***

Richard Luck went for an early morning swim every day. He padded out to the pool from the kitchen carrying a towel over his shoulders and a glass of orange juice. He was wearing blue tropical-print swim trunks on his trim, handsome frame.

He walked past the lounge chair where his wife's body had been found, looked at it vaguely like it held no particular significance. He set the towel and the orange juice on a picnic table with an umbrella, kicked off his sandals and dove into the pool.

Richard liked to swim underwater, believing it freed up his thinking, as though he left this world and entered one of his own design. That morning, the thought that occurred to him was that he now had a clear path to becoming a US Senator. Lisa believed she could divorce him? That was never going to happen.

Now she was gone. He had little remorse. She was the one who spread her legs for some young guy in Mexico while he was busting his ass trying to negotiate a bright future for them with investors down there.

No one could possibly tie Lisa's death to him. He was free.

The thought of finding a new girlfriend, a future Senator's wife, thrilled him. He knew his bed would not be lonely for long.

Richard Luck broke the surface of the water, saw the brilliant sunshine sparkling on the waves he created. He was ready to fulfill his destiny. *Think of the power a US Senator has!*

Tom Continues Our Story:

In the morning I went out to talk with Mondo Gonzalez, the gardener. He was scheduled to work at the Gould's property that day, I was told by Missy.

I found Gonzalez trimming the oleander bushes that served as a privacy fence at the east end of the Gould's property. *This guy really was a master gardener,* I thought as I approached him. Missy and Sterling's lawns and gardens had never looked healthier.

I recognized the unmistakable scent of steer manure, then noticed bags of it stacked nearby. It was used to fertilize lawns.

Gonzalez was a hulking guy with thick, short legs, dark curly hair and one of those mustaches that curved down at the corners and made a fella look menacing. He walked with an odd, side-to-side gait like he was slightly crippled.

"Good morning, Mr. Gonzalez," I said.

He turned, eyed me with suspicion. "Yes?"

"My name is Tom Colt. I'm assisting the police with looking into the death of Lisa Luck."

I saw a bushy left eyebrow twitch. "I didn't know the woman, Senor." He went back to his pruning.

"You were reported to have told one of your employees that you were glad she was gone, something to the effect that, we're better off."

He turned back to me and spat. Since he wasn't chewing tobacco and probably had not had a bug fly into his mouth, I assumed there was a message in the spittle for me.

"Puta," he said.

"Please go on, sir."

"We all knew she was a whore. Sen. Luck deserved a good wife, a loyal one to give him children. He is going to make life better for us little people. My dream is, we will live in houses like this one day instead of mowing the lawns and spreading manure."

Even I at 27, who didn't give a rat's ass about politics, knew what Gonzalez said was 100 percent steer manure. Politicians are mainly focused on making their dreams come true and putting their interests first, not ours. I had to suppress a laugh at his little people comment. I pictured Luck being lustily cheered by a room full of dwarfs.

I wondered which of the loyal household staff members eavesdropped at the Luck residence and then blabbed the tidbit about the Lucks not being able to conceive a child. But I didn't know whether this information had any bearing on the case.

So I continued: "You were on the Luck property the day she was killed."

He nodded. "So."

"So tell me what you saw."

I think he wanted to say he didn't have to tell me anything. But my purposely vague reference of "assisting the police" contained just enough authority to keep him talking.

"She was swimming. She stepped out of the pool and wanted me to look at her body, which was wrong."

"You could have averted your eyes." Ha! Remember the asshole who taught me that phrase!

"She liked for us to look, staff, servants, whatever you wish to call us. She was proud of her body."

"Was she naked?"

"No. White bathing suit. But almost..."

"Transparent when wet."

He didn't know what I meant. "You could see," I tried.

He nodded.

"No one else was at the house?"

"I worked all over the grounds that day. Saw no one but...her."

"Did you hear any cars drive up?"

"No, senor."

I knew Gonzalez was lying about Lisa getting nearly naked by the pool so she could torment the gardening staff. That would've been something Julia Wilkinson would have done, not Lisa.

Richard Luck's supporters--apparently including Gonzalez--had developed a narrative that Lisa was a slut, and they were going to stick with it. Mathers has an acronym for this type of behavior BTOB, Believe Their Own Bullshit.

But I also knew, at that moment, that Gonzalez had nothing to do with Lisa's murder. The guy was dedicated to growing beautiful things, not destroying them. And I'm seldom wrong about people.

See, Mathers' acronym especially applies to me.

"You do amazing work out here, Mr. Gonzalez," I said. I thanked him for his time and left. But, I detested the man's characterization of Lisa as a whore. I didn't see her that way at all. There was much more to her story.

The mystery of Lisa's death could only be solved if I solved the mystery of Lisa's life. I mean, if Det. Mathers and I did. And Caroline.

The most compelling piece of information was that Gonzalez did not hear any cars. I doubted the killer would have parked on the street and hoofed it up the long driveway to the home. The car would have been visible to a half-dozen neighbors.

I closed my eyes and did a 360-degree memory tour of the Luck's property, from a position by the pool. There were low hills behind the property, as far as I remember uninhabited desert. Could a killer have parked on the other side of those hills and hiked to the Luck residence, unseen? If so, we had our premeditation sewn up. The killer, it would seem, knew the Lucks at least fairly well and had most likely been to the house before.

When I got back to the guest house, I called Mathers and told him what I learned. He said he would send an officer to check out my hunch.

Chapter Twenty-One
The Photos That Changed Everything

Judge Roy Wilkinson prided himself on knowing everything of significance that was happening in his city, but it took a meeting with none other than Marco Greene to bring him up to speed on the looming political disaster. Marco had called the Judge to meet at a coffee shop on Central Avenue, not far from the Judge's office.

They sat down at a corner table, greeted each other in an unfriendly but businesslike fashion, and then Marco slid a manila envelope across the table to the Judge. Wilkinson opened the envelope and examined the contents--photos.

"How did you get these?"

"That's not important. The important question is, what are you prepared to do about it?"

The Judge looked through the photos again. Four whores cavorting," he said.

"Politicians...they lack even basic morality," Marco summed up.

And the meeting was over. Marco Greene got up and walked out. Meetings with gangsters tend to be brief. They don't go in for small talk.

Coming out of yet another locksmith shop in search of the secret to the elusive key, Tom Colt saw Marco Greene leave, the Judge coming out moments later. He remembered the Judge saying he wanted to rid the business community of the Marco Greenes. Tom wondered if the Judge had found a way to get Greene to leave town.

***

Tom Continues Our Story:

I was new to the detective biz but I already recognized that prospecting for clues is like prospecting for gold. In the old West, if you weren't sure where to look, you just kept digging. Sometimes, you hit the mother lode when you least expected it. My lucky break came while I was driving through Scottsdale, which calls itself 'The West's Most Western Town'.

I was picking up some new McGregor 'golden tee' golf slacks I had taken to my favorite tailor for minor alterations. My waist size was between 34" and 36" so it was hard to find a perfect fit off the rack. Katrina pointed out that if I ate less red meat I might slim down to a perfect 34. Not going to happen.

Walking down the sidewalk, I saw yet another locksmith/key shop. I went inside. Behind the counter was a very young Mexican man, early 20s. Perhaps the business was started by his father. Even the shopkeepers tried to fit in with the Old West theme. He was wearing an ornate, dark outfit of the vaquero, or Mexican cowboy. He stopped grinding keys and introduced himself as Jamie. I told him who I was, explained my dilemma and handed him the key.

"Naranja!" he exclaimed.

"What does that mean?"

"Orange in my language. This belongs to the Valenzuela Trucking Company. Also known as The Naranja Company in Mexico because their trucks are orange, their buildings are painted orange. Their drivers wear orange hats. My uncle drives for them, the Los Angeles to Phoenix route. This key opens a locker. My uncle has one just like it."

I was beaming.

"Can you tell me anything about the company?"

"The Valenzuelas are wonderful people. My uncle has worked for them for 20 years. They live near Hermosillo, Sonora. What else...their Arizona headquarters is way out in the west part of town, 59th Avenue, I think."

"I can't thank you enough, Jamie."

"What do you think you will find in the locker, Mr. Colt?"

"Trouble with a Capital T."

"El Conflicto."

"Right. What is your favorite beverage, Jamie?"

"Cerveza."

A day later two cases of Dos Equis lager were waiting on the back doorstep when Jamie arrived to open the shop.

***

Now, I'm cooking with gas, I thought as I dialed 'information' from a pay phone near the locksmith shop on 5th Avenue in Scottsdale. Valenzuela Trucking Co., as my helpful friend Jamie had told me, was on 59th Avenue and Thomas Road. I was on 70th Street, so it would be a long boring drive out there. I picked up two roast beef sandwiches with my favorite spicy mustard at a nearby deli, and set off with renewed hope.

I wondered, though, how I was going to just sashay into a place of business and ask directions to the employee locker room.

When I arrived at the front gate of this truck depot, where trucks came to be serviced and drivers came to get their assignments from the dispatcher, I saw my concerns were unwarranted. There was a 8 foot high carport-like structure outside, with numerous storage lockers on a wall, protected from the weather, about 5' high and 25' long.

How does one pose as a trucker? I had my golf clothes on, my own kind of uniform. Should I go to a store that supplies jeans, working boots and flannel shirts? No, I decided that behaving like you belong was the most important thing. I walked up with a confident stride into the locker area.

As I scanned the bank of lockers for 27B, a real trucker walked up to his locker, a burly guy with jeans, scuffed yellow work boots and a checked red and grey flannel shirt. He had a huge head and a thick mustache.

"Hey, how ya' doin'," he said as he turned the key in the lock.

"Great, man, except for that fog coming out of Monterey Bay. Hate driving through that stuff." My extensive geography and meteorology knowledge came courtesy of playing the Bing Crosby Invitational Pro-Am out there.

"You doin' that run out of Salinas?"

"Yep. Truck full of artichokes."

All would have been well if I hadn't added, "Love dipping those leaves in garlic butter, maybe a little tarragon."

I found 27B and turned the key in the lock, hoping the trucker wouldn't be staring at me like he wanted to stuff me in the locker.

He said, "I like 'em that way too, but the wife says they're too expensive at the grocery sometimes."

With a heavy-legged gait, he went back to his truck. I breathed a sigh of relief. What do I so often say? It's all about fitting in.

And I now had a white 10"x13" envelope in my hand. I hurried back to my car, put the envelope on the front seat. I had been having serious guilt pangs about not telling Det. Mathers about the key. Who knows, maybe the police could have found the locker before I did. Maybe they even have directories of keys to reference, like Sherlock Holmes had penned a monograph about types of cigarettes and tobacco.

I looked at the envelope. It was sealed with thick packing tape. On the front, in Lisa's pretty, flowing handwriting was:

> For Tom Colt   xxxxoooo
> I will be at the Valenzuelas. Could you and Caroline join me there? I need your help. I need you guys.

Now, I really felt guilty. Why couldn't I have done more to help this lovely girl?

I drove out of the truck stop lot and stopped at the nearest pay phone to call Mathers. We arranged to meet at the guest house at 4PM. I decided to keep the envelope sealed until he got there.

***

Brooks Continues Our Story:

Dominic Lucato, patriarch of his clan, stood on the hill overlooking the lush, healthy terraces of grapevines of his vineyard, and equally healthy patches of marijuana, actually his most profitable cash crop. In his hand was a piece of paper with a handwritten note that said simply, "Honor Our Agreement."

His hard 70 years had given him a bowling-ball paunch, a stooped back, white hair which he trimmed to short bristles and arthritis in both knees. He walked slowly and with discomfort.

Dominic had lied to the police about not knowing the identity of the body that was found on his vineyard property. The man had been employed at his vineyard for ten years before leaving to take a higher paying job with the Morales Group in Mexico.

The note referenced the agreement they had made with Roman Morales to obtain the funding for his son's campaign. Dominic suspected that Morales had seen that Sen. Luck was, in his campaign speeches and interviews, waffling on, if not absolutely breaking, certain key provisions of the agreement they had made.

Dominic also did not share the note, which he found on the dead body, with the police. His generation had a deep distrust of cops.

The Old Man looked over his beautiful vineyard, raised up from rough desert soil, with great pride, but there was also a weariness in his eyes. Was everything they built about to come crashing down?

He said, in a whisper, "Everything I did, it was for a good cause, it was for my beautiful boy."

***

The oval dining room table in the Guest House was now sort of a crime lab analysis table. Mathers and Tom were seated there, with assorted documents relating to the Lisa Luck murder spread out over the table, and even on the floor. They were looking at THE PHOTOS Tom had retrieved.

The photos depicted two naked Caucasian males and two naked, voluptuous, highly energetic Mexican females, both with long dark, untamed hair, engaged in every combination of vigorous sexual activity that 4 bodies could comfortably contort themselves into. The two girls took on each man, while the sidelined man watched with unabashed excitement, knowing his turn was next. The photos were both riveting and disgusting to Tom.

The two men were Sen. Richard Luck and the campaign manager for his opponent, Devin Hughes.

Ed looked through the dozen or so photos without much visible reaction. Tom chose to change the subject, from the cringe-worthy subjects of the photos.

"These photos were taken in a darkened hotel room. Why didn't either of them see the flash?"

"You're thinking of those cheap Made-In-Japan cameras they sell to consumers. The military and the government, like the CIA, have miniaturized cameras that can be placed in tight spots, and don't need flash equipment to work in poor light. The latest in technology."

"Sounds very James Bond."

"I read a lot of Ian Fleming's novels on stakeouts. My fav is *Goldfinger*. I've read that golf match scene between James Bond and Auric Goldfinger a dozen times."

"I do believe Det. Mathers, that you are just as obsessed with golf as I am."

"And I believe you are almost as obsessed with justice in this world as I am."

Tom laughed. "I think you're right."

"Well, then, let's us get out there and find us a killer. But first a double-decker hamburger at Bob's Big Boy might be good."

"And chocolate shakes. Detectives need their strength."

"We're gonna really need it now, my friend. Maybe a double order of fries."

Caroline came in weighted down with two bags of groceries. She set them on the counter. "I've never seen two guys who eat as much as you two do."

Her eyes bulged when she spotted the famous photos. She picked one up, examined it closely.

"What a horrid bastard Richard Luck is. Lisa deserved so much better."

She fumed for a few more seconds then said, "Wait...I know where these were taken."

Mathers bristled with anticipation.

"It's a hot-sheet motel on 36th Street. It's where...I was arrested. Ed, I...worked a temp job as a filing clerk for a law firm downtown. On my lunch hour I would give the firm's senior partners blow jobs there."

Mathers' turn to look startled.

"Lemme tell you, the BJs paid a lot better than the temp position."

"I used to work Vice," Mathers commented. "Surprised we didn't cross paths."

"I was too elusive for you, Ed. The charges were dropped due to diligent efforts on my behalf by the firm's Senior Managing Partner, my best customer."

Tom said, "So do you remember the name of the motel?"

Caroline revolved in a little circle, trying to conjure up a memory. "It was the Shangri-La, but it had a guy's name on it...ahhh...think, Caroline."

She got a look of triumph. "Marco's Shangri-La was the name of it."

Mathers jumped out of his chair. "Could it be?" he said to Tom.

"Yes it could," Tom said with a grin. "Marco Greene."

Mathers walked around the room saying, "YES!" over and over.

"Evidently, I made a significant contribution to your investigation, Detective. And please Ed, don't judge me. I know Tom doesn't. I was 20 and broke."

"Judge you? I feel like kissing you. Caroline, you just busted this case wide open."

"A cop wants to kiss me," she mused, looking dazed as she returned to the kitchen.

Tom and Mathers resumed looking at the photos. "Ed, these pictures, they're considered pornography by law enforcement, right?"

"Yes they are. They include images of erect male organs and oral-genital contact."

"I don't think I've ever seen pornography before."

"Good. Stay away from that stuff." He continued: "It is illegal to transmit images like this through the US Mail. I believe we can use them to put the squeeze on Marco Greene."

"Let me go over to his office--during the day. He's married to my ex-wife."

Det. Mathers already knew this. He had Tom thoroughly checked out before inviting him to assist with the investigation.

"Dunno if that's a good idea, Tom. Let me think on it."

***

Tom Continues Our Story:

Marco Greene's offices were located just off 32nd Street and Camelback Road, the northern boundary of the city's business district at that time. It was primarily a residential area. Four older homes on a quiet side street had been spruced up and converted into office space for professionals. The four professional tenants were a CPA, an Attorney, an Architect and a Gangster.

I walked up to the latter's office. The sign on the door was a series of rolling hills painted gold, above it printed Marco Greene & Associates, in bright green. Very classy. I'm sure Miss Stirdivant, my high school English teacher, would have recognized the significance of the colors on the sign. I expected a sign that said: *Warning! Dangerous Mobsters Inside. Enter at Your Own Risk. And Wipe Your Shoes on the Mat, If Youse Know What's Good for Youse.*

I rang the buzzer. Marco's secretary, a curvy thing with frightful blue eye makeup and long red dagger-like fingernails, answered and showed me with crisp efficiency to Marco's office in the back, which had been converted from a master bedroom.

Marco greeted me warmly, with a hug of all things. He pointed me to a nearby couch and he sat in an armchair. Up close, he looked older than I thought he was, probably mid-50s. His face looked puffy and he had a day or two of stubble. Marco also had the biggest hands I had ever seen on a Homo Sapiens. Great hands for strangling, I observed.

He also had a giant personality. He was almost affable. When I told Mathers I was going to make an appointment to meet with Marco, which he strongly advised against, he said the cops call Marco, The Happy Gangster.

He popped up from his chair and said with a note of embarrassment, "What kind of host am I? Would you like a refreshment?"

"No, thank you. I don't really care for Chianti this early in the day."

"Thomas, try to avoid stereotypes."

Marco noticed Tom looking at his feet.

"Why are you staring at my shoes?"

"Just seeing if you wore spats, like George Raft's character in *Some Like It Hot*. Remember that movie...Marilyn Monroe was terrific."

"His character was a gangster."

"Really..."

"You misjudge me, my friend. You think I leave here in the evening and take my Tommy Gun and shoot out store windows of shopkeepers who didn't pay the protection money on time."

"Seems plausible."

"No. I drive up the street to my beautiful home in the Biltmore District, where my beautiful wife, Mandy, your ex-wife, has prepared a delicious meal. We enjoy good wine and light romantic conversation, then go out to our yard and play with our two cocker spaniels we just adopted from Missy Gould's dog shelter."

"What are their names, Vinnie and Rocco?"

He laughed, that Happy Gangster. "Again with the stereotypes. Mandy will get a chuckle when I tell her that one. Their names are Lucy and Desi."

"So, what business <u>are</u> you in?"

He took a biz card out of an impressive silver holder on the end table and gave it to me:

Marco Greene
Private Equity

My turn to laugh. The card was identical to Judge Wilkinson's. Marco looked puzzled. Then cross, like I was making fun of him. He took the card back.

"Let us get down to the reason for your visit. You want to know whether I own a hotel on 36th Street, the Shangri-La. I do."

I opened my sport coat and pulled out three of THE PHOTOS, held together by a paper clip.

Marco's brown eyes narrowed just enough that I could tell he was surprised I had them.

"These were taken at your hotel."

Marco shrugged.

"And you paid a sleazebag photographer to install a secret camera and take them."

"I have better things to do with my time."

"The photographer is deceased. Det. Mathers with Phoenix PD found receipts from your company in the photographer's files."

A total bluff. No such receipts were found. The really cool thing about being a young-looking, harmless golfer boy was that people tended to believe you.

Marco bit without hesitation. "NO law on the books against taking pictures at your own place of business. I was at my motel one day urging my General Manager to cut down on laundering expenses—sheets, not money."

I smiled. Score one for the Happy Gangster.

"And who should I see go into Unit 7 but Senator Richard Luck, followed 5 minutes later by Devin Hughes, who I was led to believe worked for his opponent, Sen. Vance. And then two beautiful and barely clothed Mexican chicks drove up and joined them. My manager reported to me that this scene was repeated each Tuesday afternoon. I saw opportunity. I called Monty Cummings and he installed the camera."

"You sent the photos to Lisa. She sent them to me. The photos got Lisa killed."

Marco sat quietly, steepled his fingers and thought about my allegation. In general, I find steepled fingers irritating.

"I had nothing to gain by her death. And the photographer was probably killed because he got greedy and tried to get hush money from Luck's organization. My hands are clean."

He held them up to me. They were clean, and beautifully manicured. He veered off the Happy Gangster persona for a bit.

"What are you anyway? A detective now? I thought Mandy said you were a golfer."

"I'm both."

"How can that be?"

"Why not...Bobby Jones is a lawyer, and a good one."

Marco ran his hand through his curly permed hair, it sprang right back in place. It was probably afraid not to.

"The photos destroyed Luck's political career. Which you know they would. Why do you hate him so much?"

"My reasons go back a generation, and they are valid ones. His family's corrupt business practices harmed my family's business to the point of bankruptcy. My Uncle Tony committed suicide. Shot himself with me and my father in the room." For emphasis, he made a gun from his hand and pointed it at his head.

I mentally chastised myself for the empathy I suddenly felt for Greene. The man is a terrible human being.

"Tom, what is your family heritage?"

"Poverty, mostly."

A bellowing laugh from Marco. Score one for the young detective. "I mean your nationality."

"Italian and Irish."

"I'm Italian and Jewish. Since we're halfway the same, let's meet halfway and not pursue this further. Richard Luck got what he deserved. I was not the married man having dirty sex with Mexican prostitutes while his lovely wife sat home alone."

"How do you know they were prostitutes?"

"Okay, Mexican nurses. Why do I care who they are?"

"Because I thought you might be able to tell me if the Lucatos had a connection to business people in Mexico. No one seems to know where their money comes from."

"I can't help you with that." But the glint in his eyes told me he could. Also, Greene was starting to sweat. *Could we be dealing with criminal activity in Mexico?*

"Perhaps Det. Mathers could talk with you about it."

Out of the blue, Greene exploded, his face turning bright red. He stood up, shook a massive, hammy fist at me. "Do not threaten me with the police. You're a fucking golf pro..."

Score one, a big one, for the gangster. I backed down. Marco quickly calmed down and took his seat. He was genial again. "You see, Tom, you're the nice guy everybody likes and most women love. My wife Mandy still adores you. I'm the ugly thug who gets all the dirty work done so people like you can spend your time playing your little golf game at the posh Valley Vista Club, safe behind the high walls. You know, I haven't had more than two consecutive days off in 10 years."

I leaned forward, tried to look sincere. "I had <u>no</u> idea ugly thugs worked that hard."

He tried hard not to chuckle.

"So it's like this. Because Mandy loves you so much, I will leave you alone as long you leave me and my business alone. If you cross me, or cause my business harm, I will kill you."

I knew it was time for me to exit. I nodded that I understood, got up and walked to the door.

"Stay well, Tom. Mandy still talks about how you could cheer her up, no matter how bad a day she had working at the telephone company."

He followed me out. Safely on the porch, I said, "Well, I suppose she didn't marry me for my money."

The Happy Gangster's scowl was genuinely malevolent. But score one for the young detective, now scurrying for his car like a frightened little rat.

Chapter Twenty-Two
A Lovely Day for a Break-in

Brooks Continues Our Story:

Sunday morning, the Guest House, 5AM. Tom walked into Caroline's bedroom, opened the curtain. "Wakey, wakey," he said cheerfully.

Caroline stirred, slightly. "Shit, Tom, it's the middle of the night."

"No. Morning's almost here. A beautiful sunny morning. I have a fun activity planned for us."

"You go have fun for the both of us. I'm going back to sleep."

Tom pulled the covers off of her. She woke with a start, sat up.

"What if I slept naked?" she said.

"Then I would've screamed, I imagine."

"You do wonders for my self-confidence." She yawned and stretched. She was wearing very baggy pajamas with an image of Minnie Mouse on the top.

"So tough badass chicks wear Minnie Mouse jammies these days."

"Minnie has to be tough to put up with Mickey's antics. What's the big adventure?"

"We're going to be criminals for a morning. We're breaking into the Lucato Industrial Corp. warehouse. We don't have to actually break in because I borrowed a key from the Luck homestead."

Caroline brightened. "Count me in. Quick shower, some coffee and two chocolate doughnuts and I'll be ready."

Over said coffee and doughnuts Tom remarked, "You're going to be lookout and I'm going to be the Private Eye."

Caroline shook her head. "I wanna be the detective. You be the lookout."

"We can discuss it on the way."

The warehouse was located in what we term The Bowels of Phoenix, south of the central business district. The area was a mix of blighted housing and industrial buildings that tended to be under constant police surveillance. Trash banked up against the wicked barbed wire fences, an occasional mangy dog barked. Not a place to visit after dark. Or ever, if you could avoid it.

Tom drove, taking the direct route down Central Avenue, which at 6AM on Sunday was devoid of traffic.

Caroline took a piece of paper out of her pocket when their progress was stalled by a passing train. "I made a logo for us." On the left side it depicted three vertical interlocking Cs, to the right it said:

COLT & COLT CONFIDENTIAL
Discreet and Professional Investigators

"This looks great. You sure you want to get involved in this detective business?"

"We are a great team, "You're the debonair golfer boy who blends in with the rich, and as I tell you over and over, I'm the lean mean, streetwise girl."

"You never say which street. The yellow brick road?"

"They'll come a time when you'll need my skills."

"I always need you."

They shared a smile of solidarity. Caroline was thrilled. She now had a job that didn't entail setting out green peppers, squash and tomatoes at the corner market. The train passed, the road opened again.

Caroline asked, "Did Lisa ever hit on you?"

"Nope. Never."

"She asked me what to wear to her lessons with you. I thought she might be romantically interested. I mean, two attractive people out in the warm sunshine by themselves. No smooching behind the greens keeper's shed?"

"No such smooches ever happened."

"But she slept with those two old farts Carter and Sterling."

The Carter disclosure was new and important information to Tom.

"You're certain of this."

"Tom, girls share all sorts of secrets. Carter's wife Babs found out and threw a huge fit--she's Greek--so he ended it before she turned his life into a Greek Tragedy. Then he atoned by making a donation to Luck's campaign. How ridiculous is that!"

"He came to me with this lame idea that the gardener killed Lisa."

"That was to distract you...us. He was afraid one of his buddies was the killer. These people stick together, no matter what. Lisa told me that."

"Carter and Sterling. Both staunch supporters of the opposition party. Why would Lisa choose them?"

"Fucking them was a 'fuck you' to her husband's political ambitions."

"Of course. Brilliant, Caroline."

"I know."

"You told me Lisa was once prim and proper. What happened to her?"

"Richard Sleazeball Luck is what happened to her."

They continued on in silence a few moments until Caroline said, "In a way, I wish Lisa would have made a play for you. You would've been a perfect couple. Could've had two adorable blond children--no more than two, mind you--and taught them to play golf with a strong Vardon grip."

"You've been reading your P.G. Wodehouse again."

"I love his stories. With all the shit going on, sometimes I just need to laugh."

They arrived at the street where the warehouse was located.

Tom said, with perhaps mock seriousness, "Before we team up on this PI business, are you sure you don't mind working for me?"

"No problem with that at all."

And so after further negotiations, as you might expect, it was decided that Tom was the lookout that day, Caroline was the Chief Investigator for Colt & Colt Confidential.

The key Tom had purloined from Richard Luck's home worked the lock on the front gate. The warehouse and the buildings around it were deserted on this Sunday morning. Tom gave the key to his sister.

Caroline hurried to the front entrance, turned the key--it worked again. She went inside, leaving the door open. Tom stayed by the gate and watched for approaching vehicles.

Caroline scanned the warehouse. Boxes of various sizes were stacked on conveyor belts that ran in the direction of a large metal sliding door in the rear. Stacked high were cardboard bales which she assumed were boxes that were not yet assembled.

She walked over to one of the conveyor belts. The boxes had various labels on them: Toys, electronic components, cosmetics, garden tools--even sportswear and lingerie. The shipping labels of each one showed destinations in Mexico. The Lucatos were evidently engaged in a large-scale import-export business.

She took out a small notepad and pencil and wrote down the addresses the boxes were being sent to. They were going to eight different places, all businesses in Mexico. The most frequently shown name was The Morales Group in Hermosillo, Sonora, Mexico.

She then took out her trusty switchblade and slit open six of the boxes. The contents of four of them were as labeled. Two of the boxes however contained packing paper and inside the packing paper was a small burlap sack full of-- sand.

"TOM!" Caroline hollered.

He rushed in and went through what she had found. He was as astonished as she was. They opened a few more boxes and found the same pattern, every third one contained sand. They went into the only office in the warehouse and looked at the files in a--surprisingly unlocked--cabinet.

Expensive sacks of sand, these. The invoices ranged from $1,000 to $15,000.

Back in the warehouse, they carefully re-taped the boxes they had opened, and carefully locked up. They hurried to Tom's car, drove off quickly to tell Det. Mathers what they had found. They didn't notice a solitary individual leaning against a lamppost, enjoying a smoke on this cool, sunny Sunday morning. The man made a mental note of Tom's vehicle license.

"What does it all mean?" Caroline asked in a state of confusion.

Tom stopped at a pay phone to call Mathers. At the Parks Cafeteria on E. McDowell St., over plates of crispy, delicious Southern-style fried chicken and savory mashed potatoes--all three of them loved this place--Mathers said to Tom and Caroline, "It means a scam. Luck's family set up a dummy corporation to funnel money from Mexico into his senatorial campaign."

"Who is The Morales Group?" Caroline enquired.

Mathers tried to imitate the sound effects of a scary movie. "A company owned by Roman Morales, one of the most dangerous men in Mexico. You, my friends, are going to stay as far away from him as possible."

He picked up a chicken breast and attacked it with his usual zeal. He chewed a moment then said, "I don't approve of what you did this morning. I don't disapprove of it. Stellar detective work, by the way. But now is the time to let me and my colleagues--who wear .38 caliber guns--move this investigation forward."

Tom said, "Ed, we need to go to Mexico. Remember the message on the envelope with the nasty photos. Lisa wanted Caroline and me to meet her at the home of the Valenzuela family. They live in a town west of Hermosillo, toward the coast."

Mathers dabbed about a half pound of butter on his mashed potatoes and considered Tom's request.

"That should be OK. Far as I know, that family is completely clean, honest business people, good citizens--in both countries. Bring me back some tequila."

"Not good for your putting stroke, Ed."

"Oh...well, forget it then."

***

By 1962, Marco Greene had become so successful that his business empire practically ran itself. His strongest skill as a manager was being able to spot great talent to bring into his organization, not just great in terms of experience or knowledge, but hard-nosed men and women he could trust.

He also had developed a network of informants that provided a constant flow of business intelligence to help him spot opportunities and just as importantly, the emergence of potential rivals. Also valuable was intelligence he could use as leverage against these rivals.

That day he had in front of him on the green blotter on his desk a slender manila file folder with information that, if not financially valuable to him, was certainly fascinating and curious.

Records of juvenile offenders are normally sealed and protected from public view, but Marco had one such, very old, record in front of him, from a wealthy municipality in Massachusetts. The information may have dated back to the time just after Arizona became a state, but the contents of the folder still gave Marco a jolt when he read it.

A young man had been arrested when he badly injured a classmate who had defeated him in a golf match at one of the famous country clubs in the East. The injury was a blow to the head with a golf club, a 5-iron to be exact. The motive? He believed his opponent had cheated to win the match.

The young offender had grown up to become rich and a member of Valley Vista Country Club in Scottsdale, Arizona-- with a seat on the Club's Board of Directors no less.

Marco, after he got over the initial shock at reading the file, thought, *This could help Det. Mathers with his investigation.* But he quickly reconsidered, thinking, *Why do I care if that nitwit copper solves the murder?* The foundational element of Marco's business philosophy had always been, Take Care of Yourself First.

He got up from his chair, picked up the file and deposited it in the elegant light oakwood cabinet, with shiny brass handles, in the corner of his office. *Who knows, I might be able to use the information someday.*

Chapter Twenty-Three
A Night Passage to Mexico

They left for Mexico at midnight, Tom driving the T-Bird, looking like prosperous Americans going on a holiday. Tom wore sharply creased grey slacks and a royal blue, long-sleeved shirt. Caroline wore a rose-colored satin blouse and cream-colored slacks.

Tom Continues Our Story...

Det. Mathers was able to give us the address of the Valenzuela family hacienda, or with their wealth perhaps it was more of an estancia.

Caroline asked reasonably, "Why didn't we call ahead?"

"They might have said, no, don't come. This way we will use our charm and sincerity to get them to invite us in and give us the whole story. We'll arrive like humble sojourners. They'll probably give us lunch."

"Or they could say, go home, gringo."

We drove in silence for many miles. It was a lovely night for travel. No rain, no wind to blow dust along the highway, bright stars over our heads. The mighty Thunderbird V8 engine roared down the highway.

Caroline said, "Don't be mad at me."

I laughed. "Do you notice so many of our conversations have begun this way?"

"Probably hundreds. Tonight's featured topic is: Julia is not the woman for you."

"And how do you know that?"

"After we watched *Have Gun Will Travel* the other night, she invited me to come to her room. Suite of rooms, actually. She even has a piano in the living room area. On one wall there are photos of her with all the guys she's dated. It looks like the wall at a big game hunter's lodge."

"Is there a photo of me?"

"Yes, Mr. Narcissist. I mean Mr. Popularity. There surely is. And she has a closet with all these stuffed animals from her childhood, like she doesn't want them anymore but can't bear to let them go."

"That's a bit strange..."

"She has all these unfinished projects. Like half-finished songs scribbled on music composition paper. Pretty good songs, but they have no endings. Songs need happy endings.

She bounces from dream to dream."

"Not sure what this means for me."

Caroline smacked her forehead. "Duh. It means she'll never be with you because she'll never finish what she started with the other guys."

"You're right."

"What do you mean, I'm right? You hardly ever say that."

"Let me see this through with Julia. We'll see how it plays out. We all grow and change."

Caroline looked skeptical.

We arrived at the little village of Magdalena de Kino, an hour or so south of the border, just after 6AM. The first thing we did was have a snack of chocolate pastry and that strong Mexican coffee I love.

Driving the sharp looking T-Bird instead of that old junker gave me a tremendous boost in confidence. I used to feel, to borrow a term from my sister, like po' folk. But I was to learn that having flashy wheels makes you noticeable. Not always a good thing.

We asked the friendly café owner for directions to the Valenzuela home. The woman lit up with joy, gave us directions and said, "They are the nicest people. Please tell Eduardo that my daughter Consuela says hello and hopes he is well."

Caroline then asked the woman if she knew Senor Roman Morales. The reaction was quite a bit different. She shook her head so vigorously I feared she might injure her neck. *Who is this guy--Vlad the Impaler?* I wondered.

Turning west from the larger city of Hermosillo, the drive to the Valenzuelas was a picturesque 2 ½ hour trip through gently rolling green hills dotted with farms and ranches. Our destination was not far from the Gulf of California. We saw crops as varied as wheat and walnuts and lots of beef cattle grazing.

The Valenzuela property was precisely as we anticipated: vast, with high whitewashed brick walls with colorful bougainvillea plants all along the perimeter. What we didn't anticipate was the security station, complete with armed, surly guard, at the entrance.

"Well," Caroline commented philosophically, "At least I got to see a new part of Mexico. A lot hotter down here than I expected."

Luckily the guard spoke passable English. We told him our names, apologized for not calling ahead.

He picked up a phone. An animated conversation ensued in Spanish. The only thing I understood was, "Yes! It is them!" The guard retuned, surly no longer, all smiles. "We are honored you came to visit. Please follow the road to the hacienda."

As I drove the winding tree-lined road, dappled with the pretty morning sunshine, Caroline said, "Why do I waste my precious time in Phoenix when it appears I'm a VIP down here?"

We stopped in front of an enormous home—more white walls then an interior courtyard, then the main house. The gate to the courtyard was wide open. We walked in and saw 4 people emerge from the 8 ft. high carved wooden door. A strikingly handsome man of about 30, a lovely but anxious woman in her 50s, a tall and almost imperial grey-haired man about the same age as the woman, and apparently the nonna, a woman with grey hair in a bun, an ample bosom, ample hips and more than ample warmth and graciousness.

I wish I had known how to say Day of Surprises in Spanish, because when the group saw us walking toward them, they all, except for the nonna, began to weep.

Caroline looked at me with imploring eyes that said, "What's going on, Tom?"

The nonna stepped forward, grabbed Caroline and kissed her on both cheeks, then did the same to me. She had a lovely fragrance, like orange blossoms. *In keeping with their orange theme,* I supposed.

"Please excuse our sadness. We are thrilled and honored you have come. It is just that...Lisa told us if two attractive Americans came, driving a new red car, it means..." Now, the nonna broke down in tears. "Lisa said it would mean, she is dead."

The nonna grabbed me again and sobbed onto my shoulder. Caroline, for reasons I did not understand, ran to the crying young man and put her arms around him, exclaiming, "Eduardo! I am so sorry."

I learned later that Caroline had met Eduardo during a trip she made to Mexico with Lisa. She was not told his last name--or that he was from a wealthy family.

The nonna released me and I took my sodden shoulder and introduced myself to the father, Ben, and his wife Amelia. "I am Tom Colt. This is my sister Caroline. Lisa Prentiss Luck was our friend. Did you not know she was killed in Phoenix?"

Ben, with sad, watery eyes, said, "We know, but we still cannot accept it. When you came up our driveway, it brought all the pain back."

They invited us to join them on the spacious back patio for a late breakfast/early lunch.

Once the shock at seeing us was over, the family turned into warm, friendly almost lighthearted people. I could see why everyone loved working for them. They were without pretense—some of the most down-to-earth people I have ever met. I half expected Caroline to beg them to adopt her.

Their staff served us dish after dish of fabulous food. I tucked into a dish of sunny-side-up eggs over tortilla chips with salsa and grilled chicken. It was wonderful. The morning was exceptionally warm. I welcomed the cold beverage they served, watermelon and mint infused water, or Agua Fresca; I probably had three glasses.

And with each dish, there seemed to be a new revelation about Lisa.

The handsome but quiet Eduardo was the father of her child. When the baby was born, they said an American named Les Levine flew down there and attempted to have the child adopted to a Mexican family.

The father, Ben, said, "Eduardo had not told us of his responsibility to Lisa and the child. When he told us, I stepped in and had the adoption stopped. The child was familia—family. We were—are—so grateful to have her."

I asked, "How did you connect with Lisa, if she thought her baby had been adopted?"

Ben smiled. "She remembered seeing Eduardo in one of the orange hats we wear at my company. In Phoenix, she saw one of our trucks, the driver wearing the same hat. She found out the address of our company, and contacted us. Very smart young woman."

Ace detective Tom Colt was humbled, remembering how long it took me to find the locker that fit the orange key.

Caroline, listening intently between crunching the delicious breakfast tacos--spicy chorizo sausage, scrambled eggs and potatoes--asked, "Does Kathleen know who her mother...was?"

Amelia, the mother, said, "We have given her information in small doses. We maintained hope that Lisa would return to us. And then our prayers were answered. Lisa wrote to us and asked if she divorced the man she to whom she was married, could she come and live with us."

I said, "You answer must have been yes. Her bags were packed the day she was killed."

A gloomy silence fell over the table.

Overly direct Caroline turned to Eduardo and asked, "Did you love Lisa? Would you have married her?"

The father stepped in. "He would have married her, yes."

Eduardo nodded, but it could not be described as emphatic. All familias, on both sides of the border, have a few cracks in the high walls they erect to protect themselves.

The family cook brought out a tray of churros, cinnamon-dusted fried cruller-type pastries and a dish of rich hot chocolate to dip them in. Caroline and I devoured those as though we'd never seen chocolate before.

And then a young girl, maybe 7 or 8 years old, came up the path to the patio with her dog, a feisty, wooly terrier puppy. Caroline and I could do nothing but stare. The child was a miniature Lisa, complete with her violet eyes. She even walked with the relaxed grace I recalled from seeing Lisa walk barefoot on the golf course.

The nonna decided it wasn't the right time to introduce the child to us, got up and said to the little girl, "Would you like to take your puppy for a walk? I will go with you." She tapped one hip. "I need the exercise after this fine meal. We'll go to the duck pond. He can swim there."

The child's expression bloomed into joy and the three of them descended the path to the lush gardens.

Eduardo got up, excused himself in a formal manner and said he had to get back to work, adding that it was a pleasure to meet us. The father and mother invited us to come inside to the cooler living room. The morning sun had invaded the patio. They, too, excused themselves, saying they would return in a few minutes.

Caroline stood at the window, her eyes fixed on the young happy girl down at the pond. I joined her.

"Lisa wasn't a slut or a whore, Caroline. Far from it. She was a beautiful young women whose dream was—"

"To be a mom." Caroline finished my sentence.

Amelia did not return. Ben, the father, did and sat down across from Caroline and I who shared a sofa. He had a serious look on his face, almost grave.

"My new friends, I hope you do not take offence at the questions I must ask."

"You don't have to worry Senor Valenzuela," I said.

He nodded, a brief smile appearing. "Why did a lovely young woman like Lisa have no friends in America except you two?"

"She became a political liability for her ambitious husband. She was like a prisoner—at least since I met her. I gave her golf lessons. My sister had known her much longer, since school days."

Caroline said, "At first, she came to Mexico with Richard, when he was working on some kind of business deals here. Later, after she met your son Eduardo, she came by herself. A few times I came with her. We always met at a beach village." Caroline continued, "She and her husband Richard Luck could not have a child together—which was Lisa's dream."

We were quiet a few moments, until Caroline asked, too directly I thought given our tenuous status as uninvited guests, "Did Eduardo love her?"

The father studied Caroline a few moments, then said, "That does not matter now, does it my friends from Phoenix. The important thing is the welfare of young Kathleen."

Then he asked Caroline to leave for a moment. She made a face, but complied and went back outside. Man to man talk coming, I assumed.

"I was looking in your eyes, Tom, when you talked of Lisa. Did you love her?"

"Sir, no I did not love her. But I believe I could have."

Ben nodded with lively eyes as though that was an outstanding, truthful answer.

I asked him, "Can you tell me anything about Roman Morales?"

My question seemed to sting him. "Only to stay away from him, far away."

"Good advice, sir, thank you."

Unfortunately for Caroline and me, it was already too late.

Brooks Continues Our Story:

Tom and Caroline had booked a room in a small hotel near the town of Magdalena de Kino, not knowing how long their visit with the Valenzuelas would take. It was, early, just after 4PM when they got back to the village where their day in Mexico began, so they decided to get back home that night.

They passed through a narrow alleyway on the way from the hotel to the parking lot. Three men followed them, catching up quickly. One grabbed Tom, one opened a door to a small dark room, the third one roughly tossed Caroline into the low-ceilinged room, and before she could react, hand-cuffed her left hand to a water pipe above her head. The other two men tag-teamed Tom and threw him onto the cement floor.

Caroline screamed. One of the men slapped her. With a raised, opened hand, he communicated to Caroline what would happen if she screamed again. The third man closed the door.

Two of the men drew short night-stick type weapons and beat Tom with them. They worked methodically, professionally, and completely without emotion. The room was nearly dark, save for the weak light from the alley coming through a narrow window. Caroline couldn't see what the weapons were, but Tom was quickly bloodied. He gasped and groaned as they beat him over and over, the terrified Caroline looking on, yanking on the rough handcuff so hard her own wrist bled.

She screamed again, one of them punched her in the face and her lower lip split open. She tasted blood.

Just like that, the beating ended. Two of the men exited quickly, the third took a key from his pocket and tossed it to Caroline, who deftly caught it on the fly with her free hand.

"Getta fug bag te Feenis and mine yeronn beesniss," the man said as he hurried out the door. Caroline unhooked her left wrist, went to the doorway and called out, "Tell whoever sent you..." and she couldn't think of how to finish the sentence. Blood was running down her chin.

She knelt by Tom and asked him if he could walk. He nodded, but not with any resolve. She helped him up and led him to their car, opened the door and helped him settle into the back seat.

She could see his shirt and pants were torn and he was bleeding from about 25 small cuts. *The sticks the men beat him with must have had sharp points or abrasive edges*, she thought.

She took her switchblade from her purse and cut swatches of bandages from her once-beautiful rose satin blouse. She wrapped the cuts on his arms, praying the men hadn't broken any bones—and then wrapped her own bleeding wrist. She took a tissue from her purse and tried to stop the bleeding from her lip.

Caroline got in the driver's seat and the Thunderbird's V8 roared to life. She pushed the speed to 80 mph, trying to leave Mexico as fast as the powerful machine would take her. Across the border an hour later, she stopped on the side of the road, took off her bloodied, tattered blouse and said, "Fuck it, just fuck it."

She tossed the blouse away and thundered down the Interstate toward home.

Tom stayed awake the whole time, but was in considerable pain. Caroline stopped at a small grocery store south of Tucson and bought three 16-oz bottles of beer. The small, jittery store clerk seemed afraid of her when she plunked the money on the counter. She looked a fright: Tom's blood on her light-colored slacks, a swollen, blood-crusted lip and wearing only a blue lacy bra for a top.

She got them back on the Interstate, gave a bottle of beer to Tom and drank the other two as she drove. "Not my Mexican dream vacation, but for once I got to save you."

Tom tried to laugh, it came out a hoarse groan.

Fifty miles later, Caroline said to Tom, "I've changed my mind about something. I think you'll find true love someday. You're so determined, you'll keep looking until you're 70 if that's what it takes to find her. Hope I'm still here to go to your wedding."

She glanced in the back seat. Tom was asleep.

Thankfully arriving at the Wilkinson estate, Caroline helped Tom into bed, took his clothes off, cleaned the worst of his wounds with mercurochrome, an antiseptic containing mercury that besides stinging like hell, left a strange reddish-brown stain where it was applied. Then she gave him a sleeping pill.

She phoned Det. Mathers, didn't let him get a word in, her mouth running as fast as the RPMs of the T-Bird's V8 could do. "Ed, please come over first thing in the morning. Tom and I have tons to tell you. Lisa had a child in Mexico. We met her. She's beautiful and healthy and loved by the Valenzuelas. On our way back, we were jumped by thugs and Tom was badly beaten." She paused due to the necessity of breathing in oxygen.

"Get the coffee on, Caroline, I'll be there at 7AM."

"You got it, Chief."

"Thanks for the promotion."

She checked on Tom once more. He was sleeping as comfortably as could be expected. She went into her own room and did something she hadn't done since she was a little girl. She knelt beside her bed, put her hands together, like her dad had taught her and said:

"God, I know I don't talk to you very much, but my mother goes to church so much I thought she prayed enough for both of us. I was wrong. Tom and I were almost killed tonight in Mexico, and it was a miracle I got us back home safely. Thank you for that miracle. And please take care of Tom. Very bad people want to hurt him. And...he's all I've got in this world."

And then our tough, streetwise chick sat on the soft caramel carpet, folded her knees together and cried and cried and cried.

***

At 7:01 the next morning, Mathers knocked on the Guest House door. The suddenly domestic Caroline who was in the kitchen making coffee and baking cinnamon muffins, let him in.

Mathers was taken aback when he saw the battered, bruised, Tom lying on the couch. He tried his best to not let it show.

"Hey, guy, just stopped by to see if you had time for a quick 18 holes."

"Ha, ha," Tom said, trying to smile.

Caroline said, "Nothing's broken. The Bad Guys knew how to cause serious pain without doing serious damage.

Mathers observed, "We should always appreciate practitioners who are skilled at their craft."

Caroline returned to the kitchen and poured three cups of strong coffee. Mathers glanced at The Leaderboard, lamenting how long and vague a list it was. More than a dozen names!

> Richard Luck
> Les Levine
> Dominic Lucato
> Marco Greene
> Devin Hughes
> Mysterious Prowler
> Jordan Lucato
> Carter VonEssen
> Or his wife Babs
> Sterling Gould
> Or is wife Missy
> Roman Morales
> TBA Member of Luck Campaign

TBA Supporter of Sen. Vance

Mathers rubbed his forehead. "This Leaderboard...we're missing something. And scratch the Prowler. Buncha flimsy nonsense to mislead us. These people think we're stupid."

Tom sat up and Caroline brought him coffee. She handed a cup to Mathers. Tom and Caroline took turns telling Mathers all they had learned on their memorable one day trip to Old Mexico.

"Slow down, you guys. Can I play too? You're solving the crime without me."

After they recounted the events of the last 30 hours, Mathers summed it up: "That is what I call NETO. Nifty Effort, Terrible Outcome."

"All roads seem to lead to Mexico, Ed," Tom said.

"Not necessarily. Lisa tossed a large wrench into the Lucato money making political works. I'm still going with old man Lucato, maybe the dim brother, or another person in their organization. I was talking to the Chief last night. He agrees with us the body dumped at the vineyard looked like the work of Morales' people--a warning shot, just like you two got last night. I liked Marco Greene for the shot-up body until the Chief and I got to talking. Marco is nothing if not smart. Word is he had some beef with Lucato, but he'd find a more diabolical way to get back at the old man."

We three considered what Mathers said for a few moments, then he looked startled, like he flashed on something important. To Caroline, he said, "They didn't do anything to you..."

Caroline struck a pose and said in an exaggerated Southern accent: "Why detective, I am flattered that you are worried I was de-flowered south of the border. But I am pleased to say, not this time."

Mathers' narrowed, curious eyes suggested he didn't know quite what to make of Caroline but would like to learn more.

Her decorative touch was to purchase two bar stools with red leather seats and place them at the kitchen counter. Mathers sat on one.

"My next step is to pay a visit to Lucato Vineyards. I think the old man knows why the body was dumped there, in a mob-style hit job. I want to go at night and not give him advance warning. If you're up to it Tom, I'd like you to go with me. I don't want to sail up with a flotilla of armed cops and spook the Lucatos. But another pair of eyes would be helpful."

"I'll be ready in two or three days."

"I'll come too," Caroline said eagerly.

"Why not," Mathers said. "I bring a golfer and his 'cute and leggy' sister, it'll really throw them a curve."

"You read the column in the paper!"

"Yes ma'am I did."

Caroline brightened. *Always a sucker for applause*, Tom thought. He never admitted to himself, of course, that he was much, much worse.

"I'm going to whip up cheese omelets. Would you care for one, Ed?"

"Sure. I'm famished. Could you put some bacon in mine? Maybe some mushrooms?

Caroline displayed a totally insincere dutiful housewife-style smile as seen on TV commercials. "Certainly, dear. Would you care for portabella mushrooms or shitakes?"

"Ah, either one."

Tom laughed and stretched out on the couch.

Caroline said, "This is just like being married. The hubby lies on the couch while the wife-y serves everybody."

Mathers said brightly, "That's the natural order of things, I believe."

"Your wife's a lucky woman," Caroline replied.

"That's what she told the Judge that day in court two years ago, when he granted her a divorce from me."

***

The next day, Mathers drove out to the desert road in back of the small hills that surrounded the Luck home. He started his trek at 7AM before the merciless desert sun had risen too high.

He lived for this phase of an investigation when he knew he was close to the solution of a difficult crime puzzle. There were some crimes that were, to use a golf term, gimmes, easy to solve with little effort because most criminals are just plain dumb.

But the Lisa Luck murder required all of the skills and savvy he had.

He tromped over a rise and saw a very rough path to the Luck home. It was an area that was popular with hikers who wanted to get away from the city for a while.

Young officer Rudy had combed through this same desert—for an entire afternoon and hadn't come up with any meaningful evidence--just a few sharp cactus thorns in his backside. Mathers had a hunch that it was worth spending a few hours giving it a fresh look-see.

Mathers also wanted some time away from the office to think about how best to utilize Tom Colt's skills. Tom had the gift that all good detectives share—he observes and really sees. Most of us wander through our lives with our eyes half closed. Not Tom. And for a young man, Tom had a unusually strong feel for human motivation, what makes an individual tick.

Mathers wondered how Tom was able to focus completely on golf when he was playing in tournaments. Keen observational skills are not something you can turn on and off. Mathers didn't realize the truth was: Tom was easily distracted while playing. And not just by pretty girls in the gallery like the golf writers thought.

Mathers knew it wasn't fair to ask Tom to help him with cases. He was so excited about and dedicated to his tournament golf career. But on the other hand, when you have a valuable police resource that costs nothing except the occasional lunch tab, it was Mathers' duty to utilize it. The population of Phoenix—and along with it the number and complexity of crimes—was growing faster than the tax base that supported government services, including law enforcement. Mathers knew he even would've had difficulty getting budgetary approval to go to Mexico with Tom and Caroline. It made him feel twice as bad after they were attacked there.

Mathers decided to take things one case at a time and see what happens. He really enjoyed working with Tom, and maybe even with Caroline.

A glint of metal caught his eye, near the base of a staghorn cholla cactus. He knelt down and reached for the item, careful to not let the wicked thorns stick him.

The object was a metal button. He turned it over. It was a campaign button with the slogan, "LUCK '62—The Best Way to Grow."

Mathers hated politicians and their empty slogans. *What the hell was this one supposed to mean?* he thought, placing the button in a small paper bag to take back to the station. "*What are you growing besides grapes and marijuana?*"

***

Even though being a hapless dupe is not necessarily a criminal act, Mathers called Devin Hughes into his office at the police station for a little chat later that day. Hughes, now a permanently unemployable political operative, agreed without hesitation. He looked to be one dispirited guy, when he took a seat across Mather's desk. Ed had the famous photographs strategically placed at the side of his desk.

"I met Richard at a conference in LA, three years ago. I was managing another campaign. He said he was moving to Arizona, planning to run for office, and he and I should stay in touch. A year ago he called me and flew out to LA to meet me. We met in a small conference room at a hotel near my office. He didn't want to meet me where I worked. He told me Sen. Prescott Vance had an opening for a campaign manager, and I would be the perfect man for the job. I was confused. I mean, my job would be to make sure Richard didn't win the Senate race."

Mathers observed, "You must have been more than confused. It made no sense."

"Until he told me my job was to run, as he termed it, a less than optimal campaign. And I was to be paid $50,000 the morning after Sen. Vance lost the election; the money was coming from a wealthy gentleman in Mexico. Richard said the man was helping fund his campaign, so he was definitely good for the money. Do you know how much $50,000 is, Detective?"

Mathers doodled some numbers on a note pad, frowned. "A little more than 6 times my salary."

"I like Richard. He's a blast to be around. He lies like a son-of-a-gun when he makes speeches, but no one seems to care. He told me losing the race wouldn't hurt my career in the long run. Everyone knew Prescott Vance is a doddering old fool. It wouldn't be my fault if he lost."

"So you bit."

"I bit hook, line, and sinker. This rich Mexican even provided us with...girls. More beautiful girls than I've ever been with in my life. I mean, look at me."

Mathers picked up the photos and looked at them.

"Detective, remember Richard's famous speech 'A Return to Moral and Ethical Capitalism'? That was a Tuesday night dinner event at the Arizona Biltmore for the Young Voters

Association. Where do you think Richard and I had been on Tuesday afternoon?" He pointed at the photos.

"Topic shoulda been 'How to Stimulate a Rising Economy'," Mathers said.

"For a cop, you have a good sense of humor."

"Keeps me sane. That and playing golf."

Mathers arranged one of the photos that depicted Hughes' erect penis so it faced him. He wanted Hughes to squirm with embarrassment, which he did. "Very sexy girls. Who wouldn't be tempted...do you speak Spanish, Devin?'

"Yes, Richard and I are both fluent. Why do you ask?"

"Just wondered how you and Luck got the girls to do some of the things they did." Mathers put the photos down. "Did you ever meet with this rich Mexican? Seems like he was putting up an awful lot of money to help a run-of-the-mill political hack like Richard Luck."

Hughes didn't get to be a political operative without knowing how to be sly. "The more I learned, Detective, the more it became clear our benefactor was buying a seat in the United States Senate. How much is that worth?"

"You didn't answer my question, Mr. Hughes."

"No, I didn't, Detective. It would put my life in jeopardy. I've already lost everything else."

Chapter Twenty-Four
Who is this New Katrina Stern?

THE NEW IMPROVED Katrina Stern, after her wardrobe makeover by Jilly Flannery, and her shall we say personality makeover by Tom Colt, stood on the 18th tee in the last round of the Desert Dreams Ladies Invitational in Tucson tied for the lead. Unfortunately, the woman with whom she was tied had won the most tournaments on tour so far that year, was the leading money winner, and the leader in scoring average per round by a remarkable full stroke.

That week, for the first time in her playing career, Katrina noticed that the golf fans liked her. They cheered for her. They offered words of encouragement to her. She, for the first time in her golf career, made it a point to smile back and say, "Thank you." When she made a critical putt and heard applause, she responded with her brightest smile and a wave. Many fans had never seen that beautiful smile before.

Katrina was wearing dark red shorts--Jilly had insisted that they be a full 2 inches above the knee--a tight royal blue sleeveless top and matching golf shoes. She had exchanged her men's style rounded golf hat for a sporty, dark red visor to match her shorts.

On the 1st tee, her playing partners commented on how nice she looked, as did the gentleman known as The Starter, who announced the names of each player before they teed off. Kat was unsettled by the attention at first, but quickly came to like it.

She found, to her surprise, that her game did not suffer one bit from interacting with the paying customers. If anything, it pumped her up. She found herself wanting to play well not just for herself, but for them.

And now, on the 18th hole, she took a sip of water from a paper cup to deal with her tension-dried throat, took a deep breath and surveyed the challenge she faced.

It was a classic "sucker" hole, designed to tempt the golfer into taking a potentially foolish risk, a dogleg right with a lake running down the length of the hole on the right, and an equally daunting hazard made up of cactus and rock-strewn desert on the left. From the tees the ladies were playing for this event, the hole measured 340 yards. They were playing from tees that were halfway between the men's championship tees and the ladies tees used by the club members.

The smart way to play the hole was to take a 4-wood or long iron and place your tee shot in the center of the narrow fairway, then hit an 8 or 9-iron to the green. But for the bold player it was hard to resist trying to cut the corner.

Kat looked up ahead and saw that her opponent was in the middle of the fairway. She had a shot of 110 yards to the green. Kat watched this great player select a club and take her stance. Kat admired this woman. She had incredible power off the tee, accuracy with her irons and finesse around the greens. In short, she was THE BEST. She was what Kat aspired to be--and no golfer tried harder than Katrina Stern.

Kat watched as she hit her approach shot. A beautiful one, that bounced on the green and stopped 10 feet from the hole. The way this great woman putted, Kat was almost assured her opponent would make a birdie 3.

Kat thought, in conservative Kat fashion, that if she made a par 4, she would earn a second place position and a nice check. Katrina loved nice checks.

Kat's playing partners were up on the tee first. She saw they both selected 2-irons.

She had not yet tried to hit a tee shot the way Tom had suggested--with the substantially longer swing. *Enough changes for one week,* Kat had thought, again reasonably.

One of the bedeviling aspects of golf is that a competitor has too much time to think between shots. Stray thoughts come into your head unbidden to interrupt the concentration that is so vital to sustaining great play throughout a round.

As Kat waited for her playing partners to tee off, she was visited by her past. She saw images of the dangerous passage 8-year-old Kat had made from Germany to Brazil, and then the trip 8 years later to America, where her family had to start all over with very little money and no friends. How incredibly brave they had been.

She looked down the fairway, thinking: What Am I So Afraid Of? Failure? As Tom told her, there's no such thing as failure, because no matter what happens, there's another tournament next week. Tom...Why Am I So Afraid of Him?

Kat looked at the faces of the fans following her group. Her fans. That seemed so strange to say. Some of them smiled at her as she glanced across the tee and down the fairway. How startling it was for Kat to realize that strangers cared whether she won or lost that afternoon. A young girl, maybe 12, gave her the "thumb's up" sign.

She walked over to her caddie and said, "Give me the Driver, please." Her caddie was a freckle-faced freshman at ASU named Brenda, an aspiring golfer who really needed a job to cover tuition and of course beer expenses. Kat gave her one, just as a veteran player had done for her when she was 18. That veteran player was her opponent she was tied with on this day.

Brenda's freckled face looked puzzled. "Kat...um...you always lay up with an iron on this hole."

"The Driver, Brenda."

The caddie complied. The fans in the gallery buzzed with excitement when they saw the big club coming out of the bag, Brenda even removing the head cover with a flourish.

To her playing partners, Kat said, "Ladies, they'll be a slight delay. I'm going with the Big Gun." Translated from Golf to English, Kat was telling them she was going to wait until the group ahead had finished on the 18th green, because she was hitting a Driver off the tee, the club she could hit the farthest, and try to fly the ball over the length of the water and onto the green in one majestic stroke.

Given the astonished looks that were returned to her from her playing partners, she might as well had said, "Ladies, I'm going to crawl into a Mercury space capsule with Alan Shepard and orbit the earth for a while." They backed away, like you do when you see a crazy person ranting on the street.

Brenda said in the most timorous voice imaginable, "I don't know if _we_ can hit it that far, Kat."

"I don't know either. Why don't _we_ find out?"

Kat took a total of 5 practice swings, each one longer until she stretched her swing arc to the maximum length she had achieved with Tom coaching her.

From the fans up at the green came the OHHHHHHH! sound that accompanies a critical missed putt. Kat saw the woman she was tied with walk disgustedly up to the hole and tap the ball into the cup. Now, Kat didn't have to try to drive the green in 1 stroke. She could play safe and try to make a birdie 3 for the win or a par 4 to tie and go into a playoff.

She didn't give it a second thought. She placed her ball on the tee, took her stance, focused on a mental image of hitting the perfect shot and swung. She made the long, strong swing that Tom had shown her, but with Kat's own superior rhythm and timing. Even so, she nearly fell over on her follow through. It was the most ungainly swing of her career, and the one she would never forget.

She hit the perfect shot, the kind of shot that every professional golfer dreams of hitting when the game is on the line. She watched the ball soar, curve ever so slightly to the right, around the water, following the contour of the hole like a small plane flying along the coast.

The ball landed in the tiny opening beyond the water and in front of the green, took two bounces on the hard sun-kissed ground and rolled onto the green--20 feet from the hole. Two putts from there and Katrina Stern was The Champion.

She smiled as she handed the Driver to the stunned Brenda. The fans were screaming, clapping, cheering with voices that rose to a roar. They streamed down the fairway to get a prime spot to witness the climactic shots of the tournament. Kat and Brenda let her playing partners walk down the fairway first. As Kat followed 30 yards behind, she smiled and waved at every person she saw smiling and cheering for her.

Kat didn't two-putt for the victory, she rammed the 20-footer home for an eagle two and a two-shot victory. The first person to step onto the green to congratulate Kat was the woman she had just defeated, the greatest player in the game. "You got guts," she commented to Kat. "No one tried that shot all week, not even me."

THE NEW IMPROVED Kat Stern remained there after the trophy ceremony and signed autographs for every person who asked. The last autograph seeker was the little girl who gave her the thumb's up when she needed it the most.

"You're my favorite player, Miss Stern," the little girl said.

"Thank you," Kat said simply.

Kat finally made the solitary walk to her car. Carrying her trophy. She got in behind the wheel, sighed with understandable fatigue, and then began laughing, almost hysterically. "I won! I won! I won!" And then she remembered the little girl saying, "You're my favorite player, Miss Stern," and it so touched Katrina's heart that her emotions swung to tears. She looked in the rear-view mirror. *What is the matter with me?* she thought. *Get it together, will you.*

When her eyes cleared enough to be able to drive, Kat started for home.

***

Tom was a quick healer. Although the cuts and bruises still looked bad, internally he was feeling much better. He was healthy enough to drive over to Valley Vista to get in some practice on the driving range. Afterward, he sat on the patio and enjoyed a tall glass of beer. He overheard the ladies seated at the next table talking about Kat's amazing victory and her miracle shot on the final hole. Her victory made Tom feel really, really good. He all but forgot about the injuries he sustained in Mexico--for a few minutes at least.

It's too bad, thought Tom, that Kat wasn't interested in romance. He resolved to call her later that night and ask her out on a real date. He called Kat's apartment number at 8PM. She didn't arrive home 'til 8:15.

When Kat came through the door, she realized she didn't have anyone to celebrate with. Her stewardess roommate Pauline was working a flight from Dallas and had not yet returned. Her brainy sister Ingrid was teaching a seminar on business planning in San Diego.

She poured herself a glass of German beer, set the trophy on the dining room table, and smiled.

At 8:30, her roommate Pauline Kramer came home, wheeling a suitcase and looking exhausted.

"How was work?" Kat asked, still sitting at the table with her trophy.

"Nice smooth flight. And I only got pinched on the fanny twice. 'Course the second one felt like a lobster claw." Pauline noticed the trophy. "I heard in the concourse that you won! Good for you!" She walked over and peered at the trophy inscribed with Kat's name. "So this is why you pros hit golf balls 75 hours a week--to get one of these little guys."

Pauline saw Kat's dark scowl. "Sorry. That was rude. Long day, that's all."

Victory had put Kat in a feisty mood. "At least our customers don't pinch us in the butt."

"Good point." Pauline went to the refrigerator and took out a beer. "And I got newz for youz from two Western Airlines Stewz."

Kat left the table and took a seat on the sofa. "What?"

"You know that guy you went out with, Tom Colt...well, this is third hand information from a cop's wife, but he and his sister went on a holiday to Mexico and were beaten up and robbed by outlaws--right in the middle of a peaceful little village."

Kat looked stricken. "Were they hurt?"

"The sister wasn't hurt, but Tom was beaten badly."

Kat, without warning, burst into tears. "No! No!"

Pauline hurried over to Kat, sat down and put an arm around her. Kat sobbed so deeply her breath came in gasps.

"This can't be. He was the reason I won today." Kat was crying so hard that Pauline could barely make out what she was saying.

Pauline was worried: she had never seen the self-controlled Kat fall to pieces.

Pauline was a woman with considerable mileage on her, and not just miles in the air. "It's OK, Kat. His injuries weren't life threatening, they said." Pauline smiled. She placed her hand on Kat's forehead, as though taking her temperature. "Just as I suspected. A slight fever. You're not having a breakdown, kiddo. My diagnosis is, you're in the beginning stages of falling in love."

Kat blew air through her nose, which unfortunately created snot bubbles.

"No. Tom doesn't see me in that way."

"How do you know that? Have you ever asked him? Have you ever kissed him?"

"I've tried," she said weakly, her head down.

"The Katrina I know just doesn't try. She prevails, no matter the odds."

Kat nodded, with resolve. "This wasn't like me. I'm stronger than that. It's just...everything was going so well."

Whatever storm had blown through Kat began to subside. Kat stood up, went to the bathroom and washed her face with cold water. "Thank you, P.K. I'm good now."

"My advice, go to him. Tonight. See for yourself that he's OK. Put on one of those pretty outfits your Fairy Godmother bought you and get over there."

"I paid for half!"

Kat reappeared in the living room. "You're absolutely right."

Pauline looked like she wanted to say one more thing but was hesitant. Kat perceived that. "What?"

"If you golf pros get this upset when you win, what the hell happens when you lose?"

Kat finally smiled. "You don't want to be around us."

***

Forty-five minutes later, Katrina knocked on the door of the Guest House at the Wilkinson Estate. The door opened and Katrina met Caroline. They both burst out laughing. They were wearing the exact same outfit: Teal pullover wool sweaters, white blouses, tan slacks and black flat shoes.

"I'm Tom's sister Caroline."

"I'm Katrina Stern."

They continued to laugh. "Where do you shop...that new Scottsdale boutique, Chez Jilly?"

More happy-girl laughter. "Is Tom in?"

Caroline, equal the detective to Tom, quickly assessed the situation. "C'mon in. I have to make a run to the liquor store. My favorite store is in Albuquerque, so I'll be a while." Caroline winked at Kat.

Tom appeared. He pitched the keys to the T-Bird to Caroline. "Take my car, but don't go over 70!"

"My brother is overly cautious. Maybe you can work on him. He needs to cut loose."

Caroline grinned. Caroline split.

Walking into the well-lighted living room, Kat could finally see all the cuts and bruises on Tom, who was wearing Bermuda shorts and a t-shirt. Her expression conveyed worry, even alarm.

"I look worse than I feel," he said with typical Tom nonchalance. "Just a little accident."

Kat shook her head. "Not what I heard. What were you doing in Mexico?"

Tom thought for a few moments. "Caroline wanted to go shopping there."

Kat didn't believe that for an instant, but didn't pursue it. What if she had pursued the issue and Tom told the truth: "I'm an undercover operative for the Phoenix Police Department. We're working on the murder of Lisa Luck."

"I came by to see for myself if you're OK and to thank you from the bottom of my heart for your help with my game-- and for your encouragement. I won today--against the best player on tour."

Tom's eyes shone with excitement. "I know. You were the talk of Valley Vista this evening. The sky's the limit for you in golf, Kat."

They smiled at each other. There was an air of anticipation in the room.

Katrina had cut loose on the 18th tee that afternoon, and she did again that night at 9:53. Trembling with expectation, she extended her hands. He took her hands in his.

She said, "Can you make love?"

"Yes I can. I have two manuals on the subject, one with pictures and detailed diagrams."

Kat laughed, stopped trembling. "No, fool. I mean will it be too painful--your injuries."

"Oh, yes. The pain will be excruciating. But I'm willing to sacrifice--for you."

Kat giggled. "Where do we start?"

"I believe Chapter One of the manual says, we quickly remove our clothes."

She giggled again. She was totally at ease with this wonderful guy--and she could tell he was thrilled that she was there.

She pulled the sweater over her head. She began to unbutton her blouse. Per her roommate Pauline's suggestion, she hadn't bothered with a bra. He slipped the t-shirt over his head, as she removed her blouse, and set it on the back of the green couch.

"Look at those Little Beauties!" he exclaimed when he saw her breasts. He lightly kissed both of her hardening nipples. "Nice to finally meet you both."

Yet again, Kat giggled.

Tom took her by the hand and led her to his bedroom. Both of them cut loose than night. Two superbly conditioned athletes using all of their athletic prowess to please each other more than either had ever experienced before. They took their passion to the physical limit, holding nothing back. Two people of limitless will to win encouraging each other with every touch, every tumble in the sheets, every kiss.

And so a love affair began that night that would last the rest of their lives—but featured many, many interruptions, some for years. Tom remained Tom and Katrina remained Katrina. This presented numerous barriers, even to people who were most likely soul mates.

The tremendous, glowing passions that had brought them together: for achievement, for victory, for justice, for honor, for loyalty, for liberty, for pleasure—were the same ones that prevented either of them from ever asking, Would You Marry Me? Tom and Katrina, above all else, wanted to give flight to their dreams. There were too many times each of them had to soar alone, because the nature and importance of their dreams were so different.

And of course there was the persistent complication named Julia Wilkinson.

That night, though, was the time Kat would finally recognize that Tom was thrilled with every inch of her. Her alabaster skin untouched by even a single blemish, unless you count the sweet tiny dimples on her back. Her green eyes that shone with mystery and promise in the throes of passion. Her legs, as strong as his, so thrust was matched by energetic thrust.

As they contentedly dozed, Kat lying on her stomach, Tom lying on his side, he woke and enjoyed casting his eyes on the loveliest round little backside he had ever seen.

She woke, too, saw him admiring her. "To think I said I had no time for romance. What a double dummkopf I was."

"What you didn't know was that love and golf go together very well."

She pushed herself up, leaned over and drowsily kissed him. "In college I dreamed of you and I doing this."

"How does the reality compare with your dream?"

"We'll need to do a lot more research before I can give you an answer. Remember, I was a chemistry major."

"Must have been Good Chemistry you majored in."

She kissed Tom once more.

Chapter Twenty-Five
Why Mathers Became a Cop

"Coulda had this meeting at the station house," JB Leeves grumped.

"What do I always say," Det. Mathers replied. "Confined spaces lead to confined thinking."

On this bright morning in May, Ed had brought JB and Officer Rudy out to Wickenburg, AZ, a 40 minute drive north and west of Phoenix. He was taking them on a horseback ride.

JB wasn't looking forward to hefting his bulk up onto a saddle. The horse probably wasn't either.

Mathers was dissatisfied with the progress they were making in the Lisa Luck murder case. "Too many suspects," he was heard muttering to himself in the station house, nearly every day. His goal for the horseback ride was to have them compare notes on the information they each had gathered and to winnow the list down to a manageable number.

They arrived at a dude ranch, Rancho de Los Caballeros, a favorite winter and spring destination for tourists from all over the US who wanted to experience the Old West, or at least a version of the Old West that featured comfortable accommodations, maid service and great food. The ranch was expertly run by Dallas Gant and his family.

Ed had an acquaintance who worked as a wrangler at the ranch, Lucas T. Boone. Lucas was a weathered, bow-legged authentic cowboy who was born on a nearby ranch in 1907. Under the wide Stetson he always wore, there were just a few wisps of brown hair on either temple.

Lucas was very patient with the 'dudes' who came out to stay at the ranch; he particularly liked teaching youngsters how to ride and rope.

The tourists would have been amazed to learn that this soft-spoken, laconic Westerner had a collection of over 100 firearms of all types, from Old West revolvers to modern semi-automatic rifles. From time-to-time Mathers had called upon Lucas T. Boone to assist him when a case took a dangerous turn. Lucas had no compunction, as he said, about "doin' difficult thangs".

When the police officers arrived to get their mounts for the day's ride, Lucas was finishing up teaching a young lad of about 10 years old how to saddle a horse and ride. The boy looked a bit unsure of himself atop the powerful steed.

"Officers, meet young Brian. He and his family have come all the way from Wisconsin. He wants to learn how to be a cowboy, wants to own a ranch someday."

The police officers, schooled in Public Relations, smiled amiably at Brian and said hello. Mathers added, "Looking good on that horse young man." The polite young man beamed and said, "Very nice to meet you, Sir."

Young Brian didn't grow up to own that ranch, but did grow up to write Western screenplays. Lucas never completely recognized the impact on these youngsters of the campfire tales about the Old West he told. What Lucas taught them about the heroic settling of The West, stayed with them. Lucas didn't read these stories in books; his pioneer ancestors lived them and handed them down in a treasured oral tradition.

As the officers started down the wide desert trail, Mathers said, "We lack focus. We're looking at everyone and learning nothing. I want this to be unfiltered today. There's no right or wrong answer. So speak up, Rudy."

"Yessir," Rudy replied.

Only Mathers wore cowboy boots on the ride. The other two had on sneakers. Although in keeping with the Western theme, JB had a chaw of tobacco in his mouth.

Mathers noticed that JB looked more uncomfortable on his horse than young Brian did, which pleased him. Comfortable cops can become lazy cops.

Mathers glanced over at his colleagues and his mood darkened. *This is my elite investigative unit,* he thought. *I'm screwed.* Then he remembered he also had Tom Colt, and cheered right up.

The desert was gorgeous that morning. Arizona had sufficient winter and spring rains to bring forth a colorful bloom of wildflowers, bright yellow and purple and red, that ran up the sides of the craggy brown hills they rode through. The trail was wide enough that they could ride side-by-side.

Mathers began, "Okay, guys. Let's throw out some names. I'll start with Dominic Lucato, Richard Luck's father."

Eager Rudy jumped right in. "I interviewed Luck's brother Jordan. He told me the Old Man blew his stack when he found out Lisa had a child fathered by someone other than his son. Jordan said he called Lisa ever vile name in the book."

"Good work, Rudy. But 7 years is a long time to wait to act upon that anger."

"Maybe it just festered, waiting for the right moment," Rudy said reasonably.

"Anyone know where Dominic was on the day of the murder?"

JB and Rudy shrugged.

Mathers responded, "I will pay Mr. Lucato a visit at his vineyard. I would say he's definitely a viable candidate."

JB Leeves said, "I'm leaning toward Marco Greene. Those dirty pictures he took showed he's capable of a sex crime. Remember the revenge angle."

Mathers shook his head. "Not his style. The photos he shipped to Lisa set the events in motion to ruin Luck's career without putting Marco in any jeopardy. Pretty slick of the Happy Gangster."

"I think you're wrong, Ed. Some of the shit he's been accused of..."

"But never convicted of, or even arrested for that matter. Marco is all about money now. And he's happily married to a great gal."

"Rudy, you look like you want to say something."

"I think someone on Sen. Vance's team, or his supporters did it."

JB scoffed. "Rich people don't take risks like that. Besides, I've talked to at least a half dozen of them. None thought Luck had a chance in hell to beat Sen. Vance anyway. What would they gain by offing her?"

Mathers started to see the shadow of an idea, but it was one of those nagging notions that serve to frustrate and never resolve into a clear image.

"That broad slept around," JB said. "It was one of those spurned lovers. Think about the anger it took to whack her in the head, repeatedly, with a golf club."

Mathers said, "She is 'the deceased', JB, not 'the broad'."

JB huffed. "I don't give respect that isn't earned." Then he spit a wad of tobacco for emphasis.

They came upon a watering trough. They dismounted and let their horses take a drink.

JB continued, "Devin Hughes is another good bet. Getting rid of Lisa is stirring up sympathy votes for Richard."

Rudy chimed in, "He says he was in LA the day of the murder, but we're still trying to confirm."

"Stay on top of that, Rudy," Mathers said. "Luck got that fool to throw away his career for 50k. Who knows what else he could have convinced him to do if the money was there."

"And don't forget those boys enjoyed kinky sex together." JB grinned. He kept one of those FAMOUS PHOTOS in his desk and reviewed it over his lunch hour, by himself with the door closed.

Mathers tried to ignore that comment. "Les Levine is an obvious suspect. But I have a problem with that one. Can't imagine him having a passion for anything except where his next fat fee was coming from, like most lawyers. His idea of getting rid of Lisa would have been to keep her quiet and happy until the election was over, not kill her and stir up a huge mess. My guess is he was convincing her she could have a quick divorce after the election. But still...something doesn't pass the sniff test."

Rudy contributed, "What if Lisa just said no, I'm leaving, and was preparing to file for divorce."

"Excellent observation, Rudy."

Inspired by praise from his boss, Rudy continued, "A smart lawyer like Levine would be smart enough to set up the murder to look like a crime of passion."

Mathers nodded affirmatively. Oddly his big roan horse bobbed its head up and down, too. The three men chuckled. Mathers patted the horse's neck. "Should we deputize him?"

Quickly, Mathers turned serious. "We have to face the reality that Luck could've hired a hit man coming out of Mexico—since he himself had the perfect alibi—and that person is long gone."

JB shook his head. "Gotta say, Luck isn't that smart. He just an empty suit with a winning smile."

Mathers said, "I agree completely with you JB."

They got back on their horses--JB stiff and in noticeable pain--and started back down the trail to the ranch.

"Guys, we have to keep Roman Morales on the list, even though logic says he'd be more likely to take out Richard Luck, not Luck's wife, if he was seeking revenge."

JB said, "Morales is capable of anything. He had a guy shot up the ass just to make a statement—and no one seems to know that the statement was."

"That's another thing I'm going to go over with Dominic Lucato. You're certain you can trace the dead man back to Morales..."

"Yes, on occasion my informants in Mexico come through for me."

"How do we pay them?"

JB said nothing. Kept his head straight ahead. They got back to the corral and returned their horses. Mathers told his team, "I feel better about what we know and what we need to find out."

JB said, "I do too, but damn this case is complicated."

Mathers asked, "You guys ever heard of a Rube Goldberg contraption?"

They shook their heads. "That's what this case is," Mathers said.

As they walked back to their car, they saw a group of young buckaroos, boys and girls, maybe 7-12, including young Brian they met earlier. They were eating mesquite-broiled hamburgers prepared by wrangler Lucas T. Boone. They were laughing and telling stories about their horseback riding adventure.

"I hope we don't get scalped when we go out riding tomorrow," a little red-headed girl named Darlene said to Lucas.

"Won't happen unless you and your momma go shopping at those tourist traps in Scottsdale," Lucas replied.

The kids never got that joke, but he always enjoyed telling it.

Mathers reflected on his own carefree childhood in the cattle ranching community of Springerville, Arizona, turned to his colleagues, pointed to the happy group of kids and said, "That's why we do this job gentlemen. That's why we work sometimes 15 hours a day, or 7 days a week. Why we put up with crappy pay and abuse from the press. To keep them safe."

Officer Rudy nodded thoughtfully.

JB Leeves chuckled. "Ed, you are such a softie."

"The criminals don't know that."

Chapter Twenty-Six
The Judge Kicks Ass All Over Downtown

Brooks Continues Our Story:

Leaving his office on the fourth floor of the Guaranty Bank Building on Central Avenue, Judge Wilkinson walked the four blocks to Luck Campaign Headquarters. He marched in, saw Sen. Luck in an office in the back, and continued on through the room. None of the campaign staffers dared to stop him. Remember what Tom had observed about the Judge having gravitas—and Mana.

He strode into Luck's office.

"What are you doing here? Finally see the light and want to join our movement?"

The Judge threw down the envelope with the photos. Luck opened the envelope with calm assurance. He flinched just very slightly when he looked at them.

"I've seen these already Wilkinson. Where did you get them?"

"I'm not going to tell you."

Luck looked at the Judge like he was trying to read his mind, or his soul.

"You know what you have to do, Lucato. Discontinue your campaign. You will say to the press that losing your beloved Lisa has been too devastating. You cannot give the people of Arizona the focused and dedicated representation they deserve. If you do this by 2PM today I will make sure these photos do not reach the press. You can keep your seat in the State Senate if you wish. You hardly ever show up at the state capitol, anyway."

The room went silent for thirty seconds.

Luck visibly deflated, like all the air left this puffed-up political balloon. Moments later, though Luck almost looked relieved.

"Lisa stopped loving me. She began to hate me after she found out I couldn't get her pregnant. You know who she loved? Tom Colt, your little protégé. I'm sure he fucked her after those golf lessons I paid for. She all but admitted it at a party in February. Something for you to think about before he asks for your daughter's hand in marriage. Yes, you old bastard. I have information sources, too."

Luck stood up and went to the window, leaned against it. "And that plane crash your son was killed in. You were supposed to be on that plane that day, weren't you. I guess you have enemies, too, Roy."

The Judge's face reddened with rage. "Don't you ever talk about my son, you miserable little dago punk."

"You and your crowd just couldn't deal with a reformer coming to town, someone who cared about the poor and the downtrodden, the marginalized."

"Bloody hypocrite, you are. The only person you ever cared about was yourself. And reform what? That's just a word, a bunch of political bullshit. Our city and state are prospering like never before--and you contributed nothing to that growth and prosperity."

Luck shook his head. "You know what it's like to see...an army come together to bring about change. An army of people who believe in you." Luck's gaze passed out the door to the desk where his personal secretary Dottie Petersen, the person who had believed in him the most, from the beginning, sat. She was watching and listening to the proceedings in the room with a look of unmasked horror. "I came so close to gaining that power, Wilkinson. I planned on making your life miserable."

Luck went back to his desk and turned the photos face down on the green blotter. The Judge walked over, grabbed the photos and stuffed them back into the envelope.

"I have a question for you, Wilkinson. Who loves you? Anyone?"

"You go to hell," the Judge growled as he turned for the door and walked out.

"I expect you'll get there ahead of me."

***

The Judge walked to Durant's Restaurant on Central Avenue, the gathering place for the movers and shakers, the city's good old boys, to have power lunches and even more powerful drinks. He sat at the bar, ordered a scotch on the rocks, downed it in four gulps, paid the tab and walked out. Even mighty Judge Roy Wilkinson needed liquid courage sometimes.

He went another 4 blocks up Central Avenue to the Office of the United States Senator, Prescott Vance. He walked through the small lobby and smiled at the Senator's long-time secretary, Beth-Anne, who greeted him warmly.

"Roy! How nice to see you. It's been a while."

"Is the Senator in today?"

"For you, yes. He's in a sour mood though. Just be aware."

She picked up her phone and dialed into the Senator. In a few moments the heavy door swung open and Senator (Alvin) Prescott Vance, 81, appeared. He had a white hair and white eyebrows, stood an erect 6'3", and wore a western style suit with a bola tie.

Vance was born on Oct. 26, 1881, a full 30 years before Arizona achieved statehood. It was a famous date in Arizona history—the Gunfight at the OK Corral in Tombstone was on that day. It is entirely likely that if Wyatt Earp and his brothers were around in 1962, they would have voted for Sen. Prescott Vance.

His heavily wrinkled, pinkish face broke into a broad smile when he saw the Judge. The Judge did not return the smile. He strode into the office, set the envelope on the desk and sat down on the high-backed leather chair that sat opposite the Senator's even more massive chair.

His curiosity, or perhaps it was fear, on full alert, the Senator came in, sat down and opened the envelope. Seeing the photos, he looked stricken, his pink face turning full red.

"Alvin, your stupidity in hiring Devin Hughes to manage your campaign almost cost us a Senate seat. You're thinking isn't clear anymore. No 81-year-old man can be as effective as he was when he was 60. Hell, I'm only 62 and I can feel my life force starting to abate. I shudder every time you go to the podium at a campaign event. What idiocy is going to come out of your mouth next?"

The Senator didn't seem to be paying attention to the Judge. He was still staring at the photos.

"How could the young man betray me? I gave him a job that was a wonderful opportunity. He seemed so earnest."

"He was planted to run a shitty campaign and make sure you lose--to a slimeball, an opportunist--from out of state, just like Devin Hughes is. He sabotaged your campaign, and I bet I will find out he was paid handsomely to do it. Not the first time it's happened in politics."

"What shall we do, Roy?" The Senator asked softly, meekly. The energy was draining out of him. He looked every one of his 81 years.

"I want you to resign. Let us nominate someone who's in his prime, who can fight for us."

The Senator angrily pushed the photos away, onto the floor. The Judge said nothing. He desperately wanted this man, his old, old friend and ally, to do the right thing.

The Senator looked down at his hands, which he folded in front of him. "I'm done, Roy. I'm done. What reason shall I give for quitting?"

"You are worried about your declining health. You cannot any longer give the good people of Arizona the energetic and passionate representation they have come to expect from you."

The old Senator, first elected in 1938, reached a gnarled arthritic hand across the table to the Judge, the fingers twisted every which way. They shook hands, warm friendship still enduring despite the harsh words the Judge had said that day.

"I want confirmation of your resignation in writing, by 2PM."

***

Back to Durant's for another scotch. The restaurant, which opened in 1950, already had a retro feel by 1962. Dim lighting. Red flocked wallpaper. Leather booths or banquettes as they were called. The waiters wore red tuxedo vests. In speakeasy fashion, the restaurant's regulars entered through the back door and passed through the kitchen. In the 1940s, the owner Jack Durant had worked as a pit boss at the Flamingo Hotel in Vegas, employed by gangster Bugsy Siegel.

The Judge wondered if Marco Greene knew him. Bugsy, not Jack.

As he was escorted to his regular booth, Judge Wilkinson perused the B&W photos on the walls of the celebrities who visited Durant's. His own photo was on the wall behind his booth.

He could have used one of Durant's signature martinis, but he still had serious work to do that day. He ordered a t-bone steak with garlic mashed potatoes. At half hour intervals, two couriers brought the Judge envelopes, one on Luck Campaign letterhead and one with the august letterhead of a US Senator. He read both with satisfaction.

"Best steaks in town," he commented affably to his red-vested waiter when he paid his tab.

***

From his office phone, Det. Mathers called Marco Greene to set up a meeting to find out what he knew about Roman Morales.

"Ed, I don't have time for meetings right now. This is my busy season."

Mathers thought, *Organized crime is a cyclical business? Who knew.*

The Happy Gangster continued: "But again, as always, I try to help my friends the LEOs. And in this case, you're off in left field. I didn't send Lisa Luck the photos in the US Mail. I believe that would have been against the law."

Mathers hoped Greene didn't hear him chuckle.

"Ed, I'm not sure what penalties are on the books for a man entering the Ladies Locker Room at a private club at 9PM and setting an envelope in a woman's locker."

"I think I can set your mind at ease. Probably won't pursue a prosecution at this time."

"That's a good one!" Greene laughed. "Regarding Roman Morales, he has a wide range of business interests here and in Mexico. He's a tiger as a businessman. Shrewd as hell. Knows how to identify and opportunity and seize it before other guys—myself included—move in."

Mathers could hear Marco's fingers drumming on his desk. "What else can I tell you. He was born Ramon Morales. He became fascinated with Ancient Roman History, changed his name to Roman. He has an obsession with...he belongs to this nutso group that wants to conquer and annex the American Southwest. Crackpot stuff if you ask me."

"How does this relate to him funneling money to Luck's campaign?"

"Maybe Roman thought that controlling a US Senator would...shit, Ed, I have no idea. I don't get involved in politics. It's too dirty."

Mathers let Marco think some more without interruption. A standard Mathers technique.

"Let me bottom line it for you, Ed. This Morales is one of the most dangerous men you'll ever meet. He has this idea that he has a grand destiny to fulfill. It makes guys do crazy things. My advice, leave him be. His hacienda down there is like a military compound."

"Suppose someone betrayed him, misled him, cheated him. What would happen?"

"That person, and his whole family would soon be dead."

"I appreciate your input, Mr. Greene." Marco's stark tone gave Mathers the willies. He hoped he never had to deal with Roman Morales.

"Ed, one other thing. Do you not have the budget for a police training academy anymore? Why are you recruiting golfers?"

"Did you realize that when Tom Colt met with you, you gave him information that is vital to our ongoing investigation?"

Marco was nonplussed. "I did? I didn't mean to. What the hell did I say?"

"That's why I recruited a golfer."

Mathers hung up before Marco could slam the phone down.

***

At the Founders Roundtable Club, a members-only dining club atop one of the few high rises in the youthful city of Phoenix, the men who considered themselves the city fathers had been gathered at the request of Judge Roy Wilkinson-- who told them they had an emergency to deal with. The walls of the club were crammed with photographs that celebrated Arizona's history going all the way back to the days prior to statehood in 1912.

The dining room was a sea of about 30 very apprehensive faces. Among them were Sterling Gould, Carter VonEssen, and Jilly's ex-husband Steven. Others included the senior partners of the major downtown law firms, top bankers, leaders of major corporations and of course the biggest real estate developers.

The Judge strode to the front of the room at 2:07PM. He was in full Judge Roy Bean Wilkinson hanging judge mode. A number of these industry titans were frightened of the Judge. Conversation in the room was quickly hushed.

"My friends," this has been quite a day in our state's history. We woke up to read opinion polls in all three major newspapers saying that Sen. Richard Luck had taken the lead in the Senate race. Well, things have changed dramatically since this morning."

A few quiet voices broke out into confused discussions.

"State Sen. Richard Luck has withdrawn from the race for personal reasons. As you know he suffered an unspeakable tragedy recently. And United States of America Senator

Prescott Vance has withdrawn because of health concerns." He held up the letters from both.

The room broke out into chaotic chatter. The business community, like the stock market, wants nothing more from politics than stability.

"If any of you have ever desired to enter the political arena, this is your chance. I have been in contact with the state Chairmen of both major parties and a new nomination process will begin immediately."

A voice from the back of the room, the founder of a major law firm, yelled, "How about you, Roy?"

"Frank, I have so many skeletons in my closet there's barely room for my overcoat."

The room erupted in laughter.

"I like making money. It's my calling in life. And as Harry Truman said, the only people who make money in politics are crooks."

More laughter. Roy had such, that word again--gravitas--that the Founders Club members seemed reassured that the sky was not falling.

A man in front of the room stood up, "I'll be happy to run, Roy."

The Judge walked over to him. It was Bob Bland, owner of three very profitable car dealerships in the East Valley of Phoenix. His family were Mormon pioneers who came to Arizona in the 1860s. He married his high school sweetheart and they had 6 beautiful children, three boys, three girls. He was a Boy Scout troop leader and contributed his time and money to a charity that gave food to the poor. And was of course visibly active in his Church.

"That's wonderful news, Bob. Best news we've had all day."

The Judge knew Bob Bland wouldn't accomplish a damn thing of significance in Washington. Just what Judge Roy Wilkinson wanted from his United States Senator.

***

The Judge went to his own office, returned phone calls from everyone but the press, then drove home. When he pulled into the garage, he finally felt the exhaustion that had been postponed by his will to save his beloved city. He walked inside, into the living room and filled the biggest glass he could find with scotch. Julia heard him and appeared in the living room. She had her own glass of Jack Daniels.

"How was your day?" she said cheerily.

"Productive but hectic. I'm bushed."

"What happened?"

"I decided who our next US Senator is going to be."

"It's not Tom..."

The Judge laughed. "No, not Tom. He's much too nice to get involved in politics. You see, Julia, politics is the art of pretending you care about your fellow man when in fact you don't. You care about power. Tom is someone who genuinely cares."

With Julia, every conversation eventually was re-routed to be about her. "Does Tom care for me?"

Another big gulp of scotch. "More than you will ever know. But you need to let your relationship develop slowly. He told me he is enjoying getting to know you better, each day."

Julia considered that for a few moments, twisted her lips into a thoughtful, though pouty, expression, and said, "Did he care about Lisa Luck? She was beautiful."

"I doubt it. He cares about justice, sweetheart. You need to be patient with him. He and Detective Ed Mathers are working hard to find out which one of Sen. Luck's malicious entourage took her life. Tom is a damn smart detective. Better detective than golfer, actually. Don't tell him I said that, though."

***

Terrell's 7th Street Gym was a favorite hangout for serious body builders and amateur and aspiring professional boxers. Inside, it smelled like 20 years of sweat and tireless effort. The failed dreams of hundreds of pugilists haunted the place like ghosts. Inside, it looked like no one cared how it looked inside.

Dottie Petersen trained there. Not that she was an aspiring boxer. She just liked beating the crap out of the heavy bag. It helped her dissipate the stress of political campaigns she worked on. Every campaign generated its own stress. Guaranteed.

The fickleness of voters astounded her. Dottie was the opposite: she was the true believer in every candidate she worked for, but never more so than with Richard Luck. She idolized the man.

That day, she gave the heavy bag a particularly brutal beating. She was mad to the core of her being that Sen. Luck had quit the race, particularly without consulting her.

Dottie had always been an athlete. She participated in every sport she could in high school. She was bigger than the girls she competed against, with particularly large hands and feet.

She was the most honored female athlete on Graduation Day, and the class Valedictorian. She'd been a winner all of her life.

Chapter Twenty-Seven
A Bitter Harvest at the Vineyard

Tom Continues Our Story:

Mathers picked us up at 5PM on Friday for the trip to the Lucato Vineyard and Winery, southeast of Tucson. The mood in the car was upbeat. We three shared a belief that we were making progress. I sat in the front seat with Ed, Caroline in the back.

"How come you didn't take the squad car, Ed?" Caroline asked.

"Wanted this to be informal. Just a chat with the Lucatos. My hope is we get a read on the family conflicts. Maybe the two of you could take a winery tour and buy a couple of bottles. Their chardonnay is supposedly pretty good."

I said, "She just wanted to ride in the back seat of a black and white, for old times sake."

Mathers laughed.

"Can't you arrest Tom for making bad jokes? Time in solitary would do him good."

"Wouldn't work, Caroline. He'd figure out a way to smuggle in girls."

"True, true," my sister said.

The highway from Phoenix to Tucson is one of the most boring stretches of asphalt imaginable. No pretty desert, just brown scrubby stuff and flat terrain, covered with motorists' litter. Even when we get summer rains, it never greens up.

We arrived at the gates to the Lucato vineyard at 7PM. It was an impressive property. There was still enough waning light to see the broad terraces of grapevines.

The winery and retail operation, housed in Spanish Mission-style buildings, had a large courtyard in the middle of it. There were 15-ft. high l-shaped lights set around the perimeter. Dominic Lucato hosted wine tasting parties and also catered events there.

We parked at the far end of the parking lot. Then walked toward the entrance to the winery. We saw the lights were on. And we saw there were perhaps 15 Mexican men in military-style uniforms, and with the cohesion of a military unit, armed with automatic rifles, stationed all around the courtyard.

To our horror, in one corner of the courtyard, Sen. Richard Luck was standing on two stacked wine barrels. A stout rope hung from the overhanging light post and was attached to his neck. He was clad in only his white undershorts, the front of which had a wide yellow stain. He was trembling from fright and from the cool night air. In another corner of the courtyard, the other ten members of the Lucato clan were huddled together, armed Mexicans on either side of them.

We were in the shadows of the dark winery building. Mathers swallowed hard. "I'm calling for backup. Wait here and don't make any noise."

As Mathers turned, two of the armed Mexicans strolled up with what appeared to be smashed pieces of a police radio. They held the pieces up to us and laughed. Another man motioned for Mathers to give him his service revolver. Mathers complied immediately.

At the prompting of a gun barrel poked in my ribs, I walked toward the center of the courtyard.

"I've seen this movie," Caroline said softly. "It's called 'The Alamo'."

And right on cue, the Mexican leader strolled out of the breezeway between the buildings and into the lighted courtyard. We knew it was Roman Morales himself. He was dressed all in black, and wore a black beret. He had the most frighteningly focused eyes I had ever seen, and a mouth that looked like it had never formed a smile since early childhood. He was such a dark and furious force that I had no idea how tall he was. Could've been 5'7", could've been 6'4".

I had thought Judge Wilkinson had gravitas, but in comparison to Senor Morales, the Judge was Daffy Duck.

I looked over at Mathers. He was making a gum-chewing sound even though there was no gum in his mouth. Probably just trying to summon saliva so he could speak.

Sen. Luck, teetering on the unstable barrels, spoke first. "Please cut me down, Roman. I can get some of your money back to you. Don't hurt my family."

Roman Morales shook his head solemnly.

It looked like the yellow stain on Sen. Luck's undershorts was growing wider.

I'll never forget how long we all stood there. Hours, it seemed. No one moved. No one made a sound. The night breeze even stopped.

And then from the south end of the courtyard, another group of men strode into the courtyard. It was a motley crew of fat guys, thin guys, white guys, black guys, Mexican guys. They were dressed like the thugs you see loitering with intended menace on every street corner in every big city when the sun goes down. They were armed with an array of weapons, from automatic rifles to machetes. The contrast between these men and Morales' lean and smartly dressed troops was striking. Who are these guys? They only thing they had in common was they were ugly and they were willing.

And then I saw Marco Greene. He walked almost casually to the front of the group of men he had apparently brought. He smiled, that Happy Gangster he. Morales, of course, did not smile back.

I finally got it: The Americans had arrived. And we would shortly be at war with Morales and his men. One of the many remarkable things about America is that we are always able to produce an abundance of tough, hard, dedicated men to volunteer for whatever harsh duty comes up to save our land.

I looked over at Caroline. She was silent, and trembling. She took my hand like she did when we were walking home from the park after dark when we were little kids and the bigger sinister kids were watching us.

It was as though all these men were waiting for the first twitch. I looked over at Sen. Luck. He was shaking so hard the barrels were wobbling beneath him. In a few moments, he would be hanging himself.

I saw movement out of my right field of vision. A chuckle of amazement bubbled out of me. It was Judge Roy Wilkinson. He walked into the courtyard, to the middle of the action, only perhaps 25 yards from Morales. The Judge was wearing black trousers and a long-sleeved bright white shirt, with the sleeves partially rolled up. The implication was clear: he was ready for the fight.

I mentally withdrew my foolish Daffy Duck remark. The Judge oozed gravitas from his pores. I looked at these two great men, Wilkinson and Morales, and realized they had another quality in common, Mana--the force of nature itself was embodied in them. Marco Greene had the same quality. I thought to myself that the three of them, together, could whip up a tornado.

Morales had barely acknowledged that Marco Greene had arrived, but now he said: "Roy Wilkinson. We finally meet."

"Cut that useless Sen. Luck down, Roman. And let his family go."

Morales shook his head.

The Judge didn't step back, he stepped forward, ten paces from Morales. I saw several of his men ready their guns.

"You made a bad investment, Roman. It happens to the best of us. I've written off $1 million of sour deals in my career. Your mistake was trying to buy a US Senator. It would have gotten you nothing. With a few exceptions, all Senators in our country do is talk. I know you're a student of history. In ancient times Senators had the guts to stand against all-powerful Julius Caesar. Now all we have are puffed up little men like the one you are about to hang, strutting around and pretending to be Caesars. So go home, Roman. You got your revenge."

Morales' sharp eyes betrayed that he was considering what the Judge said.

"And another thing. Give up your foolish dream of conquering the Southwest and annexing it for Mexico. In my country, the patriots all own guns. Lots of them. Even the Japanese weren't stupid enough to invade the United States in World War II, for that very reason."

I stood there riveted with admiration and respect for Judge Wilkinson. Did he really say what I thought I heard him say to Morales?

The Judge continued: "I have a better idea for us tonight than more death and destruction."

"What is your proposal?"

"You and I do business together. I would be honored to develop resort properties with you in your magnificent country."

"I own 500 acres that run along the seashore on the Gulf of California. One of the most beautiful spots on this earth."

"Let's do it, then. Build a golf resort that will be the envy of every other developer in the world. I have a young protégé, Tom Colt, who's here tonight. He could host a tournament for our Grand Opening."

I thought, *Oh shit, oh shit, please don't single me out.* I knew there were more wine barrels in the vineyard, and surely more rope.

"Step forward, Tom."

I thought again, *Oh shit, oh shit.* But I stepped forward. Morales' expression changed.

He...smiled. "Tomas Colt! I saw you win Vegas. A miracle that was, that final shot, mi amigo."

"I thought so, too. Do you play, sir?" A truly idiotic thing to say under the circumstances, I know, but what the hell was I supposed to say?

Suddenly, with my mention of golf, Morales got so excited that he dropped the measured, menacing cadence of his speech, and lapsed into a chattery Ricky Ricardo sort of dialect.

"I do, I do, but not well, I'm afraid. I need lessons. My tee shots are shaped like, the plantano." He made a half-moon gesture with his right hand.

Caroline nudged me. "The banana. He hits banana balls off the tee." This meant the ball veers off target with a wicked left to right arc.

"Not good, not good," he added dejectedly. "Perhaps you could help me, Senor Tomas. And permit me ask to you, could you bring the other Great Players besides yourself to this Grand Opening Senor Judge Wilkinson is proposing?"

"Ah...yes."

"Sansnee?"

"Sure."

"Binogann?"

"Absolutely."

"Rneepulmair?"

"You betcha...sir."

And that was the precise moment in my life I became a real estate developer. Because I flat out lied about the amenities I could provide the prospective customers. The Judge of course had never been so proud of me.

"I would be glad to help you with your golf swing, Senor."

Morales barked: "Cut him down."

I almost crapped in my Izod slacks. I thought he meant me. Swiftly, one of Morales' troops emerged with a long knife, scrambled up the light post and cut the rope around Sen. Luck's neck. The barrels gave way and Luck tumbled to the ground, groaned, barely moved.

Curiously, no one seemed to look at Sen. Luck. All eyes were still on Morales and Wilkinson.

The Judge turned to Det. Mathers. "I would like it to be stricken from the record that Senor Morales was ever here tonight, including the incident with Sen. Luck and the rope. I would also like it stricken that Marco Greene and his associates were ever here. Is that acceptable to you, Senior Detective Edward Mathers of the Phoenix Police Department?"

"Just don't strike out that the miserable dirtbag pissed himself," Caroline muttered.

While Mathers considered that, I stepped over to the Judge and whispered in his ear. As I finished, Mathers said, "Fine."

Morales nodded and he and his men disappeared into the darkness of the high desert night. Marco Greene gave a, I am pleased to say, stereotypical gangster hand signal to his associates and they also left the scene.

Marco walked over to the still trembling Sen. Luck and said, "Looks like you had a swinging time tonight, Sen-A-Tor." Just for grins, he shoved the still fear-stricken Senator, who fell to the ground. He walked over to us, smiling.

"I heard there might be a rumble here tonight. Brought The Boys. Mandy sent me. She said that if anything happened to Tom, I would be locked out of the house. I never liked sleeping outdoors." He saluted the Judge, strolled away, smiling as usual.

The terrified Lucatos finally emerged from their protective huddle. I noticed not one offered Sen. Luck pants, a shirt or sweater. He stood alone and shivering in the cooling night, with that widening, humiliating, yellow stain on his underwear.

Then Richard Luck cracked under the stress of almost being hanged by the neck that evening. He whined, "The campaign was ruined anyway. Les didn't have to..."

Under questioning later at the police station, Luck finished the sentence: "...kill that photographer."

Les Levine was in police custody at 2AM.

Det. Mathers motioned for me to join him for a private conversation.

"You doing OK?" I asked. I'd never seen Mathers so downcast.

"Peachy, pal. I just violated the oath I took as a police officer, and every rule I've ever been taught on the force. And what's worse, I cowered in the face of the Mighty Judge Roy Wilkinson, in front of gangsters from two countries. I should turn in my badge and then my balls."

"But you averted a bloodbath here tonight. And solved the photographer's murder."

"Well, there's that. What did you whisper to the Judge?"

"I got you a ten-year membership at Valley Vista Country Club, initiation fee and dues prepaid. In the club by-laws, they can give free memberships to the Reverend clergy. I told him you pray frequently and sometimes take confessions. So you qualify."

Mathers burst out laughing, releasing all the fear and stress of that night. He twirled around with sheer joy, did a few inferior dance steps, went over to Caroline and kissed her on the mouth.

"Why did you do that?" my surprised sister asked.

"Because it would've looked peculiar if I kissed Tom. Did you like it?"

"Um...well...yes."

Mathers asked: "Tom, tee it up on Monday? Got a day off."

"See you at 10AM. My friend. Or as I guess we say now, mi amigo."

He strolled off to his car. Caroline sat down on the ground. "I need to rest a moment. This is all too much. We nearly were executed by gangsters tonight and then I had a positive interaction with a law enforcement officer."

But I noticed the trace of a smile on her face.

Judge Wilkinson, hands nonchalantly in his pockets, strolled over to us. I was amazed how cool and collected he was. My own heart had not yet stopped racing. "C'mon, kids. Let's go home," he said.

***

The next day I went to Valley Vista and resumed giving lessons. I had four clients scheduled for that morning. I greeted each of them with enthusiasm, chatted about the weather and how nice the course was looking, like nothing had happened last night--such as nearly being a part of a gang war, a massacre and witnessing a Senator hung in his underwear.

As I reflected on last night's events, I realized I had learned my Business Axiom #1: Enemies who figure out how to make big money by working together are less likely to kill each other. This axiom served me well in my real estate development career later on in life.

Chapter Twenty-Eight
A Tale from the Campaign Crypt
Terror on Lincoln Drive

Brooks Continues Our Story:

If you think the offices of losing political campaigns are grim the morning after, an aborted campaign that didn't even make it to election day is even worse. Richard Luck sat on the edge of a desk in the tomb-like main room of his campaign headquarters.

He couldn't quite believe it was all over. A few short weeks ago he had been the darling of his political party and the local media. His campaign had even garnered national publicity. Now, all the phones around the room were eerily silent.

Mathers and Tom walked in. Sen. Luck didn't seem the least bit embarrassed to see them, even though the last time they'd been together, he was shivering in piss-stained underwear. Politicians apparently had a unique ability to shrug off the worst humiliations, the embarrassments that would mortify the rest of us, send us into hiding for months.

Mathers began, "Thank you for taking this meeting, Senator." Luck nodded and extended his hand toward two chairs near the desk.

On the floor were boxes of campaign buttons. One button was for staff and volunteers, another for the public, the voters.

"Can't quite throw them out yet. The last remnants of my glorious dream." He handed Mathers stapled sheets of paper, a legal document it appeared to Tom.

Mathers read it. "This is what you promised Roman Morales? A US Senator can't do any of this stuff. The President couldn't."

With that irritating fake smile, Luck said, "I know that, but Morales didn't. He studied Roman history, not US history. Detective, political promises last about as long as farts in the wind."

Mathers scowled. "Not to Roman Morales. You violated his code of honor. To a man like that, honor is everything."

Tom said, "You started waffling on the agreement, so Morales leaves the dead body at your family vineyard."

"My father found a note on the body that said, 'Honor Our Agreement.' I guess that was a Morales hit job, as you call it."

Mathers folded his arms and said, "Good of your old Pop to tell us about that."

A woman appeared from one of the outer offices. She was a tall brunette with hard looking features, a long horsey face. Even in a nicely tailored tan business suit, skirt and matching jacket, she looked mannish, Tom thought.

"I'm taking off, Richard. Good luck. Please take care and stay in touch."

"You too, Dottie. And my sincere thanks for your years of service to our cause."

Mathers didn't believe that professional politicians should be allowed to use the word sincere in a sentence.

Dottie made an odd snorting and sniffing sound. "Yes, my years of service." She exited with a heavy-legged clomping gait.

Luck observed, "She took it really hard, the campaign shutting down. I almost think she wanted this more than I did."

***

No one will really know what transpired that afternoon in a casita at a luxury resort on Lincoln Drive. All we know is what Julia said when she banged on Tom and Caroline's door just before nightfall.

Caroline answered the door, was shocked when she saw Julia. She took Julia's trembling hand and led her inside. "Tom!" Caroline called out urgently. He came in from the patio.

Tom, too, was shocked to see Julia. She was absurdly stuffed into a white shirt that was two sizes too small, didn't even cover her midriff. The shirt had the name of a resort stitched on the pocket. It was a maid's shirt.

The back of the shirt was stained with blood. Her makeup was streaked and her normally perfect hair tangled and disheveled. She looked like a frightened, abandoned child.

Julia said, almost apologetically, "He beat me."

"Who," Tom asked, putting his hand lightly on her shoulder, not certain the extent of her injuries.

"Derrick."

"Sit down," Tom asked gently. Please tell us what happened." Julia did. He saw the blood on her shirt. From Caroline's POV, Tom looked both angered and helpless.

"Derrick flew in this morning and asked me to go with him to a late lunch by the pool at the resort. It was fine until we finished eating, then he started to become agitated. I didn't know why. He invited me to join him in one of the little casitas at the resort. I did. Laying with me usually calms him down."

She paused for breath. Tom fetched a glass of water for her, which she acknowledged with a wan smile and quickly drank it halfway down.

"The minute we got inside, he threw me down on the bed—and attacked me." She gasped. "He tore my shirt away. Took off his belt. He has this huge silver belt buckle that was made from the first silver strike his family made in 1885. The buckle has sharp images of miners' pickaxes carved on it."

She had to pause again. Tom and Caroline both perceived that Julia didn't believe the terror of that day was over.

"I had never seen a look in his eyes like that. I was too terrified to move. I couldn't understand what was happening."

She paused and gulped down air.

"He whipped me over and over with the belt buckle. I curled into a ball, hoping he wouldn't hit my face. My face is my livelihood. He must have hit me 20 times. He said it was one for each time I kissed Tom. He saw us that night at the gazebo."

Julia reached out for Tom's hand. He squeezed hers.

"Then, he left. I lay there for a long time—in shock I guess. The maid came in, saw me, and got this shirt for me to leave in. I called a cab and came home."

Complete silence gripped the room—Tom and Caroline were stunned.

Julia stood up and pulled up the back of her shirt so they could see the ugly welts on her back.

To Caroline, Tom said, "Please go to my bathroom and get the mercurochrome and bandages."

Caroline hurried off. "Right."

When Caroline came back, she led Julia into her bedroom and helped her out of the tight and bloody shirt.

Julia lay face down on the bed and Tom applied the disinfectant, which made Julia wince. Caroline put square gauze bandages over the worst of the abrasions, which were nasty looking—but the pain of the humiliation Julia had suffered was much worse.

Caroline said, "Please stay here tonight. Tom and I will keep you safe." She loaned Julia the Minnie Mouse pajama set. She didn't know exactly why. Perhaps so Julia could pretend to be an innocent young girl again.

Julia used the phone by Caroline's bed to call her Father and let him know she would be staying at Tom's. She summoned that iron will that Tom had seen before and sounded genuinely cheerful, "We're going to have a late supper and then listen to records. You know how much I enjoy being with Tom and Caroline."

Julia rejoined Tom and Caroline in the living room. Tom got beers for each of them.

"You need to call the police," Caroline said in a sharp, instructing tone.

"NO!" Julia said, almost yelling. "Derrick's father puts up the lion's share of the capital for each of our real estate projects. It lets my father spread the risk and be able to do more deals. I can't say a word about this to anyone—and you mustn't either."

"But he assaulted you," Tom said incredulously but without accusation.

"He's never done anything like that before. He just can't stand that you and I are close."

Caroline, emotions on fire, paced the room. She truly couldn't believe what she had just heard. "Derrick must know you go out with other guys. You showed me the photos in your room."

Julia took a replenishing swig of the beer, which until tonight she didn't like. "Derrick hates Tom because he's a champion golfer."

This surprised Tom. Derrick Rhodes seemed like the type of man who automatically assumed he was superior to other men in all ways.

Another swig. "Derrick is shitty at golf—his mom and dad are both club champions at the Broadmoor.   He's weak at all sports really, the runt of the Rhodes family litter. And remember, the first time we saw Tom he was playing in the US Open! Derrick hates it when he can't be the best."

Caroline had had enough. "Why do you people let money rule your lives?"

Now Julia had had enough. "You don't understand." She pointed at the brilliantly lit mansion on the hill and continued: "You come up and eat our fabulous food and drink our expensive liquor. You look right at home lying with your feet up on the soft leather sofa in the TV room. You and your brother live in a house we paid for!" She hiked up the pajama top and pointed again at the orange wounds on her back. "This is the price to have all these things. And you will never even know the price my father has paid. A much greater one."

Julia began to weep. Real tears. Not acting, Tom and his sister both recognized. "We've treated you both like family, so try to understand."

The room went completely silent except for Julia's quiet sobs.

Then Caroline did one of the most un-Caroline things Tom had ever seen. She said, "I am sorry. What I said was stupid. I'm a smart person with a stupid mouth."

Julia nodded, acknowledging the apology. She said, "I'm worn out. I have to sit down." She did, on that famous green couch where once a dream of Tom's had come alive.

Caroline sat down next to her and gently stroked Julia's forehead, and repeated, "I am so, so sorry."

Caroline got up, went to that all-night pharmacy known as her purse and pulled out a pill bottle. Tom noticed it did not have a pharmacy label. It never did. She opened the bottle, took two pills out and gave them to Julia. "These will help you get some rest."

Julia took the pills with a swallow from the water glass.

Caroline asked, "Do you think Derrick might come here, Julia? He knows where Tom lives."

Julia offered no answer. Shrugged.

Tom went to the kitchen drawer and took out his gun, the snub-nosed .32 caliber revolver. "Don't worry. We'll be safe. I keep the bullets in the other drawer."

Caroline said, "Tom got his advanced weapons training from Deputy Barney Fife when he visited Mayberry."

Julia smiled. Tom said, "Keeping a loaded gun in the house could lead to accidents."

Caroline had a wry grin. "I know that, good brother. I thought some levity would help."

"I have to admit that was funny," Tom conceded.

An hour later, Julia was asleep in Caroline's room. Caroline set up the living room sofa with a pillow and a blanket for her to sleep. Tom sat thoughtfully on the bar stool, sipping his beer. Caroline looked at Tom and thought, but wisely did not say, *Guess that's it for poor Katrina. If Julia were a popsicle flavor she'd be Sex on a Stick. I look like a sack of potatoes in those pajamas. Julia looks like a fashion model on a runway in Paris.*

At that moment, Julia walked into the room, drowsily. She had shed the pajama bottoms. She walked over to Tom, who hopped off the bar stool, and kissed him with a passion that surprised Caroline. Then she went over to Caroline, kissed her as well, then hugged her tightly and said, "I love you," which in her sleep-drugged state came out as "I wuv you." She let go of Caroline, padded back toward the bedroom, turned and said, "I wuv bof of you."

Tom got another beer for Caroline and they sat on the patio, trying to make sense of the evening's events.

"She wuvs us," Caroline commented.

Tom chuckled. "Lots of rich folks seem to wuv us these days."

"If they do, how come we're not rich?"

"They don't wuv us quite that much."

Tom and Caroline clinked their beer bottles and laughed, as much from relief from shock and stress as from the humor of the remark.

"I have a question for you," Caroline said. "Why did she just lie there and take the beating? I would've clawed the fucker's eyes out."

"I don't have an answer. These people have a social order that you and I don't understand." Tom thought a few moments. "Maybe it was what Julia said. She was trying to protect her face. If you look at her chin, there is a scar on it."

"We can guess where that came from," Caroline said.

After Caroline went inside to get ready for bed, Tom wondered, if Derrick came to the house intending to do them harm, would he have the courage to put actual bullets into his gun and shoot Derrick.

The honest answer was, he was not at all sure he could. And to Tom, raised to believe the iron laws of right vs. wrong from detective and Western movies in the '50s and '60s, this meant he wasn't a genuine crime fighter. He was merely playing at being a private detective. And he was just playing at and imitating his hero and that of his father, John Wayne. The real lawman has to be able to pull the trigger.

Tom shuddered at the unaccustomed emotion that gripped him. It was fear.

Chapter Twenty-Nine
Colt and Mathers Solve the Case

Tom Continues Our Story:

I sank a twisty 20-foot putt on the final hole of the US Open Qualifying event in Broadmoor, Colorado. Yes--I sank a putt when it mattered, really mattered, because I qualified by one slender stroke. I was going to Oakmont to play in the Open! Our National Championship!

When the ball disappeared into the hole, I burst into song, kind of an opera-like thing. The fellows I was paired with me looked at me like I was an imbecile. I did not care. They failed to qualify. I made it. So there, losers.

How splendid it was to be competing again. I felt great, no lingering effects of the beating I took in Mexico.

The US Open is always played on a brutally difficult course that the US Golf Association, which puts on the event, works diligently in the months leading up to the Open to make even tougher. This year, the venue was Oakmont CC in Pennsylvania. I wasn't certain that my putting, though improved, was up to the challenge of Oakmont's huge, legendary greens. But I was eager to find out.

A cynic might say, Tom, you're just pumped up because you're falling in love with Katrina and she's falling in love with you. And the cynic would be right. But there's nothin' wrong with falling in love.

This same cynic might add, borrowing a line from Sam Snead, Young Tom, Oakmont will eat your lunch and the paper bag you packed it in. But for once I managed to put all those cynical voices out of my head.

I entered a tournament two weeks before the Open, so I could get used to the turbulent and tense atmosphere of competition again.

This tournament was The Rocky Mountain Roundup in Denver, a place that will always be special for me. Rust showed in my game in the first round. I shot a 2-over-par 74, but rebounded with a crisp 69 in round 2. Sheboygan, though, noticed my mind wasn't totally on golf.

"I can't get the investigation out of my mind," I confessed to my caddie. Golfers confess everything to their caddies.

"Hoss, why don't you think about the 'vestigation after the round is over. Just an idea."

"My mind doesn't work that way. It's open for business 24/7."

At that moment, my mind was beginning to form an idea, perhaps a break in this frustrating case. I swung way too fast on a relatively easy 5-iron shot, and pulled the ball to the left of the green.

Sheboygan shook his head. "Hoss, hoss."

"Why do you call me Hoss? That's the big man on *Bonanza* on TV. You look like him more than I do. I see myself more as James Bond."

Sheboygan chuckled at that one. "I guess I could call you Little Joe."

I laughed. Our lighthearted mood began producing results. I birdied three holes in a row and was within striking distance of the lead. Not bad after a four-week layoff.

I was standing in the tee of the next hole waiting to hit my drive when the emotional equivalent of a thunderclap hit me.

"That voice," I said aloud. "I've heard that voice before."

I looked so exultant, Sheboygan tried to join in my triumph. "I'm so glad. Now let's focus on the next shot. And make some money for da both of us."

I was already jogging off toward the clubhouse. Sheboygan hollered, "Hoss, what are you doing?"

"I have to make a phone call."

Like all great caddies, Sheboygan followed me without question or complaint. On the steps of the clubhouse, Tournament Official Seamus O'Flaherty was waiting for me.

"Ach! You can't leave the course during a round! Get back to your place in the playing field!" He spoke with a thick Scottish brogue.

"Need to use the phone in the clubhouse. It's urgent."

"I'll disqualify you, I swear. Mr. Popularity or no."

He pronounced it like Poop-u-larr-etee.

A pond fronted the 18th green. I walked back over to it. "You're not disqualifying me." I opened the zippered compartment where I kept my golf balls and one by one tossed the 7 balls into the pond until I had none left.

"I am forced to withdraw because I ran out of golf balls."

"I'm reporting you to the rules committee Tom Colt!" He wagged a finger at me. "What could be more important than golf?"

"Solving a murder," I said irritably.

"What that? What?" Seamus exclaimed. "No one's been killed at my tournament, I hope..."

I climbed the steps and pushed Seamus out of the way. "Fuck it, just fuck it." That's how pissed off I was: I was starting to sound like Caroline.

"And quit with the fake Scottish accent. You're from Indiana."

I sprinted to the locker room and found a phone. Thankfully, I got connected to Det. Ed Mathers right away.

"Ed, at the Goulds' New Year's Eve party I heard an angry conversation between Lisa and someone whose voice I didn't recognize. She accused Lisa of ruining, destroying the Senator's campaign. The voice was Dottie Petersen's."

I could hear Mathers' old desk chair squeak, like he was leaning forward with great attention. "You're certain."

"Absolutely. I walked off the course in the middle of a tournament when I was only one stroke out of the lead, to call you."

"Got it."

"When we looked at who was at Valley Vista CC the day of Lisa's death to see who could have taken the golf club, the murder weapon, we only looked at the men who were at the Club--it was Men's Day and hardly any women were there anyway. I'll bet if we check the records, Dottie was a guest of a member that day."

"If this checks out, you're a genius!"

"Ed, that badge you found in the desert by the Luck home was the key. It was the badge that campaign staff and volunteers were given to wear. A minor staffer wouldn't have killed Lisa. It had to be a higher-up in the campaign, someone with a lot to lose if Richard Luck lost."

"Let's catch a killer. I'll get a search warrant for her house. There were partials of bloody footprints near the door to Lisa's bedroom. Looked like hiking boots. We thought they were a small man's--like Les Levine. Could have been from a big girl."

"That's what we overlooked. Did you see how big and strong Dottie Petersen was? Her boots could have been men's sized."

"We got a new leader on our Leaderboard. Call me when you get back, and I mean immediately. We have to act fast. Remember she told Luck she was leaving town."

"Sure thing, Chief."

Brooks Continues Our Story:

Things came together quickly. Mathers found hiking boots at Dottie Petersen's pad, that had tread similar to the partial prints found at the crime scene. They had been scrubbed clean. But as Mathers always said, blood is stubborn stuff and the police lab experts found traces of Lisa's blood on the boots. Why didn't Dottie Petersen dispose of the boots? That's another Mathers axiom: most crooks are stupid, especially the ones who think they're so damn smart.

Dottie Petersen was indeed a guest of a member the day of the murder: none other than shifty little Les Levine. The good guys got another break when one of the waitresses identified Dottie as being the one who lifted the golf club--the murder weapon--from the hallway by the pro shop. At the time, she thought it odd, but not odd enough to tell the police about.

***

Mathers had sent JB Leeves to bring in Dottie Petersen for questioning. He looked at his watch as he sat at his tiny desk in his tiny office. The interrogation would begin in roughly two hours. He spent as little time as possible in his office. As he often said, he believed confined spaces led to confined thinking. Truth was, he suffered from fairly debilitating claustrophobia, but didn't tell anyone.

He preferred the wide open spaces. He had solved several crimes while horseback riding by himself in the pristine desert country outside of the city. Maybe that was one of the reasons he loved the solitude of golf so much.

Mathers had a problem. They had as the Chief would say, 'buncha evidence' that Dottie committed the crime. But he also could imagine a smart defense lawyer smashing his case to smithereens. 'Buncha evidence' isn't always the same as quality evidence.

He reviewed the key pieces in his mind. Tom overhears a conversation with Lisa and Miss Petersen which sounds like she was accusing Lisa of ruining the Senator's campaign. Could Tom testify under oath that he was absolutely certain that was Miss Petersen's voice—which he heard from the other side of a closed door?

Then we have the scant traces of Lisa's blood on Miss Petersen's hiking boots. Juries can be skeptical of scant traces. They prefer more graphic evidence, such as a shirt splashed with the victim's blood. Suppose the defense concocts a story like good friends Lisa and Dottie went hiking together, and Lisa cut herself, Dottie stepping on the blood when she provided first aid to her good friend.

The campaign button Mathers found in the desert—the type of button given to staff and volunteers—well, there were probably 100 staff and volunteers in a campaign for the United States Senate.

And Dottie was a guest at the Valley Vista CC the day the murder weapon, the golf club, was taken. And a witness even says Dottie removed the club—she thought. All the defense would have to do is present the list of the 120 men who had access to the same golf club that day.

Mathers could hear the Defense's closing argument: "*The police and the prosecutor, unable to make any progress in this high-profile murder case, have collected a basketful of irrelevant items, and presented a farrago of confusing, conflicting suppositions, and tried to pass them off as decisive evidence.*"

Lawyers like to use words like farrago, thinking cops like Mathers wouldn't understand them. They were wrong, in Ed's case.

Nonetheless, Mathers' gut told him Dottie Petersen committed the crime. The anger it must have taken to murder Lisa in that brutal manner, with a golf club, made Mathers shudder. It seemed subhuman to him. But one of the problems he had in this case was remaining impartial, because he had met Lisa, and liked her. He could tell, Tom did too.

What Mathers needed was a confession. Police investigators learn to present various personas, depending on the needs of a particular case, or a particular suspect. The most well-known is probably the Good Cop/Bad Cop tandem interrogation, which emerged from the Film Noir genre in the '40s and '50s, because it makes for great drama. To Mathers, the problem with that method was it doesn't work as well in real life. Perps watch movies, too.

An hour before the Petersen interrogation, Mathers had no clear-cut strategy to elicit a confession. He had a sour stomach from all the worrying he was doing over this thorny case. He took a green bottle of Mylanta anta-acid from his desk drawer and slugged down much more than the suggested dose.

With dumb suspects a bluff can sometimes manipulate them to start babbling their guilt, but this Petersen woman was a savvy political operative. She was skilled at being the manipulator.

At 11:30 JB Leeves escorted Dottie Petersen into the interrogation room, which had no window, 3 uncomfortable metal chairs and a small table with a wobbly leg. On the table was a 9"x12" envelope, unlabeled.

She wore a summer-y white dress and a light blue jacket. Crisp and cool. *The woman looked too cool of demeanor, would be hard to rattle,* Mathers thought. Officer Rudy manned the reel-to-reel tape recorder in a corner of the room.

Mathers stepped in, with a smile on his face, like greeting an old friend. "Miss Petersen, thank you for accepting our invitation to come in and talk to us today. I am Detective Mathers. We met briefly at Sen. Luck's campaign headquarters."

"Am I under arrest? She asked placidly, maybe mockingly. "If I am, I want my attorney here."

Mathers smiled. "No, no. Nothing like that. Please sit down and relax."

Mathers noticed JB's incredulous stare. "Thank you, JB. That will be all for now."

Leeves left. Outside the closed door, he muttered, "Anything you say, Beav. But what the fuck are you doing?"

Mathers and Dottie P sat down. She said, "You searched my house. Why?"

"Just routine. We have to chase down every lead. This case is a frustrating one for us."

Now officer Rudy looked incredulous.

"Tell me, what was your impression of Lisa Luck?"

Mathers took note of the instant fire in Dottie's eyes.

Dottie laughed with a sneer. "I hated that bitch. She was taking a wrecking ball to everything we had worked so hard to achieve—and why? Because she was angry that she and Richard couldn't have a baby. There's more to life than children."

Mathers tried to make an exaggerated face to express that he didn't understand.

Dottie asked, "What about acquiring power and using that power to change this country?"

"Change it into what," Mathers asked levelly.

She glowered and gave no answer.

"We could have gone all the way to the White House. I could have been the first female Chief of Staff!" She slapped her large hand on the table for emphasis.

"I met Lisa a few times at Valley Vista CC. She seemed beautiful and charming to me."

Dottie sprang to her feet. "Detective, she was a damned whore." Dottie's long horsey face was alight with anger. "And I didn't know cops could afford to hang out at Valley Vista."

"Only the best ones."

Mathers calmly, gently motioned for her to sit back down. She did.

"There's no evidence she was anything but a wonderful wife, Miss Petersen."

Dottie raised her voice. "No evidence? What kind of cop are you? She humiliated my Richard every chance she got."

Mathers took note of the 'my Richard' remark.

Mathers' smile was clearly dismissive of her comment. "I think Lisa deserved a better husband. Richard Luck is as phony as a 3-dollar bill."

Mathers opened the envelope and removed one of the famous photos of Sen. Luck and the prostitutes. He turned the photo right side up and slid it over to Dottie P.

She looked at it, became apoplectic. "This is fake. Trick photography."

"No, ma'am. You can't fake sexual excitement like that. Sen. Luck, a married man, who tells the voters he's a devout Catholic, consorted with whores on a regular basis. You probably remember him leaving the office early on Tuesdays."

"No!" Dottie cried out.

Mathers stood up and strolled over to the door, leaned on it. "Sorry, Miss Petersen. I have to disagree with you. Our conclusion is that the problem was Lisa being trapped in a marriage with a jerk of a politician, a professional liar." Mathers stroked his chin. "You know Luck had no chance of winning against an Arizona legend like Sen. Vance."

"You're wrong! Legend? That senile old coot! He keeps us in the Dark Ages."

"Luck is as phony as a 3-dollar bill," Mathers repeated, even more confidently.

"Stop this!!"

"That's why Luck had to cheat, and bribe Devin Hughes to run an incompetent campaign."

This was apparently the first Dottie had heard of Hughes' strange, key role.

"What? What do you mean?" Dottie Petersen exhibited such psychotic fury in her eyes that even inexperienced officer Rudy could perceive it.

With calm assurance, Mathers said, "I don't believe a thing you've told me. Lisa Prentiss Luck was a fine young woman. Anything to the contrary is just lies and slander. You made up a story to destroy the reputation of a blameless young woman who just wanted to be a mom. You know it and I know it."

Dottie was visibly shaking.

Mathers did not betray how good he was starting to feel. He sat back down, this time in a chair next to her, not across from her. He idly, coolly, picked some lint from his suit coat. He could hear Dottie's accelerated breathing. If Dottie were an older, less in-shape person, he might wonder if she were going to pass out.

"I've never understood how a human being could take the life of another," Mathers said with great synthetic sincerity.

"It's easier than you think, Detective," Dottie Petersen said.

TOTAL SILENCE IN THE ROOM. Maybe in the entire city. Mathers let the silence build emotional heat in the confined space, like a summer storm about to unleash its fury.

In a soft, gentle guidance-counselor voice, Det. Ed Mathers said, "Lisa Luck's blood was on your hiking boots. When you went to her house that afternoon you dropped a Luck campaign staff button in the desert. A waitress at Valley Vista saw you take the murder weapon out of the clubhouse and to the parking lot. She remembered it because it seemed odd you took out a man's golf club. You were overheard by a credible police witness making direct threats to Lisa Luck at a party. Shall I go on?"

Mathers let the silence build again. Rudy was watching with such rapt attention, like watching an absorbing stage play, Mathers hoped the tape recorder was still running.

Oddly, Dottie Petersen looked relaxed, almost at peace. Mathers thought to himself, this crazy woman thinks she did a good thing for the people of Arizona, or at least for her political party, killing Lisa Luck.

Dottie began, "I didn't really decide to kill her until I saw the golf club in the hallway. I had lunch that afternoon with Les Levine, who thought we were pretty much done for. Lisa had the upper hand. And now she was filing for divorce. So it all came together. She slept with those old men at the Club to get back at Richard. I wasn't a member of The Club. They'd think a man did it. I don't even play golf. It's a stupid game for stupid old men."

If he could, Mathers would have incarcerated Dottie P. just for saying that.

She continued: "I knew no one would be at the house except Lisa."

Mathers glanced over at Rudy. Tape recorder still running, plenty of tape.

"I knocked on the kitchen door. She came out in a bathrobe. Must've thought I was the gardener waiting to be paid. When she walked past me I hit her—again and again."

Mathers checked on Rudy. The young man's eyes were so wide with fright he knew Rudy would be transferring out of homicide soon.

"Why did you pose the body that way?"

Dottie smiled, apparently carried away by her own cleverness. "A sexual thing. You'd think a man did it. Apparently you did, so my idea worked. I tore the robe off her body and ripped the sleeve, like an angry male would do in a sexual fury. And I posed her so the last pictures taken of her would show the slut she was."

Mathers went to the door, opened it and called out to a nearby cop, "Please send Det. Leeves in. Thank you."

Mathers turned back to Dottie: "All that pain, all that death, for what--power."

"Yes, power to do good."

"Sorry, don't buy it. Your motive was one of the oldest: you wanted Richard Luck to yourself. Poor Lisa was in the way. And the hell of it is, I don't think Richard Luck wanted you."

Dottie shot a look at Mathers that was malevolence to the max.

"Just one more question. Why didn't you get rid of the hiking boots?"

Dottie didn't hesitate. "They were my most comfortable pair. It takes forever to break in a new pair of boots."

"Thank you for clearing that up."

JB Leeves appeared. "You do the honors, JB. Miss Petersen has confessed to the murder of Lisa Luck. We have it on tape. Please book her into the custody of the great and sovereign State of Arizona."

Leeves looked stupefied as he led Dottie P. away. Mathers rather enjoyed that. Rudy stopped the tape, stood up and said, "You were amazing, sir."

"It was three-quarters bluff. I correctly read that the woman was being consumed by hatred. I thought she'd crack and she did."

"She didn't just crack, she shattered. You broke her by breaking Sen. Luck. Brilliant, sir."

Mathers walked past Rudy, patted him on the shoulder and said, "Get that tape to the transcript desk ASAP. See you in the morning."

***

Detective Ed Mathers, an emotional stew of exhaustion, elation, triumph and relief, bolted out of the police station. His first stop was Bob's Big Boy restaurant at Central Avenue and Thomas, conveniently located for hungry LEOs, where he had two cheeseburgers and a large chocolate shake. He hadn't eaten all day, his stomach so roiled by the struggle for a strategy to force a confession from Dottie Petersen.

He drove to the Valley Vista CC. He walked, no strode into the Men's Locker Room. He passed down the rows of lockers until he found one with a plaque that said, Det. Edward Mathers, Phoenix Police Department.

He looked inside the locker. A set of two keys sat on the top shelf, one for his locker and one for the clubhouse door. On the second shelf was a thick 9"x12" envelope that said, "Welcome to THE CLUB!" on the front, signed by Club President Wesley Stoneman III. Inside was the latest Club news bulletin and a calendar of events. There was also a thick book of Club rules and regulations.

Mathers smiled. He liked rules and regulations.

He sat down on the bench by his locker, looked up to heaven and said, in almost a shout, "Dad, I made it!"

Chapter Thirty
Mathers Shares Credit
Katrina Learns that Sex Sells
Aunt Felicity Shares a Warning

Two days later, a press conference was held outside downtown police headquarters. Chief of Police James Flannery presided over the event and revealed the steps that led to the apprehension of Lisa Luck's killer. Tom Colt attended the press conference, seated on the back row.

The Chief looked like an old-style Irish cop from Chicago, which he was. His face was fleshy and florid. His uniform clean and crisp. His manner professional and smooth. He was a stellar leader of men.

Flannery was skilled at spreading the credit around to those below him in the chain of command, which energized and inspired the troops he led. Unlike many men in a position of authority, he was a man without any insecurity. To his troops, he was solid as a rock.

The Chief was Jilly Flannery's older half-brother. Phoenix was still a small city in '62.

The Chief heaped accolades on Det. Mathers until Ed was almost embarrassed. He spoke of what a complex case this was, with numerous potential suspects. He concluded his remarks with how proud he was to lead the officers on the force. Then he turned the microphone over to Ed.

"I want to thank Chief Flannery for his kind remarks. He was correct in saying how difficult a case this was. But..." He paused and looked over the assembled reporters. "I need to recognize the man, a civilian, who teamed up with me to solve these crimes. And remember, we're talking about three deaths. Some of the key breaks in the case came from his diligent efforts and brilliant...well, brilliance. He took time away from his own busy career to assist the Police because he, like us, believes in...justice."

The members of the press were intrigued and peeved. The press hate it when a cop is one step ahead of them. Their little heads popped up and craned like prairie dogs on the Serengeti picking up a scent. Who is this mystery man?

"He's my friend, Tom Colt. If you read the sports pages in the local fish wrap, you know who he is. Please stand up, Tom."

Tom did. The reporters turned and looked at him. He saluted Ed. Both men had broad smiles on their faces.

Tom Continues Our Story:

When I got back to The Club after the press conference, I ran into the General Manager, Basil Hedgerow, in the hallway near the locker rooms. I ran an idea by him which, surprisingly, he immediately endorsed. Usually he just said, NO! to my ideas, with narrowing eyes and the condescending droop of a pencil-thin grey eyebrow.

Golf pros who play the professional tour are said to 'play out of' a given club. When they are announced on the first tee, the Starter of a tournament will say "Now on the tee, playing out of Valley Vista Country Club in Scottsdale, Arizona, the Winner of Exactly One Measly Event in His Whole Miserable Career, Tom Colt." Well, it's not exactly like that, but that's how it sounds to me.

My idea was to have Hedgerow invite Katrina to play out of Valley Vista. Would this be immense generosity on my part or a desire to see her more often? We all know the answer to that question.

I asked Basil to call her and invite her to The Club. She arrived about an hour later and Basil told her the good news. Valley Vista was already a prestigious club to 'play out of'. She was thrilled, and I could tell by the look in her sharp green eyes she knew who was behind the whole thing. She went up to Hedgerow's office to sign some papers to make things official and came bounding back down the stairs, grabbed me and kissed me with great enthusiasm and joy. As we all know, good deeds are their own reward.

I had a copy of the latest issue of *Championship Golf Weekly* in my hand. I opened it to page 14, where there was a story titled, "What's Happened to Katrina Stern?"

I gave the magazine to her. She looked dazed. She wasn't used to, and never sought out, publicity. I on the other hand...you've already seen how I loved to see my name in print.

The Article said:

The slender proette from Brazil has earned a reputation as a dour technician on the golf course who exhibited little joy during her career. Suddenly, her sunny side has broken out. She smiles with the galleries and chats animatedly with her growing ranks of fans. Katrina, who goes by Kat, is finally sharing the bright, fun personality we all know she had.

But that's not all that this writer noticed when he followed her at a recent event in Tucson, Arizona, which she won in dramatic, heroic fashion. Kat had been known as a timid player who hit every approach shot to the middle of the green, and was so careful off the tee she routinely gave up 20 or more yards to her playing competitors.

Now, Kat has adopted an exciting, bold style of play. She plays like she is intent on making a birdie on every hole.

And there's more: she used to dress like a dowdy schoolmarm who shopped at thrift stores. No more. Her wardrobe has been updated and features equally bold colors. Her shorts are shorter, her tops are tighter. We finally get to see her shapely, long legs and cute figure.

Golf fans have embraced this new Katrina Stern as well. And this reporter noticed she takes the time to sign every autograph request, particularly from the young girls who really love her, as a hero and positive role model.

At Championship Golf Weekly, we have to say WE LOVE this new Katrina Stern. A proette to keep your eyes on for the remainder of '62 and beyond. The men's tour has Mr. Popularity, Tom Colt. Maybe Katrina will become Miss Popularity on the ladies' tour. Keep up the great work, pretty lady.

I was watching Kat to gauge her reaction. She had that frowny face, a particularly dark one. Oh, oh.

"Great article," I exclaimed. "Congratulations."

"Proette?" she spat out. "Why do they call us 'proettes'? Are we not real pro golfers? Do we not practice even harder than the men do, and do we not give our best out there every damn round even though our prize money is puny?"

I thought she was going to chuck the magazine at me.

"With publicity, it's always you take the good with the bad. What's the matter with being a winner, who's beautiful and popular--especially with the young fans. I mean, you're inspiring the next generation of golfers."

Fortunately for me, my words soothed her.

"You're right. I just hate that term 'proette'. I'm sorry I got cross. This is lovely, actually. With help from you and Jillian, I've got a whole new image, and now I play out of this posh club instead of a dusty public course off the Interstate."

I gave her a hug. "As I've said before, the sky's the limit for you."

"I even got an offer to do commercial endorsements." She pulled a letter out of her purse and showed it to me.

It was a German beer bottler. They wanted her to appear in print ads for their brand they were introducing to the American market. The ads were going to feature Kat at a pool party with a bunch of hunky muscular guys. She was going to wear, for the time, a very brief bikini and hold up a bottle of their beer.

"I'm turning it down of course."

"Why?"

"I'll be half-naked in those ads."

"Kat, this is a great opportunity for you to become even more popular. Remember about busting loose?

She looked at the ceiling and exclaimed, "ACH!! I am so tired of hearing that!!! I've busted as loose as I can!!!"

The ads came out two months later. Damn she looked good. And so did that bikini. The photographer angled the shot to emphasize her lean torso and memorably cute ass. Good Job!

***

Brooks Continues Our Story:

Tom's monthly expense check from Judge Wilkinson included a $30,000 bonus, apparently a reward for solving Lisa's murder--and most probably for not implicating any of the Judge's friends. In 1962 dollars that was enough to pay cash for 3-bedroom, spacious home in one of the new middle-class neighborhoods that were popping up like spring flowers in Phoenix in all directions.

Tom didn't buy a house though. He set part of the bonus aside, and then asked the Judge for the name of a stockbroker to help him invest the rest. The broker convinced Tom to put the money in some up-and-coming technology stocks he had never heard of.   Familiar names to us now, the high-flyers of the '60s:

*Polaroid   *Xerox   *Texas Instruments   *ITT   *Teledyne

This was another wonderful turn the Judge did for Tom. The Dow Jones Industrial Average hit its low point for the 1960s on June 26, 1962. By 1966, it had soared above the 1,000 mark. The Judge's broker made Tom over $100,000 in that time.

***

Caroline came home late that night. Tom was already asleep. He had finally admitted to himself how exhausted he was. She took off her shoes and brushed silently across the cushy carpet. She looked through her mail which was on the kitchen counter. She saw one of those ominous letters from Valley National Bank. *Oh, crap, I'm overdrawn again. But I was so careful this month. Get your head in the game, Caroline.*

Opening it like there might be a bomb inside, she pulled out a small pink piece of paper.

It was a Notice of Deposit for $10,000. For a few moments, she thought it must be a mistake. She bit her lip really hard to hold back tears. "Tom," she said quietly.

She walked into his room and kissed him lightly on the forehead. "You are truly different and special. And I am starting to see, so am I. I'm just not quite there yet." She silently left the room.

Tom wasn't asleep any longer. He smiled.

***

Tom Continues Our Story:

I was so ready to get back to my life as a pro golfer. The US Open was a little over a week away. I was practicing harder than I ever had before. I invited Kat to coach me on The Mental Game, the most elusive part of golf. Kat and I managed to incorporate some vigorous nighttime physical activity into the practice regimen.

After working on my game at Valley Vista all day, at 4PM I was still on the practice green tinkering with my putting stroke to deal with the treacherous greens at Oakmont CC, where the Open was being held. Also worrying me were the reports that they had grown the rough at Oakmont as high as 5 inches. I would be under immense pressure to keep my drives in the fairway.

I saw someone walking toward me from the clubhouse. It was Felicity Greyhawk, who was married briefly to my Uncle Kevin. Felicity, pushing 40, I would guess, had been a B-movie star in her 20s and 30s, usually playing the beautiful and well-endowed Indian maiden in Westerns.

Her character was either kidnapped and ravished by a young, buff Indian Chief, or taken by a young, buff settler and ravished. Of course, in those days a lot of the ravishing action was portrayed through dialogue and innuendo. She got to keep her buckskin dress on (mostly) during these films. Strangely, the actual Indian maidens I've seen in vintage photos didn't usually reveal as much cleavage as Felicity's film characters did.

She was a very popular and busy actress for a ten-year period, taking advantage of what was evidently a critical shortage of authentic Indians to play these roles. Her real name was Florence Plotnik. She put her film earnings into California real estate and had done quite well.

After leaving H-Wood, she kept the Indian image. She annually bought enough Indian jewelry, turquoise and silver, to keep the economy in Navajo County, Arizona humming nicely. Her skin was burnt a copper color, like the pre-mummified ladies you see lounging by the pools in Palm Springs. Felicity wore her long dark hair braided in the back.

Felicity's gestures were flamboyant. Her hands fluttered as she spoke like bright, startled birds in the rainforest. One of her trademarks was wearing alternating shades of garish nail polish on her fingers.

As if that wasn't enough personality for one woman, Felicity believed she was psychic. She had a little shop in the fashionable shopping district of Scottsdale where she gave psychic readings and sold autographed photos from her 45 films. She did a brisk business during the tourist season. Her film career may have faded but her cleavage was still outstanding.

"Tom!" she exclaimed using those fluttery bird hands to signal me. She padded quietly onto the putting green in her beaded moccasins. "I've missed you! We shouldn't be such strangers just because your Uncle was a dickhead and I had to cut him loose. I'm still your Auntie!"

I always cringed when she reminded me of that. "It's wonderful to see you, too."

Felicity was a get-right-to-the-point kind of gal. "I wanted to make sure I caught you before you departed for the US Open in Pennsylvania." She pronounced it pencil-vannnn-ya, like it was a potentially scary place. "I'm afraid I have dark premonition about you. And it is a very strong one. I had to have two vodka tonics this morning to calm myself down."

I tried to look concerned instead of my first inclination, which was to break out laughing. "What is it?" I asked with faux shock in my voice. "Did you get a vision of how many greens I am going to three-putt at Oakmont? Or that I'm going to be paired with that prick Rodney Burkett and punch his lights out in the locker room?"

She wagged an index finger at me. I think it was a puce index finger. "You have always been a funny boy, but this is serious. You must heed what I have to say."

"What do you want me to do? Withdraw from the Open and stay home with the doors locked and the windows shuttered?" Her whole face darkened and her eyes had the glow of warning. *Shit,* I thought. *This woman really is a good actress.*

"My vision showed you will not make it to play in the United States Open."

This gave me momentary pause, but only momentary.

"Thanks for the timely heads-up, but I need to get back to my practicing now. I fly out early next week. This is how I make my living."

"Fine. Don't listen. You were always a stubborn boy, too." She abruptly turned and tried to stomp off. Doesn't really come off too well in moccasins. On a soft putting green.

What a daffy dame, I thought.

Chapter Thirty-One
Tom Saddles Up Anyway

Brooks Continues Our Story:

Sunday night the week before the US Open. Tom felt great, no lingering effects of his injuries sustained in Mexico. He had booked an early morning flight to Pennsylvania on Monday, would play practice rounds at Oakmont CC Tuesday and Wednesday, and then compete in the premier golf event in the United States.

He was relieved when he saw he was paired with relatively benign players in the first two rounds. No one obnoxious like Rodney Burkett, no one so famous that the crowds following Tom's group would be too large and noisy.

Tom couldn't wait to get there. He was driving the ball as long and straight as he ever had, which was critical to success in a US Open venue, where the rough was reportedly very high.

It was 9PM. Tom was on the little putting green at the Guest House, practicing his stroke with the porch light as illumination. He had a bad case of US Open butterflies in his stomach. Caroline was inside, catching up on her reading.

The Judge had stocked a little bookshelf in the living room with bestsellers, fiction and non-fiction. She picked up a few books, saw Tom was reading *Success Through a Positive Mental Attitude*, by Napoleon Hill. He had placed little pieces of paper in key sections he wanted to remember. *No, Tom. Not this book. If you were any more positive I couldn't stand to be around you.*

She took out *Tropic of Cancer* by Henry Miller and put it on the nightstand in his bedroom. *Yes, even Mr. Popularity with the Ladies can learn a few things from great steamy literature, especially from a book that was banned for 20 years in the good ol' freedom-loving USA.*

For herself, she picked out *To Kill a Mockingbird* and went back to her bedroom. She had read it twice before. She adored the father character, Atticus Finch. The passages of reassuring dialogue between Atticus and his young children that Harper Lee wrote made Caroline feel so calm and safe that she usually went right to sleep, with the book in her hand.

Outside, Tom lined up a 20-foot putt and in a quiet golf announcer voice said, "Tom Colt, who as you know is an accomplished detective as well as a fine golfer, has this putt to become the US Open Champion for 1962." He stroked the putt. It came up three inches short.

In the distance, over toward the gazebo at the other end of the Wilkinsons' property, Tom heard voices. Angry voices. He halted his putting practice and walked in the direction of the sounds. His detective instinct told him the situation may be dangerous. He walked back inside the Guest House, went to the kitchen and opened the drawer where he kept his gun. It was gone, along with a handful of bullets. He hurried out the door and sprinted toward the angry voices. He feared the worst. But somehow was not afraid for himself.

The gazebo light was on. Tom stopped dead in his tracks when he saw Julia holding the gun, aimed at Derrick Rhodes, who was standing no more than 20 feet from her. At first, neither noticed Tom was there.

"You aren't going to shoot me. You love me," Derrick said.

Tom saw that Julia's gun hand was remarkably steady. He wished it weren't. Derrick might have half a chance.

"You beat me with your belt, you miserable bastard," Julia spat out.

"I had to get through to you, darling, that it is not acceptable to run around with that golfer when I am out of town. You belong to me."

She shook her head with great furious resolve. Rhodes took several steps toward her. "Give me that gun. It won't be easy to forgive you, Julia, but I will try. We owe it to our families."

"Don't come another step closer. I'm never going to see you again. Caroline is right, the money isn't worth it."

"Who in the world is Caroline?"

"My sister," Tom said as he stepped out of the shadows into the light thrown from the gazebo. They both looked at him strangely.

"Go back, Tom. I have to take care of this myself."

Very calmly, Tom said, "You can't shoot him, Julia. You'll go to prison. This jerk isn't worth it."

Derrick looked at Tom like the uppity hired help had just cussed at him.

"I'll say it was self-defense. I can show Det. Mathers the scars on my back from Derrick beating me."

"It still would be voluntary manslaughter." Tom took slow tentative steps toward her. The look in her eyes was unlike anything he had ever seen. A kind of manic light shown in them.

Tom thought, *Julia knows Mathers worked homicides. Julia fully intends to put Derrick 6 feet under tonight.* Tom made the irrevocable decision to intervene. He stepped forward and very smoothly placed his hands on her hand that held the gun.

"You don't have to do this. He will never bother you after tonight. We can make sure of that."

The three participants stood completely still for 15 seconds. Tom kept his hands over hers, securely but lightly. He hoped his touch might have a calming effect.

But Rhodes, like all arrogant men used to getting their way, couldn't keep his mouth shut.

"I'll decide whether I see Julia again, not you, little golfer boy. And I may sue you for not keeping your gun in a secure place. Yes, I've been in the guest house. Julia and I shared hot, unforgettable sex in the guest bedroom. I mean, why not. It's the Judge's house, not yours."

Tom didn't hear anything Rhodes said. His attention was riveted on Julia. He thought he was making progress calming her down. He had slowly, deliberately adjusted the gun barrel's aim away from Derrick's head.

Derrick said, with cruel mockery, "You know, Julia, I'm starting to see that you aren't good enough for me. This stunt with the gun proves it. Crazy stuff. Didn't you take your medication? Maybe we'll pull the plug on the investments we make with your Old Man."

Derrick turned and began walking away.

Julia screamed, "No!" She jerked the gun but Tom held fast to her hand.

"Let go of me!"

Tom held fast. She jerked the gun again and--it is hoped-- accidentally pulled the trigger.

The bullet hit Tom in the left shoulder. The blast knocked him over. Julia stood in shock for a few seconds, then dropped the gun and put her hands over her eyes.

Tom's first thoughts were how much it hurt to be shot. It felt like fire burning through his shoulder. It wasn't like when Matt Dillon got shot every few weeks on *Gunsmoke* and then was fine the next episode.

Tom could feel the blood pouring out of him. The bullet had entered his shoulder just two inches above his heart. He saw Derrick hurry off in one direction, Julia in the other direction toward the main house. Tom said aloud something he had once read, "They retreated into their vast carelessness." Then added, "See Miss Stirdivant, I read '*The Great Gatsby*', the whole book."

His literary quote wasn't completely accurate, but shit, he'd just been shot.

He saw the gun on the ground. He took out his handkerchief with his right, his good hand, and wiped the gun handle clean. Then he passed out.

Caroline was in full sprint toward the direction the gunshot came from. She had checked the kitchen drawer and saw the gun was gone. Her first thought was that Tom had gone after a prowler.

When she found Tom, she had to stifle a scream in her throat. She thought he was dead. A thick ring of blood had seeped through his t-shirt. He was completely still.

Caroline was surprisingly level-headed in a crisis, probably because she had created so many of them. She checked Tom's pulse to confirm he was still with her. She ran full speed back to the Guest House and wheezing from the exertion, vowing to get in better physical condition, phoned the police and called for medical help.

The help arrived with remarkable speed. One of the benefits of living in a wealthy neighborhood.

While the paramedics were tending to Tom, she picked up the gun with the sleeve of her shirt. Only one shot had been fired.

What happened next was a blur. She remembered driving 75 miles an hour in the T-Bird back into town and to Doctors' Hospital. She remembered sitting in the waiting room seemingly forever. She flipped through five magazines, but couldn't have told you anything she'd seen or read.

A doctor with short grey hair, the kind of physician that exudes experience and calm competence--finally came over to her and reported that Tom, healthy young athlete that he was, had sailed through surgery. The doctor inquired, "Who is Miss Stirdivant?"

Caroline, puzzled, said, "Our high school English teacher."

"Before the surgery, he mentioned her name. And said, 'I read the book'."

"Tom never got over getting a C+ for his essay: Fitzgerald's Use of Color in *The Great Gatsby*. I got an A for my essay on that same book."

"What did you write about?"

"My essay was titled, 'Yo, Gatsby. That Girl Just Ain't Worth the Trouble'."

The doctor laughed.

"Can I see Tom?"

"Wait an hour or so and he will be coming out of the anesthesia. He will be weak. He lost a significant amount of blood."

"There are only 5 liters of blood in our entire body," the well-read Caroline commented. She had no idea why she blurted that out, other than it was better than heaving the magazines across the room.

The unflappable Doctor replied, "Yes, I remember reading something like that during my 6 years of Medical School."

Caroline sat in Tom's room the remainder of the night. He did awaken for short stretches at a time. She had a million questions for him about what happened, but wisely chose to let him rest. Each time he awoke, she reassured him that, "I'm right here, Tom."

The next morning, he was in considerable pain. Caroline went home, showered, put on fresh clothes. Next she fixed herself an enormous sandwich made up of spicy Italian sausage, sweet peppers, tons of Mozzarella and their Mother's amazing marinara sauce, all packed into a baguette. She adored their Mother's cooking, just couldn't stand to be in the same room with the woman.

She drank two beers for vital re-hydration and returned to the hospital.

Tom was awake and sitting up when she got there. She decided she had allotted him enough recuperation time. "So what happened?" she asked as she plopped down at the edge of his large hospital bed.

"I heard something unusual while I was practicing putting, thought it might be an intruder, went to check it out and a guy shot me."

"Did you get a good look at him?'

"No. Too dark. He was wearing black clothes and a stocking mask."

"Do you think he was there to rob the Wilkinson's?"

Tom was relieved to finally tell Caroline something that wasn't a complete lie. "Yes, and maybe hurt them."

Caroline turned away and screwed up her face into a confused frown. A nurse came in and gave Tom a shot for the pain. Several minutes later he dozed off.

Caroline stayed with him another hour then endured a crappy hospital cafeteria meal, pondering the imponderables.

She only heard one shot. Her hearing was superior, as was Tom's. Either:

--Tom had accidentally shot himself. Not likely.

--The intruder jumped Tom, took his gun and shot him with it. Not likely. Must've been a big, strong intruder. Tom is 6'2" and 190 lbs., all muscle, and he never backs down.

--Someone took the gun from the Guest House and shot him. He had shown Julia where the gun and ammo were kept.

The bottom-line conclusion of Private Detective Caroline Colt's preliminary investigation:

OH CRAP!!!

Caroline returned home at dinnertime. At 7PM Katrina Stern came to visit Tom. He was enough of a local celebrity that the incident made the afternoon newspaper, *The Phoenix Gazette*.

Kat was incredibly relieved to see Tom looked OK. He was sleeping comfortably when she came into the room.

Kat got an idea. She quietly removed her shoes and the blue dress she was wearing. Silently, she slid into the bed next to Tom. His breathing sounded fine. The bullet didn't hit a lung, she thought. He felt as strong as the night they made love.

He stirred a bit. Kat felt his hand slide over her until he reached her breasts. "The little beauties!" he said in a strong voice.

Kat giggled, now even more relieved. All was right with her world. Not even a bullet could take the rascal out of her Tom.

***

A minor follow-up procedure to correct some bleeding tissue was scheduled for Thursday, so Tom was slated to stay in the hospital through the weekend. A huge bouquet of yellow roses was delivered to his room. He looked at the card:

Get Well Soon, my headstrong Young Nephew. And next time LISTEN
        --Aunt Felicity

Tom said, "Okay, okay. I give up. You really are psychic. Or something..."

He got to watch the US Open Golf Championship from Oakmont with Kat and Caroline on the TV in his deluxe, state-of-the-art hospital room at Doctors Hospital.

Kat gave Caroline insights into what it was like to compete in a Major Championship. The two of them were going to be good friends, Tom was pleased to see. Because now, and Tom was quite clear on this in his mind, pain killers or no, that these two women along with his mom were the most important women in his life.

Kat noticed with some concern that Tom seemed distant and reflective at times when watching the US Open on TV. She wondered how it felt to have missed playing in the event he was most looking forward to.

What Tom was thinking was, *it hurt more than being shot.*

The winner was Jack Nicklaus over Arnold Palmer in a stirring Sunday playoff after they tied at the end of 4 rounds. It was Jack's first victory as a pro. What a way to start an epic career!

Would Tom have beaten Jack Nicklaus that week? He knew, of course not. But to Tom Colt, the joy was and always would be in the trying, the adventure of being there, in the middle of the action. Only one player gets to be Jack Nicklaus, after all.

***

On Tuesday morning, Tom, antsy to be released from the hospital, was sitting in the courtyard waiting for the Doctor to sign off on his discharge. He sat on an iron bench and enjoyed the sunshine. Golfers work outdoors. They get depressed when they are forced to be inside. They are the opposite of vampires.

The officious, overly starched (her personality, not her uniform) nurse, who was beginning to annoy him with all of her petty orders, insisted she take him out to the courtyard in a wheelchair, but he popped out of it the minute she was out of sight.

Tom still felt weak, but surprisingly the bullet hole in his shoulder didn't hurt that much. He was also surprised to see Judge Wilkinson stride up the sidewalk to the courtyard.

"You're looking good, Tom. I am so glad."

"Thank you." He omitted the customary, Sir, since the guy's daughter had shot him and all. "What brings you here?"

"Wanted to see how you were progressing after the...accident."

Tom's brow furrowed. He stood up, leaning on the back of the iron bench for support. He was going to be damned before he let the Judge tower over him.

In a strong, clear voice Tom said: "I want a 5% interest in your next 6 real estate deals. I will pay you a grand total of $1."

The Judge sputtered, "For what?"

"For services rendered."

"That's outrageous. You can't extort me. Who do you think you are?"

"I kept your daughter from going to prison for murder and assault with a deadly weapon."

"You couldn't prove--"

"Her fingerprints are on the gun. Her footprints are at the crime scene, along with your partner Derrick Rhodes' size 8½ Italian loafers. Tiny little feet that fella has."

The Judge turned away. Tom could sense the wheels turning in his head. The Judge lit a cigarette.

"I may never play golf again, at least at the pro level. I protected your daughter. What would you do if you were in my position?"

Tom was having trouble standing up, but he would not sit down.

The Judge puffed nonchalantly for a few moments, then crushed the cigarette on the concrete. Judge Wilkinson smiled that unique smile of his that contained no mirth, no joy, but certainly contempt.

"I would have demanded 10%, is what I would have done." Noticing Tom's stunned reaction, he kept that smile. "Never propose what you think your adversary will readily accept. Propose something that causes them obvious pain, then when you back significantly off that position they will feel you are relieving that pain."

Tom nodded, not certain whether he had won or had lost.

The Judge said, "Great. We have a deal. Of course, it's contingent on your complete silence about this matter between now and the end of time. I'll tell Marjorie to put you on the mailing list for the prospectuses. We have some peachy-sweet deals in the pipeline--even a golf resort in Mexico with a gentleman you recently met. He said you owe him a golf lesson."

The Judge winked at Tom, then started to walk off. Tom said, "I'm probably not going to marry your daughter."

The Judge turned back. "That's a shame. Think of the stories you'd have--to tell your kids."

He resumed walking and said, "I took care of your hospital bill, by the way."

Tom, moments before he would have fallen over, sat back down on the hard iron hospital bench.

***

When Tom got home from the hospital, he found a terse note tacked on his door, from Marjorie, saying that Julia was spending the rest of the summer in New York City with the Judge's sister Judith. And Julia was sorry she missed him before she had to leave.

Only missed by two inches, Tom thought, tracing a line from the still healing bullet wound to his heart. Kind of an impersonal way to deliver the message. But he understood there was a clear message within the message: there would be no further discussion of the night Tom was shot, or Julia's role in what happened.

***

Two days later, there was a knock on the front door at 9AM. Tom, feeling much better than he expected to, answered it. It was Detective Mathers, who smiled at Tom and said, "Good to see you up and around, guy. I've been shot and I know how weak and shaky it makes you."

"Thank you. I can't believe how much better I feel than just a few days ago."

"Do you have time for a walk? Just a short one."

"Sure."

Mathers led Tom to exactly where he knew he would be led: to the gazebo. Mathers got right to it. "I don't believe your story about an intruder jumping you. They break into houses, not invite the occupants to come outside. We found the print of a woman's sandals, a man's shoe--and yours of course."

"Ed, the gazebo is a popular place to come and sit. There's probably lots of prints."

"This isn't how it works, pal."

Tom sat down on the bench at the gazebo. He was still so easily tired. "At least you didn't call me Ace or Slick."

Mathers smiled briefly then got serious again. "You and I, we work on the side of the good guys, the side that seeks justice for everybody, whether they are rich or poor, butt-ugly, or rose-gold gorgeous."

"I absolutely agree."

"If that bullet had been coupla inches lower, we wouldn't be having this conversation, unless I was standing at your grave talking to you. And believe me, I've visited lotsa graves in my time."

"I was lucky, I know."

"Double lucky. Bullet went right through you. Minimal damage." Mathers pointed to tree, then took a bullet out of his pocket. "Officer Rudy dug it out of that eucalyptus."

Mathers tossed the bullet to Tom, who caught it with athletic ease. "Souvenir for you." Mathers was irritated with Tom's seeming evasion. He half-revolved in place. "You love her, don't you."

Mathers was taken aback, then pleased, by how direct and certain Tom sounded with his reply. "No, Ed, I do not love her. But I care for her. I care how her life ends up."

"We can't have one set of rules for the rich and politically connected and another set for the rest of us. Societies that do end up collapsing. Remember the glory that was once Rome's. Now, it's ruins. We can't let that happen to the USA. Not on my watch."

Mathers could not know, at that time, that Tom had saved Derrick Rhodes' life that night and kept Julia from going to prison. Somehow after all the suffering she had inflicted on him, emotional and now physical, he still could not bear the thought of being responsible for putting her behind bars.

Tom reflected for a few moments. "Ed, I've read that the trauma of being shot, the loss of blood and all, can cause a temporary amnesia. But the person's memory of the traumatic event often later returns."

Mathers smile knowingly. "Okay, my friend, that's how we'll play it."

Mathers handed Tom a paper sack with a heavy object in it.

"What's this?"

"Your gun. No prints whatsoever on it. Yours or anyone else's. Wonder who wiped it clean. Maybe that mysterious intruder, all dressed in black. Sporting of him to not steal your gun. Nice piece. A gun for a professional private investigator."

Tom took the sack and shrugged.

"Get well, my amazing friend. Let me know when you're up to giving me another golf lesson. I have a notion of entering the Valley Vista Club championship."

"With you in the field, maybe the rich old boys won't cheat as much."

"They cheat in golf, they cheat in life."

"Thank you, Ed. For listening to what I had to say."

"We may drive black and whites, but our jobs aren't always black and white." He paused and said with a genuinely sincere warmth, "I get it now, Tom. You'd be sending your dream to the slammer. No man should have to do that."

Chapter Thirty-Two
Back to 2004
Why the Bumper Sticker on Tom's '61 T-Bird says:
God Bless John Wayne

Guest Narrator Brian Continues Our Story:

Tom appeared at the door to his third-floor office at Valley Vista Country Club. He had loaned Brooks Benton the use of the space to complete the last few chapters of their manuscript, *The Mystery of the Golf Club Murder.*

Brooks had wheeled the comfy, high-backed desk chair over from Tom's desk to the little conference table, where his computer and printer were set up. Brooks was apparently dozing.

Tom walked softly to the table and flipped through the manuscript. It was complete. The last page said, THE END. He picked it up. "Hefty," he said, which caused Brooks to stir.

"Tom! We finished our story. And I have to tell you, I'm exhausted! Writing about your life and times wore me out. I can't imagine how you feel, re-living it."

Tom went behind his desk and flipped through the small pile of phone messages, then looked up at Brooks. "I'm not tired at all. I feel re-energized. I realized that after all that's happened to me, I'm lucky to be alive."

"One of our great mystery novelists said that when she finishes writing a book, she feels like an empty shell washed up on the beach. Now I know how she feels."

"I feel like a young pup romping on the beach. Cheer up Brooks-y. You want to play a late afternoon 9 holes to celebrate our achievement?"

"Oh hell, no. I'm going home, having a scotch and going to bed." He added, "Anyway, we did it."

Tom paused then said with warm sincerity, "And you were right. I'm glad you talked me into putting my story on paper. Could you please print out another copy. I want to share this with Carmen."

Brooks had a wry grin. "Sure thing. I had a little feeling you wanted to write this book for her."

Tom's smile was enigmatic, not the least bit revealing.

"And Brooks, my friend, you did a brilliant job telling my story. I am proud of what we created here. You amazed me how you could take the sketchy details I gave you and bring events from all those years ago to life. You are an outstanding writer. You have that special gift. I am totally impressed."

Hearing Tom's words, Brooks had to remind himself that he was an abrasive, sometimes rude sportswriter guy from New York, who never let sentiment overwhelm him.

For many writers, compliments, not to mention paychecks, can be few and far between. The struggles Brooks faced early in his journalism career were still fresh in his memory, despite all he had achieved. It meant the world to Brooks that Tom loved their book.

Brooks thought, *Tom Colt is one of the most generous people I have ever met, including being generous with gratitude.*

Brooks remembered a quote from Cicero: *Gratitude is not only the greatest of virtues, but the parent of all others.*

Brooks thought, *I love this man. I am honored to tell his story.*

Tom said, "I was pleasantly surprised to see how you expanded my vocabulary. I've never used the word 'impactful' in my life."

"You have now. When it's in print, it becomes the truth."

Tom smiled, walked out of his office and bounded down the stairs like a thirty-year-old to the second floor where the casual dining room was located. Lovely Carmen Lopez was putting out place settings for the dinner crowd.

Carmen and Tom smiled at each other with the amazing warm chemistry they shared, unlike anything either one had felt before.

"Hey, when do I get to read this famous book?"

"My faithful chronicler Brooks Benton is delivering a copy to you later this afternoon."

Carmen put her hands together in soft applause. One mustn't make excessive noise at The Club. "Congratulations! You finished it."

Tom paused, shifted his weight from foot to foot, as though considering something weighty.

"I have a question, a strange question to ask."

Carmen's smile faded. "Sure. But this sounds serious. Should I be worried?"

"Do you like John Wayne?"

Carmen burst out laughing. "That's your Big Question? You've never been to my house, have you…"

Tom shook his head, no.

"My grandpa Ernie was a stuntman in Duke's movies. I have all sorts of pictures on the walls of him with John Wayne in classic westerns like *Hondo* and *The Searchers*. I have a DVD collection of the movies the two of them were in." She reached into her pocket and took out a key ring, walked over and handed it to Tom. The key fob read, 'Hurry it up, We're Burnin' Daylight.'--a John Wayne line from the classic Western *The Cowboys*.

Tom handed the key chain back to her. They briefly held hands.

Carmen said, "I have an idea. Come over tomorrow night for dinner. I'll show you the photo albums Grandpa left me. Wonderful memories. What an exciting life he had!"

"I'd like that very much. I will bring the wine."

Carmen looked elated. She wasn't at all sure he would say yes to the invitation. He never had before, all the times she had asked.

"So I guess I answered your question."

"You did. In many different ways."

"Maybe you and I could make some memories of our own tomorrow night."

"Let's find out. That's why we get up each morning, after all."

But, would inveterate risk-taker Tom take that one last risk--to let himself fall in love with a woman he admired so much--almost from the first moment they met--that she could break his heart like a matchstick if she didn't feel the same way?

No matter how many years passed, Tom Colt would, like most of us, retain those lingering doubts about himself he started his adult life with. But, no matter what fears visited him, he always saddled up and rode straight for the challenge, anyway.

And it finally occurred to Carmen that Tom was afraid, if he pursued her too passionately, too actively, she would reject him. She found this revelation almost impossibly endearing and made her love Tom all the more.

Tom had finally met someone with the same luminous romantic spirit he had. He made a mental note to call his auto mechanic to give the '61 T-Bird a tune-up. He had his own little feeling, that he should arrive at Carmen's house in that powerful, memory-evoking machine tomorrow night. First dates are scary things.

Chapter Thirty-Three
We Return to 1962
Mathers Makes Tom an Official Detective
A Quiet, Hopeful New Year's Eve

Tom Continues Our Story:

A hot September afternoon, 105 degrees at least, just after Labor Day 1962. My shoulder still ached from the torn muscles the bullet ripped through. For some reason I especially got a sharp twinge whenever I saw a busty blonde walking down the street.

The Doctor gave me the green light to resume 'light' practicing. He's evidently never seen me play golf. I never did anything 'light'. I can't explain what it felt like to know I could play golf again--and the Doc assured me--at a high level again. I would never complain about having to go out and practice. It was sheer joy to hold a club in my hand, to feel that lusty contact with the ball.

I was giving Det. Ed Mathers a lesson on the driving range at Valley Vista CC. When Ed first began coming to the club for lessons, our wonderful, tolerant members pretty much shunned him. Now, with his status elevated to Full Golf Member, some of them still could not understand why this guy who had formerly been relegated to the far end of the driving range was suddenly allowed--gasp--inside the clubhouse.

But I was amused to find, once everyone realized Mathers and I were the ones who solved the Lisa Luck murder case, it all changed. Now the members set up near us on the driving range, hoping to hear snatches of conversation about another sensational scandal or murder.

I couldn't believe a whole year had passed since I started giving Ed lessons. He now had a strong, repeatable, respectable swing. He understood that swinging fast doesn't necessarily generate more power. I got through to him by using the analogy of a gunfighter in the Old West. Wyatt Earp and others had observed that the fastest gun doesn't necessarily win the fight--it's the smoothest and steadiest one. Ed's swing now had a rhythm of SLOW, SMOOTH, POP!

Ed had graduated to the point I didn't have to stand and coach him on every shot. I practiced next to him and offered tips as needed. I also didn't charge Ed for the lessons anymore.

He stopped practicing and looked back at me, bashfully it seemed. "Tom, do you think Caroline would enjoy going out with me?"

Tom flashed his Smile of the Rascal. "I knew you were a little sweet on my sister."

"She has a quality..."

"That she does. Yes, she'd like to go out with you. But I need to let you know, she's not as tough as the image she tries to present to the world."

"Good! Neither am I." He laughed sarcastically.

Taking a break from my own practice, I pulled some letters out of my golf bag that I wanted to show him.

"What are these?"

"Fan mail from crime buffs. Can you believe it?"

"You get fan mail? I don't--what gives?"

"It doesn't amaze people when cops solve crimes. It does when golfers do."

He laughed. I saw a twinkle of mischief in his eyes. "You know, I still can't get over that your ex-wife is married to Marco Greene. That's like going from a Mouseketeer to a Racketeer."

"Funny stuff. But I'd keep the day job."

He hit a crisp 5-iron about 180 yards. The man is an athlete. He stopped to take a few swigs from a bottle of Pepsi-Cola. A shadow fell across his face.

"I've been thinking about this whole Luck family mess. Maybe The Church in Rome should revise the Seven Deadly Sins. Split off the Lust for Power from other types of Lust, make it a Deadly Sin on its own. It is so corrupting."

"Good idea. What these people did to acquire power over their fellow citizens...it made them insane."

"And crazy attracts crazy. Sen. Luck's closest advisor was Dottie Petersen and his de-facto business partner was Roman Morales, the psychotic would-be conqueror of the Southwest. Morales and Luck wanted to set themselves up as dictators, petty tyrants, after the election."

"There must be a bullying gene that some people are born with. My dad told me once, 'freedom is a fragile thing that must always be protected and defended'."

"And to think the asshole crime reporter at the fish wrap says cops are the bullies." Mathers shook his head in disgust. "All we ask is that citizens get up in the morning and at least attempt to do the right thing. Is that too much to ask?"

"Nope."

I hit several of my patented booming tee shots, tried not to let Mathers see that it still really hurt to swing that hard.

He finished his Pepsi, set the bottle down. He looked pensive. "I need to ask you something, Tom. I know you're a busy guy. Would you like to work with me on cases in the future? You won this year on the big tour. I can't ask you to take too much time away from--"

"YES!!" I exclaimed as emphatically as I could.

"OKAY!" Ed said just as emphatically. I could see some of the members craning their heads our way, but trying to appear they were not really listening in.

"Chief gave me permission to have you registered as a Police Consultant, which means access to info on cases. We can't pay you anything...they can barely pay me...but..."

"Do I get a badge?"

"Not exactly...it's not quite as metallic as a badge. It's more of a...cardboard thing-y...but it says 'Police' on it."

"Deal."

I extended my hand. Mathers and I shook firmly, for a long sequence of seconds, ratifying our partnership, with a kind of expectant joy on both of our faces.

Ah, the adventures yet to come.

Mathers couldn't resist this. He said, loudly in his tough cop voice so the craning members could hear, "And remember, Tom, we uncover any corruption at this Club, we'll nail 'em."

Several of the eavesdropping members seemed to back away from us.

I said, "Next week, let's have your lesson on the course. If you have time, we can play a full 18 holes."

"This course? Really? Valley Vista?"

With mock solemnity, I said, "You are ready Detective Ed Mathers."

"I'm ready. Wow. You think I'm ready. You're sure..."

He looked at me with apprehension, like I was sending him off to war.

"I've only played the muni layouts before. Never a ball-busting, professional kick-ass course like this."

Mathers swallowed. Hard. I grinned.

I love this course. I love this game. I love my life.

***

Brooks Continues Our Story:

After Ed left, Tom practiced for a half hour or so longer. Kat Stern arrived at the practice range, carrying her golf bag on her shoulder and toting not one, but two wire buckets of practice balls. "Nice afternoon for a practice session," Tom said, smiling.

Kat smiled back. "So good to see you out here again!" Her eyes conveyed both warmth and concern. Tom was touched. It gave him an idea.

He walked over to her spot on the driving range. Then he got down on one knee and extended his hand to Kat.

Now the look on her face was a blend of thrilled, curious and scared.

"Katrina Stern," he asked as he took her hand. He cleared his throat and paused as if drinking deeply from the cup of courage.

"Yes," she said in a much tinier voice than normal.

"Would you...be my partner...in the Rising Stars Golf Challenge the first week of January?"

She put her hands to her face in a mock expression of deep surprise.

"Why, yes, Tom, I would." Then she fashioned that cute frown of hers, made an equally cute fist and firmly tapped Tom on the shoulder. *Rascal*, she thought, but an irresistible one as far as she was concerned.

"The event is at an island in the Caribbean. Brand new course owned by a rich dude from Scottsdale. The tournament is to promote the grand opening of a hotel and golf course there."

"Sounds like great fun."

That was the closest either Tom or Katrina ever got to proposing to each another, over the subsequent 40 years. They continued their conversation on the practice range that afternoon, a light and forward-looking one. But Tom and Katrina each had a thoughtful, private moment wondering what would have happened if he really had proposed to her that day. But they both told themselves, *they'll be plenty of time for that. We have our whole lives ahead.*

***

New Year's Eve, 1962

Tom Finishes Our Story:

The Valley Vista golf course was deserted. It had been a cold grey day, typical for late December in the desert, that gave way to warm sunshine late in the afternoon, in perfect harmony with the sunny mood I was in. The members were at home getting ready for various kinds of New Year's Eve celebrations.

I went for a walk on the course, starting on the 10th hole and then all the way to the 18th green. I had always loved walking golf courses at the end of the day after the players had left. From the very first time my dad took me with him to play, I've thought a golf course is just about the most beautiful thing in the world.

That afternoon, I used the quiet time to reflect on the crazy, spectacular and sometimes painful year of 1962.

Financially, the year had been a smashing success. Believe it or not, I needed to hire a CPA to help me organize my finances, investments and taxes. I couldn't have imagined needing financial guidance a year ago. All I had to do then was be able to add up to about $500 in my bank account.

I remembered a CPA's office was located two doors down from Marco Greene's office. I called the CPA and casually mentioned I knew Marco. He rushed me in for an appointment that afternoon and gave me a substantially discounted rate. Go figure.

Caroline and I had formally launched Colt & Colt Confidential investigations services. We installed a 2nd phone line in the guest house to answer calls for our detective biz. Several club members had already discreetly asked me for our business cards, the nifty new ones creative Caroline designed.

As I walked the course my mind inevitably turned to reflecting on Lisa Prentiss Luck. Det. Mathers' case file on her murder may be closed but my emotional file with her name on it was not. I only now realized how much she meant to me. She was able to express her feelings toward me in the letter she wrote when she sent me the orange key. I never got the chance.

Caroline, as you know, blurts out things in a brash, unfiltered manner, but sometimes she is spot on with her observations. When she told me Lisa and I would make a great couple, I dismissed it at first. But now, I believe Caroline may have been right. When I gave Lisa golf lessons, there were sparks between us. But there were many times when her warm, fun personality was buried beneath the pressure she was under.

Buried. Maybe not the best choice of words. But I'll never be the marvelous wordsmith Brooks Benton is.

This was the first time since my father disappeared in the Korean War that I lost someone truly important to me, which may sound odd because I spent so little time with Lisa.

Try as the evil Dottie Petersen might, my lingering image of Lisa was not naked and battered and dead, lying on the chair by the pool. It was of a young, lovely, classy girl with long tanned legs and a soft voice like the breath of springtime, walking barefoot on the warm, welcoming turf of this magnificent course, where she felt briefly at peace being with a guy she knew could have loved her.

And if I were even close to being the detective/knight/hero some people apparently thought I was, I would have at least held her hand as we walked that day.

This gorgeous, doomed girl was the first ghost who would walk beside me all the fairways of my life, forever.

Why did I say she was the first ghost? Because down the years unfortunately there would be many more.

When I climbed the steep hill that took me up to the 18th green, I focused on the everlasting stone clubhouse, festooned with 'Happy New Year' banners in anticipation of the dinner/dance there that night. I felt energy surge through me and I renewed, but modified, a dream I first had in 1953 and said aloud, "I'm going to own this Country Club someday."

A foolish, extravagant dream to be sure, given I was merely an employee of the Club. But why not aim high? That's what Americans do. Not too many years later, we would be landing astronauts on the moon.

Caroline and I had enough money for each of us to rent a new place of our own in the nicest part of Scottsdale, but the Judge insisted we stayed at the guest house, rent free. "I will need you two even more in the upcoming year," he said, adding, "You both are immensely valuable to me."

Judge Roy Wilkinson was the one person I would never even partially understand. He was always a few steps ahead of us. A brilliant man, on occasion a very kind and generous man, usually a hard man. But I was never sure, a good man.

Caroline and I decided to have a quiet New Year's Eve at the Guest House, cooking a massive 7 lb. prime rib roast and of course sharing a bottle or two or three of champagne. Kat was spending the evening with her visiting sister Ingrid. Our mom was working of course, catering the Goulds' New Year's Eve party.

Caroline had been a little pissed off at me for not admitting that Julia was the one who shot me. But I knew she solved that mystery before I got out of the hospital.

That night she came to terms with it, as Mathers had. "I got sucked in too, Tom. Julia is like, grand and terrible adventures seek her out and it makes you want to be a part of them. You couldn't be the one who sent her to jail. By taking a bullet from her, you saved her."

"So you forgive me for letting her skate."

"There was never anything to forgive."

The wonderful beefy aroma coming from the kitchen was making us famished. While we anxiously awaited our prime rib to be ready, Caroline told me, "Det. Mathers is taking me out horseback riding at a dude ranch in Wickenburg. He has a friend who's a wrangler there. Afterwards there's a cookout in the desert. Porterhouse steaks cooked over a mesquite fire, under the stars. Yum!"

I smiled in a smug but congratulatory way. "So you're going on a date with Ed...cool."

She shook her head a bit too vehemently. "No. It's not a date. Just a day enjoying our beautiful desert scenery."

"Sound like great fun. Since it's not a date, maybe I'll come too."

She sputtered, her eyes wide. "No...ah...I don't think that's a good idea."

"Aha! It is a Date."

"Well, ain't you the hot shit detective!" she quoted Sheboygan.

We were getting a little tipsy. We laughed and laughed like we hadn't since we were kids and allowed to laugh whenever we wanted to.

After dinner we put on Perry Como's new Christmas album and enjoyed Mr. C's warm and rich voice, as warm as sitting by the fire on a cold winter night. Which we don't have too often in Phoenix, so we have to use our imagination. With shared good feeling we stood by the record player and enthusiastically sang along with *There's No Place Like Home for The Holidays,* Caroline of course with a much better voice than mine.

Thumbtacked on the wall above the record player were the Christmas cards we had received. Caroline chuckled when she saw one from The Greene Family. It was a photo of Marco in a Santa outfit, with Mandy seated on his lap, taken by their pool with festive bright red bougainvillea plants in the background. Their two spaniels, Luci and Desi, had reindeer antlers on.

Caroline commented, "We got cards from Chief of Police Flannery, US Senator-elect Robert Bland, and from a notorious gangster. Don't you find a moral inconsistency in that?"

"You're right, as usual, dear sister. Next Christmas we'll toss out any cards from politicians."

"Damn straight."

At the stroke of midnight, Caroline lifted her glass to me. "Happy New Year, partner."

"And an especially Happy New Year to you, partner."

Full of hope, not to mention perfectly prepared prime beef and outstanding champagne, cheered by my return to robust health, I decided as the brand-new year of 1963 arrived that this would be My Year.

I'm going to focus on golf and win at least two tournaments. I'm not going to get beaten up by gangsters in Mexico. I'm certainly not going to get shot by a girl I believed I loved--at least not with my own gun.

What could go wrong? I thought as I swallowed the last of the champagne that Caroline poured for me.

Never ask that question. Nope. Never. Just don't do it.

--THE END--

Tom Colt will return in *Murder on Bogey Island*...

Printed in Great Britain
by Amazon

87680387R00192